THE BETRAYAL

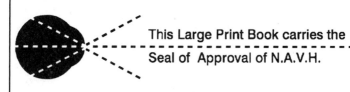

This Large Print Book carries the
Seal of Approval of N.A.V.H.

THE BETRAYAL

HELEN DUNMORE

THORNDIKE PRESS

A part of Gale, Cengage Learning

Detroit • New York • San Francisco • New Haven, Conn • Waterville, Maine • London

GALE
CENGAGE Learning·

LIBRARY OF CONGRESS CATALOGING-IN-PUBLICATION DATA

Dunmore, Helen, 1952–
   The betrayal / by Helen Dunmore.
     p. cm. — (Thorndike Press large print core)
   ISBN-13: 978-1-4104-4425-7 (hardcover)
   ISBN-10: 1-4104-4425-2 (hardcover)
   1. Saint Petersburg (Russia)—Fiction. 2. Large type books. I. Title.
PR6054.U528B48 2012
823'.914—dc23   2011037975

Published in 2012 by arrangement with Grove/Atlantic, Inc.

Printed in the United States of America
1 2 3 4 5 6 7 16 15 14 13 12

To Patrick and Alexa

1

It's a fresh June morning, without a trace of humidity, but Russov is sweating. Sunlight from the hospital corridor's high window glints on his forehead. Andrei's attention sharpens. The man is pale, too, and his eyes are pouched with shadow.

It could be a hangover, but Russov rarely drinks more than a single glass of beer. He's not overweight. A touch of flu then, even though it's June? Or maybe he needs a check-up. He's in his mid-forties; the zone of heart disease.

Russov comes close, closer than two people should stand. His breath is in Andrei's face, and suddenly Andrei stops diagnosing, stops being at a comfortable doctorly distance from the symptoms of a colleague. His skin prickles. His body knows more than his mind does. Russov smells of fear, and his conciliating smile cannot hide it. He wants something, but he is afraid.

'Andrei Mikhailovich . . .'

'What is it?'

'Oh, it's nothing important. Only if you've got a moment . . .'

His face is glistening all over now. Drops of sweat are beginning to form.

Suddenly Russov whips out his handkerchief and wipes his forehead as if he were polishing a piece of furniture.

'Excuse me, I'm feeling the heat . . . I don't know when they're going to get around to turning off these radiators. You'd think our patients had all been prescribed steam baths.'

The hospital's radiators are cold.

'I wanted to ask your advice, if you've got a moment. As a diagnostician there's no one whose opinion I respect more.'

Now why is he saying that? Only last week there was an idiotically petty and irritable 'professional disagreement' over a little girl with an enlarged spleen following a serious fall. Russov had gone on about 'scientific accountability' while he tapped his pen scornfully on the table. He hadn't appeared very impressed by Andrei's diagnostic skills then. Andrei always spent far too much time with his patients. This was a clear-cut case of splenic trauma following an abdominal injury. The only question was whether it could be treated non-operatively, or whether an immediate operation was advisable.

When it turned out that the child's swollen spleen had indeed nothing to do with the accident, and was due to undiagnosed leukaemia, Russov muttered about 'flukes' and 'all this hands-on mumbo-jumbo'. But all the same, Russov is a reasonably good physician. Hard-working, responsible and extremely keen to write up as many cases as possible, in the hope of raising his research profile. He's certainly getting noticed. One day no doubt he'll produce that definitive research paper which will unlock the door to a paradise of conferences and the golden promise of a trip abroad. Andrei's gift for diagnosis annoys him. It isn't classifiable and it hasn't been achieved in the correct way, through study and examination. The two men have never become friends.

'So what's the problem, Boris Ivanovich?' asks Andrei.

Russov glances down the corridor. A radiographer is wheeling a trolley-load of X-ray files towards them.

'Let's go outside for a breath of air.'

The courtyard is large enough to be planted with lime trees and rose bushes. It's good

9

for the patients to look out and see living things. Andrei remembers the time when they grew vegetables here: onions and carrots and cabbages, rows and rows of them packed together. Every green space in Leningrad became a vegetable plot, that first summer of the siege. Strange how close it still feels, as if those times have such power that they still exist, just out of sight.

These limes are young trees, less than ten years old. The former trees were all chopped up for the hospital stoves in the winter of '41/2. But the wood ran out at last, no matter how much they scavenged. Andrei's fingers still remember the icy, barren touch of the unlit stoves.

Two paths run criss-cross through the courtyard. In its centre there's a circle of gravel, and a bench. Russov remains standing. His feet shift, crunching the gravel, as he takes out a packet of Primas and offers it to Andrei.

'Thank you.'

The business of lighting the cigarettes draws them close. Russov seems calmer now. Although his fingers fumble with the lighter's catch, they don't tremble.

'Good to get a breath of fresh air.'

'Yes,' Andrei agrees, 'but you'll have to excuse me in a minute. I have a patient going into X-ray at two, and I need a word with the radiographer first —'

'Of course. This won't take a moment.'

But still he won't come to the point. Just keeps on dragging at his cigarette and blowing out jerky puffs, like a boy who is smoking for the first time. Like Kolya.

'It's a new patient. A tricky case.'

Andrei nods. 'Would you like me to take a look?'

Russov's face twitches into a smile. 'It's not a question of diagnosis precisely,' he says, with an attempt at his usual manner of lofty certainty, 'but of defining exactly what tests ought to be carried out at this stage.'

'So what are the symptoms?'

'In a case such as this . . . Well, in such a case one needs to be a hundred per cent certain before one takes the next step.'

'I'm not sure I understand you. What are your initial findings?'

Russov gives a sudden harsh bark of laughter which transforms his face completely. He looks almost savage. His short hair seems to bristle.

'My "initial findings" are that this patient is the son of — of an extremely influential person.'

'Ah. And how old is the boy?'

'Ten.'

'And so it's a joint problem, is it? Is that why you've come to me?' Why doesn't Russov get to the point?

'He's Volkov's son,' says Russov abruptly.

'Volkov's?' My God. It's one of those names you only have to say once, like Yezhov or Beria. Andrei's heart thuds, and he has to clear his throat before speaking. *'The* Volkov, you mean?'

Russov just nods, and then rushes on. 'A joint problem, yes, I'm pretty sure that's what it is. There's swelling and redness and so on, pain on articulation, heat to the touch. That's why I've come to you. All the symptoms point to juvenile arthritis and you're the man for that. I haven't ordered tests yet, it's pure guesswork,' he adds hastily.

'You'd like me to take a look.'

'If you would. If you would, my dear chap, I tell you, I'd be eternally grateful.'

My dear chap? Eternally grateful? Sweat is still leaking from the pores of dry, competent Russov. He never talks like this. What the hell is going on?

The breeze is warm and sweet, but ice touches Andrei. There's much more here than he's being told. Russov fears that this child is seriously ill. He wants Andrei to see the boy, take on the case, order the tests and then give the verdict to the family. Russov will do anything not to be the bearer of bad news to Volkov. It won't be Russov's face that Volkov will remember with the cold, hard rage that such a man will feel for anything he can't control.

Russov drops his cigarette butt, grinds it into the path and then smoothes clean gravel over the spot with his heel. Andrei says nothing. He finds himself staring at the lime leaves as if he's never seen them before. They are so fresh and vigorous. Amazing how trees always look as if they've been there for ever, even when you can remember the women stamping down earth over their bare roots.

Russov clears his throat. 'It struck me as just possible that there might be something I've overlooked. There's a risk of setting off in the wrong direction — ordering the wrong tests, for instance. In a case of such significance for . . . for the hospital, we can't afford any margin of error.' And he actually has the nerve to look at Andrei self-righteously, as if Andrei is the one who has neglected to think about the greater good of the hospital community. Andrei stares back blankly. Russov's eyes drop. 'For example . . .' he mumbles. 'For example, you'll recall the little girl with the spleen.'

How the man is abasing himself. He will hate Andrei for it afterwards, once all this is over. No one makes a better enemy than a man who has had to beg for your help.

But perhaps Russov really *has* missed something. He's thorough, but he goes by the book. It's also just conceivable that he's aware of this — that he's not as self-satisfied as he always seems . . . In which case he might be doing exactly what ought to be done in such a case: seeking a second opinion.

'You still haven't told me anything about this child,' says Andrei.

Another throat-clearing. Russov's hand strays to his jacket pocket, where he keeps his cigarettes, and then falls to his side. His eyes stare into Andrei's, but remain opaque.

'My thinking was that it would be best for you to come to the case quite fresh.'

A rising breeze makes the lime trees shiver all over. *Hold back,* thinks Andrei. *Don't commit yourself. Not instantly, like this.* He recognizes it already as one of those moments that has the power to change everything. Perhaps he won't be able to avoid it. If you put everything else aside, there's still a sick child here, and he needs the best possible treatment. What if Russov gets it wrong again?

But Andrei has Anna to think of, and Kolya.

Their faces rise up in his mind, oblivious. There's a knot of tiny lines on Anna's forehead, but when she looks up and sees him that knot will clear. And there is Kolya, tall and thin, narrow-shouldered because he hasn't grown into his height yet. Kolya frowning at his homework, then suddenly jumping up and crashing across the living room because he's spotted a mouse under the table. Or claims he's spotted one — Kolya wants a cat, and Anna isn't keen.

Kolya, lunging between child and man, and out of step with both.

Andrei's heart beats hard. Whatever happens, these two mustn't be touched.

But Russov didn't want any of this, either. He's just a trapped, ordinary man. Reasonably competent, reasonably conscientious. And now quite reasonably afraid.

'So, you'll see the boy?' asks Russov.

'Have you got the case notes with you?'

His colleague hesitates.

'It was just a preliminary examination, you understand. I've done no tests. There's been no possibility of making any sort of diagnosis. The boy was brought in last night with certain symptoms, that's all. By private ambulance,' he adds, as if this hopelessly irrelevant detail will make up for all the blanks.

In a flash, Andrei does understand. The bare minimum has been put into writing.

'But you must have ordered tests. You must have thought about what would be needed.'

'I don't want to prejudice your own examination.'

Andrei feels himself recoil. Even here, out in the courtyard where surely nobody can be listening, his so-called colleague won't talk. He's studied hard all right, in the unwritten subject that runs through every other course of study. Keep your tongue and your hands still, unless you are absolutely sure that it's safe to move them. Don't take risks. Don't stand out. Be anonymous and average; keep in step.

'It was Doctor B. I. Russov, of course, who made the initial examination and first suggested the diagnosis that was later confirmed . . .' He'll do anything to avoid that. Much better for Russov to be able to say: *'I asked a colleague — a first-rate general paediatric physician and one of our finest diagnosticians — if he would examine the patient. Dr Alekseyev has a particular interest in juvenile arthritic disease, and given that my own caseload does not permit me to take the*

special interest in this case which it requires, it seemed the best course of action to hand over the case as soon as possible. Consistency of care, you understand, is of the utmost importance.'

That's how it will be.

What does Russov take me for? Does he think I'm a complete idiot?

Russov looks down at the gravel. His shoulders sag. He thinks he's lost, thinks Andrei. He thinks I'm going to tell him to sod off. And of course that's what I've got to do. Let Russov carry his own can. He's always trying to make himself conspicuous, and now fate has found a way. He'll 'raise his profile' with Volkov all right . . .

Russov got the case. That's all the difference there is between us.

He could say yes. That's what he always says. Andrei has never been one of those doctors who keep their expertise only for their own patients. He doesn't spare his energy either. Sometimes it seems that the more he uses up his energy, the more he has, as if he's got access to some secret principle of acceleration that overrides the normal rules of fatigue. Everybody knows they can count on Andrei. Russov will be counting on that.

'You want me to take on the case,' says Andrei.

'I didn't say that.'

'Listen, Boris Ivanovich —'

'I'm only asking you to take a look at the boy.'

'Not today. It's impossible. I've got two clinics, and then a meeting until nine.'

'But you will?'

'I can't promise. I've got to go, my patient is waiting, and the radiographer. I'll speak to you tomorrow.'

Russov puts a hand on Andrei's sleeve. Shadows flicker on the dusty brownish-grey cloth. 'I appreciate your cooperation,' he says. He wants to sound as a man should sound after a normal professional discussion with a colleague, but in spite of himself his voice pleads.

'These trees have done well,' says Andrei.

Russov looks up impatiently. Trees! For heaven's sake, aren't there more important things to talk about? His grip tightens on Andrei's arm, then he recalls himself, and says with forced civility, 'Splendid things, trees.'

Anna worked from first light to darkness on the big October tree-planting day, the year the war ended, Andrei remembers. He didn't take part, because he was on duty all day. She came home exhausted — she had certainly 'fulfilled her norm of unpaid labour'. He was annoyed with her for doing so much — all that slog on top of a week's work. Surely she could have come home earlier, look at her, she was going to make herself ill. But Anna said, 'It's trees, Andryusha. Something for the children. Just think, one day Kolya will be able to take his children out to the new parks and walk under the shade of the trees we've planted today.'

Andrei walks down the corridor towards the Radiology Department. He can feel the tension in the back of his neck. He pauses for a moment, drops his shoulders, rotates them, lets them fall. Sick children are very quick to spot signs of adult anxiety.

'Hello, Tanichka, how's Mama behaving herself today?'

Tanya and her mother both laugh. It's an old joke between them. Tanya's mother used to scuttle in and out of the hospital, head down, terrified of breaking imaginary rules, terrified that Tanya would show her up. On one occasion all her fears came true when Tanya couldn't get to the toilet in time and wet herself, right there on the floor. But they've all got to know one another now.

Just as well, since Tanya has had to be hospitalized several times with acute attacks. There is a new treatment based on extracts from animal adrenal glands, but he thinks it is still too risky for Tanya, given her weight and generally poor condition.

'You remember how I told you, Tanya, that your joint mobility depends on you too now, not just on the doctors and nurses? How have those exercises been going?'

Andrei has prescribed a course of isometric and isotonic exercise for Tanya, plus massages.

'Very well, doctor, she's been doing her exercises every morning and every evening, just like you said,' Tanya's mother answers.

'Even when they hurt I do them,' says Tanya proudly.

'That's right. Remember what I told you, it may hurt but it will never harm you. You're not putting any weight on your knees, you see. You're just helping them to learn how to move again. And how about the cod liver oil?'

'She takes it every day, good as gold, don't you, Tanya?'

What he'd really like to do is send Tanya to a sanatorium that specializes in arthritis. There's no father: dead in the war, like so many of his children's fathers. Probably never even saw his daughter. The mother is from Kingisepp originally, but she and all her family fled east as the Germans advanced, and were sent on to the Urals. Tanya and her mother must have returned as part of Leningrad's post-war influx. And now Tanya's seven, and her mother works in a tailoring shop. Their chance of a ticket to a children's sanatorium looks slim, but it's still worth pursuing.

'And you've kept all the physiotherapy appointments?'

Tanya's mother can manage these hospital visits, but each physiotherapy session means that her own mother, who went back to live in Kingisepp, must travel to Leningrad, stay over and take Tanya to the clinic. *She'd live with me if it would help, but in a communal apartment like ours it's not really possible. Our room is very small. And besides, she grows vegetables, and that's how I get extra eggs and milk for Tanya.'*

'Yes, Tanya's been to her appointments as regular as clockwork,' says her mother with pride. 'She's never missed a single one.'

'That's really excellent,' says Andrei warmly. 'Now, please wait just a moment while I have a quick word with the radiographer. Tanya, I'm going to ask Sofya Vasilievna to look especially carefully today.'

He spends too long with patients. He talks to them too much. He's been criticized for it, but he points out in his defence that in the long term his approach is efficient. It enables him to spot problems as they develop, or even before. He achieves 'exceptionally high levels of patient compliance with treatment', which is certainly something that can be ticked off on the targets. It's not all 'yes doctor no doctor' and then go home and swallow some decoction their grandmas swear by, and not bother with the exercises because the poor little thing is sick, isn't she, so what's the good of wearing her out?

Also, Andrei believes that children want to know far more than we think they do. They get less frightened that way. He has known children close to death who have understood it in a strangely matter-of-fact way, but have suffered because their parents, in grief and terror, refused to acknowledge what was happening.

He's on his way up to the ward when someone behind him calls his name. He turns. 'Lena! Sorry, I'm in a rush —'

She's panting, and her face is flushed. She must have run after him. 'I saw you coming out of Radiology.'

'Is everything all right?'

'I've got to talk to you. It's important. It'll only take a minute.'

'What's wrong?'

She glances up and down the corridor, puts a hand on his arm and steers him a few metres away from the half-open door to their left.

'You were in the courtyard with Russov.'

'Yes?'

'It's about the boy who came in last night, isn't it? He's in a private room, but Lyuba saw the name. What's going on? Don't for God's sake let Russov drag you into this.'

'Lena, is it true that this is Volkov's boy?'

Again that quick look up and down the corridor. 'Yes. They say it's the only child.'

Andrei feels a plunge in his stomach, as if he were standing on a cliff and had suddenly looked down.

'He was, wasn't he?' asks Lena.

'What?'

'Russov. Trying to dump the case on you. It's so typical —'

'I suppose we can't blame him, Lena. If we were in his shoes —'

'You soon will be, if he has his way. And he'll be out of them.' Lena's clever, slanting green eyes scan his face anxiously. 'You've never agreed?'

'I've said I'll talk to him tomorrow.'

'Listen to me. I know about these things. Tomorrow you'll call in sick. Promise me.'

'I can't do that.'

'Do you think Russov would do anything for you if you were in his position?'

'No. Probably not.'

'Well, then.'

'But, Lena, we're medics; we have to co-operate. It's perfectly legitimate for Russov to call on a second opinion.'

'Is that what he calls it? He's going to be the first opinion, then?'

'Well —'

'Just as I thought. It'll be you in the firing line, and no one else.' She lowers her voice again. 'You should keep out of it. Remember *Court of Honour.*'

Of course he had seen the film. He and Anna had watched it in silence, and left the cinema without comment. She had held his arm very tightly on the walk home. The film was fiction, but its targets were real.

Kliueva, Roskin and Vasili Parin. Brilliant, innovative research scientists. Kliueva and Roskin pioneered biological drug treatments to shrink tumours. They'd seemed invulnerable. State funds poured into their research institute. Kliueva was awarded a Stalin Prize.

The charges brought against them were that they'd betrayed Soviet scientific research secrets, which belonged to the State. Either they'd been tricked by the Americans into disclosure, or there was a more sinister explanation. But everyone knew it was inconceivable that they'd made these contacts with the Americans without permission. No scientist travelled to the USA without a full and thoroughly understood set of instructions. Whispers said that everything was done on clear State orders. Policy had changed overnight, as it did so often, and the scientists paid the price. Parin, who'd actually handed over the research material, was sentenced to twenty-five years as a spy for the Americans. Somehow, by the skin of their teeth, Roskin and Kliueva survived their Court of Honour, their severe reprimand and the barrage of claims that they too were spies, hoodwinked by the Americans.

They'd been unbelievably lucky; Parin not so. The warning was there. Don't think, however eminent and crowned with prizes you may be, that you can't be destroyed. Don't think that the scientific or medical community can expect any special favours because of its particular expertise. The same stringent standards apply to everyone.

Scientists can be spies; doctors can be anti-patriotic saboteurs. Anybody can go out of favour in the blink of an eye. The State is tireless in exercising the utmost vigilance over scientists and doctors who present themselves as 'do-gooders', thinking only of the needs of humanity and of their patients.

Lena is watching him. She'll know exactly what he's thinking. Everyone saw *Court of Honour*. She glances around her again, and says very quietly, 'I know it's not quite the same thing, but it'll turn out the same way, believe me. *They* believed that they were acting in good faith and so they would be all right. All they were thinking about was the cure. That was their mistake.'

He nods. Not for the first time, he's amazed by Lena's trust in him. 'I understand what you're saying, Lena,' he answers.

'Do you? I hope so. You've got too much faith in people, but to me all this smells wrong. Did he tell you what's wrong with the boy?'

'Not yet. What do you know, Lena?'

'Not a lot. No one's been allowed near him except Russov. He's had X-rays done already, did he tell you that?'

A wave of anger courses through Andrei. How can that be possible? To have X-rays done, but not to tell him! Was Andrei supposed to order more X-rays and so give the patient a double dose of radiation?

'Retinskaya did the X-rays out of hours,' says Lena, naming a radiographer who is new to the department and whom Andrei scarcely knows. 'She's like *that* with Russov.'

'Lena, how do you know all these things?'

'Because I've got kids. There's only me to look after them, and so I have to know things. Listen, we've been talking too long. Promise me you won't go in for any heroics. A man like Volkov, you don't want him even to know your name. You just have to not be here, that's all it'll take. Call in sick tomorrow.'

The children. Yes, Lena has two children. And no husband, like so many. Andrei never knew him, because Lena's not a Leningrader. She's a Muscovite who moved here after the war. Her husband was a prisoner of war and he died in a German camp. He left behind a girl who must be fourteen now, tall, with long plaits, and a boy a year or so younger. Both of them are much fairer than Lena, and the girl is as slender as a willow, quite different from her dark, stocky mother. The dead man moves inside them like a shadow, in the turn of a head or the gesture of a hand.

27

Anna has always liked Lena. Kolya likes the girl, too: Vava.

Call in sick! If only he could. Anna could call in sick too — a double miracle — and they'd take their bikes and some bread and sausage and cycle out to the dacha for the day. Kolya would be at school, so it would be a real holiday, just the two of them. He'd repair the shutters, and Anna would dig the vegetable garden and then make tea.

But Russov must be crazy to take such a risk with the X-rays. It's inconceivable that he's simply destroyed them. There must be a record.

Crazy, or very, very frightened. What can those X-rays have shown?

If it's some form of juvenile arthritic disease, then it's legitimate — or at least, semi-legitimate — to shunt the case on to Andrei. Everyone in the hospital knows he runs two JA clinics a week. But X-rays reveal many things —

He fights down an urge to find Russov and shake him until he disgorges every bit of information he's got. Let's see if he dares to lie about those X-rays when Andrei's hands are around his throat!

Russov would still lie. What's he got to lose by it? And the radiographer, what's her name, she'll lie too. They'll have calculated that the worst that could happen is that the child might remember being X-rayed; but no one takes much notice of what children say.

Another wave passes through him, but this time it's revulsion rather than anger. The child, in the middle of all this, not suspecting a thing. He's been told what doctors are for: doctors are there to make you better. What have we come to, thinks Andrei, when our patients can make us ashamed of ourselves.

Call in sick . . . An attack of flu, even though it's midsummer. He can smell the earth as Anna pulls weeds from between her rows of carrots. The soil will be moist after all this rain. The weeds will come out easily, and Anna will throw them on to a heap to wilt and die.

He blinks. The blob of sun on the corridor wall wavers. The day shines before him, impossibly ordinary and beautiful. This must be how the dead think of life. All those things they used to take for granted, and can never have again.

He is no brilliant Roskin. He's never likely to be offered trips to America, or the chance to be bamboozled by American spies posing as disinterested fellow researchers who care for nothing but the good of humanity. He's just an ordinary doctor; a good one, it would be false modesty not to recognize that, but still — just a doctor.

That's all he wants; no more, but no less. He wants to live out an ordinary, valuable life. He wants Anna, and their life together, and Kolya too, maddening as Kolya so often is. He wants to come into work early and smile as he passes a colleague in the corridor, with her arms full of files.

'Busy day?'

'Yes, isn't it always?'

He wants to sit in his vest by the wide-open window on the first warm day of spring, drinking a beer, with Anna somewhere in the room behind him, sorting the little brown envelopes of seeds she's saved from last summer. Each envelope is labelled in her beautiful slanted handwriting. She has what he always thinks of as 'an artist's hand'. His own writing is cramped and hard to read. But they've never needed to send each other letters, because they've always been together.

That child in his private room doesn't know it and can't help it, but he carries a disease that destroys ordinary life as fast as the plague corrupts a living body. His father is high up in the Ministry for State Security, and their mothers are so tired too, after long days at work. It's important to manage things so that everyone stays calm. There seems to be more noise than usual — someone's crying . . .

At last all the noise fades away. The scratching of her pen is loud. Surely that head measurement can't be right — or only if a child had hydrocephalus —

Just then Irina pokes her head around the door. 'You finished in here, Anna? I'm off in a minute.'

Anna stands up. 'I've got a few last measurements to put on the chart, and then I thought I'd stay on a bit to work out the averages.'

' "Averages"? That's ridiculous. Isn't it enough to keep a record of each child?'

'Apparently not.'

'Well, if you will keep on "showing a special interest" . . .'

They both laugh. This is a favourite phrase of the nursery head, Larissa Nikolayevna Morozova. She is a tiny woman who barely comes up to Anna's shoulder, but is packed with dynamic force. She has a way of making all her staff do far more work than they ever intended, by divining a 'special interest' in everyone. Irina's is hygiene. Anna's is nutrition, and Larissa Nikolayevna has

and he has one of those names that is spoken only in whispers: *Volkov.*

2

'That's right, heels against the wall, and now stand up as straight as you can.'

Anna is kneeling so that her eyes are level with little Vasya's. He stands proudly, chin up.

'Not on tiptoe, Vasya. You see, if you stand on tiptoe now and next time you forget, I'll think you've shrunk and I'll get worried.'

Vasya looks at her sternly, as if to say: *This is no time for jokes!*

'All done. Do you want to look at your graph?'

Anna is responsible for keeping the children's height and weight charts. Three years ago she gained a qualification in child nutrition, after two years' study at night school. Now she has special responsibility for monitoring the children's diet and preparing information sheets on nutrition, which are put up on the walls for the nursery parents.

'You see that curve, Vasya? That's where you started, there, when they measured you right after you were born.'

'When I was a baby.'

'Yes, when you were a baby. And they measured your head, too: look, that's a separate chart. These are all the measurements we got from the clinic. This is where you are now . . . And look, this is how tall we think you will be, when you're a man, if you keep on following the curve.'

She shows him the place on the wall measure. Vasya gazes upwards, his eyes wide.

'One hundred and seventy-six centimetres. That's a good height for a man. Now, go and put your shoes on and find the others. It's home time.'

When Vasya has gone, Anna sits back on her heels, and sighs. It's been a long day, and her back aches. She stretches her arms up high above her head, keeping balance. Just a short break, then she'll get back to the figures.

Dimly she hears the hubbub of the children leaving. She's being covered for home time today. Alla is helping arms into sleeves, crossing thick scarves over chests, cramming thumbs into mitten holes. The children are so tired and fractious by the end of the day,

every intention of sending her on further courses. 'You're an intelligent woman,' she says to Anna, as if this is something Anna's unlikely to have spotted for herself. Larissa Nikolayevna wants her to create a subset within her statistics, to track the growth of children born to *blokadnitsa* mothers. What are the effects, if any, of maternal starvation? Such statistics would be an invaluable basis for future research. In addition there's a ready-made control group, because so many of the nursery mothers were post-war immigrants to Leningrad.

'So how's the hand-washing campaign going, Irinochka?'

Irina sighs.

'Germs on your fingers, germs on your
    palms,
Germs on your wrists and germs on your
    thumbs.
When you come here to the sink you
    must fly,
And kill those germs before they
    multi-PLY!
Wash those germs away!
Wash those germs A-WA-AA-AAAY!'

'My God, did you make that up?'
'I'm afraid so. The kids love singing it,

though. Apparently the incidence of colds and flu can be reduced by up to thirty per cent if children wash their hands each time they come indoors after using public transport. We're touching germs all the time — the whole world is contaminated, Anna. And the rule applies to adults too, of course. Imagine the number of working days that are being lost quite unnecessarily. Children can become their parents' educators!'

'Each time? But the soap's so harsh. Won't their hands get chapped?'

'Don't. Just don't. I've still got to write the hand-washing hygiene fact sheet for the parents not to read. All the same, it's got to be pinned up and then taken down after a decent interval. And by that time the next campaign will be starting.'

'Irina . . .' Anna wants to say, *'Be careful . . .'* but of course you can't say such a thing.

Irina winks. 'I am getting support at the highest level for the cross-generational, outreach and home-penetrational aspects of the campaign.'

'It sounds a lot of work. You picked the wrong special interest.'

'*I* picked it? But don't worry, I have a new one in mind.'

'What can it be?'

Irina flicks Anna a look from under her lashes. 'I am making a full-time, one-hundred-per-cent-committed study of available men within the twenty-five-to-forty-five-year age group.'

'And reporting back, I hope?'

'If it seems "appropriate",' says Irina, with a sanctimonious smile and perfect mimicry of another pet word of Larissa Nikolayevna's.

'You're not fair to her. She's transformed this place,' says Anna. 'You've got to admit she's the best we've ever had.'

'I know. I know,' says Irina, suddenly sounding so weary that Anna looks at her in surprise. 'It's all right for Morozova, though, isn't it? A husband, three children — I ask you, whoever has three children these days? — a good job, and she'll get a better one, she's on the move all right, that one. And she's only thirty-seven. It's not even as if she's ugly. Have you seen her husband?'

'Mmm, yes, I did once.'

'Mmm, yes, exactly. What I want to know is, how did she get hold of him? There aren't any men like that around any more. And you know what, Anna, he takes her dancing on Saturday nights.'

'She moves well, even though she's tiny,'

says Anna thoughtfully. 'She'd be a good dancer.'

'The whole thing makes me sick,' says Irina. 'Do you know what I'm doing on my Saturday night?'

'No, what?'

'Going to the flicks with my sister. She'll chomp her way through a whole bag of sunflower seeds, and cry at the soppy bits.'

'Don't, Irinochka. You've got loads of time, you're only twenty-eight. Look at your hair. I wish mine was as lovely and thick as yours. And you've got beautiful eyes.'

'It's not enough, though, is it, not when there are ten women to one decent man. You've done all right, Anna, you've got Andrei. You were lucky. Go on, tell me what you'll be doing on Saturday night. Rub salt in the wound.'

Anna laughs. 'Andrei's taking Kolya on a fishing trip, so they'll be away overnight. I'm going to work on my dress.'

'Oh — you mean *the* dress? Has he found out about it yet?'

'No, and he's not going to until the evening of the ball.'

'You see, there you are. A perfect place for me to research my special subject, but it'll be you going. What a waste.'

'I think you've got the wrong idea of what

a hospital ball is like,' says Anna, thinking of the crowded floor, the women doctors with their hair tightly curled and their ill-fitting, hopeful dresses, the men outnumbered and drinking too much.

'The thing is,' says Irina with a sudden passion that catches Anna off guard, 'I wish it *was* a joke, but it's not. I'm so sick of it all. The way things are. Never anything happening except what you know is going to happen. Is this how it's meant to be?'

Anna glances at the door. But it's all right, Irina isn't really talking loudly. Like everyone else, she's so much in the habit of being careful that she never really loses control. 'I don't know how things are meant to be,' she says quietly, and there is a short silence. Then, 'Listen, when the ball is over, why don't you borrow the dress one evening? We're about the same size, and the colour would be lovely on you. You could go dancing.'

Irina has seen the fabric. Anna brought it in, a beautiful soft dark green glazed cotton. You couldn't buy such quality nowadays. It was something from long ago, which came out of a small travelling trunk that a theatre friend of Marina's had brought from Moscow, years after the war. He had kept it safe. The trunk was valuable in itself, because it was covered in fine leather and had a lock that still clicked open as smoothly as the day it was made. It contained two parcels of material and a pair of red satin slippers that were too small for Anna. Marina's slippers. Anna weighed them in her hand, thinking of the dead woman, her father's friend. Her father's lover, who had loved him all her life, and now lay with him in the same communal grave.

There was a dress-length of red silk in one of the parcels, but the colour was too striking. It would make her stand out. To arouse envy was dangerous. Silk, after all . . .

The silk fetched a good price, and Anna put the money towards Kolya's school clothes, and new winter boots. She kept the slippers. They seemed too personal to sell; they had the faintest imprint of Marina's feet in them. She thought of Marina walking around their apartment with her quick, light steps and her beautiful actress's carriage. But she'd proved how tough she was. Marina had fought for life and she'd kept them all fighting. It wasn't until Anna's father died that she gave up.

Anna closed her eyes, holding the slippers. She saw her father, wrapped in frost, and Marina clinging to his body.

They were gone. How crazy it seemed,

that a fragile luxury like these slippers should survive when Marina and her father were dead. She folded them back in the tissue paper, and replaced them in the chest. But she would use the green cotton.

'Really? You're sure you wouldn't mind lending it?' Irina was asking eagerly.

'Quite sure. Besides, we all have a duty to share the fruits of our special-interest research with one another.' She smiles, but Irina doesn't smile back. She's looking over Anna's shoulder.

Anna hasn't heard the light footsteps. The first she knows of Larissa Nikolayevna's presence is her crisply approving, 'My own view exactly, Anna Mikhailovna.'

A wave of heat rushes through Anna's body, but long habit supports her. 'We were discussing the children's measurements, Larissa Nikolayevna.'

'You've established your subset?'

'I think so.'

'Excellent. I look forward to hearing your outcomes. But surely you should be going, both of you?'

'I'm just going to do a little more on the averages,' murmurs Anna, pushing back her hair and stifling the faint unease she always feels when talking to a woman who is so much shorter than she is, and so much higher up. Morozova is finished and perfect in her tailored cream blouse and a dark skirt and jacket which look as if they've been made to some special, miniature pattern. They are office clothes. They tell the world that while the nursery has to be a place of overalls, mopped floors and the smell of children sleeping in the early afternoons, it is also a proper, scientifically managed workplace with targets to meet and an impressive reputation in the wider pedagogical world. Anna looks measuringly at the waist and lapels of the dark suit.

Morozova nods once more, and then gives them both her sudden, vivid smile. That smile never fails to weaken Anna. Just when she thinks she has got the measure of Morozova and her ambitions, that smile says something quite different. There is a captivating warmth behind its brilliance. In spite of herself, Anna finds herself wanting to please, to fulfil, to present her statistics immaculately and slightly ahead of the target time.

'Excellent,' Morozova repeats. 'Well, I'm in my office if you have any difficulties.'

As if that needs to be said. She won't leave before eight. There's an inspection coming up, and then a Professor of Child Development is bringing students here on Friday as part of their fieldwork. The nursery is becoming known as a first-rate site for research. As the inspection approaches, everyone works later and later. Better to be bog-eyed than caught out. There must be no sign of slackness. One set of poorly kept records might be enough to wreck the collective effort. Morozova doesn't need to point this out. The pressure is within each one of them, and there will be no letting up.

A few weeks earlier, Anna was called into Morozova's office 'for a chat'. 'I've been observing your work, Anna Mikhailovna. I am happy to tell you that you're doing very well. But you know that already, and I want to talk to you about something else. It still seems to me that you are not reaching your potential. Your organizational skills are excellent. You have a strong grasp of statistics, even though I understand that you have no qualifications in the field. In fact, I would go so far as to say that you have a mathematical brain.' Morozova looked expectant. This was high praise and she would want Anna to acknowledge it as such. Anna bowed her head, feeling awkward. 'Your relationships with other staff are very good,' Morozova continued, 'and so, all in all, in my opinion, you have unused capacity. Obviously you need training; you will have to attend further courses. Ideally you require a pedagogical qualification, but I understand that full-time study for a degree may not be feasible?' She paused. The word 'degree' resonated in the silence.

'No,' said Anna. Better say too little than too much. Certainly better than allowing anyone to guess the real reason she would never apply for a university course.

It was the forms. They asked for too much information. Those lethal questions about family and background would reveal her class origins and allow an experienced reader to trace her father's long years out of favour, unpublished and suspect. Kolya must never be tainted. He would need to apply to university one day, but she wasn't going to think of that yet. He was only sixteen. Things might have changed by then. Meanwhile, the stupidest thing you could do, if there happened to be any blot on your copybook, was to remind the high-ups that you existed at all.

'In that case,' went on Morozova briskly, 'let's focus on what can be achieved by further part-time study. Courses in mathematics and statistics would be particularly appropriate for the development of your career. I shall most certainly support your application, Anna Mikhailovna.'

'It's very good of you —'

'You can achieve valuable qualifications. You need to be thinking about promotion prospects.'

Anna's mind raced. She must be very careful. 'I'm very grateful,' she said.

The other woman looked at her sharply. 'But? Do I hear a "but" coming?'

'It's — well, it's difficult for me. Andrei works long hours at the hospital. Kolya's studying hard and it's important for me to be there in the evenings.'

Morozova poked her head forward, like a blackbird considering a worm. 'Surely it's possible to organize your domestic life so that your career isn't held back.'

Anna bit back a reply. She thought of lunch hours spent rushing from queue to queue, of peeling the potatoes for supper before taking off her coat, of nights when Kolya coughed and coughed and she knew that next morning bronchitis would have set in. Of endless negotiations over the cleaning of the common ways, and the fact that she usually ended up sweeping and scrubbing the stairs herself, because she can't bear how dirty they get.

But Morozova has three children, and she

45

has never been known to take a day off. One adolescent boy is no argument. Morozova is a graduate of the Herzen Pedagogical Institute. She possesses a masters in pre-school education. In time she will complete the research and write up her doctoral thesis: 'A Consideration of Primary Aspects of Goal-identification in Target-setting for Language Skills in the Under-sevens'. She'd be bound to think that if Anna defined her goals she'd be able to sail past dirty floors.

'I like working here, with the children,' said Anna.

But Morozova wasn't going to let that pass, either. 'Look at it another way, Anna Mikhailovna. A worker who consistently underperforms — that is, fails to fulfil her potential — might, in a sense, be seen as stealing.'

' "Stealing"!'

'Yes. Such a person might be seen as depriving society of what it has a right to expect: that is, the fullest possible engagement.'

Anna was silenced. To say nothing was risky, but not as risky as saying the wrong thing at such a moment. But suddenly Morozova relented, allowing a kindlier smile to settle on her lips.

'Of course I am not saying that you are

46

such a person. Gracious me, this is just a private chat between the two of us. As I've said to you before, you are doing well. But think about it, Anna Mikhailovna. Let me share something a little more personal with you. It has always been my policy never — *never* — to fail in seizing an opportunity. And it's because I've been watching you — and because of my respect for your work — that I want to be sure that you take the opportunities that are offered to you.'

Anna hasn't mentioned this conversation to Andrei. Partly it's because she's still not quite sure of her own position. Has Morozova spotted something real, which Anna ought to address?

Morozova is from Moscow. She didn't live through the siege. Hard as life probably was for her — and Anna knows that she lost a brother — she has a kind of energy, even an innocence, which Anna no longer possesses.

All she wanted, as those terrible months stretched out as if they would never end, was to live, to be on this earth, to put food into Kolya's mouth, to sit in the radiating heat of a lit stove. All these things seemed as remote as miracles.

She had survived. She'd lived so much with the dead that she had felt like one of

47

them. Their hands had reached out for her, and she'd almost clasped them. Her father had lain frozen in the next room, long day after long day, waiting for Anna to come to him. Marina had died, too. The streets had been full of people waiting curled up under snowdrifts with one blackened hand clutching at the air, or seated in trams that were frozen to the tracks, as powder snow blew in and filled the caves of their eyes. In the city's parks they sat on benches, slumped like people tired after long days at work, fallen asleep while they waited for a summer that would never warm them.

It had finished. Green had broken over the city like a tide. But sometimes Anna still sees them, out of the corner of her eye. The grass has grown thick over their communal graves, but they are still waiting. When she struggles home through a February blizzard she seems to see them, leaning heavily on sticks, stopping every five paces to catch their breath, making their way to the bread queue.

But she has survived. She has left them behind, walking with the quick pace of someone who now eats three meals a day. Sometimes Anna feels a clench in her stomach, almost like fear, as if she's lost something she'll never be able to find again.

She's never mentioned this to anyone, but she thinks other people must share that feeling. It's better not to talk about the things that really frighten you.

Andrei's different. He talks about Mikhail and Marina quite naturally, as if they died in the ordinary way, and are safe in the past. When Kolya was little, Andrei would tell him the story of how he first met 'your father'. 'We were both in the People's Volunteers, and we used to sit round the fire and talk. Once a woman gave us eggs and we cooked and shared them.'

'And after that my father was wounded,' Kolya would say, knowing the story, wanting to hear it again.

Kolya would be all right at school, with such stories to tell. He had a father who had fought and been wounded and then had died of his wounds, like so many fathers. The dark years before the war — the years of the Terror — could be covered up by this acceptable death. Little Kolya didn't know about the friends who disappeared, or the fellow writers who sat on editorial boards and told Mikhail that really, no one wanted his kind of stuff these days.

'And when Father was wounded, that's how you met Anna,' Kolya would say triumphantly, when he was seven or eight and believed in a past that fitted together as neatly as a jigsaw puzzle. His father had died, but Andrei had met Anna and now he lived with them. Most people who didn't really know the family thought they were his parents. People would look surprised when he called them 'Anna' or 'Andrei'.

But now he's sixteen and the old stories don't satisfy him. Talk of the past bores him. Even when his friends aren't round, he still spends hours in his room, choosing to be alone rather than with either of them. What he does in there, she has no idea. Kolya takes the luxury of a private space for granted, because he's always had it. Sometimes she wants to shake him and shout: 'Don't you know how privileged you are? Don't you realize how other people have to live?'

But of course he knows. He visits his friends. A boy like Kolya is aware of everything. It's just — well, just that he doesn't want to seem aware. At sixteen, you don't want to be grateful.

She knows that Andrei wants a child. Andrei is like a father to Kolya, thinks Anna loyally, but it's natural for a man to want a child of his own.

Is he really like a father, or is Anna just parroting what other people say about their little family? Does Kolya think that Andrei is a father to him?

It's impossible to know what kind of father Mikhail might have been to a moody, strong-willed teenage boy. She's slipped into the habit of thinking about her own father as if he were Kolya's grandfather.

Kolya has changed so much in the past couple of years. He never confides in Anna these days. He seems wary, defensive, sometimes even ironic. He says he wants the right to drink beer, but he longs for sweet things like a baby. In fact, he's greedy. You can't leave a loaf of bread out on the table.

Anna thought that all adolescents devoured poetry; but not Kolya. He hardly opens a book and seems to regard Anna and Andrei's reading as a foible he's willing to put up with for the sake of peace. *'All these books everywhere! Can't we get rid of some of them?'* Once he came in from school and wrinkled his nose critically before pronouncing, *'Do you know what this place smells of? Mouldy books!'* What her father would have said to this, she can't begin to imagine.

At school most of the teachers tell the same story. Kolya gets by, causes no trouble, is an easygoing, well-liked student. His

51

marks keep him safely in the middle of the class. They're reasonably satisfied with his progress.

Only the occasional teacher has mentioned that Kolya is not really fulfilling his potential. Immediately her whole being sprang to Kolya's defence. Or was it to her own? Was she really afraid that there was something in the life they led that had quenched Kolya's ambition? *You've made him like yourself,* said a small, cold voice deep inside her. But no, that isn't true. Kolya is entirely different.

Anna thinks of how Kolya would listen to stories when he was seven. His face was wide open, as if it were a window through which the stories flowed. He would put one hand on her arm, urging her on. He used to ask her the most astonishing questions, and she would think: *Are all children like this?*

He is often critical of her these days. 'You're always . . .' 'You never . . .' Andrei says it's not worth getting upset. It's just Kolya's age, and they have to expect it.

It's a long time since she and Andrei talked about having children of their own. Towards the end of the war, when Kolya was eight or so, they began to imagine it. The siege was broken. Our forces were driving westward, sweeping back over the land that had been swallowed by the Germans.

They could begin to think of a future.

'When we have children . . .'

'Which do you think would be better, a girl first or a boy?'

'Maybe a girl. Kolya might be jealous of a boy.'

'He won't be jealous if we handle it right.'

'It's just as well really, isn't it, that you can't choose?'

'No, you have to take what comes.'

Take what comes. They'd laughed then. They had a future. Not only had they not died, but their children would be born and would survive them. They would become parents. A boy with Andrei's eyes; a girl who walked as if she was only just managing not to break into a run, like Anna. But different, too; entirely different. Children who would grow up in better times. They wouldn't remember the war, and they'd only know about hunger from books.

She'd allowed herself to drop her guard. She'd believed that things really might be different, after the war. Surely people would have had enough of death. And Andrei, too, had hoped for better things. Otherwise, suffering was just suffering; purposeless and mechanical. You couldn't allow yourself to believe that.

People said that Leningrad's heroism

would be rewarded. No other city had held out for so long. Paris had fallen in forty days. Leningrad had held out for nine hundred, and had never fallen, no matter how many shells rained down on it. They had starved in thousands, and then in hundreds of thousands, but in the end it had been the Germans who retreated.

It seemed impossible now that they had really done the things they'd done. That they'd lived, let alone continued to work and to fight.

But so soon after, the signs of hope began to disappear. Exhibitions that showed the life of the city under siege were dismantled, and the exhibits scattered. Plays were written, but never put on. Memoirs were put away in drawers. *What has happened to you is not as important as you think. We intend to tell this story in a different way.*

The visionary reconstruction was a pipe dream. Money was needed elsewhere, and Leningrad must accept that there were other priorities. It was a provincial city and due for relegation. If Leningrad thought it had deserved better, it was naive. *We don't mind hearing about the battles and the shells, but the appalling details of starvation are not required. Besides, it raises unpleasant questions. Please keep your personal stories where they belong, inside your heads.*

Every hope had been smashed.

But maybe some time, in the not too distant future, things would start to get easier. *'No one can live for ever,'* they whispered to each other. Even now, when they're alone, they go no further than that. *He* is an old man, even though his polished-up photographs make him look young as he presides over the great parades. Over seventy now.

'Georgians live for a long time,' said Andrei once.

'Only if they stay in Georgia,' Anna replied.

'Kolya might be jealous of a boy.'

'He won't be jealous if we handle it right.'

'It's just as well really, isn't it, that you can't choose?'

'No, you have to take what comes.'

Take what comes.

Yes, and embrace it. In this one area of her life at least, Anna wasn't going to struggle and organize and plan and budget. She thought of the warm wind that blew from the south-west after winter had broken, and the way the earth seemed to spread itself out in its nakedness and wait.

■ ■ ■ ■

She can hardly bear to think of all that now. She'd known nothing, and she'd been punished for it. That wind certainly hadn't blown anywhere near her. She was twenty-six, then twenty-eight, and then suddenly she was over thirty and beginning to be frightened. Now she is thirty-four. Sometimes, when Andrei's out, she secretly takes down his medical textbooks. She scours through them, as hot and scared as a kid trying to find out about sex. The diagrams and cold descriptive paragraphs repel her. They talk about abnormalities, and propose investigations on defective lumps of flesh.

She can't talk to Andrei about it. She can't bear to bring her failure out into the open between them. Besides, Andrei works such long hours, and Kolya never seems to go to bed now. It was easier when he was little and after eight o'clock the evening was their own.

She shouldn't be thinking like this.

The ball is a month away, at midsummer. Andrei has been lucky in the draw this year, and is neither on duty nor on call. Kolya suddenly decided that he'd like to stay in the city that night, but Anna wasn't giving way.

'No, you're going with Grisha to his uncle's. It's all arranged, and you agreed.'

'Only because *you* wanted me to. "Acquiesced" is the word, not "agreed". Grisha's uncle lives way out in the sticks.'

'There'll be a bonfire, and loads of food. There are five or six boys from your class going.'

'I'd rather stay here in the city. I'm not really friends with Grisha.'

'It's not going to happen, Kolya. I don't want you hanging around the parks all night with Sasha and Lev.'

'*Their* parents think they're old enough.'

'You know what the white nights are like. There'll be too much drinking going on.'

'We won't be drinking much,' said Kolya, with a weary, scornful air.

'No, you won't, because you won't be here, you'll be at Grisha's uncle's.'

Kolya shrugged in a way that always made Anna feel as if she were the childish, unreasonable one.

Well, maybe she is being selfish, but for one night she doesn't want to have to worry about Kolya. She and Andrei will be free. They'll be able to wander through the white night as long as they like, and when they get back the apartment will be empty, all theirs. Kolya stays up so late, and often Sasha and Lev are there too. Adolescent voices boom and crack. Sometimes it sounds as if they're making speeches, not talking to one another. The bed creaks, chairs scrape, laughter bellies out, or someone starts to play the piano . . .

She can't remember things ever being like that for her. She and her mother always had to be careful, because of her father. He was so sensitive.

You can't blame the boys for wanting to be round here. Sasha shares a room with his grandfather and younger brother. Lev, his mother and his grandparents are squeezed into one room in a communal apartment. It's a big room, Lev said, but his grandfather snores whenever he rolls on to his back. They wedge him with pillows, but it doesn't work. And he farts, too, Kolya told Anna later. All night long.

Kolya has that miracle, a room of his own. God knows how they've managed to hold on to the apartment, with its two good-sized rooms. Anna and Andrei sleep in the living room. They've put up a rail and made curtains which they can draw around their bed at night. Kolya might wander through at any time, to the toilet or for a drink of water. He takes after their father; he's a nightbird. But sometimes, with three boys tiptoeing through the room in procession and then collapsing with laughter as soon as they're back behind a shut door, it can be a bit much.

At least Kolya never tries to play the piano at night. The neighbours won't stand for that. Even in daytime Anna has to be careful. If the Maleviches were to put in a complaint it might start an investigation into their living space. She's warned Kolya, but she doesn't want to keep on nagging him all the time.

You want them to be spontaneous, even though of course they can't be. Her friend Evgenia, in the war, used to have a saying: *'He's swallowed the rule book, and now he shits out rules.'*

3

'Where's Kolya?'

'Out.' Anna lifts the pot from the stove, and places it on the wooden mat.

'Has he eaten?'

'Of course. When does Kolya ever miss a meal?' She gives him the glint of a smile before her face turns solemn as she lifts the lid on her stew, releasing a puff of savoury steam.

'I made the stock with the last of that boiling fowl,' she murmurs, as she ladles two generous helpings into bowls. For the hundredth time Andrei marvels at the time and trouble Anna takes, and the way she can transform a handful of dried mushrooms, a few onions, barley and a chicken carcass into a potful of thick, rich golden stew. 'It needs a bit more pepper,' she says critically, after tasting a drop from the side of her spoon.

'What are those dark bits?'

'Chopped nettles. I've only used the tips. I brought a bagful back from the dacha.'

'I've told you, Anna, for heaven's sake, just go to the market and buy fresh greens. We've got the money.'

'Nettles are full of iron.'

He gives up. Anna's like that. She'll spend hours hunting for puffballs in the forest until she finds one the size of a melon to bring home. She slices and fries the thick creamy flesh, and they eat it just as it is, smoking hot. Every time, one or other of them will say, 'Don't you think it tastes like chicken?' Anna claims to be able to pick nettles without gloves — 'It's fine, you just have to grasp them tight and then they can't sting you' — and she'll walk miles in search of wild raspberries. But she can be extravagant too. He's shocked sometimes by what she'll pay for a bunch of the earliest lilac.

Anna smiles. 'Kolya had two platefuls.' He always eats too fast. At least they've got him out of the habit of curving his arm around his plate as if someone were about to snatch it. People say that children forget, but Kolya hasn't forgotten. Hunger is imprinted in him.

'I suppose he's gone off with his friends,' says Andrei.

'They've gone to the Summer Garden. He

61

said he wouldn't be back late. Anyway, they'll be kicked out of there at ten.'

The apartment seems many times larger when Kolya's not at home. Andrei takes a breath, feeling his lungs expand. It's so good to be alone with Anna for once, although of course he'll never say so. It's ironic, really, that they've had a child with them from the day they met, and yet their own child, the child they once took for granted and expected to come along just as surely as a train will grow from a speck in the distance until it reaches the platform . . . That child has never come.

They have each other. They have Kolya. Anna doesn't want tests and examinations, and he's not going to force them on her. The one time he suggested it, as tactfully as he could, she backed away from him. Her eyes were narrow with anger. *'Just because you're a doctor, you think I'm nothing more than a broken-down machine.'* Besides, the thought of Anna with her legs in stirrups while one of his colleagues levers a speculum into her vagina makes him recoil. This is enough: the two of them alone together in the apartment, the rich steam, Anna's hair escaping into curls around her forehead.

Anna thinks, disloyally, of how calm it is.

Kolya and Andrei both put pressure on her, because they both want to come first with her. They don't mean to do it, but sometimes she feels as if she is being sawn in half.

'It's after nine,' Andrei says. 'He stays out later and later.'

'I know. But they're all out in the streets these light evenings. They can't stay indoors. You remember how it was when we were young ourselves.'

It stabs him, that she should speak as if she weren't young any more. She's not much over thirty, for God's sake.

'Do you know, Andrei, it was the funniest thing. Just as Kolya went out of the door, I caught a glimpse of his back view — and you know how sometimes you suddenly see someone not as the person you know they are, but objectively? I mean, when you come across one of your family in the street when you aren't expecting it, and you see them as other people do, who don't know them?'

'Yes?'

'He looked so different suddenly — quite old, like a student. And I've never thought Kolya looked like my father, but he's beginning to. He pulled his cap forward and then he ducked down to see himself in the mirror and he looked exactly like my father.

They must be almost the same height now, Kolya's grown so much this year.'

He notices two things: that she has slipped into speaking of her father in the present tense, and that even though Mikhail is Kolya's father as much as he is Anna's, Anna never refers to 'our father'.

'He reminded me so much of my father,' Anna goes on, in a low voice. 'You know how he was, always so absorbed in whatever he was doing.'

'Yes.' *And so far from being absorbed in you,* thinks Andrei.

'He couldn't get outside himself, that was the trouble,' Anna says, her voice even lower. 'He was trapped. I used to hear him in the night, walking about.'

'That doesn't mean Kolya won't be happy.'

'I know. Did you have a good day?' She says it casually, as she spoons the last of the stew on to his plate.

'Quite good.'

'Morozova wants me to go on a maths course, and statistics as well. She's got her eye on me.'

'Sounds ominous,' says Andrei lightly. He can see that Anna really is worried.

'I'm not "fulfilling my potential" apparently.'

'My God, that woman wouldn't reco[g]
your potential if it jumped up and bit [.]
It drives him mad, this obsession w[ith]
status, position, qualifications. The qu[es]
tions that check and place you in less than [a]
minute: your current research interest? You[r]
publications? Party membership?

He's even been infected by it himself. The
fear of being left behind, and becoming one
of those doctors whose opinion no one ever
seeks. You have to go to meetings. You have
to be seen, and be heard saying the right
things. Someone whose clinical work you
really respect puts an arm around your
shoulders one day as you're both walking
down a corridor and says: *You know, young
man, I've been thinking that you'd have a lot
to offer to the hospital liaison committee. It's
so important for the decision-makers to be
kept in touch with our rising clinicians . . .*

And, of course, it is. He understands
exactly what good will be done, and to
whom. Doctors who want to develop their
careers must learn to sit on committees and
talk about the public good rather than getting bogged down in the detail of individual
cases. Besides, it's in the interests of the
patients as well. A doctor with 'pull' can
secure the latest equipment and drugs for
his clinics. Keep yourself pure as the driven

65

snow if you want, but there's a cost attached, and it's not just you who'll pay it. The brotherly arm will fall from your shoulders. The minutes of the meetings will never reach you. Much better roll up your sleeves and *get stuck in.*

The arm around his shoulders gives an encouraging squeeze. *We're all in this together.*

Andrei crumbles bread into his stew. Already the moment when he should have said something about Russov and the child has passed. He looks at Anna, willing her to break through the fog that wraps itself around him.

'I shall have to do something,' says Anna, 'Morozova's not going to leave me alone. It's not as if I didn't respect her —'

He gets up and comes round the table, behind her chair. She leans back, pressing her head against him. He bends over her, and kisses her cheek because he cannot reach her mouth. Her eyes are closed as she takes his hand and kisses it, then continues to hold it against her face. Another light kiss touches him, and then another. There'll just be time, before Kolya gets back, if they're quick —

But he can't. He's got to tell her.

'Anna.'

'Yes?'

'Something happened today.'

She twists around to face him and looks up, her eyes wide and searching. Her body has stiffened. 'What?'

'It might turn out to be nothing. But Russov asked me to look at one of his patients today.'

She says nothing, waiting.

'It's a child, a boy of ten. The father — well, I've only had it from Lena. He's MGB. Volkov.'

'Volkov!' She starts as if an electric shock has gone through her.

'I know.'

There's a long silence between them, and then Anna rises from her chair, walks to the window and looks out. After another little while she turns back to him. He can't see her expression clearly, because she's standing against the light.

'*The* Volkov, you mean?'

'Yes. There's only one, I should hope.'

'My God.' Instinctively, she has lowered her voice. 'What's the matter with the child?'

'Russov wouldn't tell me; he made out he had the usual symptoms of some form of juvenile arthritis. Swelling, pain, redness. I haven't got anything like the whole picture.

67

It's all been completely unprofessional. But Lena says it's serious.'

'How would she know?'

'Apparently Russov's had X-rays done on the quiet.'

'But you can't do that, can you?'

'It seems Russov has. There are no records, so I don't know what the results were.'

'But that's —'

'You don't need to tell me.'

'It's something bad. That's why he doesn't want you to know.'

'It's hard not to come to that conclusion,' says Andrei drily.

'My God.' Anna's quiet for a moment, then she says, 'I should be thinking of the child but I'm only thinking of you.'

'I was the same. As soon as Russov told me all I could think about was you and Kolya.'

Slowly, Anna stands up, pressing her palms down on the table as if she needs to support herself. 'Let's go out. There's no air here. Let's go down by the water.'

'But we won't be back in time for Kolya,' says Andrei, surprised to find that he's the one who remembers this.

'He can let himself in for once, he's got his key. I'll write a note for him.'

They walk in silence, arm in arm, through streets that are washed with evening light. The sun is hidden by a thin fleece of cloud. It will scarcely grow dark tonight. The main streets are busy, but Anna and Andrei keep to the back ways, along potholed roads, past damaged buildings.

'Let's go down to the Neva.'

The whole city seems to be out of doors, moving slowly, as if heading to a destination that everybody has agreed on. But there's no destination, only the summer night itself. That's enough for everyone. You stroll like this, relaxed, expectant, swinging hands, when you've got a whole summer night ahead of you. Girls' cotton dresses billow against their bodies as they lick their ice-creams. Young men in naval uniform link arms. An old woman in rusty black with a kerchief on her head hobbles very slowly along the centre of the pavement in front of Anna and Andrei, leaning on her stick. Anna hops off the kerb to pass her, followed by Andrei, and followed by the old granny's voice, grumbling, 'It's all very well when you're young, just wait until you're old like me.'

But she and Andrei are not so young any more, thinks Anna. That girl who's crossing the road, in her white dress splashed with red flowers: she's really young. She looks back, laughing, at the rest of the gaggle of high-school girls who are running to catch up with her. Her hair flies up and her silver necklace jumps against her collarbone. She's very pretty. Anna slides a look at Andrei to see if he's watching, too.

No. Andrei's staring ahead, frowning. Anna's stomach lurches as the fear she'd almost left behind catches up with her. My God, what's she doing, worrying about such a thing when — ? But all the same she can't help being glad Andrei wasn't watching the girl.

'Let's get away from all these people,' says Andrei. At the next corner he turns left, into an even narrower, dustier and more pot-holed street.

'This isn't the way to the river.'

'It'll be quiet along here.'

They wander on, more slowly now. Maybe it's better to avoid the water, Anna thinks. She and Andrei would be like a couple of black crows among the summer faces.

A memory rises up in Anna's mind. Her mother kneels at her feet, tying the sash of Anna's best dress. She glances up at her little girl. Maybe Anna is frowning, or tear-stained, because her mother says, *'You don't go to parties with a long face.'*

A thin, scabby cat hurtles out of an entrance, ears back, yowling. Anna stops, and peers into the courtyard. In the shadows a circle of children bunches. They stare at the couple defiantly. *This is our world. You can't come in.* Anna and Andrei walk on. Suddenly she stops and leans against a pock-marked stone wall. Shell splinters, probably.

'Are you all right?'

'What are we going to do? What are we going to do, Andrei?'

Even the stone might be listening. She'd been desperate to get out of the apartment. Some nights she can almost hear the Maleviches breathing through the walls. She'd thought they would be freer out here in the summer night, but they are more exposed. His face is close to hers, anxious, drawn. He mustn't be worried about her, on top of everything.

'I'm sorry, I was being stupid,' she says. 'Of course we will be all right.'

'Of course we will,' he says, and pulls her close. She feels his heart beating like hers, too fast. She says nothing.

In bed that night, they talk quietly, because

71

they know that Kolya will be awake.

'He never seems to sleep.'

'No wonder he's so pale.'

'And he's like death warmed up in the mornings.'

'When you think how he used to get us up at five in summer.'

' *"It's not time to sleep! The sun's shining!"* '

'And you had to have the curtains relined.'

They grumble quietly, holding each other, avoiding the subject that burns in both their minds.

'Andrei?'

'Yes?'

'Move your arm a bit . . . Listen, you can't get involved. Why should you do this for Russov? He wouldn't do it for you. Lena's right, you'll have to call in sick.'

'For how many days?'

She's silent, calculating.

'Russov will have given Volkov my name already,' goes on Andrei. 'I know him.'

'Then let's go away.'

' "Go away"? What do you mean?'

'Just . . . not be here.'

'I can't leave the hospital. You can't leave the nursery. Besides, Kolya's got exams coming up.'

'I know all that, Andrei. But why not? We could go to the dacha. It's safe there. No one would know we were there —'

'Someone always knows.'

'Not if we're careful.'

'People would see us coming and going. There'd be smoke from the chimney.'

They are talking as if they really might do it, he thinks in amazement. Go away, lie low, let the storm pass. Lose their careers and their livelihoods, but keep their lives. No. It's absurd. Anna is overreacting. Things are not so bad as they used to be. The Terror is over; Yezhov is dead, after causing so many deaths. People aren't vanishing in their hundreds of thousands, as they were in Yezhov's time.

'It's impossible,' says Andrei flatly.

'No, don't you see, it's the only thing to do? The only thing, Andryusha! Once they get hold of you they never let go. They go on and on, and then they go on some more. Once they've got your name on a list they never forget it. They can make up whatever they like. But you can be ill, my darling. You work so hard, you need rest. It's perfectly legitimate. We do nothing but work and work. I want to cultivate more ground at the dacha, anyway. Kolya won't like it, but he'll have to understand. It's for his sake too, Andrei! We can't let his life be wrecked before it's even started.'

Thank God that Kolya is older now. She thinks of them often, those ranks of bewildered children parted from parents and then from grandparents, sent off to children's homes where they got TB and faded away from sheer lack of the will to live. But on the other hand Kolya is almost old enough to be sent to the camps himself. Once the contamination gets into a family, it spreads to every member of it.

'His life won't be wrecked,' says Andrei. His voice sounds cold but she knows he isn't cold, not really. It's just that he's been forced into a corner. 'Nothing's even happened yet. For God's sake, I'm a doctor. Russov's asked me to make an examination, that's all. They can't make much out of that. If the boy's got arthritis, they can hardly blame the doctor.'

'But that's exactly what they will do. It wouldn't be any trouble to them to make a criminal out of you, simply because you've been involved with the treatment. If anything goes wrong, there you are: they've got a scapegoat. You'll have ordered the wrong tests, or they won't have been carried out properly, or something. Russov knows that. Lena knows it. She's trying to help you, only you won't listen. You won't see what's going to happen, because you're too pure and you want to think that everyone's like you.'

'I do see it,' says Andrei quietly. 'Only there isn't an alternative. So we go to the dacha . . . but everyone knows where that is, so it's no solution.'

'We could go to Irkutsk.'

'For heaven's sake, Anna! What on earth would we do there?'

'We could stay with your uncle. You told me he's got two rooms, and the boys have left home, haven't they? They're family. They'd help us until we could find work.'

'That's just crazy, Anna. You're panicking. We haven't got the right papers, we'd never get a residence permit just like that. We live here in Leningrad and our work is here. These are our lives. Are you suggesting that we run away from everything — destroy everything we've built up — just because there might — *might* — be trouble?'

Anna sighs deeply. She knows he understands her, and yet he's pretending not to.

'We *should* panic,' she says. 'People are destroyed because they don't panic in time. They think it won't happen to them.'

He feels her sigh become a shudder, shaking her body.

'Anna. Anna!'

He clasps her tighter, wrapping her in his arms. Her warmth and her softness sur-

75

round him. He could vanish into her, be hidden as she longs to be hidden. He could stop the world from dragging them away from where they want to be.

'Anna!'

She sighs again, differently. Her body moves against his, yielding to his touch so that the melt and flow of sex can begin. He smells her hair and the skin of her neck. She twists round and licks his face, then dives to kiss his belly, following down the dark line of hair that leads to his penis. She rubs her face against it until he groans aloud.

'Shh, Kolya'll hear,' she mutters automatically from the depths of the bed, but it's too late for him to care. They are moving out together, far from their creaking bed and the listening walls, to the place where they are always together and always safe.

4

In the light of the next morning, Andrei is confident that he and Anna have let themselves get worked up over nothing. For heaven's sake, all Russov has asked him to do is to see the boy. He and Anna have given way to paranoia. Easy enough to do, but not very creditable, he tells himself, as he walks to work through the calm grey morning. This mist will lift later on, and it'll be a fine day. Not too hot. He doesn't mind that. Humid, stifling days are bad for his patients. The whole hospital simmers with suppressed irritation once the mercury reaches the high twenties.

His heels strike firmly on the pavement. Anna has had his shoes resoled and the cobbler put metal tips on, as if he were a kid. But he likes the sound.

In bad weather he might take the tram, but on a morning like this half an hour of brisk walking is just what it takes to clear his mind. Everything will be all right. That hollow feeling in his stomach is because he's eaten nothing. They overslept. Anna was rushing around the apartment and there was barely time to gulp a glass of tea.

The boy is a patient who requires diagnosis and treatment: not only requires it, but has a right to it. This has got nothing to do with Russov now.

The figure sitting outside the private room is a Ministry of State Security policeman; one of Volkov's men. Andrei barely glances at him. He's heard of this happening, although high-ups often go to private clinics or have medical treatment in their own homes. But with children it's another matter. Andrei's mouth tightens in anger. The boy's ill, and they prop a goon outside his door.

In the door's name-slot there is one typewritten word: VOLKOV. Information, threat or warning? It could be, and probably is, all three.

'Your papers,' says the policeman, holding out a hand.

'I am Doctor Alekseyev, a paediatrician here. I've been asked to examine this patient.'

'Your papers.'

■ ■ ■ ■

The door of the private room closes behind Andrei with a soft, firm click. The boy is propped up on a heap of pillows. He has a miniature screwdriver in one hand, and an engine on a wooden tray in front of him. He does not look up at Andrei, but the woman sitting at the bedside gets to her feet with convulsive suddenness. She is expensively dressed and her face is thick with make-up, but her body is strong and square. The body of a peasant.

'Good morning,' says Andrei.

Still the boy doesn't look up, but the mother says hastily, 'Say good morning to the doctor, Gorya.'

The boy's fingers tighten on the screwdriver. Andrei measures the outline of his body under the bedclothes. He's tall for ten, and slender for his age. They have fixed a cage over his right leg. Andrei advances slowly and casually towards the bed, as a horseman might approach a nervous foal. The child keeps his head down, but Andrei catches the glint of his eye as he steals a look upwards, towards the doctor.

He's afraid. Arrogant too, maybe, but that's scarcely his fault.

Andrei takes a chair on the opposite side of the bed to the mother.

'That's a fine engine,' he says.

The boy doesn't answer. His face is pale and pinched. Andrei judges that he is in moderately severe pain.

'He's got dozens of them at home, a real collection,' breaks in the mother. 'There's nothing he likes better than putting them to rights when they go wrong. Wherever the fault is, he'll always find it . . .'

'That's good,' says Andrei, and then to the boy, 'I'm Doctor Alekseyev. My father was an engineer; he worked on the design of railway bridges.' Still the boy won't look up, but Andrei knows that he's listening. 'He worked in Siberia. There are a lot of special problems when you're building on permafrost, as you can imagine. He was like you: he could repair anything —'

'He's been in such pain, doctor, you can't imagine,' the mother interrupts again. 'All night, he's been waking up every hour.'

Andrei stands up, and holds out his hand across the bed. 'Excuse me, I should have introduced myself to you. Andrei Mikhailovich Alekseyev. As you probably know, Dr Russov has requested me to do an examination.'

The mother nods, slowly. Her wide brown

eyes may look bovine, but they are shrewd too, sharp even. She's not happy with the way things have gone so far. This hospital has let her boy suffer, that's what she thinks. Such things shouldn't happen, not to people in their position. And yet her peasant self, deep within her, is telling her not to cross Andrei, because he is 'the doctor' and his powers have a touch of magic in them.

Suddenly she remembers her manners. 'Polina Vasilievna Volkova,' she says. She doesn't want to cross him, but at the same time she knows who she is, and what her entitlements are.

'I wonder if you'd be good enough to leave me with Gorya for a little while?' he asks.

She stares at him. 'But I'm his mother. He needs me here.'

'Of course. But in this case I consider it the best approach,' he says firmly, deciding neither to apologize nor to explain. 'And I can see that you're exhausted. You've been up all night with him, I expect?'

'Not just last night,' says the mother with grim pride. 'It's more than a week since I've lain in my bed. Before he got taken in here, I was up with him night after night. Never had my clothes off. You can't leave a child to the servants.'

The effrontery of it makes him smile in

spite of himself. Quickly, he recomposes his face. 'I thought as much. It's what any mother would want to do,' he says. 'I understand that you won't feel able to take a nap, even though that's what you need, but some tea and a breath of fresh air would do you good. There's a courtyard where you can go. Any of the staff will show you.'

Her face eases. She nods again, this time in acquiescence. She wants to be looked after too. 'It's true. It's stuffy in here, even with the fan.'

Yes, they've got a fan. And a bunch of grapes in a bowl on the bedside table. And a handsome bar of chocolate with a wrapper he doesn't even recognize. But he doesn't want to think about all that.

The mother pauses, holding the door handle, and looks back at Andrei. 'He's my only one,' she says, and he can't tell from her tone if it's a plea, a threat or a warning.

The door closes behind the mother. He has lost Gorya again, who is twiddling his screwdriver in a minute screw. Andrei sits down. The screwdriver slips out of the groove, because the boy's hand is so tense. As if there's been no interruption to their conversation, Andrei says, 'I used to love watching my father repair our radio. If he couldn't get hold of the correct part then he was always able to improvise.'

'That's stupid,' says Gorya in a low voice. 'You should always use the correct part, or you'll damage the mechanism. Or, if the radio is no good, then you should replace it.'

Andrei looks at the boy with something close to pity. How has this boy been brought up? He's like the citizen of a foreign country. 'But sometimes that's not possible,' he says. 'You have to make use of what you can get hold of. Who put that cage over your leg?'

'One of the nurses.'

'Don't you know her name?'

The boy shrugs. 'I can't know all of their names.'

'So, does it keep the weight off your leg satisfactorily? Does it ease the pain?'

'My leg doesn't hurt,' says the boy savagely. 'I only feel ill because I'm stuck in this stupid hospital. I'd be all right if I could go home. It's just swollen because an idiot called Vanka whacked me with his racket when we were playing doubles.'

'Oh — you play tennis?'

'I don't like it. I like football.'

'I see. So the important thing is to try to get you fit for next season.'

For the first time, Gorya's face relaxes. 'Of course.'

'Right. That means we're going to have to do some tests. They won't be particularly comfortable, but they're essential. You understand? Blood tests, X-rays and so on. But first of all I need to take a close look at your leg and ask you some questions, which will probably sound very boring, but are all quite important. If you like, your mother can come in and help you with the answers; but you're ten, aren't you?'

'Nearly eleven.'

'Then I expect you can tell me everything I need to know.'

'She gets things wrong, anyway.'

There's a knock on the door, a light tap. It's Lyuba.

'Russov said you'd want me to take the bloods.'

'In a while. We're just going to have a look at Gorya's leg first.'

Carefully, he lifts the bedcovers off the cage, and draws them to the foot of the bed. He lifts the cage away, and puts it on the floor. The boy is wearing expensive dark blue pyjamas, but the right leg of them has been cut off at the thigh.

'Mum did that,' says Gorya, with a trace of animation. 'She got the scissors and cut right through the leg of all my pyjamas, because they were hurting me.'

84

'Were they?'

He can see the swelling on the tibia, just below the knee joint. He touches the child's skin gently. The swelling feels warm. 'This is where it hurts?'

'It's where Vanka whacked me.'

'Very clumsy . . . How long ago was that?'

'I can't remember.'

'It's still tender . . . and quite red, too. Has it been that colour for long?'

'I don't remember.'

'You know, Gorya, a machine can tell you that something's wrong by overheating or simply by failing to work any more. But your body works differently. It will give you clues, and sometimes they are quite hard to read. So a doctor has to understand the design but he also has to be a detective. You see this redness and swelling?'

'Yes.' Gorya barely glances. He's dropped the screwdriver and his hands are balled into fists. It's hurting.

'Look just here. Don't worry, it's still your own leg, the same as always.' Slowly, reluctantly, Gorya lets his gaze drop below his knee. 'There,' Andrei continues, 'that swelling tells us there's something wrong. Maybe it's been caused by the blow from your friend Vanka's racket; maybe it's something else. It's our job to find out, so we can try to make it better. A detective has to search for every clue. Perhaps you'll be able to remember things that will help us.'

His fingers gently trace the outline of the swelling. He glances up at Lyuba. Her arms are folded and she's watching intently, frowning.

'It's been like this for a while, hasn't it, Gorya? It's been hurting you like this, but perhaps no one else noticed? And maybe you've been a bit tired and sometimes you've been limping, even though you haven't fallen over?' murmurs Andrei, not looking at the boy's face. As if unconsciously, Gorya nods his agreement. 'But have you got this type of pain anywhere else?'

'No.'

'Not in the other leg? Good. Not in your back or your shoulders?'

'Not anywhere. It wouldn't be, because Vanka only whacked me here.'

'That's true. Move your arms for me, forward and back, like this. That's right. Now, try to think back, Gorya. Have you had pain and swelling like this anywhere else in your body that you remember? Not in the last few months, maybe, but any other time?'

'I told you, it's only where I got hit.'

'Good, you've got an excellent memory. There, that's enough. Let's put this cage back over your leg, and then we can drape the bedclothes back. It's surprising how you can get chilly when you're lying in bed, even in a warm room. We'll be doing an X-ray, Gorya — you know what that is? You've had one before?'

'Yes, it's a picture of my bones, the X-rays make them show,' says the child, so glibly that Andrei knows Lena was right. Russov has already had X-rays done, and has disposed of them rather than adding them to Gorya's file. He must keep his temper. Children are so quick to spot anger, and think that it's directed against them.

'Fine, Gorya, we'll do X-rays, and Nurse Osipova here will take some blood so that we can do tests on that. None of it will hurt more than a little, but the problem is that your leg hurts when you move it, doesn't it — and we shall have to take you to the Radiology Department to do the X-rays.'

'How do you know it hurts when I move?'

'You keep it so still. We'll bring a wheel-chair, and Nurse Osipova will help you. She's very strong.' And no doubt that policeman will come traipsing after us, all the way to the door of the Radiology Department. Russov must have calculated that

87

the policeman didn't matter; he wouldn't have the medical knowledge to see anything wrong with doing two sets of X-rays. But the name Russov will already be in the police file; didn't he understand that?

Gorya looks at Lyuba's broad forearms. His body has relaxed slightly. He is beginning to trust these people to look after him.

'So will my leg be better in time for preseason training?'

'I hope so. That's what we all want. But at this point I can't say yes or no, Gorya, because I haven't got the evidence.'

The boy sniffs loudly. He's looking straight at Andrei now, taking in everything. Lyuba has turned away and is washing her hands at the corner basin in preparation for taking the bloods. Andrei can tell from the vigorous splashing and scrubbing that there's a lot she'd like to say.

'My dad'll be angry if I'm not better by then. He wants me to be in the underelevens first team this year.'

'Is that what you want, too?'

'Course it is. It's what everyone wants. Vanka won't get in though, he's not fit enough. He could be, but he hasn't got the commitment. Dad takes me to training every Saturday morning, or if he can't our chauffeur does. Even if you miss a week it affects your fitness. I run, too. My dad's made a running track at our dacha.'

Andrei nods. Some patients give way to hospital life almost at once, others fight it every step of the way, insisting that really they still belong to the world outside. They can't be ill, because they haven't got time. Besides, they're going to a wedding next weekend, or they're expecting a promotion. *Don't you understand, doctor, I'm not a patient like all the rest.* Children cling to what was going to happen on the day they got ill. That cinema trip hasn't been abandoned, it's just been postponed. Even months later, when the programme has changed dozens of times, they keep on asking.

Normal life is where Gorya knows that he belongs. Privileged, extraordinary, normal life, with a running track at the dacha and a car to take him to football training. Poor kid.

'You know you said I limp?' says Gorya.

'Yes?'

'Well, I don't. Only when I forget. Dad's never even noticed.'

'You don't want him to know.'

'No. He'll be —' But whatever it is that Volkov will be, Gorya can't quite get it out. Perhaps he's afraid of his father, like everyone else. Andrei just nods, as if nothing

89

Gorya might say could surprise him. The boy shifts a little, and Andrei notices the way his lips tighten with the pain of movement.

'You're managing well,' he says to Gorya. 'Some people can't handle pain.'

The boy's face flushes faintly. 'I'm all right,' he says, then looks into Andrei's face. Yes, Gorya has definitely decided to trust him now. 'He'll be so angry if I don't get better soon,' he mutters, and although his eyes are fixed on Andrei's, there is still something hidden there: a shadow that only the child can see.

'No one's going to be angry,' says Lyuba, taking the boy's arm and turning it over. Expertly, her fingers rub the skin to bring up the vein, but Gorya takes no notice of her.

'I think this lump's like a balloon. If I stuck a pin in it, it would just burst,' he says to Andrei, with a forced smile and a look of such desperate hope that Andrei bends forward and adjusts the bedclothes so as not to meet the boy's eyes.

'No,' he says gently, 'it doesn't work like that. We're going to do the very best we can, Gorya.'

'Have you seen a boy with a leg like mine before?'

Andrei's mind switches back. Yes, the first one was during the siege, but in the second year, when they had supplies of anaesthetic again. The boy was older than Gorya; about Kolya's age. They amputated above the knee. Everything went well.

'Yes,' he says. 'We treat most illnesses in this hospital, you know.'

The child nods, satisfied. Andrei can see how tired he is. 'Then you know what to do,' he says, and closes his eyes.

'I am only seeing what I expected to see,' Andrei tells himself, as he stands in front of the X-ray. The light shines from behind and shows quite clearly the tumour deep in the bone and swelling out beyond it. The tumour is hard, star-shaped. He moves to the second plate, and then to the third. 'Sofya, what do you think of this?' he murmurs, but he already knows what Sofya Vasilievna thinks. There's no other way of interpreting the X-ray.

Sofya moves up close to the image. Her face shows little expression, but her voice is warm and full as she says, 'Poor kid. How old is he?'

'Ten.'

'They're usually a little older.'

'Yes. Of course it may be benign. We have

91

to do the biopsy.'

Sofya studies the images in silence. 'It doesn't look good,' she says. 'It looks like an osteosarcoma to me.'

As soon as the word is out in the space between them, it becomes true. It's been true for months already.

'Unusual at that age though,' says Sofya. 'Poor kid. But sometimes I think it's almost worse for the parents.'

'Yes,' he says absently, thinking, *She doesn't know, or she'd never talk about 'the parents' like that.*

She unclips the X-ray plate, and hands it to him. 'The others are on the table,' she says. 'So who's going to do the biopsy?'

'I don't know yet.'

'Why not go and see Brodskaya? She has orthopaedic oncological experience, and she's an excellent surgeon. This isn't your field.'

'Yes. Yes, I probably will. Thanks, Sofya.'

'I'm only doing my job.' *Unlike some . . .* he thinks he hears her add in a murmur. His mind jumps. So she knows about Ret-inskaya and the X-rays she did for Russov. But she's not saying anything. Why wade in shit if you don't have to?

I'm a paediatric physician with a special interest in juvenile arthritic disease, Andrei tells himself. Facts are what's needed here. I'm not an oncologist. Sofya's right. This isn't my area.

Russov is drinking tea in the canteen. His pale, pouchy face sharpens when he sees Andrei. Andrei puts down his dish of meatballs, and sits opposite Russov.

'So, how was it?'

'You know how it was.'

Russov's hands fiddle with an unlit cigarette. 'What do you mean?' he mutters, but not as if expecting an answer.

'He needs a biopsy. You've seen the X-rays, don't pretend you haven't. I'm not an oncologist, Boris Ivanovich. You knew that. You're going to have to find someone else.'

Andrei hears the piano before he even puts his key in the door. His heart sinks. He's going to have to speak to Kolya again. The neighbours will be complaining. The Rostovs are fine — they even claim to love the sound of Kolya playing — but the Maleviches complain regularly. They have a right to live in peace, don't they? If they want to listen to someone playing a piano, which they don't, they'll go to a concert hall, thank you very much. Rachmaninov, is it? Well, it's just a racket, as far as they're

93

concerned.

Andrei is pretty sure it's Rachmaninov again today. Sure enough, the Malevich door opens. The son, Petya, 'the Weasel', as Kolya calls him, comes out, dressed for the office although he's probably been home for hours already. He smells of bureaucracy.

'If this goes on, we'll have to put in a formal complaint.'

Andrei looks at him, keeping the door open, keeping his face impassive. 'I'll have a word,' he says.

'You'd better make sure you do,' says the Weasel, and goes back inside his apartment, shutting the door.

Andrei's fists clench at his sides. He'd like to get hold of the man's shoulders, screw his head round, force him to listen. He'd say, 'What the hell do you think you're doing? You're talking about a boy playing the piano. Don't you know how lucky we are, living here? These apartments have thick walls. You could be sharing a communal apartment with a family who fight all day long and would beat the shit out of you if you said a word about it.'

No, it's worse than that. He'd like to get the Weasel around the throat, or lift him up and shake him until his hair flies out of its carefully pomaded quiff. It wouldn't even be a fight. All the Maleviches are puny, apart from the mother.

But he can't do any of it. People like the Maleviches can be dangerous and they have their own weapons. The mother never goes out. She's the eyes and ears of the whole building. Andrei's fists clench tighter. Deliberately, he loosens his shoulders and makes his hands drop to his sides. If he goes into the apartment in this state, he'll only have a row with Kolya.

It's just as well that the Maleviches aren't interested in music and probably haven't heard of Rachmaninov, otherwise they'd put in a 'further and additional' complaint about having their ears sullied by the work of an émigré. Their 'further and additional' complaints are well known throughout the building.

Andrei knocks on Kolya's bedroom door.

'The Weasel's been round again. You'll have to keep it down, Kolya.'

'What? I can't hear you!'

'The Maleviches. There'll be a formal complaint if we don't watch out.'

The bedroom door flies open. 'No one else says anything! I don't even believe they can hear it, the walls are much thicker on that side than they are on the Rostov side, and the piano's not against their wall, anyway.' Kolya glowers as if Andrei is the enemy, not the messenger.

'It was pretty loud.'

'All right then, if you're going to take *their* side, I'll stop. I suppose I should have known you wouldn't back me up. But next time I see that Weasel —'

Andrei knows that Kolya has far too much sense to say anything to any of the Maleviches. He watches as the boy goes back to the piano, lowers the lid with exaggerated, furious care and then brushes his hands as if wiping dirt off them.

'Cretins,' he says. 'Idiots.'

'What were you playing?'

'The second sonata.'

'But isn't that very difficult?'

Kolya frowns. 'Too difficult for me, you mean? Thanks.'

'No — I'm just — well, impressed. You know how little I know about music.'

All at once Kolya softens. A smile that is both older and younger than his adolescent scowl lights up his face. 'You don't need to be too impressed. It's not difficult, it's impossible. I tried the *allegro molto* — it sounded like saucepans falling out of a cupboard. But if I were Horovitz they'd still be banging on the walls. And do you know what, that Weasel told Anna his mother thought I was growing up into a hooligan. My God! She ought to get out more.'

'We don't want to get on the wrong side of them.'

'I know. No point giving them a chance to overfulfil their norms for behaving like bastards.'

Andrei laughs. Suddenly, as if through a window into the future, he sees a time when he and Kolya will be able to go out for a drink together. The real Kolya is still in there, behind the mask of adolescence. 'We should be grateful that they have two rooms, like us,' he says. 'In fact I think they have slightly more living space, so we shouldn't have to fear an "apartment denunciation".'

Kolya's face takes on a shrewd, calculating look. 'Yes, but there are five of them and, technically, wouldn't they count as two families? So, they've only got one room per family.'

'I suppose you're right. But my guess is they won't want to stir things up. They've got much more than the norm of living space.'

'So have we,' Kolya points out.

'I know, I know — let's forget about them. They're not worth talking about.'

'So when's Anna home?' asks Kolya casually, but Andrei knows that he really wants to know. He doesn't like it when Anna's late, or out without an explanation. Anna thinks it all goes back to the siege, when she had to go out on long, freezing forays to fetch the bread ration or search for firewood. On the worst days, in the December of '41, Marina would bless Anna before she left the apartment. Everyone knew the risks. Kolya must have known that one day she might not come back. Weakened, starving people collapsed in the streets, and no one had the strength to help them. And then there were bread thieves who preyed on the fallen. 'People think children don't know what's going on,' Anna used to say, 'but they always do. Kolya knows. That's why he's frightened.' Sometimes, before Kolya grew too feeble to protest, Marina would have to peel his hands from Anna's coat.

'She's got a meeting after work,' says Andrei now.

'How late?'

'It goes on until nine.'

'My God,' says Kolya again. His finger-nails score the margin of a music sheet. 'I suppose we won't be eating until ten.'

'Have some bread if you're hungry.'

'She's always out in the evenings these days.'

'Not as often as you are.'

Kolya turns a surprised face to Andrei. *That's entirely different,* his face says. *When I go out, well, that's natural. But Anna should be here.*

'Why don't you play something for me, Kolya?'

'I thought I wasn't supposed to touch the piano.'

'What was that piece you used to play — the eerie one — something to do with glass, I think it was. Mozart.'

'Adagio for Glass Harmonica. I haven't played that for years,' says Kolya, with a touch of scorn, whether for Mozart or for Andrei, who can say.

'I liked it.'

'Did you? I thought you were fed up with me playing all the time.'

'No. It's only' — Andrei gestures towards the door — 'the way we live. You can't go looking for trouble.'

'But if everyone's always not looking for trouble, that's why *they* win. We do what *they* want.'

'Yes,' says Andrei, 'you're right, I suppose. No: you *are* right, there's no suppose about it. But —' He shrugs. A weight seems to sit on him, not heavy but suffocating, like a cloud come to earth.

'I'll play like a mouse,' Kolya promises. 'A

Mozartian mouse.'

Andrei leans back in the chair that Anna still sometimes calls 'father's chair', and closes his eyes. The notes steal out, eerie, as he remembered them, yes, and glassy too, pure. *Not very human music,* he thinks. As soon as it finishes, you want to hear it again.

Kolya obliges. He plays still more softly this time, even during the crescendo. No one outside the walls of the room could possibly hear it. Andrei wishes Anna would come home now, this moment. They should all be together. If only he could stop thinking about that boy. If Brodskaya does the biopsy then they'll soon know for sure. They are professionals. The patient is their concern, not the politics.

But why should Brodskaya want to be dragged into it?

He has seen the boy, and that's the end of it. It's not even his field, for God's sake. He'll have to tell Anna what's going on. Anna's face will get that strained look that he hates.

Relax. Just relax, can't you? Listen to the boy playing.

5

'You understand, don't you, that the correct procedure is for the surgeon who carries out the biopsy to go on and perform whatever surgery is required?'

'Yes.'

Brodskaya folds her arms, and frowns. 'Very well. I'll see the patient today, get an anaesthetist to check him over, and we'll do the biopsy in the morning. You know that it has to be done under general anaesthetic?'

'Yes, I've been reading up on it. But, Riva Grigorievna, you do realize, don't you, the implications of all this? This boy is Volkov's son. I'd understand completely if you didn't want to become involved.'

'You've already told me that.'

Her lack of reaction amazes him. Her strong, broad face is calm. 'I'll see him today,' she repeats. 'The sooner the biopsy is done, the better. I can't imagine why Russov ever thought you should examine the boy, given that you're neither an on-cologist nor an orthopaedic surgeon.'

'He thought the swelling might be due to arthritis, I suppose.'

'Really? Did you think that, after you'd examined the child?'

'No.'

'Exactly.'

'I suppose there's still the possibility that the tumour is benign.'

Brodskaya shakes her head briskly. 'I would doubt that very much. From the X-rays you showed me, the form and location of the tumour are absolutely consistent with osteosarcoma. But let's get that biopsy done and then we'll talk again. Assuming that you intend to remain in contact with the case?'

'I — I'm not sure.'

She gives him a look that isn't remotely critical, but is full of such comprehension that he has to turn away. Brodskaya is a single woman. As far as anyone knows, she's never had any attachments. She maintains a cool, equal friendliness with all her colleagues. Suddenly, fiercely, he envies her. This is a filthy business. Each person passes the poison on to the next. If only he could just —

But maybe, even if he hadn't got Anna

and Kolya to think of, he wouldn't be as heroically disinterested as he'd like to think. *Don't stick your neck out. Be careful. Put a padlock on your tongue unless you're within the four walls of home, and even then —*

He's saturated with it. He's no better than anyone else.

'Thank you, Riva Grigorievna,' he says quietly, hoping that she knows how much he means it.

All day an uneasy part of his mind tracks what will be going on in that private room. Brodskaya will be in there now. Maybe she's already face to face with the Volkovs. She'll be explaining that the swelling is due to a tumour, which has to be analysed in order to determine the treatment. The biopsy will require a general anaesthetic, and she will take charge of the surgery. He hopes they don't talk in front of Gorya. Too many doctors assume that a child won't understand words like 'tumour' or 'biopsy'. But children don't need to understand the medical terms. They pick up the meaning from their parents' reaction.

Brodskaya does some paediatric work, but she's spent most of her career in adult orthopaedics. She has a fine wartime record; her work on limb salvage was pioneering. A

103

good surgeon, and a strong, determined woman. But she's not made the progress in her career that you'd expect. She doesn't sit on the important committees.

Andrei works late. It's after seven when Brodskaya comes to find him. Her face is as calm as ever as she sits down opposite him and says, 'It's impossible for me to treat this patient satisfactorily.'

He knows immediately that she's talking about the Volkov boy.

'But why? What's happened, Riva Grigorievna?'

'The family lacks confidence in the investigations that I proposed. They've asked to discuss the case and the course of treatment with you again.' She shrugs. 'I have to admit defeat.'

'My God, I'm so sorry — what on earth were they thinking of?'

'Who knows?'

'I'll go and see them, of course. It's probably the shock. They don't want to believe that the boy needs surgery. But you told them there was a tumour — didn't they realize what it meant?'

'Apparently not.' She leans forward a little. 'Or perhaps they feel that they need a different surgeon. They may not like my name.'

He stares at her. She looks at him with a touch of derisive pity, for all the things he doesn't have to reckon with. *'Brodskaya,'* she says. 'Surely you understand.'

And of course he does. They might prefer a doctor who is not Jewish. But she must be mistaken. As if a parent with a sick child would care about anything but getting that child well again. If the doctor had two heads, it would scarcely matter.

'You'd better prepare yourself,' she says, and this time the pity is definitely there. 'It's you that they want. You can be sure that Volkov has checked the personnel files. Probably he finds that my "autobiography" is not to his taste. Well, there we are. Allow me to give you back these X-rays.' She slides the brown folders across the table to him.

'Was he there — Volkov?' asks Andrei.

'Yes. He's still there now. He wants to see you.'

'What — this evening?'

'Yes.'

He looks down at the folders, then up at Brodskaya again.

'Be careful,' she says. 'And if Volkov changes his mind, come back to me. It's an interesting case. I know exactly how I would approach it. But if he doesn't, I'd recommend Andropov to do the surgery. He's good. The quality of the work makes all the difference to the outcome in such a case. The biopsy must be done in such a way that it won't compromise further treatment. And when it comes to surgery, the judgement of the margin must be absolutely accurate. I remember a case where the surgeon was too conservative. He operated without leaving a sufficient margin. It's vital not to be over-influenced by the desire to preserve the limb. A few months down the road, and what have you got? Seeding of malignant osteoblastic cells at the site, tumour re-growth, and very probably metastasis as well.'

'I understand.' Andrei stands up, holds out his hand. 'Thank you, Riva Grigorievna.'

But she shakes her head again and the corners of her mouth crease in a small ironic smile. 'You've got nothing to thank me for, Andrei Mikhailovich. Come back to me if you wish.'

Andrei makes himself walk more slowly as he approaches the door of the private room. It's important that Volkov doesn't hear him hurrying along, like one of his subordinates. Another policeman stands there, thickset,

Apparently' — he lays a stress on the word which makes it sound ironic — 'apparently you're a well-regarded paediatrician here. You have a notable skill for the diagnosis of difficult cases. Is my son a "difficult case"?'

'To diagnose, you mean?'

'Let's begin with that.'

'We're still at the stage of preliminary investigation. So far what's clear from the X-rays is that your son has a tumour which is growing within the proximal tibia — that is, the shin bone — very close to the knee. The expansion of the tumour beyond the bone is leading to the pain and swelling. I believe that Dr Brodskaya showed you the X-rays?'

The man nods.

'We need to discover the nature of the tumour as soon as possible. For this reason a biopsy has to be done. It has to be what we call an "open biopsy", which requires an operation in order to take a sample of the tumour.'

' "What we call",' grumbles Volkov. 'You doctors are not a secret society, I take it?'

It's a fair point, but Andrei decides not to concede it. 'In order to achieve the best possible outcome for the patient, the surgeon who does the biopsy should be the surgeon who is to perform any subsequent surgery

109

that's required.'

At this moment, for the first time, Volkov reacts like any other parent. He blinks as the words 'subsequent surgery' hit his understanding. Normally, at such a moment, Andrei would offer some reassurance, not to pull the punch but at least to soften it. But this time he says nothing. He doesn't understand this man, and instinct tells him that it would be dangerous to pretend to do so.

'You're not a surgeon yourself, then?' says Volkov, as if he's exposed a flaw which Andrei has tried to conceal.

'No. I'm a paediatric physician. I have a special interest in juvenile arthritis, which is why Dr Russov referred your son's case on to me initially. The symptoms Gorya was experiencing when he was admitted might well have been due to arthritis.'

'So, you're telling me that a fully trained and experienced doctor in one of our finest hospitals knows nothing about tumours?'

'My knowledge of them is general rather than expert. I do see patients with tumours in clinic, I examine them, I might order tests, but I would then refer them.' He could add that there is a shortage of paediatric oncologists, which means that most of the hospital's physicians have gained more experience with cancer patients than might be ideal for the patients. But to say any of that would be premature. He should not speak of cancer until the biopsy has confirmed it. It would be rash, anyway, to imply any criticism of the hospital's staffing levels.

Volkov leans forward. His light, clear eyes are compelling. 'Let me get this clear. Do you correctly understand my son's illness, or don't you?'

'There are other doctors who would understand it better than I do. You need a good surgeon, although the surgeon wouldn't necessarily take overall charge of the case.'

'But you know what you're doing. Remember, I've read your file. I know the extent of your experience. During the war years you weren't referring patients here, there and everywhere. You had to treat them on the spot. You had to operate with your own hands. Didn't you? Isn't that the way it was?'

'Yes, I suppose it was.'

'You "suppose it was"? You know it was. You're a *blokadnik*. So am I. We know how things were.'

Do we? thinks Andrei. Were things the same for the high-ups as they were for us? I doubt if there were many cases of alimentary

111

dystrophy at the top level. But, then again, Volkov wasn't at the top during the war. His rise is recent. The first Andrei heard of him was a few years ago, when a group of spies was unmasked within the Jewish Anti-Fascist Committee, and Volkov was named in *Pravda* as 'the tireless investigator whose vigilance led to the downfall of these scum infected with private-ownership psychology, who plotted against the people'.

'Let's look at it another way,' says Volkov. 'A good surgeon isn't hard to find. There are plenty in this hospital. You know who's the best. A professional always does. You've got the laboratories, you've got access to the latest treatments. What I want is someone I can trust, to take charge of the case and keep on top of it. My boy likes you. I don't want him messed around by some "surgeon-shmurgeon".'

Andrei takes a breath. 'I have to say, with respect, that's not how we do things here.'

'Hospital protocol, eh? You don't have to worry about that. Listen to me. I like the look of your file. You were with the People's Volunteers. You worked throughout the siege. But you're not a Leningrader, are you?'

'Not originally.'

'No. You're from Irkutsk. A Siberian, eh?

You don't believe that Leningrad's the only place on earth. Your parents volunteered as settlers.'

Andrei looks down at his hands. He can barely believe this conversation. The man's son has a tumour in the bone of his leg. Volkov is an intelligent man. He must, surely, understand what that means. And yet here he is, reciting the contents of Andrei's personal file to him, as if this were an —

Don't think of that.

'As I said, I went through the siege myself,' Volkov goes on, as if he's about to recite his own autobiography in exchange for reading Andrei's. 'So these Leningraders have got nothing on me, any more than they have on you. But I was born in Krasnoyarsk.'

'Really?' In spite of himself, Andrei can't help a surge of fellow feeling. Krasnoyarsk may be four hundred miles from Irkutsk but it's the same world, and a world away from this city.

'The reports on you are excellent,' says Volkov.

'I'm an ordinary doctor, that's all.'

'Exactly.' Volkov smiles approvingly. 'That's what we need. The people don't want cosmopolitan pretensions. They want ordinary, dedicated men. Apparently you have a high reputation as a diagnostician and your outcomes are exceptionally positive.'

Andrei sees that Volkov has actually forgotten that he is here as the parent of a seriously ill child. He looks down, so that Volkov won't catch him watching at the moment when he remembers it again. There is a silence. The scent of the lilac seems very strong.

'My boy wants you,' says Volkov. 'You've taken his fancy. He thinks you're the best doctor here. He didn't think much of your Dr Russov or your Brodskaya.'

'Excuse me, but I have to tell you that the surgeon I would recommend in this case is precisely Riva Grigorievna Brodskaya. She's not only a first-rate orthopaedic surgeon, but she also has the necessary special experience with . . . tumours. And she also has experience in paediatric orthopaedics. It's a particularly valuable combination of expertise.'

Volkov half closes his eyes. 'I don't like the look of her,' he says.

Andrei leans forward. It's a risk, but he needs to take it. 'Can I ask you to reconsider? In a case like your son's — if further surgery should be needed after we know the result of the biopsy — then it's very important that we have a surgeon who can evaluate the site of the tumour as accurately as possible at the time of the biopsy. In that way, she can base later decisions on firm ground. Obviously the section of tumour has to be analysed by the pathology lab, but a really good, experienced surgeon can gain a great deal of knowledge during the biopsy process. In my opinion, Brodskaya is best qualified to do this.'

'There must be others.'

'Of course. In the end it's a question of confidence. I'd have confidence in her to make the most precise, impartial clinical judgement.'

Volkov nods slowly. 'So you're telling me that it's definitely Brodskaya you want, and no one else.'

'There are other surgeons, as you say. But if it were my son . . .' he pauses, suddenly aware of danger. You should never so much as hint at your private life in front of such a man, who can so easily turn it into a weapon to use against you.

'You have a son?'

'A stepson,' says Andrei, because this has always been the easiest way of describing Kolya. 'My wife's younger brother' has never sounded right.

'Hmm. And you're telling me that all this

should be done as soon as possible?'

Andrei can't remember saying that. Perhaps Brodskaya made it clear to Volkov. 'Yes. The biopsy should be done tomorrow, so that the results can be obtained as quickly as possible, and then treatment can begin. We've got Gorya's medical records. As far as I can remember there's nothing that would complicate anaesthesia or surgery, but obviously all that will need to be checked. He'll need to be examined by both the anaesthetist and the surgeon.'

'So you've got it all planned,' says Volkov. His face is still hard and shrewd, but at this moment Andrei's sure that he's thinking only as a parent. The fear and anger in his voice are only what any father would feel. You have to be so careful, as a doctor, not to assume that because a procedure is routine to you, it is remotely normal to the families. To cut into a child's leg, after all, is monstrous. To a father, the flesh and blood the scalpel touches is far more precious than his own.

'It's what we have to do, to give Gorya the best possible treatment.' *The best possible chance* would come closer to the truth, but that can't be said; not to any parent and certainly not to this one.

'You say, "we",' observes Volkov. 'You'll

take the case, then? The surgeon — the on-cologist — whoever you need. Let them report to you. You're the one I want to look after my son.'

There's no way out of this. Hospital protocol and correct practice will count for nothing. Besides, in this particular case no one's going to feel demeaned by not having ultimate responsibility for the boy.

'We haven't had the biopsy yet,' says Andrei. 'You'll appreciate that I can't prejudge the results. But you must understand that there's a strong possibility that your son may be very seriously ill.'

'Do you think I'm not aware of that?' At that moment, suddenly and without warning, Volkov bangs his fist on the table. Andrei just manages to prevent himself from reacting. 'Do you doctors think we're all fools? Don't you know who I am?' He hasn't been able to resist it, in the end. For all his intelligence, he's like his wife, not quite able to believe that 'who he is' will make no difference to the cells that are proliferating in his child's body.

Andrei lays his own hands on the table, palms down. There is silence. For one thing, Andrei cannot think of anything to say; for another, he suspects that whatever he says might be construed as a provocation. It's

117

quite natural for parents in this situation to vent their feelings. Volkov, above all, has to feel that here, in this hospital, he is a parent and nothing else.

Suddenly the tension relaxes. Volkov leans back in his chair and folds his arms. 'You're an Irkutsk boy,' he says. 'You don't flinch.'

6

Anna guides the fabric over the foot of the sewing machine with her left hand, while she turns the handle smoothly with her right. The needle stabs up and down, the seam lengthens, and the stitched fabric pours satisfyingly over the side of the table.

Julia has lent her the sewing machine for a week. Anna had the dress cut out and tacked, all ready so that she could make maximum use of the time. Julia has lent her the pattern, too.

The dress is sleeveless, with a full skirt that comes a little below the knee. The shoulder straps and the neck are the most difficult to get right. If the neck doesn't fit properly, she'll end up having to improvise a scarf out of the leftover fabric. That would look awful.

Anna peers at the fabric. Yes, the seam is straight. She's almost there.

She can start to gather the skirt with running stitch, and then pin skirt to bodice.

'What about shoes?' Julia had asked.

'I've got these ones.' They'd been Vera's; Anna's feet are exactly the same size as her mother's. The shoes are silver brocade, with a little heel and a button fastening that Anna used to love fiddling with as a child. Vera must have bought those evening shoes long ago, before she met Anna's father, who never danced. Anna has had them resoled. Fortunately the style is classic.

'Mmm.' Julia had nodded without enthusiasm.

'They're very comfortable. Don't look like that, it's a hospital ball, Julia, not some grand event at the Astoria. No one's going to be staring at my feet.'

'Oh my God, Anna, don't say that. I can't bear women who say, "After all, no one'll be looking at me," as if it were a point in their favour. Isn't the world dull enough without filling it with dowdy women? You're going to a ball. It calls for maximum effort. I always look at people's shoes. It's a pity our feet aren't the same size or you could borrow my satin pumps.'

But Anna could never fit into Julia Slatkina's pretty little shoes. She smoothes out the fabric again, and turns the sewing-machine handle faster. It'll be such a beauti-

120

ful dress. Andrei will love it. The kind of dress you put away and keep for your daughter —

No. She'll lend it to Irina.

Julia dresses beautifully, and she's so completely at ease in her skin. She doesn't even notice other women's glances. She offered Anna one of her own dresses to wear for the ball, but Anna refused. She wanted to feel like herself.

She wonders if she would become friends with Julia if they were to meet for the first time now. She was Julia Slatkina before she married; one of the little Slatkins who were so much part of Anna's childhood. They all lived together, in the same communal apartment. Julia was like a sister, but when the Slatkin parents separated it all came to an end. Julia's mother went off without the children. She worked for Lenfilm, Anna remembers that. Anna assumed that Julia must have moved away from Leningrad with her father, or died in the war, until the day a well-dressed woman approached her in the crowded foyer of the Philharmonic Hall. And there was Julia's voice, full of doubt and hope. 'Anna? Is it really you? Anna Levina?'

Julia and Anna knew each other almost before they knew their own names. They played together under the kitchen table while the grown-ups talked endlessly. Slatkins, Levins and God knows how many other assorted writers and musicians and idealists of the new dawn. There was a man who used to smoke a pipe and sit Anna on his knee while he declaimed poetry in a growly voice. In her memory, the people who actually lived in the apartment, the procession of temporary residents who just needed a mattress to sleep on, and the visitors who dropped in and out at all hours are mixed up together. The adults' faces are indistinct. She can remember their shoes and their voices, the smell of cigarettes, the endless glasses of tea that gave way to beer and vodka when there was enough money. She can remember her mother's impatient voice: 'Aren't you lot ever going to bed? I have to go to work early tomorrow.' Even Vera's face is shadowy, but Julia was under the table with her. Julia's vivid features, her hazel eyes and sharp pinching fingers are as clear to Anna as the grain of the table's wood, when they traced it with their fingers.

She had never expected to see Julia again.

'Anna? Is it really you? It's me, Julia. Julia Slatkina!'

Memory surged back. Yes, the eyes were the same, thickly fringed with the dark eyelashes that used to lie on her cheeks 'like butterflies' when she was asleep. Anna recalled one of the grown-ups saying that, and her own chagrin because she wasn't like a butterfly. A knot of tears thickened in her throat.

'Julia!'

It was Julia who reached out for her, Julia who held Anna tight, as if she might vanish again. A rich scent enfolded Anna. She blinked away her tears, while Julia let hers run down to the corners of her mouth. People were looking at them.

'It's really you. I can't believe it, after all these years.'

'I thought you must have died.'

'No, I'm still here. Only I'm not Julia Slatkina now. I'm married to a wonderful man called Georgii Vesnin.' She held Anna away from her and looked expectantly into her face. Of course Anna recognized the name. A leading filmmaker who had received a Stalin Prize quite recently. Anna and Andrei had seen *Journey Across the Snow*. She hadn't found the story particularly interesting — it concerned the construction of a railway in Siberia — but Andrei had loved it. And they had both admired the style: spare, even austere, but bold too.

'A real artist,' Anna said, and Julia

123

squeezed her hand.

'He is. He really is. I've got to rush, but listen, you mustn't disappear again. Here.' She scrabbled in her bag. 'Here's my card. We must get together. How about coffee one morning next week?'

'I'll be working, Julia.'

'Oh — of course. All right, let's have supper one evening, somewhere nice. My treat. Look, write down your telephone number here . . . But look at you — you're lovely. I always thought you would be.'

'Not half as lovely as you,' Anna had said, taking in Julia's polished hair and high heels.

'Oh well, all this!' Julia made a face as she smoothed her skirt over her hips. 'It doesn't mean a thing. You should see my mother, she thinks of nothing but face massages and these wretched strip things that she sticks on her forehead at night — and she looks more of a hag than ever.'

'What — you mean Lydia Maximovna?'

'Of course. I've only got one mother, haven't I? Unfortunately. We kids didn't see her for years after she left Father, but as soon as I married Georgii she was straight back on the scene. He was worth knowing, you see. She's still writing screenplays. Not very good ones, Georgii says,' and Julia had grinned with such sparkling malice that

Anna half expected a pinch from a perfectly manicured finger and thumb. 'My God, Anna, she's indestructible. Like a rubber ball. No matter how hard she gets thrown, she only bounces higher. Listen, darling, I've got to rush, but I'll ring you. Don't you dare vanish again. I can't wait to talk about old times.'

If it weren't for her, Anna would be sewing this dress by hand. Julia brought the sewing machine round to Anna's apartment herself. When Anna opened the door, there was Julia, leaning against the wall, out of breath but triumphant. She must have lugged the machine all the way up, staggering in her high heels.

'Julia, you shouldn't have, I'd have come to yours and fetched it —'

'I came by taxi, idiot. A few stairs are good for the health. Now, let me show you how it works . . . My God, Anna, what a wonderful apartment. It's so — so Levinish!'

'Well, it was my parents' apartment. We've been here ever since we left the *kommunalka*.'

'All those paintings . . . And isn't that a piano through there?'

'It's Kolya who plays. That's how we got it. His piano teacher knew a woman who was thinking of selling her upright because she had the chance of a baby grand. The teacher made sure this woman heard Kolya play, and so we got it at a bargain price. We robbed her, really, but she didn't seem to mind.'

'Kolya's got talent, then?'

'Not enough to make a career. But he's good. He practises until the neighbours start banging on the walls.'

'Neighbours. Some of them can be such bastards,' said Julia, with a strength of feeling which surprised Anna. Surely the Vesnin family didn't have troubles like that.

Julia had looked around the apartment with hunger in her face. 'Are those your father's books?' she asked.

'Yes. Of course we had to sell some of them.' She won't tell Julia about the books that had to be burned, to feed the *burzhuika*. People who weren't 'here' don't understand such things.

'It's so like the old days.'

'Julia, that's ridiculous,' said Anna, more sharply than she intended. 'The *kommunalka* wasn't like this at all.'

'But it's got the same feeling. You've kept it somehow, Anna. I don't know how you do it. It feels as if any moment one of those old poets will wander in and start declaiming.'

'What about your brothers, Julia?' asked Anna.

'They're all right. I don't see much of them,' said Julia shortly, but the next moment her face lit up again as she explored the rows of books. 'I'm sure I remember some of these . . . Isn't that your father's Dante? Yes, I thought so. And it's not even a very big book. Do you know, I used to think it was huge? And so heavy, when he let me hold it and turn the pages to look at the drawings.'

'Your hands were smaller then.'

'Here's his name on the flyleaf . . . You are so lucky, Anna.'

'Am I?'

'Yes, you are! No, don't smile like that. You really are.'

Julia's not happy. When the sparkle dies away from her face she looks drawn, exhausted. She loves her husband, though. She speaks proudly about his epic dramas of Arctic exploration and railway construction, and her whole face glows when Anna says how wonderful she and Andrei had thought some of the shots.

'But what do you do, Julia?'

They were having supper together, tucked

into a comfortable corner of a restaurant that Anna had heard about but never visited. The head waiter clearly knew Julia well. Would she be happy with this table? Or perhaps she'd prefer to sit in the window?

'The lamb's very good here,' Julia had said. 'They do a wonderful shish kebab.' The lamb was meltingly tender and succulent, pink inside and charred at the edges. Anna ate slowly, savouringly. Julia pushed most of hers to the side of her plate.

'You've told me about Georgii. But what do *you* do, Julia?'

Julia lit a cigarette, then glanced quickly at Anna's plate, and stubbed it out. 'I'm sorry, I'm so uncultured. Well, I was a dancer.'

'A dancer! Were you really?'

'Not a very well-known one, obviously.' Julia smiled ironically. 'I slogged my way through ballet school. I really liked it, though; they were hard on us but you felt looked after. I got into the corps de ballet of the Kazan Ballet Company when I was eighteen — but it was pretty obvious after a couple of years that I was never going to make it as a soloist. I was going to be dancing in the line until my hair turned grey and they booted me out. It's a tough life, being a dancer. You're smiling again, Anna, but it

128

is, it is really!'

'I believe you.'

'I kept getting injuries and generally things weren't going too well. Anyway — and then of course a bit later the war came. And everything was messed up.'

'Yes,' said Anna.

'Dancers' feet are horrible,' said Julia quickly. 'You should see mine. Excuse me a moment, I must just —'

There were too many gaps in Julia's story, Anna thought as she finished her side dish of rice. Such fine grains, each one separate, perfect, and scented with cardamom. But if it wasn't the truth, or was only part of it, it was what she wanted Anna to believe. And who could blame her? Everyone has their closed doors. Whatever it was that Julia didn't want to talk about, no doubt she had good reason. But she was all right now. She'd met Georgii, she was safe. Anna watched as Julia walked back from the Ladies. Her walk was elegant, but yes, she did limp, very slightly. So that part, at least, was true.

'And then you met Georgii,' said Anna, to help her, as Julia sat down.

'Yes, more or less then. But you, poor thing, you were here in Leningrad the whole time?'

'Yes.'

'And your mother? Your father?'

'My mother died a few years before the war, when my little brother was born. You know, Kolya. The one who plays the piano.'

'Oh my God, I didn't realize. I thought he was yours.'

'No.'

'I didn't even know your mother had another child.'

'No reason why you should. He's sixteen now, and he lives with Andrei and me. I met Andrei during the siege. That was when my father died.'

'Poor man. Do you remember how he used to write little stories for us and sew them into books?'

Anna had completely forgotten.

'Surely you must remember! Mine had a blue cover, and yours was red.'

'No, I —' But even as she said this, something swam into Anna's mind, out of the past. 'Was the story something about a wolf princess?'

'I knew you hadn't forgotten! She'd been turned into a wolf and everyone was afraid of her, until she found a little girl who was lost, wandering in the forest, and the little girl curled up against the wolf's fur and so even though it was freezing cold, she survived. The little girl loved the wolf but when her father came searching for her, with his gun, he didn't realize that the wolf princess was protecting the child. He thought the little girl was being attacked, and so he shot the wolf. But then, at the moment that she died, the wolf turned back into a beautiful young princess.'

'Good heavens. How well you remember it, Julia.'

'I've never forgotten your father's stories. How I wish I still had my little book. But it must have got lost, with everything else. And now he's dead. I'm sorry, Anna.'

'He was in the People's Volunteers. He was wounded. We nursed him, but he had no chance of recovering from a wound like that — not in those conditions,' said Anna, suddenly wanting Julia to know that her father had been a soldier.

'Poor man,' said Julia again, rather vaguely, staring at the stub of the cigarette that she'd lit as soon as she returned to the table.

'And your father?' asked Anna hesitantly.

'He died too,' said Julia, in such a tone that Anna asked no more.

The needle needs rethreading. Anna stretches, yawning. Andrei and Kolya will

131

be back soon.

The dress will be ready in good time. She and Andrei will go to the ball together. That is absolutely all she's going to think about today. Shoes, flowers, dress, bag, her best pair of stockings. She is sick to death of being so serious and careful and fearful. She's thirty-four, and life is flowing past so quickly that before she can turn round she'll be middle-aged.

Middle-aged and childless. A jolt of anguish goes through her, so sharp that she has to bite her lip. Middle-aged, fussing over poor Kolya as he tries to pull away from her and get a life of his own —

No. They'll go to the ball. It'll be just like one of her father's fairy tales. Music, light, the warmth of Andrei's hand on her shoulder blade as he steers her into the waltz.

The wolf. Volkov. No matter how determinedly she pushes him out of her mind, he comes back. Her stomach tightens. *I'm not going to think of you. You can't come in, because this is my home.*

There was a time when her father never slept properly until after dawn. He'd drop off, then wake with a jerk. He'd get up, make tea, read. She was so used to him turning night into day that it seemed normal to her. It wasn't until much later that she realized why he'd only been able to fall into a deep sleep once dawn was safely past. It was because that was the hour when they came for you, when you were weakest. Night after night he waited, listening for the tramp of boots in the stairwell, boots worn by men who couldn't care less whose sleep they broke. Boots, and voices. *'One more floor. It's up here. This is the door.'*

He was afraid that they would all be destroyed, because of him. If she'd understood that then, she could have been more help to him, or at least she'd have been less impatient. She hopes he never realized quite how impatient she used to become when he sat there sunk in gloom hour after hour, not moving from his chair, bestirring himself only to drink another glass of tea if she placed it at his right hand. He seemed so cold and distant, even towards Kolya. He brooded endlessly on the course of his life. Could it have been different? Could or should he have acted differently?

Such questions led nowhere. They served only to paralyse his will to live, write, love. She'd known that he felt isolated. She'd thought she understood what it was like for him to be rejected and a failure whose work nobody would publish. But she'd understood nothing, it seems to her now. She was too young and, although she'd thought she was a realist, she was still wrapped in the envelope of optimism that surrounds the young. Now, since his death, she is beginning to understand him better.

Did she show him enough love? This is the question that torments her now these days. She was always so busy. She had Kolya to bring up, the endless shopping and queueing and cleaning. She had her job.

But maybe her constant busyness seemed to him like a criticism of his own stalled life.

At least she has the consolation that she showed him love when he was dying. Oh God, maybe even that isn't completely true. She was angry with him, even then, because he refused to fight for life. She thought he was giving up the struggle, when there was still a chance of recovery. Looking back on those times, she can see her judgement wasn't normal. It couldn't have been. She was beside herself with cold and hunger, and the fear that the others wouldn't survive. That was the worst terror of all: that you might be the last one left alive. This terror made her angry. Why should her father sink into death, leaving her to carry the burden of life?

But there was love there too, even in those

times. A window had opened into her father's soul towards the end and he had allowed her to become close to him. He spoke to her with a tenderness that had been hidden away for years. *'I'm not really hungry, Anna,* moya dusha. *Just tired.'* He had smiled, reached out, and taken her hand. Everything became simple. She was his daughter and he loved her. He didn't have to be frightened any more about what he might bring down on her head, because he knew that he was going to die.

Now that she fully realizes how afraid he was, it makes sense of something else he'd said, which had puzzled her at the time: *'They'll soon forget about me, once I'm dead.'* He'd said it without a trace of bitterness; in fact there'd been a faint smile on his face, as if something worthwhile had been accomplished. He'd meant that the name of Mikhail Ilyich Levin would soon fade, and so his family would be safer. He could no longer be summoned before committees. His work could not be picked apart and then rejected. No other writer could denounce him to save his own skin. There'd be no more risk of expulsion from the Writers' Union, after which it would be open season on him and all who were connected to him.

But the man who haunted her father's nights is still alive. Thousands — millions — perish around him, but Stalin appears immortal, like the pitiless gods of the Ancient Greeks. They think, *Surely he must die soon,* but he does not die. And now there is Volkov.

Anna had to accept, once Andrei had explained it all, that there was no choice. He had to take on the boy. It would be worse than useless to argue with Volkov, even on the basis that it wasn't a professionally sound decision. All Volkov would think was that Andrei was trying — for reasons which were certainly discreditable — to avoid a professional relationship with him. He'd know why — of course he would — and probably he'd take pleasure in it. *They like us being afraid,* thinks Anna. *It makes them strong.*

The fact that Volkov has taken to Andrei is one of those things that even years of being careful can't protect you against. A red, tender swelling on a child's leg, that's all it takes to destroy years of caution.

'It's me Volkov wants. He thinks I'm the one to look after his boy,' Andrei said.

The favour of such a man is as random and potentially lethal as the cancer that brought the child to hospital in the first place. Andrei has told her that the boy's name is Gorya, but Anna doesn't want to use it, even to herself. It makes him too real.

She's always been so careful. Hedged about with second thoughts at every step, silent when she's longed to speak, speaking when she'd prefer to be silent. If she could have thrown a cloak of invisibility around them all, she would have done so. But you can't. It's the stupidest of illusions. She is so sick of all those phrases: *Keep your nose clean; keep your head down; a fly will not get into a closed mouth . . .*

They are all lies. There's no protection in making yourself small and hoping to become invisible. All you do is make yourself small.

Anna folds her sewing, stands up, and goes to the door to Kolya's room. She glances at her watch, then very quickly goes across to the piano, kneels down by the piano stool, lifts the lid, takes out a pile of music and places it carefully on the floor. She leans forward and stays still for a moment, looking into the empty box, and then she gets up, goes back into the living room and searches through a toolbox in one of the cupboards. She returns to the piano stool, carrying a small screwdriver. She kneels

137

down again and one by one she unscrews the screws that fasten the base of the piano stool. When they are all loosened, she slips the point of the screwdriver into a groove between the side of the stool and the base, wriggles it around, and then slowly lifts.

Underneath the lifted sheet of plywood lies a small compartment in which there are several notebooks and some larger sketch-books. Layered sheets of paper line the bottom of the compartment.

Anna picks up one of the notebooks. The handwriting is her father's. Even now, after she's opened these notebooks so many times, the familiarity of it still gives her a pang. A person's handwriting is part of him. She seems to hear her father's voice.

This I should not be writing down. How can a man with children be so criminally irresponsible? But there's something deep within me that says: Write, whatever happens.

So I keep on writing. I have a little place under the floorboards, big enough to hold a couple of these notebooks. There's a rug over the floorboards, and a table covered with work planted on top of it. Anna would never dream of disturbing my work.

He'd been so sure of her. She is not sure that she recognizes the 'Anna' who emerges from her father's diaries. But he's right: she'd never have discovered them if Marina hadn't told Anna where they were, before her own death. Her father and Marina must have shared many secrets. It's terrible how bitter that can still make her feel. Death is supposed to bring reconciliation, but sometimes she feels angrier with her father than she ever did while he was alive. And with Marina, too. They've got away, they're dead, and she can never ask them what they thought they were doing.

After they died she had to turn to the future. Kolya had to survive. Those who lived through the siege were like a different race by the time they emerged. She had Andrei and they had to make a life. She didn't even try to lift that floorboard, not for a long time.

Sometimes, it has to be said, I lose that thread of hope to which I cling. I begin to believe that they are right, and I ought to change my style. No, not just my style but my content and my whole approach. The inner furnishings of my mind are wrong. I'm a relic. The future has no place for me. I'm no Tikhonov.

Anna knows that her father was a friend of the poet Tikhonov long ago, when they were both young. He thought very highly of Tikhonov's *Twelve Ballads.* 'He was the real thing then.' But since Tikhonov became a much-decorated flag-bearer for socialist realism, he'd chosen different friends.

'My God, the stuff he's been churning out!' her father said once. 'He buys his trips to congresses in Paris at a high price. And you know, Anna, a few years ago he was even kind enough to favour me with some advice, for old times' sake. I've got to "adopt a more positive perspective, let go of my individualistic neuroses and produce something that reflects the deep, pure reality of the people". But he's given up on me now. Tikhonov doesn't even look at me these days, let alone speak.'

Her father had said this as if it were a relief, but Anna wondered. It couldn't have been pleasant to be ignored by a writer as influential as Tikhonov. If he slighted her father, others would rush to slight him too. Thank God her father hadn't lived to see Tikhonov become Chairman of the Writers' Union . . .

Sometimes, especially at night, I begin to wonder. What if all the Tikhonovs are right, and their careers aren't consummate demonstrations of expediency, but the only true and possible response to our times . . . And then I'm forced to consider the possibility that I'm simply wasting my own life and whatever talent I have left. And perhaps I should admit my weakness, ask for forgiveness, start again.

If it weren't for the taste of Tikhonov's boot polish . . . No, I don't think I could quite swallow that.

Anna closes the notebook. She still feels as if she is spying on her father by looking at his diary, and yet she feels compelled to read it. It seems as if by doing so she is keeping his memory alive. The same, familiar pages yield different meanings each time.

If she had a grave to visit, perhaps the diary wouldn't matter so much. Her father and Marina are buried in the swampy, overgrown mass graves at Piskarevskoye Cemetery. At least the anniversary of his death falls in midwinter, when the graves are covered with a thick blanket of snow. The place looks less neglected then. In summer she can hardly bear to visit, because the weeds are so rank.

Andrei doesn't know that she has kept

these notebooks, although of course he always knew that her father wrote a diary. Andrei was carrying one of these notebooks the first time he came to their apartment — and Anna was terrified, because she thought he'd come to bring her the news that her father was dead. But Mikhail was only wounded, with a good chance of recovery; or so it seemed then. Andrei had known immediately that the notebook must be taken into safe keeping. It would be dangerous if it were found in her father's pocket when he was taken to hospital.

She has that notebook in front of her now. The war notebook. She opens a page at random.

Andrei and I have just eaten our eggs. Little fires are burning, Everything is calm and settled and almost like home. That's the main thing I remember from the last war. You had to make a home out of wherever you were, no matter what the place was like.

He goes on to write about Andrei, and how they'd talked about the taiga, and Andrei's home. Strange to think that her father knew and liked Andrei before Anna had even met him. In fact, if it hadn't been for her father, she would never have met Andrei at all.

It's better that Andrei and Kolya don't know about the piano stool. It's a good hiding place, she thinks. She's heard that one of the first things they do when they make an arrest is to pull up the rugs, feel for any loose floorboards and then wrench them up. At first she thought of wrapping the notebooks in oilskin and burying them at the dacha, so that they could be dug up one day 'when things are better', but then she realized that she needed to have them near her. Besides, things might never be 'better'. This is her life, her only life. Reading the diaries was like a conversation with her father, one which she had never had. As she grows older, she is coming closer to him. One day their paths will touch, and join. They will be the same age. No, she doesn't want his diaries to be mouldering under the earth.

And she, too, had things she needed to hide. It wasn't difficult to organize the piano stool's secret compartment: Anna's good with her hands. The important thing was to keep it shallow enough not to arouse suspicion if anyone ever tipped the music out of the stool. She lined the bottom edges of the compartment with narrow wooden battens, five centimetres deep, and then fitted the plywood cover so that it could be levered in and out, but would not loosen on its own.

The original label from the bottom of the stool was stuck so hard that she had to turn the stool upside down, prop it up and hold a steaming pan of water inside until the label loosened enough for her to peel it away. When it had dried, she stuck it back down on top of the plywood cover, and rubbed wax into it until the new wood looked more or less the same as the old.

The only problem with such a good hiding place is that it reveals the trouble you've taken to conceal whatever is in it.

There's one notebook that she has never read. She opened it, saw that he was writing about Marina, and closed it again. In her mind it's the 'Marina notebook', and dangerous. She's afraid of finding out her father's side of the story. She knows Marina's, and will never know her mother's.

Anna reaches for the top sketchbook, and opens it.

There is a drawing of a tram, stuck in a snowdrift. Its windows would be full of frost, except that a shell blast has shattered them. Through the gaps you can see a woman sitting, muffled in coat, hat, scarf. Her head has fallen to her chest. She is dead.

On the next page there is a snowdrift. A hand sticks out of it, but people walk by, not even noticing, intent on their next step. The drawings are made in strong, thick lines, like cartoons.

She flips over the pages. There is Kolya, in his nest of blankets, cocooned in layers of clothes. His toy horse rests on his pillow but he isn't playing with it. He stares at the window, which is criss-crossed with strips of paper as protection against blasts.

That figure which looks like an old woman — that's Tanya, her school friend. If she'd lived, she would be thirty-four now, the same age as Anna, but Anna heard that she'd died. Anna did the sketch from memory, after she'd come across Tanya crouched with her hand drill, boring through the canal ice for water. There was no water supply in Tanya's apartment building any more, and she hadn't the strength to go as far as the Neva, where the water would be cleaner.

There are dozens and dozens of drawings. Here's a loose piece of paper, torn from her father's Shakespeare. Marina asked her to do that drawing, after her father died. He lies there frozen, wasted to the bone and with ice in his hair.

Marina had said, 'You must draw everything, Anna. One day people will want to know what happened.'

But Marina was mistaken. People have to bury their stories. What's wanted is an acceptable version, not the truth. Certainly not Leningrad's truth. Anna drew the Sennaya market, with its terrifying vendors of meat whose origin mustn't be questioned too closely. She drew the face of the man who stole her sledge with the sack of wood she'd scavenged, and the face of Zina when she came to their apartment door with her dead baby in her arms. At the bottom of the secret compartment there are her larger drawings: their apartment, with the shapeless, sexless figures huddled around the *burzhuika;* her father's room, which is now Kolya's, where her father and Marina lie together, dead. The frost is all over them like fur. Anna drew as if only drawing would keep her alive. Here's Marina, alive again, carefully peeling off the top, painted layer of papier mâché from Kolya's toy fort. There is nourishment in the paste that held the layers of newspaper together. They will cook and eat the papier mâché.

She can still feel little Kolya in her arms, in the freezing darkness of the midnight apartment. He is so thin that she can touch each separate bone of his ribcage. His lips

146

move against her neck, sucking in his sleep. She holds him all night, for fear that without her warmth Kolya will die.

Why do we think that the present is stronger than the past? They are not even separate. The past is alive, waiting. She and Andrei turned away from it because they had to, but it only grew more powerful. Part of her will never leave that frozen room.

She turns the pages. Now there are drawings of dandelion leaves. Here is a row of cabbages, fat and solid. Here is Kolya, eating a bowl of porridge with a spoon, looking up at her with a self-conscious smile. His arm is curved around the bowl, but he is trying to eat 'nicely'. They are not starving any more. Here is a brigade of women sweeping the streets clean. She hears the sound of the brooms, and feels the blisters on her palms. She had to make all these sketches so quickly, and often from memory. But it's true that the more you draw, the more you can draw.

These days she finds it so hard to begin. The sense of urgency has gone and, once again, she's all too aware of her technical weaknesses. Sometimes she envies Kolya as he sits for hours at the piano, improvising, messing around, really playing.

No one would want to see her drawings

now. At one point she thought of handing them in for the blockade exhibition, but now she's glad that she didn't. The exhibition was closed down by the authorities, as if it were the scene of a crime. The exhibits were scattered. Her drawings would have been lost, or even destroyed. They recorded things that were not supposed to be part of public memory.

And besides, why should Leningrad set itself up for special treatment?

Leningrad has been punished for it.

If my drawings were destroyed, would they still exist somewhere, because they *have been drawn?* Anna has no idea what the answer to that question might be.

The sketchbook at the bottom of the compartment contains her most recent work. Among the drawings is one of Piskarevskoye. The overgrown mass graves form a vast, derelict space. Summer clouds sail high up in the sky, indifferent. Tiny figures haunt the edges of the drawing. It's said that one day the cemetery will be made beautiful, so that it will be a proper memorial to everyone who died.

Anna believes that it's not a question of remembering or of forgetting. The past is alive. It claims what is its own.

7

Andrei picks up the telephone. 'Brodskaya here,' says the voice. 'I have the results of the Volkov biopsy.' He is silent, waiting. 'Can you come over?'

'Of course.'

Galvanized, he's up and out of the door, swinging down the corridor as if eager for the meeting. Brodskaya is at her desk. The path lab report file lies in front of her, open. As soon as he closes the door behind him she says quietly, 'It's as we thought. There is osteoid throughout the lesion in the proximal tibia and the lesion has spread beyond the bone into soft tissue. Amputation of the limb above the knee is the only course of action. X-rays of the lungs show no metastasis at this point.'

'I see.'

She pushes the file towards him. Rapidly he scans it, aware that the detail will mean much more to her than it does to him.

'There's no chance of saving the limb?'

She shakes her head.

'I see.'

'So will my leg be better in time for pre-season training?'

'I hope so. That's what we all want.'

'Thank you, Riva Grigorievna. If you don't mind, I'd like to take the biopsy report with me when I talk to the child's parents.'

'Not an easy task,' says Brodskaya.

'It never is.' *Let's cling to the fiction that this is a child like any other: a straightforward case of suffering, grief, and perhaps recovery.*

'The sooner the operation is done,' says Brodskaya, 'the better for him. This is an aggressive tumour, as you know. I'd prefer to prepare the boy and operate tomorrow.'

'Yes, I understand. I'll call you as soon as I've talked to the parents.'

'This is not correct!' exclaims Brodskaya suddenly. 'I should convey this information directly — as the surgeon who carried out the biopsy —'

He looks at her, wondering if she really means it. Brodskaya doesn't strike him as the type to display professional pique. And who would make a stand on protocol in this situation, when the prize is telling a man

150

like Volkov that his son's leg must be amputated?

'I understand that,' says Andrei.

'I'm not blaming you personally, please don't think that. I know you're not responsible. But it makes me uneasy. We have developed our procedures for a reason. They protect us, just as they protect the patient.'

In such a case, nothing will protect us, thinks Andrei. With some colleagues he might even risk saying it, but he scarcely knows Brodskaya.

'Have you discussed it with Admin?' he asks instead.

'Of course. As soon as I raised the subject it was made clear to me that Volkov had already spoken to them. Every facility is to be made available. As you know, they accept your involvement in the case, despite its irregularity.'

'I see.'

'Andrei Mikhailovich, if you take my advice, you will reduce your involvement to the minimum. This is a difficult case. Postoperative care and rehabilitation take time and are not always satisfactory. The risk of complications is high, let alone the risk of metastasis. It may be that micro-metastasis has already taken place. It's impossible to tell. The outcome may be far from positive.'

151

'I may not have that choice.'

'No. But the patient will need expert nursing, physiotherapy and prosthesis. It's important that all these people who are closely involved in the treatment are able to communicate directly with the family.' She pauses. 'The responsibility for this should not be yours alone. Please tell the family that if they wish to discuss the biopsy results with me, I am happy to do so.'

He looks back at her and nods, hoping that she knows how much he respects her. It's not just professional pride that's driving her; she has courage, too.

Brodskaya's face softens, just a little.

The child is asleep. The nurse sitting by his bed looks up as Andrei pushes the door open, and puts her finger to her lips. Andrei nods.

'Is the mother in the hospital?'

'May I ask who you are?' asks the nurse in a tone that would be startling if she worked in this hospital. Andrei doesn't recognize her.

'Dr Alekseyev. I have some responsibility for Gorya.'

'Ah yes. Comrade Volkov has called Admin to say he will be in directly.'

They've made sure to find a Party member

to nurse the boy today. Perhaps she's a private nurse. This whole business is getting beyond him. He nods again, as if he understands, and starts to close the door.

'No!' comes the nurse's urgent whisper. 'You are to remain here. Comrade Volkov will be here *directly.*'

She's right. A couple of minutes later the awkward silence between the nurse and Andrei is broken by approaching footsteps. Andrei moves quickly to the door and closes it behind him before the child can be disturbed. Volkov is dressed formally in a high-collared jacket, as if he's just come from a meeting. His wife clops at his side in heels and a pale blue linen suit. Volkov's sallow, high-cheekboned face shows no expression, but Polina Vasilievna looks at Andrei with pitiful entreaty.

'So? What's the news?' Volkov asks.

'We've just received the results of the biopsy. Please come with me.'

'But we need to tell Gorya too, surely,' breaks in the mother. 'He's very anxious, you must know that. His football means so much to him, and it's the start of training —'

'Gorya is sleeping at the moment,' says Andrei.

'Yes, but when he wakes up, he'll —' She

153

knows something bad is coming. That's why she keeps talking, to fend it off.

'That's enough,' says Volkov quietly, taking her arm as if he were taking hold of a prisoner.

They follow Andrei down the corridor. He's already told Admin that he needs a room, somewhere private, and they've cleared an office for him. It smells of polish, and someone has deposited a fresh vase of tulips on the desk. Extraordinary. There are several chairs, grouped together.

'Please sit down. My colleague, Riva Grigorievna Brodskaya, carried out the biopsy, as you know. She's offered to come and discuss the results with you, if you have any questions, but I thought it best that I spoke to you first, as we agreed.'

Volkov makes a gesture as if swatting something away.

'The biopsy showed a tumour, as we expected. The results from pathology show that this tumour is an osteosarcoma. Let me explain what that means.'

The parents sit as if frozen. Volkov's eyes are still. Andrei is suddenly sure that Volkov knows what the word means, but that his wife does not.

'I am sorry to have to tell you that this is

a form of cancer,' he says.

The mother jerks in her chair. Her mouth opens and a flare of colour appears on her cheekbones. 'No, it's not so, that's impossible, you are lying to us,' she says in a high, fast monotone. 'My Gorya's not got cancer, it's not possible, tell him, Seryozha, tell him it's a mistake. They've got the results muddled up. It's sabotage, that's what it is —'

'Be quiet,' says Volkov.

'I am sorry. This is very distressing for you, Polina Vasilievna,' says Andrei.

'It's not me I'm thinking about, it's Gorya. How's he going to get better if you can't even find out what's wrong with him properly? There's no cancer in my family, there never has been. It's a mistake, I tell you —'

'If you can't sit quiet, you'll have to go out,' says her husband in the same flat voice. He reaches over, takes her left hand and folds it between his, then puts it in his lap. 'Don't talk. Listen.' And then to Andrei, 'So what are you going to do?'

Andrei pauses, glances at the mother, then back to Volkov. A wave of comprehension passes silently between them, and Volkov says, 'Polya, I want you to go to the boy. He'll be waking up and asking for you.'

She stands up. Her cheeks are drained of

155

colour now, and her eyes vacant with shock.

'Take your valerian drops in a glass of water. You don't want to upset the boy.'

She nods, fumbling in her handbag.

'I'll call a nurse for her,' says Andrei, and reaches for the phone.

Once they're alone, Volkov lights a cigarette. His hands are steady. 'I don't know much about cancer,' he says. 'So what are you going to do?'

'There's only one possible treatment, I'm afraid —'

'Amputation,' says Volkov quickly, as if he can't bear to hear the word from anyone else's mouth.

'It's the only way to stop the cancer spreading. Osteosarcoma is very aggressive.'

' "Aggressive"?' The word pushes Volkov to his feet. He stands over Andrei, his face black with anger. 'You want to cut my son's leg off, and you tell me that's not aggressive!'

Andrei holds his gaze. 'Yes, it's very bad,' he says. 'I know that.'

'You don't know. You can't know. You haven't got a son.'

So he wants me to know that he knows exactly who Kolya is. It sounds like a threat but it's also the raw feeling of a father.

'He has a chance of being picked for the A team this season.'

'He told me.'

'He can't play for the A team, hopping around on one leg. He'll be a cripple!'

'He will learn to walk again.'

' "Walk"? You mean on crutches? You mean with a wooden leg?'

'Gorya is going to need a lot of help after the operation. From everyone here, but most importantly from you and your wife. If you think he is a cripple, he will be a cripple.'

Volkov's face contorts. He makes a fist of his left hand and thuds it with all his strength into the palm of his right. And again, and again. He is sweating. The animal smell of it fills the room.

'Will *you* do it, then? Will you be the one that saws his leg off?' Volkov hisses through his teeth.

'I'm not an orthopaedic surgeon. As I said earlier, Dr Brodskaya will carry out the operation.'

'Tell me this. What do they do with the leg after it's been cut off? Throw it away?'

Andrei grasps his meaning. That precious leg; those little tootsies that you play games with when the boy is a baby. Learning to walk; learning to run. Learning to kick a

157

ball. *No, not like that, that's how girls kick!*
Watch me. Learning to dribble, learning to
pass. The baby lying on his back on a
blanket, kicking at the sun. The pudgy,
perfect foot that has not yet walked on the
hard earth.

'It would be better for him to die.'

Still Andrei says nothing. What answer can
he give? His work is based on the premise
that life is preferable to death, but when he
thinks of everything that the boy's got to go
through before he resumes his life, even
Andrei — who barely knows Gorya — has
to quail.

'Suffering, and more suffering, so that he
can be a cripple.'

'But at least it gives him a chance of
survival.'

'Survival — yes. But survival is not the
same thing as life.'

Again there's a long silence. Andrei's next
clinic is due to begin at three, and already
it's a quarter to. Usually he would spend
the lunchtime before this clinic reviewing
the files. His mind fills with the image of
the crowded waiting room, the mothers (it's
almost always mothers) with the children
sitting beside them, 'nicely'. Many of them
will be dressed in their best clothes. The
girls' hair tightly plaited, the boys' ears red

from vigorous washing. *'You don't want the doctor to think you're dirty, do you?'* The ones who are here for the first time will be afraid. His most important task on their first visit is to put those fears to rest and begin a relationship which will grow strong enough to withstand a treatment that's usually going to be long and painful, and which will need so much commitment from the parents, and cooperation from the children. You cannot sweep in and take all that for granted. It has to be built up from that first moment when you meet the child's eyes, and then the mother's, and smile.

All of them there, waiting. Does Volkov really understand what a privilege it is, never to wait? But that's impossible for anyone in his position. The more they talk about 'the people', and praise the universality of Soviet medical treatment, the further away they move from those crowded waiting rooms.

But he's being too harsh. Volkov is still a human being, and a father. There he sits, fists clenched.

'Tell me,' says Volkov at last. 'This operation. If it's carried out, I need to be sure of the outcome. Will he be cured? Will that be the end of it?'

'It's the only possible treatment. It offers

159

your son his best chance of survival.'

'What kind of chance?' snaps Volkov. 'Generalizations are no use to me. I need statistics.'

Andrei is prepared for this, and has the figures clear in his mind. But there are so many variables, and besides he has to think of the child's morale. And the parents' too, because if they lose hope at this stage then they will see the amputation not as a treatment or a possible cure but as a mutilation. He decides that with Volkov he will use technical terms, because Volkov is the type who will consider anything else at best a fobbing-off and at worst an attempt at deception.

'Gorya's tumour is in the proximal tibia, and cancerous cells have already spread into the soft tissue that surrounds it,' he says. 'As far as we can see there's no metastasis. That is, as far as we can judge from the biopsy, the X-rays and the general examination, there is no visible spread of the cancer into other areas of the body. But you want me to be honest with you. Our statistics show that the proximal tibia is a site which gives one of the better chances of survival. If the tumour were in Gorya's collarbone or his pelvis, his chances would be very much worse. A young patient whose tumour is sited below the knee has just about the best prospects. There are other factors, such as the size of the tumour and the extent of tissue involvement. But you'll understand that all patients' results are aggregated for statistical purposes, and therefore these statistics don't reflect what may happen in any particular case.'

Volkov nods. This is the kind of precision he understands and to some extent trusts.

'But the statistics themselves. The actual figures.'

Andrei pauses. 'Remember that these statistics cover all cases, including the most serious and untreatable tumours. They also cover all age groups. You'll appreciate how difficult it is to treat a case of osteosarcoma in the spine, for instance. The overall survival rate after ten years is approximately fifteen per cent.'

Volkov's eyes don't move. 'Fifteen per cent? You mean that fifteen per cent of your patients die?'

Andrei looks down. He realizes how distraught the man is, inside his carapace of calm. He will be angry that he has misunderstood. 'I am sorry,' he says, still not looking at Volkov, 'I have to inform you that fifteen per cent of them survive. That is the rate, after ten years, but as I said before

161

these statistics include many cases where there was no real possibility of successful treatment from the time of first diagnosis.' He looks up again, into Volkov's eyes. 'I must emphasize that Gorya in not in this category.'

Volkov's head jerks back. His nostrils flare. 'And if he doesn't have this operation?'

'He has no chance of survival, in that case.'

Volkov flings away from Andrei, shoves the chairs aside and begins to pace the room. Four paces, a turn, four paces again. On the next turn he comes right up to Andrei, confronting him.

'So, you advise me to permit this operation?'

Andrei can smell him. 'Yes. In these circumstances it's what I must advise.'

'You'd advise it for your own son?'

'Yes.'

'But you have no son. The boy who lives with you, he's your brother-in-law. His name's Levin.'

Andrei does not respond. Think of it as the snarl of a wounded animal, he tells himself. So he wants me to know that he's read my file, and probably Anna's and Kolya's too. Well, we always knew that would be the case.

Volkov grimaces, showing his teeth. 'And

so I have to tell my son that we intend to cut off his leg.'

Andrei notes the slightly theatrical phrasing, but also the 'we'. It's a good sign. Volkov isn't rejecting the treatment. He's even prepared to associate himself with it. But he can't be allowed to go in to the boy in this state of mind. God knows what he'd say to him. Andrei thinks quickly. It's a risk, but with a man like Volkov it's worth trying. His heart beats harder, and he despises himself for it.

'When I was working here during the siege, we saw children with their limbs blown off by shells, or crushed when a building collapsed. You know how it was, you were here yourself. We had to operate. I can't lie to you and tell you that they went back to their former lives. None of us did. But they went back to lives that they find worth living. I am still in touch with some of those patients now.'

A quick sideways glance, measuring him.

'We do everything we can with prostheses. Again, I'd be lying to you if I said it was easy to get used to an artificial limb, but the quality of prostheses is improving all the time, as our technology improves and new materials are developed. Rehabilitation here is very good. You can be assured that your

163

son will have first-rate care.'

'I realize that you've done this kind of thing many times before,' says Volkov. He speaks harshly, but his posture has changed. He's listening now.

'Would you like me to talk to your wife?'

'No. It's best she doesn't hear until we're at home.'

He's right, thinks Andrei. A woman like Polina Vasilievna will throw herself to the ground, clutching her head and screaming. Maybe that's the better way. Women like her tend to adjust more quickly than those who stare at him, frozen.

'Sometimes,' he says carefully, 'with children, it's better if the doctor prepares the ground. Or perhaps a nurse, if there's a nurse whom he particularly trusts. It's very important that Gorya believes we're trying to help him, otherwise he won't have the right attitude to his recovery. As you know, children see things differently from us. They can be very pragmatic, in my experience, as long as we don't ask them to look too far ahead.'

' "Pragmatic"!' Volkov gives an astonished bark of laughter.

'Yes. It may seem a strange word to choose; but that's been my experience. It's vital that things are explained to him clearly, as much as he wants to know. Children suffer such terrors from the things they imagine. For example, he needs to know that he won't see or hear anything of the operation. He will not see his leg severed from his body. Forgive me, these things are very hard for a parent. He must understand that he will not be alone, but will be looked after at every stage.' Andrei clears his throat. 'Perhaps I shouldn't say this. But in the siege, I used to tell the children who were brought into us that they'd been wounded in battle, exactly like the grown-up soldiers. I would tell your son that this too is a battle. After all, he might have been injured in the shelling when he was a baby, and lost his leg.'

'Gorya was not in Leningrad during the war. My wife was evacuated shortly before he was born,' says Volkov, as if denying some parental neglect on his own part. A taste of bitterness fills Andrei's mouth. They got their own children out, while ours — but he mustn't think like that. The patient is the one who matters.

'Life deals us these blows,' he goes on quietly, as if Volkov hadn't spoken. 'Gorya must fight for his health, like a soldier, and think of his scars as battle scars. And he must believe that this is how you think of it, too. He is not a cripple, but a wounded soldier whose courage makes you proud.'

Volkov's looking at him intently now. Not accepting what he says, but not pushing it away either. It's the strangest moment of intimacy.

'Those children — you said that you still see them.'

'Some of them.'

'Do they work? Have they families?'

'Some do.'

Volkov nods, lost in thought. He has sat down again by the desk and his fingers drum on its surface. 'You talk to him,' he says at last. 'I'll take his mother home.'

'My clinic begins in a couple of minutes and will last until six. As soon as it's finished, I'll be able to go and talk to Gorya.'

Volkov looks at Andrei with such absolute surprise that Andrei realizes how rarely this man doesn't get what he wants as soon as he even hints that he wants it.

'Surely your clinic can wait.'

'Explaining everything to Gorya may take some time. It isn't something I would want to rush.'

Volkov's cold, narrow stare doesn't waver. 'Very well. I'll come in again tonight, after you've seen him.'

The clinic overruns, as clinics always do,

but it's not too bad. By six thirty the last patient has gone, and the nurse is busy putting the files away and preparing the sterilizer. From the waiting room comes the clang of a bucket. The cleaners are in there already with their mops and brooms.

Time to go. He's so tired. He snatched a glass of tea between patients but it's strong coffee he needs now. No time to go to the canteen. His stomach is growling with hunger.

'Dasha, you haven't got anything to eat, have you? I need to go straight to another patient.'

She pauses, carrying an armload of buff-coloured files. 'I've got an Alyonka bar in my coat pocket. Hang on a minute.'

'Don't go giving me Ilyusha's chocolate —'

But she's gone, and back a moment later. 'There you are. You should go to the canteen for some soup, though, a bit of chocolate won't keep you going.'

'No time, I'm late as it is,' mumbles Andrei, eating the chocolate.

'You're too thin as it is. Doesn't Anna feed you?'

'She's a wonderful cook. I'm just one of those types who doesn't pay for feeding.'

'Go on, eat the lot. Ilyusha gets plenty of

chocolate. I'm too soft with him. You want to give them everything, don't you?'

'Yes. Thanks, Dasha, you've saved my life.'

He's managed to speak to both Brodskaya and the anaesthetist during the afternoon. The anaesthetist is going to see the boy later. Brodskaya was her usual cool professional self, as if this were a patient like any other. There are no blood-clotting or infection problems that might affect the operation, and the boy's general health is good. They can go ahead tomorrow morning. In fact, she's already got him booked in at ten thirty. The only problem was a shortage of matching blood — he's O Negative — but she's got that organized now. 'It's about time for another campaign on blood donations,' she observed, frowning. 'Supplies of the rarer groups should never be permitted to run down like this.'

Brodskaya really was admirable, he thinks now as he swallows the last of the chocolate. Disinterested, thorough and determined not to be panicked into anything less than her professional best. He only hopes he can match her . . . But the boy will be asleep if he doesn't get moving.

'Thank you, Dasha,' he says again. Dasha gives him a quick warm smile and then goes on with what she's doing. 'See you

168

tomorrow.'

'See you tomorrow,' she says, without looking up from the files.

Andrei recognizes the policeman, and he's sure that the policeman recognizes him. It makes no difference.

'Your papers.'

After he's checked them he opens the door grudgingly, as if Andrei were trying to obtain entry on false pretences.

The boy is lying back against his pillows, watching the door. His eyes widen and a faint look of pleasure comes into his face as he sees that it's Andrei. 'I've seen loads of doctors today,' he says. 'They keep coming in and going out, and coming in and going out.'

'You remember that I told you a lot of tests might be necessary.'

'To make me well,' says Gorya immediately. 'Is my dad coming?'

'I think he's coming later.'

'Mum went home. She usually always stays with me but Dad said she had to go home and rest.'

'Probably a good idea.'

Andrei sits down in the bedside chair, in Gorya's line of sight. 'I have something to tell you, Gorya,' he says, keeping his eyes on the child's face. Instantly, a shadow of fear moves in the boy's eyes. 'The small operation you had. You remember what it was for?'

'Taking out a little piece of the tumour so they could examine it in a laboratory,' replies Gorya. Brodskaya has done her work well.

'Yes. The surgeon looked carefully at your tumour —'

'It's not *my* tumour!'

'All right. She looked at the tumour and took out some cells for the pathologist to examine — do you know what cells are?'

'No.'

'They're like the building blocks that make up your body. But sometimes cells grow that don't build your body or help it. Instead they harm it. They make swellings, which keep growing bigger, like the one in your leg. And these swellings damage the healthy parts of your body until they can't work any more.' He pauses. Gorya says nothing, but he licks his lips. 'We could tell from the swelling on your leg, and from the X-rays, that a tumour was growing there. When tumours grow inside you they can hurt you very badly. That's why they have to be removed.'

'Then why didn't that doctor take all of it out?'

'Because she couldn't. It's too big. It's deep in the bone and it has grown into the soft parts of your leg. Gorya, you have to understand that this tumour is very serious. If it's left, it can stop you from living.'

Gorya's face contorts with what looks like anger. 'But I can't stop living. I'm not old enough.'

'No. You're only ten, and we want you to have many more years of life. We have to get rid of that tumour before it can grow any more, and make other tumours grow too. You understand, Gorya, it's deep in your leg. It can't be removed without taking away part of your leg.'

The angry look fades, as if a hand has been wiped over the child's face. He stares at Andrei. After a long silence, a look of numb, shocked comprehension steals over his face. 'What part?' he whispers.

'The part of your leg that goes from just above your knee. Here.' He points on his own leg.

'But my foot is on that part.'

'I know.'

The boy is beginning to tremble. Suddenly and without warning, he throws himself across the bed, away from Andrei.

His head buries itself in the pillows. His fists come up, covering his ears. He gives one small moan of pain, and then no more.

'Gorya. Gorya!'

'I can't hear you,' comes the child's muffled voice.

'I know you can't. But listen to me all the same.' Andrei speaks in the gentling voice he used to use when Kolya had a tantrum or a nightmare. 'Listen, Gorya. You won't be awake when it happens. You'll be fast asleep and you'll see nothing and feel nothing. When you wake up there'll be a big bandage on your leg. You'll start to get better. There are people here who will teach you to walk again on crutches, and a bit later on you'll be fitted for a prosthesis — an artificial leg.'

There's a squeak of trolley wheels from the corridor. A nurse doing the evening drug round. *Don't let her come in, not now.* As if the nurse hears him, the squeaking dies away up the corridor. Why don't they put some oil on those wheels? But perhaps it's better for the patients to have some warning —'

'Gorya.'

Gorya turns. His face is drawn with pain. It must have hurt a lot to throw himself across the bed like that. His lips are pressed tight together, and his skin is so pale it looks waxy.

'Let's get you more comfortable. Keep still while I put the cage back in place. You need to get the weight off your dressings.'

Andrei takes a little time over fixing the cage and rearranging the bedclothes. 'There, that's better. When the nurse comes I'll ask her to make up your bed —'

'I want to keep my tumour instead!' Gorya bursts out. 'I told you it doesn't hurt. I'll tell my dad and he'll take me out of here.'

'It doesn't work like that,' Andrei says. 'The tumour won't let you live. You want to live. So the only thing to do is get rid of it.'

Gorya slumps against his pillows. His chest heaves but there are no tears. He won't have taken it in, not yet, thinks Andrei. Knowledge like this is too bad to come all at once. It sinks in gradually, stage by stage, like the realization that someone is dead.

'I can't — I can't —'

'What can't you?'

'I can't — I can't —'

'Gorya, stop this. Take a deep breath and now tell me properly.'

'I can't ever be in the A team,' says Gorya in a rush, and begins to cry.

At last, exhausted, Gorya allows Andrei to

173

wipe his face and give him a drink of water.

'He'll be so angry with me. The running track cost so much money. He said if I got into the A team it would be the proudest day of his life.'

What Gorya doesn't say, but clearly thinks, is that there's no chance of his father ever being proud of a boy with one leg. And his mother won't be able to stop crying, he's sure of that. She'll cry and scream and then his father will get angry.

'You don't know how angry he gets,' Gorya mutters, glancing sideways at Andrei.

'You mustn't worry about that. It's not your responsibility.'

But Gorya only shrugs wearily, as if he'd expected more of Andrei. *We both know how things are, what's the point of pretending?*

'We have to make you better.'

'Yes, because it's your job,' Gorya points out. 'But I'm not going to let you cut off my leg. I don't care, I'll run away and you won't ever be able to catch me.'

He's only ten. Death must seem impossibly distant. It can't weigh against the fact of having your leg cut off, now, in this hospital, by people who said they were here to make you better. Andrei decides to play his last card.

'Gorya, you will have to be a man. A

soldier. I'm sure you've seen men who fought for our Motherland in the Great Patriotic War. Some of them have lost a leg, or an arm, but they are alive. If you ask them, they'll tell you that life is much more important than the leg which they've lost. You must be brave now, and make your father proud of you.'

He'd believed all these words when he said them to Volkov earlier, but now, with Gorya, they taste ugly and useless. A child wants to run about and play. He's not a soldier.

Gorya looks down, picking at the sheet. 'He'll never be proud of me,' he mutters. When he looks up again Andrei sees that his face is empty of hope. The talk of running away is over. He knows that he can't stop what's going to happen.

Volkov will be here soon, and maybe his wife too. Andrei needs to see them first, before they go in to Gorya. Oh, yes, he's the doctor and he can sort it all out. Tell the mother not to cry, tell the father to pat the boy on the back and say one leg more or less won't make any difference to him. You're such a fine doctor, you've got the answers to everything.

'Will it be you doing it?' asks the boy.

'What?'

'You know.' Gorya makes an odd tentative motion with his left hand. Andrei realizes that he's imitating the sawing of a log.

'No, I'm not a surgeon. It'll be Dr Brodskaya who does the operation. She's very good. You've seen her, she's the one who did your biopsy. You remember: she has her hair in a bun, and glasses.'

'I don't like her. Dad says she's a Jew.'

'She's an excellent surgeon,' says Andrei. The child can't be blamed; he's only parroting what he's heard at home.

'Can you be there as well?'

'Not in the operating theatre, because it has to be very clean and they don't need extra people around who aren't helping. But if you like, I can come and see you before. You remember the room where they gave you anaesthetic to make you go to sleep?'

'Yes.'

'I could be there.'

'If she tries to hurt me, you'd stop her, wouldn't you?'

'Gorya, that would never happen. She's a doctor. Her job is helping people, not hurting them.'

'My dad says you'll always find a Jew at the bottom of every nest of spies and saboteurs.'

'It would never happen, Gorya. You're safe

here. All the doctors who work in this hospital have made a promise to do everything they can to help the patients, and nothing to harm them.'

'Have they?'

'Yes.' Gorya's face relaxes a little. Andrei stands up. 'I have to go now. Your mother and father will be here very soon.'

'But you'll come back tomorrow?'

'Yes.'

'You promise?'

'I promise.'

'That means you have to do what you say. Have you got a boy at home?'

'Yes, I have a boy at home.'

'What's he called?'

'Kolya.'

'Kolya. Is he older than me or younger?'

'Older. He's sixteen.'

'And he's your only son?'

'Well — he lives with us as my son, but in fact he's my wife's younger brother.'

'Oh,' says Gorya, animated now, 'then you haven't got a son.'

'I think of Kolya as my son.'

'But he isn't really,' murmurs Gorya, on a faint note of satisfaction. His colour is better. If you didn't know, you'd never guess this boy had just been told he had to have an amputation.

8

'It's done, then?' says Anna.

'Yes. What's that you're sewing?'

Anna has given up trying to hide the dress from Andrei until the day of the ball. There's not enough time to work on it if she does that, and besides, it doesn't seem important any more.

'You know. It's my dress for the ball.'

'The ball. Of course.'

He looks exhausted.

'The stew needs another hour. How about a glass of tea?'

'Have we got any of that Stolichnaya left?'

She pauses for a fraction of a second then says easily, 'Yes, I think there's about quarter of a litre.'

Usually they open the vodka bottle only when there are guests. Anna pours a measure and hands the glass to Andrei, who tosses it back. She raises her eyebrows. He nods, and she pours another measure. This time he holds the glass in his hand, swirling the vodka gently.

'It's all right,' he says, 'you can put the bottle away.'

She puts the vodka on the table. Comments rise to her mind, such as *This isn't like you* or *Must have been a bad day,* but she rejects them. Instead she smiles. 'It's almost finished,' she says. 'Would you like to see me in it?'

'Yes.'

She picks up the heap of cloth and makes for the door to Kolya's room.

'Why can't you put it on in here?'

'It won't be a surprise.'

'But I like seeing you get undressed.'

'I know you do. Enjoy your vodka, I'll be back in a minute.'

The fabric still smells of new cotton, even after all that time put away in the chest. She pulls off her skirt and jumper, carefully slips the neck over her head and wriggles into the dress. It feels too tight, and she panics for a second before realizing that the fabric is rucked at the waistband. Carefully, she pulls it straight. The bodice and waist fit closely, as they should, and the skirt is just as full as she hoped. She moves her hips, and the skirt sways. Perfect. She runs her fingers through her hair. A dress like this needs a full petticoat, lipstick, high heels and fine stockings. Never mind, Andrei will get the idea.

The fabric moves against her legs as she goes to the door.

'There. What do you think?'

He lifts his glass, toasts her, and drinks off the vodka. 'Wonderful,' he says. 'You look wonderful. Come here.'

'Be careful, don't crush the skirt —'

'I'm not crushing anything, I'm just — you look beautiful, Anna. Really beautiful.'

'Let's dance.'

'I can't dance without music.'

'Yes, you can. *One*-two-three, *one*-two-three . . .'

They waltz with little steps around the table where Kolya does his homework, past the piano and back through the door that connects to the living room. He's forgotten how soft she feels when they dance. He smells the new dress and the scent of her body.

'Careful of the desk,' murmurs Anna as they dance towards the window. They're hardly moving at all really, just swaying together. He smells of hospitals and vodka. She reaches up, touches his cheek with her lips, and then finds his mouth.

'I could get drunk just from kissing you,'

she says, and he laughs. They dance on. She steals a glance at him and sees that the lines of strain are leaving his face. His eyes are closed, his feet out of time. He was never a good dancer, but he feels lovely —

The outer door bangs. Kolya. They spring apart. The next moment he pushes open the living-room door, frowning.

'What're you two doing? Your dress isn't done up at the back, Anna.'

'That's because I haven't finished the fastenings yet.'

He notices the Stolichnaya bottle on the table, and gives them both a stern look. 'What're you drinking that for?'

'I just had a couple of glasses,' says Andrei. *Good God,* he thinks, *here I am explaining myself to Kolya, as if he were the parent.*

'Well, you're the ones who are always lecturing me,' grumbles Kolya, 'and here you are drinking in the middle of the day.'

'It's not the middle of the day, it's after six.'

'All right, it's after six. Were you dancing?' he asks as if this were a custom he's heard of but seldom observed.

'Just practising for the ball,' says Anna lightly.

'Without music!'

'Well, you can count the steps.'

181

'I could play you a waltz if you liked. It *was* a waltz, wasn't it?' He grins at her, knowing that the waltz is the only dance Andrei can do with confidence.

'That's very good of you, Kolya,' she answers sharply, 'but the moment's past.'

They are eating their stew when Kolya suddenly asks, 'How is that boy doing?'

'Which boy?'

'You know, the one you've been talking about with Anna. The one that's having his leg chopped off —'

'Really, Kolya, can't you be a bit more . . .' breaks in Anna.

'A bit more what? It's what's happening, isn't it?'

'Yes,' says Andrei. 'He had the operation this morning. It went well.'

Kolya nods slowly, then attacks his food again. He's not insensitive really, Anna knows that. It's the way they all talk. Kolya chews and swallows a couple of mouthfuls, then says dreamily, 'I think I'd rather die than have my leg cut off.'

'He thought that, too,' says Andrei, and this time there's an unfamiliar edge to his voice. Kolya glances at him, and then down at his plate.

Andrei thinks of Gorya on the trolley,

before he went into theatre. He was sedated, but his eyes were open. There was a short delay; something to do with the preparation of the anaesthetic. A nurse was standing by the trolley; she put her fingers on his wrist and took his pulse. Gorya's pupils were dilated, and his mouth was slack. Andrei said, 'It's all right, Gorya, I'm here just like I promised. Everything's going to be fine.' He thought the boy tried to smile, but he wasn't sure, and then it was time.

He'd said to Brodskaya that he would come back when the boy was in the recovery room.

'He's really taken a fancy to you,' one of the nurses said. 'Kept asking if he was going to see you before he had his operation.'

Andrei went to Radiology. There were X-rays he had to check, and files to be ordered from Moscow, for his research. He ought to be thinking about presenting a paper by the middle of next year. They would have finished the transaction of the muscle by now. They'd have reached the distal femur. Brodskaya was very capable. She would ensure the most effective muscle reconstruction around the bone end. Someone had been messing around with these files — they were out of order. Wouldn't have been Sofya . . . The difference that the

183

quality of the surgery made to patient outcome was enormous; people didn't understand that. They thought that cutting off a leg was cutting off a leg. If they wanted to think about it in the first place, which they didn't. But as usual it was the detail that made the difference between a painful stump which would never adapt successfully to prosthesis, and one which would enable the patient to walk again.

Ah, here was the plate he'd been looking for. Not a very good image; surely there was a better one? He'd ask Sofya. The leg would be gone by now. Andrei never uses the word 'amputee', even to himself. If you talk about patients like that, you have already turned them into another species.

'Will he have a false leg?' asks Kolya, as he mops his plate with bread.

'Yes. He'll be on crutches until the wound heals, and then we'll fit him for a prosthesis.'

'A false leg . . .' Kolya shakes his head. 'I wonder where you'd put it at night.'

'Kolya —' says Anna.

'The thing is, people say, "a false leg", but they don't think about the practicalities.'

Or the reality, thinks Andrei. You don't consider that until you've got to.

There's a silence, and then Kolya asks,

'Can I have some more stew, Anna?'

'There isn't any. You've eaten the lot.'

Kolya visibly switches off. One finger taps a rhythm gently on the table. His eyes half close, gazing inward. The only sound is the scrape of Anna and Andrei's spoons.

'Shall I play something for you?' asks Kolya abruptly, in a quite different voice from before.

'That would be lovely,' says Anna, 'after you've put the plates by the sink.'

'Do you know, I'm the only boy in my class who does all this housework?' observes Kolya as he collects up plates and cutlery with his usual dexterity and scarcely a chink of china.

' "All this housework",' Anna repeats. 'I wish I were you, Kolya. Anyway, how do you know? Have they had a questionnaire?'

'I just notice these things,' says Kolya darkly. 'In Lev's *kommunalka* you have to queue for the sink. There's an old bitch who's always hogging it.'

'Don't use that word,' says Anna automatically.

'Lev can't believe we haven't been allocated another family here. Anyway, he never does a hand's turn at home, because he's never *at* home. Right, that's done. Only I suppose you'd much rather I washed up than played you a beautiful nocturne.'

'Really a nocturne? Go on then.'

It's a peace-offering. Through the open door she sees Kolya settle on the piano stool, flex his fingers and throw back his head in the way that's always reminded her of a horse being put in harness. He's no great fan of Chopin.

'Why don't you like Chopin, Kolya?'

'I don't know. He just annoys me. He tries to get you to feel the things he's already decided you're going to feel. It's like being grabbed by a fat lady and pressed to her bosom while she sobs in your ear.'

She closes her eyes as the notes begin to move. Kolya's fingers are strong now, even the ring finger on the left hand, which is always the weakest, he says, and the most difficult to move independently. It's because they are strong that he has such control and the notes can fall as lightly as drops of rain. Underneath them the swell of the nocturne rises and subsides.

'Beautiful,' she says as he finishes.

To her surprise he comes back to the table and stands behind her chair. He puts his hands on her shoulders and rocks her gently from side to side. 'You are so soppy, Anna,' he says. 'Didn't you hear me mess up that last trill?'

'Mmm, yes, I did notice the fingering was a bit slapdash.' She glances up at his surprised face, and laughs. 'I got you there, didn't I?'

'Next time,' he says grandly, 'it will be a piece of my own composition. That'll learn you.'

Andrei hears them, but doesn't listen. His mind is full of Gorya Volkov. Why has this boy got under his skin like this? Some patients do, and you have to expect it. The tension around Gorya is like a force field. Rules are broken and people who thought they were averagely brave turn out to be someone they don't want to know. Policemen settle themselves in the corridors as if they're guards patrolling a jail. In the middle of all this there's just a child.

Volkov said, 'You don't have a son.'

Gorya said of Kolya, 'But he isn't really.' *Isn't really your son,* he meant. Andrei's come across this before. Some of the young patients get possessive and they don't want to think about 'their' doctor going home to his own healthy children. They don't even want to think that you have a life outside the hospital. But the truth is that Kolya is not his son.

He looks across the table at Anna and

187

Kolya. They are laughing, but he doesn't know what about. Their eyes go into the same shape when they laugh. Kolya is often rude to Anna, rarely to Andrei. He doesn't wrap his arms around Andrei's neck like that. But that's natural, Andrei tells himself quickly.

The suturing of the wound closure has to be meticulous. Large folds of skin will cause trouble later on. Friction from the prosthesis on a carelessly sewn stump can leave it red and raw. You get sores, infections and even weeping abscesses — but Brodskaya's good. She's careful. My God, it's bad enough without some surgeon messing it up so the boy has no chance of ever getting about on anything but crutches.

An image flashes across Andrei's mind. A legless boy he saw once, propped on a wooden trolley by the entrance to a court-yard. Waiting for someone, or something. It was a cold day, between sleet and rain. Maybe they were going to take him some-where.

Gorya doesn't look much like his father. If you met him without knowing who he was, you'd just think, 'a nice boy'. No one in his right mind would envy Volkov, but all the same he's able to say, 'My son.'

'That's enough now, Kolya,' says Anna, 'you're pulling my hair.' Her face is flushed and happy. She frets when Kolya 'hides himself away from us', as she calls it, and loves it when he teases her.

'Time I was on my way,' says Kolya, and Andrei has to turn away from the disappointment in Anna's face.

'Oh — I didn't know you were going out.'

'Meeting the others. See you later — where did you put my cap, Anna?'

'I haven't had it.'

'People are always moving my stuff,' Kolya grumbles. They hear him rooting in the box under the coat pegs, and then the outer door slams.

'Don't be late!' calls Anna, a second too late. He'll be halfway down the stairs by now. He has a way of going down at full pelt, only just in control, only just not falling.

'Summer nights,' says Andrei. 'I wonder if he's got a girlfriend yet.'

'Of course he hasn't!' says Anna indignantly.

'He's sixteen.'

'Sixteen — that's still too young.'

'He's not a child. In fact, Kolya's old for his age.'

'He's still just a baby sometimes.' She goes over to the mirror on the wall. 'Look what he's done to my hair.'

'I like it,' says Andrei, and smiles at her, but she looks distracted. He's tired. The warmth of the vodka has drained away. He ought to work for a couple of hours, but he's stupidly left the files he needs at the hospital. Perhaps he ought to go back for them. He could call in and see how the boy is doing.

'You're tired,' says Anna, coming over to him and framing his face with her hands. The touch of her fingers is warm and familiar, but at the same time he seems to feel nothing. 'You're worrying about that man,' she says. 'Don't. Let's not let him in here.'

'He's in here already.'

Her hands fall to her sides. She looks around the room, 'familiar to the point of tears', as her father used to say, quoting some poet no doubt. He knew so many poets. He had so much by heart, because it couldn't be written down. There is the table; there's the low chair without arms where her mother used to sit, her father said, when she was feeding Anna. The paintings on the

190

wall are full of the stories Anna used to make up about them when she was a little girl. The cracks on the ceiling hold memories of nights of shelling. Even the damp stain is an old friend. It was too high for her to climb up there and whitewash over it. They were going to borrow a ladder, but it never happened. Andrei is far more practical than her father was, but he has so little time.

'What if someone else came to live here,' she says aloud. 'They'd never know —'

'Know what?'

She shrugs. 'Oh, I don't know. How we lived here, I suppose. They wouldn't be interested, anyway. They'd be busy with their own lives.'

He nods. 'Anna, I've been thinking about your father's manuscripts. Are they all still in the desk drawer?'

'Yes.'

'I think we should give them to somebody to look after. Just until all this is over. Who do you think would be best?' *Safest,* he means.

'I'll take them down to the dacha on Sunday,' she says. 'That way, we don't need to bother anyone else. I'll bury them. Not that they're compromising, of course they're not,' she adds hastily. She is flooded with guilt. She knows that she has no intention of burying the diaries and sketchbooks.

'That old biscuit tin would do,' says Andrei. 'The skating-girls one. If we seal the edges with tape, the manuscripts should be all right in there for a while.'

'I could bury it under the compost heap.'

'Good idea.'

'It needs forking over anyway.' She looks at him, her brow furrowed.

'It's going to be all right, Anna. This is just a precaution.'

'I know.'

At that moment the doorbell rings. A long, steady peal. Someone's holding their finger down on it. Anna and Andrei stare at each other.

'Don't answer it,' she whispers.

'Don't be silly, Anna.'

He walks through to the hallway, and opens the door. It's the Weasel.

'Good evening,' says Andrei.

Without responding to this, the Weasel taps the pile of folded paper he's holding. 'We're getting up a petition,' he says, looking not at Andrei but at a point to the side of his head.

'A petition?'

'Regarding unnecessary noise emanating from this apartment at unsocial hours. I

shall be distributing copies around the building, with the permission of the caretaker.'

'Allow me to read it,' says Andrei. With a quick movement, he reaches out and takes the papers. He riffles through them. There are ten or twelve copies. Typewritten top copies, and carbons.

Anna has come up close behind him and is scanning the 'petitions'. 'Have you a typewriter at home?' she asks pleasantly.

'No, I —' and he stops, realizing this may be a trap.

'So, you had them typed for you at work?' says Anna. 'In my workplace that would not be permitted. The use of State property and the labour of State employees for private purposes during working hours are strictly prohibited. Obviously things are different in your department.'

Malevich sniffs uneasily and makes a jabbing movement as if to snatch back his petitions.

'Ve-ry interesting,' Anna continues. 'Do you know, someone once told me that it's perfectly possible to identify the typewriter that has been used to type a particular document?'

'Give them back to me. These are not the final copies. I have some additions to make

— alterations to the text —'

'I'm sure you have,' says Anna politely, 'but we'll keep one of these, since you were good enough to bring it round for us.'

Andrei removes the top copy, gives it to Anna, and hands the rest back to Malevich. They close the door on his pale, uneasy face, and go back into the living room.

'My God,' says Andrei, 'how did you come up with that?'

'I don't know. I was so angry, it just flashed into my mind that I had to frighten him, and there's only one way to do it — fight fire with fire, I mean. But it's disgusting, all the same. Look at me, my hands are shaking.'

'You were fantastic.'

'Hmm. I just went down to his level, that's all. But I don't care. I'm not going to let him do this to us. Once he's stopped Kolya playing the piano, it'll be something else. You end up so you hardly dare breathe.' Her cheeks are flushed and her eyes glitter. She's clenched her hands to stop them from trembling. 'I don't care any more,' she repeats, 'I just don't care. I'll do anything.'

'Anna . . .' He takes hold of her hands, shakes them gently. 'It's all right. He won't bother us again for a while.'

'You're right,' she says feverishly, 'it's not

194

safe to keep all those papers in the house. And Kolya's got to be more careful, too. The things he comes out with sometimes —'

'I'm sure he wouldn't dream of coming out with them at school. He's no fool.'

'Yes, but at this age they get reckless. Besides, it's not just what he says: it's what he doesn't say. Andrei, do you really believe the boy will be all right?'

'Yes.'

'But you're not sure.'

'Of course I'm not,' he says in some irritation. 'How can I be? I'm not a faith healer. I can't control the multiplication of cancer cells. That's the problem with a man like Volkov. He's used to demanding the impossible, and no one dares tell him he can't have it.'

Anna nods. 'I've had an idea. I'll bury this so-called petition as well, then if Malevich comes after us again I can tell him it's been put in safe keeping. That'll keep him worrying. Wait a minute, I'm sure that tin is in the back of this cupboard — unless I've left it at the dacha — no, here it is.'

Andrei takes it from her. 'How old is this, Anna?'

'I don't know. We've always had it.'

'From last century, I'd say.' Andrei turns

the lid around and then picks up the base and scrutinizes it. 'The writing on the bottom is English.'

'Oh my God, it's a capitalist biscuit tin. Just as well we're going to bury it. Let's see if the manuscripts will fit.'

The tin is large and square, but of course all the manuscripts can't possibly fit into it. There are wads of stories and poems, half finished and scored through with corrections. Anna packs in as much as she can, crams on the lid, and seals it with tape. Andrei weights the remaining pile in his hands.

'I'll ask around for some oilcloth at the hospital. If it's tightly wrapped it'll be all right. How important is this stuff, Anna? Are there copies?'

Anna is taken aback by his question. No one ever asked whether or not her father's writing was important, in all the years that she was growing up. It was taken for granted, like the sun in the sky. Whether it was published or not made no difference: plenty of books were written 'for the drawer'. She had never asked herself — had never *had* to ask herself — whether her father was actually a good writer or not.

'His diary was good,' Andrei continues thoughtfully.

'How do you know?' she snaps out.

'He read out an extract one evening, when we were sitting by the campfire. You know, when we were in the People's Volunteers. It was nothing much, just a description of a deserted farm, but I've never forgotten it. He could make you see things. There'd have been a lot of fine stuff in those diaries.'

Andrei looks at the familiar handwriting, and remembers the first time he met Anna's father. For some reason he'd blurted out, *'My father is also called Mikhail,'* and then blushed. But there was a connection between them from that moment.

'He wrote his diary every day, didn't he?' he says now. 'He never failed.'

'No,' says Anna.

'Pity they've disappeared. He must have destroyed them before he died. Or else he got Marina to promise him she'd do it.'

Anna turns away. This is the moment to tell him, if she's going to, but she already knows that she won't.

Goodbye to the English skaters, goodbye to all those manuscripts her father had slaved over and never seen published.

'Better get this lot out of sight before Kolya comes back,' says Andrei.

9

Lyuba has just finished wrapping Gorya's stump. It's a long business. First the wound dressing has to be changed, and the stump examined minutely for signs of healing or infection. Dr Brodskaya's directions are specific, down to the precise width of the elastic bandage and the siting of safety pins and adhesive tape. Lyuba takes pride in carrying out the doctor's instructions to the letter. Brodskaya's not a nit-picker; she thinks like a nurse and she knows that if you put the safety pin in the wrong place it will chafe the patient's other leg.

Lyuba hasn't worked with Brodskaya before, because Brodskaya's not usually in Paediatrics, but you can see straight away that she's not just good, but tough too. The best sort, Lyuba thinks. She can't stand any kind of sloppiness herself. It was Brodskaya who got the private nurse taken off the job. 'She's not qualified to carry out this level of care.' Everyone on the ward was talking about it when Lyuba arrived that morning.

The poor kid would be better off in the main ward, in Lyuba's opinion. There's no chance of forgetting about yourself when you're all on your own. It just goes to show that the high-ups, for all their privileges, don't always get what's best. Anyway, as far as she's concerned the boy is just a boy. She's not going to think about who his father is — or at least, not unless she has to.

The mother's useless. She fusses all the time and comes in with swollen eyes, complaining about her bad nights. Just what Gorya needs to hear. She's probably not all that bright either. According to her, her little boy should just lie nice and still and get better that way. With his stump covered up in bedclothes, so she doesn't have to see it.

But Brodskaya wasn't having any nonsense. She came in a couple of days ago just when Polina Vasilievna was spooning porridge into Gorya's mouth — or trying to do so, at least. Gorya kept his lips pressed together, as mutinous as a two-year-old. Lyuba had to laugh, looking at the pair of them — although of course she didn't, not aloud.

'Please put that spoon down, Mother,' said Brodskaya in a voice so clipped and clear that Polina Vasilievna immediately dropped the spoon, turned red even through all her make-up, and started to sulk just like her son.

Brodskaya went through the rehabilitation plan while Mum sat there goggling. No one is to assist Gorya with his basic functions. He can perfectly well manage the bed-bottle himself, and tomorrow he'll be getting himself from wheelchair to toilet with the assistance of the support pole. The physiotherapist will be on hand to teach him the correct technique. The aim is to get Gorya doing as much for himself as he can. Gorya's exercises must be done exactly as directed, and at exactly the times on the exercise sheet. Painful? The correct level of analgesia will be prescribed at each stage. The physiotherapist will be in at two o'clock. The aim is to keep stump oedema to a minimum. Flexion of the hips from the earliest stage is crucial for later mobility. Gorya's exercises are designed to minimize the possibility of contracture.

Brodskaya went on and on, but Lyuba could tell that Polina Vasilievna wasn't really taking it in. Partly it was because she didn't understand the doctor's language, but mostly it was because she's mulish. The sort who'll put up with the doctor's instructions just as long as the boy's in hospital, but all the time she'll be planning to 'do things her own way' as soon as she gets Gorya home. She'll turn him into an invalid by thinking he is one. As for the father — well, Lyuba keeps her eyes down when Volkov's in the room.

Andrei Mikhailovich came in later and went through pretty much everything Brodskaya had said, but he put it into words everyone could understand, even Gorya. It was Gorya he talked to the whole time. He's good with children. Fair play to Brodskaya, though, she's not a paediatrician. It's different with Andrei Mikhailovich. He even had the mother nodding her head and agreeing that it wouldn't be long before Gorya was on the parallel bars in the hospital gym and learning to walk again. Gorya relaxed, too. As far as Andrei Mikhailovich was concerned, it was perfectly normal to have a stump. Of course there were going to be problems, but each of them could be sorted out, one day at a time. Gorya's hard work and commitment were the key to everything. Lyuba could tell that the boy liked that. He was sick of having things done to him, and his mother hanging over him, going on and on about what a tragedy the whole thing was for her poor little boy.

'Your level of fitness is going to help you, Gorya. You'll have lost a bit because of the operation, but people who've got good basic fitness get mobile really quickly. And once your stump's healed we'll be looking at the best kind of prosthesis for you. You remember what a prosthesis is?'

'It's a false leg.'

'Yes, but that's not really an accurate description. It's not a false anything. It's a real prosthesis and it's going to open up your life.'

Gorya's eyes were fixed on the doctor's face.

Poor kid. The tough time comes when they go out. In hospital people don't stare. Everyone's got something wrong with them, and often it's worse than an amputation. Well, thinks Lyuba, you can't do anything about the world. The thing is to be sure your bandage is perfectly smooth and just tight enough to support without too much compression.

'There,' she says to Gorya, smiling, 'my masterpiece is finished. Now let's get you comfortable. You remember, Dr Alekseyev's coming in again after his clinic, before you see the physio. Now, where's that book of yours?'

'Under the bed.'

'Did you just throw it under there, young man?'

'I did when Dr Brodskaya came. I didn't want her to see it.'

'That's no way to treat a book —' She bends down and retrieves it. 'There you are.'

It must have cost a fortune, that book. *Great Engines of the Soviet Union.* Thick, glossy pages, full of photographs and information. She riffles the pages. It looks a bit technical for a child of his age.

'Do you understand all this, Gorya?'

'Course I do!'

'Then you're cleverer than I am. Here you are. Going to be an engineer when you grow up, are you?'

'I don't know.' His face clouds. She knows what he's thinking.

'There's no reason why you shouldn't,' she says briskly, 'if you work hard and get your qualifications. We need engineers. Now, let me have a look at those hands . . . Even lying in bed you get dirty hands. Wait while I bring you a bowl of water and your flannel and you can give yourself a good wash.'

It's not until six days after the operation that Andrei sees Volkov again. He's intending to pop in and see Gorya on his way back

203

from a lecture on gold therapy, but Gorya's room is empty. The bed has been made, with the sheets and blankets pulled back. He looks up and down the corridor and at that moment Volkov appears, pushing his son in a wheelchair. He doesn't notice Andrei, because he's leaning forward to listen to something Gorya's saying. Their heads are close and their hair is almost exactly the same colour. Volkov looks up, sees Andrei and acknowledges him with a nod.

'We've been to the gym,' says Gorya. 'I'm not allowed on the parallel bars yet so we just had to look at them. There was a girl like me, only she lost her leg when she fell under a tram. She's got a new leg. Her leg was cut off even higher than mine, she told me. She's not in hospital any more, but she comes in for physio.'

There's a touch of colour in his face. Lyuba would have suggested going to the gym, thinks Andrei. She believes it's bad for Gorya to be stuck in a room on his own, not seeing how the other children manage. 'Let him see there are plenty worse off than he is. He'll soon be racing them on his crutches.'

'That's good. Now, are you going to show your father how you get out of that wheelchair and into bed?' asks Andrei.

'No need for that,' says Volkov. 'I can lift him.'

'He knows how to do it. It's quite a complicated technique but Gorya's a quick learner.'

Volkov frowns, but doesn't resist. They back the wheelchair parallel to the bed, and lock the wheels.

'Now, Gorya, remember: step one.'

Gorya grips the wheelchair's arms. Slowly, he levers his own weight upwards.

'Foot off the footrest. Good. Now let your weight go down on to it. Slowly. Shuffle your bottom forward, remember. Good. And now here's your right crutch. Got it? And the left one coming up. Ends of the crutch firmly on the floor. Test them. That's right, you remembered. And now, slowly, up you come. Good, Gorya, much better than yesterday. Stand still while I get the wheelchair out of your way. Excellent. Now you turn until the back of your leg touches the bed. Don't worry about looking round, the bed's not going anywhere. Let yourself down. Good. Sit back as far as you can. Check you're in position. Slowly, move yourself round, bring your leg up and use it to push yourself up the bed a little. Well done. Have a rest now, that was pretty tiring.'

Andrei adjusts the cage over Gorya's stump, and then brings up the bedclothes. The boy slides a sideways glance at his father. He wants praise, doesn't Volkov see that?

'Gorya's working very hard,' says Andrei at last, to break the silence. 'The quicker he can regain his fitness, the sooner he'll be fully mobile.'

'How long will that be?' asks Volkov abruptly.

'His wound is healing well. Dr Brodskaya's very satisfied with his progress.'

Volkov makes an impatient gesture. 'It's you I'm talking to. My son is no longer Dr Brodskaya's patient.'

Andrei looks at him. Does he means that he's spoken to Brodskaya — maybe even dismissed her, as you'd dismiss a servant? No, that's impossible.

'Excuse me,' he says quietly, 'it's vital that Dr Brodskaya continues her post-operative care.'

Volkov does not reply. Gorya has shut his eyes. Andrei knows him well enough by now to realize that this means Gorya wants to block out what's happening. Why couldn't Volkov have praised him? A few words, that's all it would have taken. The boy wants so much to please his father.

'Gorya,' he says, 'I have to go now. Remember about lying on your stomach for a while, won't you? Use the correct technique for rolling yourself over, and then you won't put pressure on your stump.'

He uses the word 'stump' deliberately. It's no good for the child to hear euphemisms, as if the reality of his body is too obscene to be named. Of course Volkov cares about the boy. Any fool can see that. But how is Gorya supposed to know that his father isn't angry with him, but with the rest of the world that is still walking around on two legs? If you want to turn your boy into a cripple, thinks Andrei furiously, just carry on like this.

Sunday is bright but cool, with a few high clouds scudding in a sky the colour of a blackbird's egg. Perfect for cycling out to the dacha. Anna cooks porridge for everyone, and packs bread, tea and sausage. Her panniers are full. As well as their own food, she's bringing goods to barter: four tins of sardines, a bag of cooking salt, a couple of school exercise books, some HB pencils, and — the big prize — the bar of Petersburg Nights Special Chocolate that the Parents' Committee gave to her on May Day. She has high hopes for what that chocolate will bring. Anna is never without her string bags, and an eye for what can be bought in the city and exchanged for butter, fresh milk, seed potatoes or a piece of pork.

For once Kolya doesn't grumble at being turfed out of bed early, and by eight o'clock they are on their way. The wind of their passage lifts Anna's hair as the scarred, exhausted city streets fly past them. The breeze is from the west today, and smells faintly of salt. It's one of those mornings when gulls wheel lazily overhead and the city is like a ship about to launch itself on to the Baltic.

It doesn't take too long to reach the edge of the city. Andrei says all this land is earmarked for housing. Nothing's happened yet, but huge developments are going to be built all around Leningrad, to house the surge of migrants who came in post-war. To replace the ghosts, Anna thinks. She remembers how empty the city was when at last the siege was lifted. Since then people have poured in from all over the Soviet Union, looking for work and a place to live. The streets are full of strangers now, not half-familiar faces. But Leningrad knows how to make the newcomers its own, just as it's always known how to transform each newborn baby into a child of the city.

She often thinks about the nursery children from before the war. She took it for granted then that they would grow up and that every so often she'd be stopped in the streets by a mother with an older child, dressed for school. 'Do you remember our Nastya? Yes, I knew you would! She still remembers you teaching her "Magpie, Magpie".'

Most of them didn't grow up, and those who survived are scattered. Starved, shelled, sent off on evacuation trains that were bombed from the air, killed in German reprisals, orphaned and taken into children's homes so that they forgot their parents and homes and even their own names. Very often those pre-war three- and four-year-olds rise into her mind, watering their sunflowers with proud concentration. *'Mine's the biggest!' 'No, it's not, Petya's is the biggest. It nearly touches the sky!'* They fly across the playground in a game of chase, shrieking with laughter. They arrive at the nursery on freezing mornings, their faces glazed with snot, and she helps to unpack them from their layers. She rubs Vaseline into their chapped cheeks.

Other children have taken their place. New little Leningraders play in the courtyards and fill up the schools. Anna glances around at the flat, marshy land with its scrub of birch and larch. It seems impossible that the city can really grow outward as far as this. People would be living so far from the centre that they'd have to get up at dawn to come into work. The thing about her city is that you learn it through the soles of your shoes. You walk it, day after day and year after year. From the day you are born you learn every possible permutation of bridge, water, stone, sky. Your own life becomes part of the alchemy. You're born, and soon you'll die, but meanwhile and for ever you're a Leningrader.

'Andrei! Kolya! Wait for me a moment!'

She cycles around a pothole. There are sharp stones all over the road and she has to swerve to avoid punctures. Has she remembered her repair kit? Yes, she put it at the bottom of her left-hand pannier. Andrei's got the pump. It's really warm now and she's sweating. You'd think those two were in a bike race, the way they rush on ahead.

It's beautiful here. Lots of people wouldn't think it was. But when you've hunted mushrooms in the woods year after year, and you know all the best places; when you've fished every pool and stream and know where the trout hide on the stony bed while water ripples over their backs; when you're covered with scratches from foraging for berries; when you come home dusty, sweaty and triumphant with a load of firewood; when the marshes have sucked at your boots as you've jumped from tuft to tuft; then you love it with all your heart. You want it to live for ever. Your own death doesn't seem to matter as much.

But people need somewhere to live. They are crammed in, three families to an apartment. What if she had to share an apartment with the Maleviches? The thought makes her shudder, but it could easily happen. Plenty of people have to live in a nest of voluntary spies, with every word censored and every thought concealed. Or they live worn down by constant rows about slivers of household soap and by accusations of bringing up their children like hooligans because they make the normal noise of children. She's had nursery mothers break down in tears after a vicious early-morning row over spending too long in the bathroom with the children.

'I just don't know what to do, Anna Mikhailovna, every morning he wakes up crying with the sheets wet and I've got to get them rinsed through and him washed, and then this old bitch starts banging on the door and screaming at me to get out —'

What's a scrub of birch or the electric green of new leaves on the larch, compared to that?

The truth is, I'm not an idealist, thinks Anna as she pedals on. I just want the children to be washed without someone screeching at them through the door. I don't suppose that woman's neighbour is really so bad. Probably just desperate to get to work on time. But we end up hating each other for lack of a bit of space.

Out here, you can breathe. They are cycling into the woods now. The road is a potholed, dusty track, running uphill. Every turn is familiar. In a few minutes they'll burst out into the sunlight again, and they'll hear dogs barking from the old Sokolov farm. They still call it that, although the Sokolovs don't live there any more. Her childhood playmate Vasya Sokolov died in the war, driving convoys over Ladoga ice. His aunt, Darya Alexandrovna, lives in a little cottage with her son, Mitya, Kolya's friend. The farm was swallowed up in the German advance, and burned to the ground when they retreated. Now it's been rebuilt as part of a huge collective.

The Levin dacha, amazingly, survived the

war. At least, the walls still stood, and there was a roof. The first time Anna came back here after the siege was lifted, she could barely recognize the place. So many trees had been cut down for fuel that the landscape looked quite different. Their plot was buried under a thick coat of weeds. Ivy, woodbine and wild clematis twined all over the dacha itself, softening the destruction. Both exterior and interior doors were gone. All the windows were smashed. Someone had chopped out the wooden floor of the verandah with an axe. Inside, there was German graffiti on the walls, and they'd lit open fires. Lucky that the place hadn't burned down, like so many other dachas — or been torched deliberately, as the Germans retreated.

Fortunately the dacha had never been much more than a glorified hut. They repaired it bit by bit, as they managed to scavenge wood and nails, corrugated iron and glass. Anna scrubbed every inch of the walls, inside and out, as if she were exorcizing evil spirits. They got hold of some exterior paint — a sombre green, and not the colour they'd have chosen, but it kept the weather out. The verandah floor was the biggest challenge. It was Andrei who fixed it. He had a contact through work: Sofya

Vasilievna, one of the radiographers, put him in touch with her father-in-law, a retired carpenter who still took on small jobs. He did the work in exchange for Kolya giving his youngest granddaughter a year's course of piano lessons. Kolya gave those lessons so well, almost like a professional. By the end of the year the little girl was able to play a concert of baby pieces for her grandpa. The floor was down and the railings fixed, waiting for varnish.

Kolya loves the dacha. Sometimes it seems to Anna as if the dacha is the one remaining beacon of family happiness. Kolya chops wood, digs up potatoes, waters the little lilacs Anna planted to replace those that the Germans chopped down and burned. Kolya's dream is that when the silver birches grow big enough again, he'll sling a hammock between them and laze in it, reading all day long. He talks about the dacha before the war as if he were talking about paradise. He was only five when the Germans came, but he says, 'I remember everything.'

The Germans must have hated trees. They snapped and uprooted even the smallest saplings, which would have been no good for fuel. They wanted not just to conquer but to erase, just as they'd wanted to wipe

Leningrad from the face of the earth. But they couldn't get rid of all the Russian trees, Anna thinks, any more than they could get rid of all the Russians. We were too many for them. Everything is growing back. Wherever she can, she plants trees.

'If they'd had enough salt, they'd have sown all our fields with it,' the old men in the village said, and then they would spit on the ground. Anna would look at them and think: *All the time we were inside Leningrad, you saw them face to face. They walked down these tracks. They took over your homes, ate your food, slaughtered the pigs and sheep, threw the chickens in a pot. Whenever they wanted, they killed you.* Marina's dacha was totally destroyed, and no one knew what had happened to her old nanny. Three entire families from the nearby village were wiped out in reprisal for a partisan attack. Seven children, aged three to fourteen. They didn't shoot them. They hanged them one by one, starting with the youngest.

They are almost at the dacha now. Andrei and Kolya are cycling abreast, talking. Anna's too far behind to hear what they're saying but she feels a surge of pleasure. Once Kolya's through this difficult stage, those two will be real friends. Not that she has anything to criticize Andrei for. He's

215

patient and consistent in just the way you need to be with a boy of Kolya's age. Sometimes, though, he withdraws. Anna hates that. They seem not to be a family any more but just three random people, forced together and ideally equipped by their intimacy to make one another un-happy.

'Anna! *Anna!*'

They are there. Anna dismounts, pushes her bike through the gate and up the little path. They prop their bikes around the back of the dacha, where the gooseberry patch is full of bright, immature fruit.

'Let's make a gooseberry pie,' says Kolya.

'They need at least three weeks more,' replies Anna. 'It'll be a good crop, look how many there are. And the white currants, too — that's the best we've had for years. But we'll have to tie string over the bushes, Kolya, or the birds will get them all.'

If only she had some muslin curtains. She saw a little cherry tree wrapped in muslin once, with all the fruit untouched —

'Can't we pick just some of them?'

'Not the currants. It's just a waste when they're not ripe. But if you and Andrei catch a trout, I'll make green gooseberry sauce.'

Even with its windows shuttered, the dacha welcomes them. There are fresh weeds pushing up everywhere in the vegetable garden. She'll have to weed by hand this time. A hoe does too much damage when the growth is young and tender. The carrots and beet are doing well, and her onion patch is coming on nicely —

'Anna, let's have some tea.'

They go inside the dacha. As always, when they first come, it smells damp and woody.

'It's all the rain we had last week,' says Andrei. 'I'm going to light the stove.'

Wood is piled beside the stove, left there to dry from last time. Arriving at the dacha is always the same. A ballet of tasks, so familiar that they could all carry them out with their eyes shut. Kolya, who doesn't lift a finger without complaint at home, is already fetching the bag of charcoal for the samovar.

'We'll have tea on the verandah,' Anna decides. She doesn't want the dacha full of smoke. Andrei is on his knees, feeding wood into the stove. This one doesn't draw as well as their old, fat-bellied cast-iron stove. That was ripped out, either by the Germans or by someone local.

'Is Galya here this weekend?' asks Andrei. Galya is an old friend and colleague of Anna's mother, and she has one of the few neighbouring dachas that survived. It was never a big dacha colony here, because the land was too poor. It's taken decades of farm manure, days and days of back-breaking trundling and muck-spreading, to make the soil at the Levin dacha as fertile as it is now. Their compost heap is a legend. After the war a new dacha area was opened up six kilometres to the south. There was enough land there for everyone to get a decent-sized plot. They are trade union plots, of course. Anna or Andrei could have applied for one, but they prefer it here. They like the uneven land, and the little gorge where the stream flows. Besides, they wouldn't want to add another six kilometres each way to their bike ride. There's a railway halt near the new plots, but Anna and Andrei prefer to cycle. The weekend trains are always so packed.

'Anna, will Galya be here?'

'She should be. Now she's retired she's here most of the time.'

The samovar hisses. They drag the wooden chairs on to the verandah, and Kolya fetches cushions. They are spotted with damp, but it doesn't matter. She'll scrub them, and put them out in the sun.

'And the sugar, Kolya!'

This is the moment she's been waiting for: the first glass of tea, with the sun coming

218

down on the pine planks, and the smell of earth all around. Anna relaxes and shuts her eyes. She can smell wild garlic. Wood pigeons are purring in the distant trees. All around her, food is growing. The day stretches ahead of them, full of work. Later on she'll take the chocolate down to Darya Alexandrovna, who has a sweet tooth and keeps chickens. Darya Alexandrovna always wants to chat these days. She used to be so brisk, but now, sometimes, you can hardly get away from her. She can't be bothered with 'all these new people'. It's people like Anna that she wants to talk to, because they remember the old days, and because Anna was her nephew Vasya's playmate when they were little. Even Andrei is of no great interest to her, although she did once remark that he had very good teeth, and Anna had done well for herself.

Vasya has no grave, of course. Darya Alexandrovna has set a stone for him in the corner of her cottage garden, beyond the hen-run. She had his name carved into it. That must have cost a chicken or two.

Anna sighs, sipping her tea, and Andrei glances at her but says nothing. She doesn't notice. Kolya's eating the sugar again. Do boys of that age ever stop eating? And the more he eats, the skinnier he seems to get.

'Leave the rest of it, Kolya, you can't just eat sugar.'

'I'm starving.'

'I'll make you a sugar sandwich. Bring me the bread, it's in my bag, and the big knife.' Thick slices of bread, spread with a smear of butter and sprinkled with sugar. Kolya will eat sugar sandwiches for as long as she's prepared to go on slicing the loaf. 'There you are, and that's got to keep you going until lunch, so don't wolf it down. I'm sure if you ate more slowly you wouldn't be so hungry.'

'Only old people eat slowly,' says Kolya.

Andrei and Kolya will go fishing. She'll sweep out the dacha and prepare the potatoes for dinner, then she'll get into the vegetable garden. There'll be radishes and lettuce thinnings to have with their bread and sausage for lunch. She'll just have five minutes in the sun before she gets to work. How good the wood smells as the sun warms it. My God, Kolya's already demolished that sandwich . . .

And later, they'll bury the manuscripts. She's decided to tell Kolya about it. If anything should happen, it's best he knows. Kolya is old enough now, and families are stronger, she thinks, when there aren't too many secrets.

She opens her eyes. 'Do you remember how Father used to smoke and keep all the mosquitoes away?' she asks Kolya. He nods, so casually that she probes further. 'When you think of Father, can you see his face?' she asks, then immediately wishes that she hadn't. Kolya drops the knife with which he's been whittling a leftover piece of pine, and chucks the wood over the railings.

'I keep telling you. I remember him perfectly,' he says in such a cold, angry voice that for Anna the light of the whole day is dimmed. Why couldn't she have kept her mouth shut? But suddenly Kolya relents. 'I'm going over to see if Mitya wants to go fishing with us, and then I'll dig the manure into the new fruit patch. We are going fishing later, aren't we, Andrei?'

'Yes, later,' says Andrei. 'I've got to fix those panels to the side of the shed first.'

Everything's all right. It will be a perfect day. But when should she tell Kolya about the manuscripts? Now, or later? After dinner, she decides, when he's full of fish; if they catch anything, that is. If not, it'll be soup with the sausage again. And then putting out the fire, closing everything up, and cycling slowly back to Leningrad in the evening light.

'Tell his mother I'll be over later,' she calls

to Kolya, who is already through the gate.

The sky has clouded over by evening. Dinner's over — one rather small trout each, and a steaming pile of potatoes — and it's too cold to sit out on the verandah any longer. It might even rain.

'Let's get it done,' says Andrei.

'You mean the manuscripts?'

'Yes.'

Andrei has told Kolya, on the way back from Mitya's place after fishing. Kolya didn't seem surprised, or even all that interested.

Anna has forked away some of the compost from the edge of the heap. It felt like sacrilege, because she grew up being told that she must never mess about with the compost heap in case it stopped heating itself up properly. She has dug down deep through the warm, crumbling soil. It's so fertile that even a manuscript might start growing there.

'Come on then. Kolya!'

They troop alongside the vegetable patch, past the raspberries and down to the compost heap. Anna glances round, but of course no one's there but themselves. Andrei produces the biscuit tin, and another, larger package wrapped in oilcloth.

'Is that hole deep enough? It doesn't look it.'

'Put the package at the bottom and then the tin can go on top of it. I dug really deep.' Kolya stands back, not committing himself to the scene, but watching everything. Once the oilcloth-wrapped package is in, Anna steps forward with the biscuit tin, and crouches down. She doesn't want to throw it in; it seems disrespectful. She has sealed all around the lid with adhesive tape. It should keep the water out once autumn comes.

Her hands are strangely reluctant to let go. She looks down at the beautiful skating ladies with their impossible arabesques. Her fingers remember them. The figures are slightly raised and she used to trace them, fascinated —

A voice calls from the dacha, 'Anna? Anna, are you there?'

'It's Galya.'

'Quick, Anna, put it in. I'll fill the hole. Hurry, before Galya comes out here looking for you.'

'Put all the compost back where it was.'

'It's like a murder,' Kolya says suddenly, 'and here we are secretly burying the corpse.'

His words come back to her later, as they're cycling the long, dusty road home. The light is grey and pallid. A grey evening will switch imperceptibly into a grey dawn. It's late — past ten already. Kolya was right. It was a rushed, guilty burial. It was her father's life-work, thrust away under the soil. His words hidden, never to be read any more. It was a kind of murder.

But it's not our fault, she argues with herself. *We didn't choose any of this.*

10

In two days' time it will be Midsummer's Day, but the weather remains cool and blowy. The surface of the Neva is chopped up into little peaks, while fresh lime leaves shiver and dust blows about the streets. Andrei is late. He hurries along, head down so that the dust won't get into his eyes, and he goes over the arguments he'll put forward at today's meeting, for the employment of another physiotherapist with experience in paediatric arthritic care. He's coming up against a blank wall. Doesn't he realize that there's a shortage of funding? The decision has been taken to prioritize an increase of 14.7 per cent in surgical beds. The plan must be adhered to.

Where do they get these figures? It's so exact, 14.7 per cent, that you could be fooled into thinking that it corresponded to reality. You get battered down by arguments on the basis of beds that don't exist yet, and probably never will. Well, he'll make his point again, even though last time he spoke out about the need for a physiotherapist, he noticed Boris Kamerevsky from Medical Personnel frowning and writing something down in a way that was meant to be noticed. *I'm becoming a problem,* thinks Andrei. *Sticking my neck out. Not a good idea.* All the same, he'll push one more time, at today's meeting.

Anna has been seconded to a one-day course on Practical Statistics. She sits cramped behind a desk, watching the lecturer draw a graph on the board and fill it in with confident squiggles of her chalk.

She's rather elegant, for a statistician. Grey skirt, freshly laundered white blouse, high heels and beautifully smooth, glossy black hair. She makes Anna feel dowdy. Although it's a cool day the room is stuffy. Too many people. The chairs are uncomfortable, but the main problem is that Anna's not used to sitting still for so long. At the nursery she's on her feet hour after hour, and at home it's often almost ten o'clock by the time she finishes all the chores and is able to sit down. There are so many things she wants to do in that precious hour that she doesn't know which to choose first. Listen to the radio, knit, sew, chat to Kolya before he goes to bed, take up the novel she's been reading on and off for months, and above all sit opposite Andrei so that every time she glances up, there he is.

Who would have thought it could take the minute hand so long to cross the small gap between the 5 and the 10? It crawls as if it were pushing its way through sand. At the nursery, time speeds by. When she's drawing, it's different again. She'll emerge to find the sun in a different place in the sky.

Her bones ache with boredom. The lecturer has a good voice, light and clear, but although Anna hears every word quite distinctly, the sentences melt away without making any sense. It's not that she couldn't understand it if she wanted to. It's more that she doesn't want this information in her head. She doesn't want to know how to collect accurate statistics about the role played by the parental level of education in the nutritional status of the child. In her experience there is very little correlation anyway. Besides, she is sick to death of handing out questionnaires to parents. They don't like it, and why should they? 'Larissa Nikolayevna will be wanting me to bring my soup pot in for inspection next,' one mother had whispered to Anna, after a particularly intrusive handout about the importance of bringing yesterday's stock to the boil for at least five minutes before adding fresh vegetables, 'in order to minimize the risk of bacterial growth and subsequent ill health'.

But she must pay attention. Morozova is bound to question her about the structure of the day and the 'learning outcomes'. Quickly, Anna jots down a few sentences, and copies the graph.

There's a good side to being bored. It's very calming. She couldn't settle last night, and finally dropped off at about four o'clock, only to wake with a jolt when the alarm went off at six. The thing is not to think about any of it. She's seen her father's life eaten to the bone by too much thinking. The Volkov boy has had his operation and is making good progress. In a few more days he'll be discharged and then Andrei will be safe. Perhaps Volkov will take his family down to the Black Sea for recuperation. There are all kinds of special Party nursing homes and rehabilitation centres down there. No problem for Volkov to get his boy into the best of them.

She'd never have thought that she could be so hard about a child. Perhaps it's because she's never met him and so he remains just a name. But it's more than indifference, if she's honest. She feels a cold opposition to the very idea of this boy and the contact Andrei's been forced to have with him. Let him see private doctors and be whisked into the most private of private clinics. Let him be anywhere, except where his existence could leak into that of Andrei and Kolya, contaminating it and threatening it. She sees the boy as a sort of Malevich writ large, with infinitely more power to do harm.

A bee buzzes at the top of the window. It's far too high for Anna to help it out. This ceiling must be almost four metres high. You'd think that would make the room airy, but it doesn't. The proportions are wrong, because it's only half of a room that has been subdivided by a stud wall. If she listens carefully, she can hear another lecturer droning on the other side. A male voice, monotonous, going on and on uninterrupted. Meanwhile, on this side, the lecturer's clear, sure voice has stopped at last.

'Any questions?' she asks them with an air of daring, as if questions are an unusual and almost illicit departure from normal procedure. Anna shifts her cramped legs and hopes that no one asks anything that might delay their release.

A woman several desks to her right pipes up in the self-righteous tone of one who knows that she's asking the correct question: 'Allow me to ask, comrade, whether or not these graphs should be prepared on graph paper, or whether it is permissible to prepare them on plain paper that is ruled for the purpose. In case of need, you understand. Some of my colleagues work in remote areas where access to the full range of stationery is not always possible. I myself am recently returned from a tour of duty in the Ufa region.'

'Tour of duty'! How ridiculous — who on earth does she think she is? We're not soldiers, for heaven's sake, thinks Anna so violently that for a moment she's afraid she may have spoken out loud.

'Graph paper is most certainly not a necessary requirement,' replies the lecturer in a voice which is even clearer and sweeter than before, as if to show how much she welcomes this question, which reveals the indomitable spirit of those who are determined to make graphs even in unfavourable territory.

'I am most grateful to you for your clarification, comrade,' says the woman, and subsides, glancing left to right with a brief, triumphant flash of her spectacles.

Anna's left-hand neighbour stirs. 'Allow me to ask,' she says, in a voice which to Anna's ear has a trace of some unusual feeling in it, 'exactly how long, in your view, it is recommended that we retain all our statistical evidence after our graphs have been completed? Or is the existence of the graphs sufficient to obviate the need for indefinite retention of such material?'

Is it mockery? Is it even, perhaps, a touch of humour? Anna glances sharply at the questioner's face, but it remains bland. As smooth as silk, like the face of a clever child who has been caught in some misdemeanour but knows he can out-think his interrogator.

The lecturer nods with sharp enthusiasm. 'A very interesting point!' she exclaims. 'Indefinite retention of evidential material is of course the ideal, but we have to also give consideration to questions of space, and indeed time.'

'Children certainly tend to take up a good deal of both,' murmurs the questioner, too low for the lecturer, but not too low for Anna.

'Excellent questions!' announces the lecturer, making it clear that she wants no more of them. Sure enough, the class begins to stir and gather up paper and pens. Anna knows the form. Most will make for the door as swiftly as they can, keeping a mask of discretion until they are out in the corridor. A toady or two will gather around the lecturer to ask 'a few questions which relate directly to their own professional formation', and to make sure that the lecturer has registered not only their enthusiasm but also who they are and where they come from. The woman on Anna's left is already putting her possessions into her bag.

'Excellent question,' Anna says to her quietly.

The woman smiles. 'Are you staying for the afternoon lecture?' she asks.

'Yes, I've been seconded for the entire day.'

'The ent-i-i-ire day . . .' The woman widens her eyes comically as she drags out the syllables so that the day sounds just as long as it's really going to be.

'But you're going now?' asks Anna.

'Yes. Fortunately they couldn't get cover for me this afternoon. Good luck.'

'I'll need it.'

By the time the meeting's over, Andrei is desperate for some air. There can be no 'additional release of hours' for the employment of a specialist physiotherapist. *No,* thinks Andrei savagely, *we've to go on admitting patients, operating on them and leaving them to sink or swim without proper rehabilitation.* It's so short-sighted that he cannot keep quiet. A 'waste of resources' of the purest kind, and surely that's what they were always preaching about, these managers and administrators who knew so much more than the clinicians. This time he's sure that he saw Boris Kamerevsky write down his name.

He'll have a cigarette in the courtyard. It seems like a while since he's been out there. In fact, he suddenly realizes that he's avoided the place since that time there with Russov.

The sky is grey and heavy. It's going to rain soon. A chilly breeze whips up leaf debris, and lets it drop again. Andrei checks his pockets, and then remembers that he'd intended to buy cigarettes from the kiosk on his way this morning, but in his rush he forgot. He'll stay out here for a few minutes anyway, to get the stale meeting room and the glances of Boris Kamerevsky out of his mind. A few minutes' peace will do him good.

The door from the corridor opens. It's Brodskaya. 'Andrei Mikhailovich, may I join you for a moment?'

'Of course.'

Brodskaya stands close to him, as Russov did, but her judgement is finer than Russov's. She doesn't crowd him. When she speaks her voice is low and clear. 'I came to tell you that I've accepted a transfer to Yerevan.'

'Yerevan!'

'Yes. I accepted the post as soon as it was offered. Medical services in Yerevan are not, of course, equal to what we have here, but there is plenty of exciting work in progress.'

Impossible to tell from her tone what she really thinks. Impossible, also, to know why the transfer is really taking place. It sounds like a demotion; the kind of thing that happens to a doctor who makes too many mistakes. Not professional mistakes, as a rule.

'So you're leaving Leningrad?'

'Yes,' she says briskly.

'But from a professional point of view —'

'There's an excellent university and Academy of Sciences in Yerevan. The climate will be good for my mother. These winters don't suit her; she has severe rheumatism.'

Clearly not a promotion then, or Brodskaya would have mentioned it. Anxiety clutches at him. He was the one who recommended her to Volkov. He committed the cardinal sin of drawing attention to her.

'You should also apply for a transfer,' she says, in a voice so low that for a moment he thinks he's misheard. 'As soon as possible. You have a family.'

'But the boy's doing well.'

'Who can say at this stage?' Brodskaya's face is sombre. 'Listen to me. Drop out of sight. You can be a doctor anywhere. You're not a Leningrader, are you? No, I thought not. So you know that life is possible elsewhere. Don't try to cling on here.'

'Riva Grigorievna, have you got a cigarette?'

She offers him a packet. Andrei fumbles for one, and lights it. What she's suggesting is impossible. He can't walk out of his life just like that. 'Nowhere's safer than anywhere else,' he says.

Brodskaya shrugs. Her eyes are experienced, ironic, even pitying. 'You may think that,' she says, 'but listen to me, because I know what I'm talking about. Get out of Leningrad as soon as you can. Discover a vocation for primary health care in a pioneer area. Out of sight is out of mind.'

'But —'

'I must go and check my list for this afternoon.'

When she's gone, he drags smoke deep

into his lungs. My God, who could have imagined it would come to this. Brodskaya giving up home, career and friends; even uprooting her mother. Is it possible that she knows something he doesn't? Or perhaps her instinct is sharper. Anna's face rises in his mind. *'We could go to the dacha. It's safe there . . . Once they get hold of you they never let go. They go on and on, and then they go on some more.'* They'd be no safer there. Anna understood that really. She knew she was panicking, and the sensible thing to do was to carry on as usual.

He would never have thought Brodskaya was the type to panic. She took a risk, though, in saying as much as she'd said to him. She must have decided he could be trusted. She's always kept herself to herself. He didn't even know she lived with her mother. But it's different for her . . .

Why?

My God, perhaps they should all get on the move. Russov — Retinskaya —

Or perhaps, he thinks grimly, those two *are* on the move already. Russov's already proved that he knows how to look after number one. He's well in with Admin too. Russov won't end up in Yerevan; it'll be something better for him.

If Brodskaya's right, though, better is

worse. Her plan is to drop out of sight by taking the kind of obscure post that won't arouse attention or envy. She's moved so quickly, too. She must have started looking out for a new post even before she operated on the boy.

He's not going to waste any more time thinking about it. He can't leave Leningrad, and that's the end of it. His patients need him. Anna's got her job, and these are important years for Kolya. Who in their right mind abandons residential status in a city like Leningrad? They would never find an apartment like theirs again. And surely Anna would never abandon the dacha?

They are all excellent reasons, but he knows they are not his real reason. Andrei is not one for imagining things, but Volkov's face is as clear in his mind as if the man were standing here in the courtyard with him. A clever face, and a compelling one. Yes, it's possible to see the boy in him. It would be possible to like the man and even to want to please him. But he's marred by an expression he can't hide. It's a deformity, but not of the flesh. A confidence that everyone who sees him will be cowed. No one should look like that.

Andrei stubs out the cigarette.

■ ■ ■ ■

'She said I had vandalized her doormat,' says Anna. Her face is flushed and her eyes sparkle with anger. 'You know it was my turn to clean the hallway and the bathroom? Well, I took the mats down to the courtyard to beat them, as usual, and when I came back upstairs old Ma Malevich was waiting for me. She grabbed the mat from me, turned it over and then said I'd torn the backing. Deliberately. Because I've got something against her and hers, apparently. And she'd left some soap in the bathroom by accident and when she came to look for it after she'd heard me cleaning in there, it was gone. So that's theft as well as vandalism.'

'But it's ridiculous, Anna. You can't take that woman seriously.'

'Can't I?'

'You don't want to let her upset you.'

'She hasn't upset me,' Anna almost shouts. 'But I tell you, she's not going to get away with any more of this.'

He looks at her sharply. She is only just holding back tears of rage and mortification. That's not like Anna. She's much better than he is with the neighbours, as a rule.

She expects nothing good of the Maleviches, and guards herself with a profound, ironic certainty that daily life just has to be dealt with.

'What did she say?' He sees her hesitate, and colour more deeply. She doesn't want to tell him. 'Anna?'

'She said we don't know how to bring up Kolya, because we have no parental instincts.'

His heart floods with anger, tenderness and pity. He wants to cover Anna up from the world, shield her so that no word or blow can ever touch her. 'Remember that what she's brought up is the Weasel,' he says.

'I shouldn't let her get to me.'

'You're worth a hundred of them, Anna. Don't listen to them.'

Anna sighs. 'I know I should have walked away. I've never thought of myself as a violent person, but I could have brained her with my broom.'

'And then you'd have been a thief, a vandal and a murderer.'

'Even worse, the broom might get damaged.'

'It doesn't sound as if she knew about the downfall of the petition.'

'He won't have told her. He was scared.'

'Do you think they'd inform on one

another, those Maleviches?'

'I'm sure they would, if it came to it. Andrei, do you think they were always like that? Sometimes I'm afraid that it's like an infection. You keep on scrubbing things and washing your hands, but it's in the air.'

'What do you mean?'

'Whatever has made the Maleviches into the Maleviches, doesn't only work on them. You know that. We think we're not like them, but perhaps we're deceiving ourselves.'

'You are the most honest person I know, Anna.'

'But perhaps that's only because I am honest with you.'

'She's really upset you, hasn't she? Come on, cheer up, Kolya will be home soon and we don't want him starting another vendetta against the Maleviches. The less he knows about all this the better.'

'You're right. He's so fiery, Kolya . . .' She smiles, rather sadly. 'Well, he'll grow out of that.'

11

It seems to Anna as if the ball has been going on for ever. Light shines palely through the high windows. It must be well after one o'clock. She's had a wonderful time, of course she has. There is Andrei again, talking to a colleague whose face she doesn't recognize. She's already been embarrassed twice tonight, by failing to recognize people to whom she's been introduced at least once, and possibly many times. They murmur compliments on her dress, or her hair. She murmurs something back, or accepts the offer of a dance so that they won't guess she doesn't know who they are. And yet she knows every child in the nursery, and every parent. She must make more effort. The truth is that she's always a little nervous with Andrei's colleagues. Sooner or later they'll ask what she does, and her answer is greeted with a surprise that they often fail to cover. They expect her to be a professional like Andrei.

She wants to dance with Andrei now. She's tired of feeling other men's hands in the small of her back, and her hand in an unfamiliar clasp. You are so close to someone when you dance: too close. Sometimes even the smell of a certain person is alienating, but you have to pretend not to notice. Not that they smell bad; everyone has made a big effort. Very probably there are some who think the same of her, because she is just not their type.

She loves Andrei's smell. It is warm and a little biscuity and so dear to her that sometimes at night when she thinks he's asleep, she'll nuzzle against him, tasting him, feeling his steady warmth against her lips. That last dance with Orlov was horrible, although at least she'd remembered his name. His plump, moist hands ended in well-kept fingernails which dug into her skin. His little twinkling eyes weren't merry at all when you looked at him close up, but cold and watchful. Anna noticed that Orlov's wife wore a black dress which had begun to look rusty with age, although she'd tried to freshen it up with a new collar. But Orlov was resplendent from the tips of his dancing shoes to the oil on his hair.

Orlov and his wife have already left. The

crowd is thinning and those who remain can dance freely. No more shuffling, elbow to elbow. A haze of smoke hangs over the dancers. When they arrived the hall had smelled of green leaves and roses. The flowers had just been sprayed with water and they were covered in glinting drops. Anna had her own rose, too: Andrei pinned a corsage to her dress; one dark red rose, sheathed in fern. It looks a little tired now, but when she gets home she'll put it in water and it will revive overnight. It had the velvety sweetness of a true rose. Now the hall smells of cigarette smoke, alcohol, sweat and Red Moscow perfume. The folds of her dress hang limply.

She'd known what the ball would be like, down to the stiff arrangements of carnations in little gilt vases on the supper tables, the spotty mirror in the Ladies' cloakroom, the bottles of Soviet champagne and Tsinandali wine (never enough of these) and the measuring smiles of Andrei's superiors.

But she'd still been excited as she got ready in the apartment. Kolya had already left for Grisha's, and Andrei was on duty until seven thirty, so she was alone. When the dress slipped over her head, stirring a current of cool air, she had shivered from the nape of her neck down to her feet. It was the smell of the fabric, perhaps, or the freshness of its touch. It was the feel of a dress in which nothing has happened yet, so that for a moment you believe that anything might be possible while you are wearing it. She looked down at her arms. They were round and strong. She flexed her fingers. They were thinner than they used to be, and the veins were more prominent. If you worked with children you couldn't avoid that, no matter how many statistics you collected or how many graphs you drew. It was physical work. The skin grew rough, and all winter her knuckles were chapped.

However, thanks to Irina, her hands were smooth tonight. *'Take half a cup of sugar, Anna, and mix it with two spoonfuls of oil in a big bowl. You rub the mixture into your hands, all over, and leave it as long as you can. You should do your elbows too. Elbows are a terrible giveaway.'*

It sounded like a waste of oil and sugar, but Irina had been so eager that Anna had tried her recipe, and she had to admit that it worked. The sugar had turned a disturbing shade of grey, but her hands felt softer than they'd done for years.

She smoothed down the dress over her hips. A good fit. If she had the time, and a sewing machine like Julia's, she'd make all her clothes herself; it's wonderful to have something that really fits and is made for you. She could see her heart beating under the fabric. It was strange how excited she felt. It had nothing to do with the excitement you feel when you are young and single, going to a dance where you think you might meet 'someone'. No, thought Anna, moving to the mirror and regarding her own face, that's not what I want. It's Andrei I want to meet, but not as we meet every day at home. We go through the routine, and that's how it has to be, but sometimes it feels as if we're sleepwalking.

Her own face looked back at her, the same as ever. But she was deceiving herself, because it was not the same. She was thirty-four and growing older by the day. If she were faced with her twenty-year-old self in the mirror she would be shocked at the change. She was on the conveyor belt that was taking her from birth to death, but so slowly and imperceptibly that it was bearable.

She clenched her fists. *You've got to stop all this.*

It was Andrei she was going to meet. Her husband. Irina thought Anna was so lucky. She thought Anna had got it made. Dear

Irinochka, it was all she wanted, to be married and to have children, to love and to be loved. I know that I'm fortunate, Anna thought. Without Andrei and Kolya, I don't know how I would live.

Sometimes she was still afraid that the dead would be angry with her, because she had survived and they had not. She had gone back to her life. The down that had grown on her arms and Kolya's had rubbed away. Andrei had told her that it would disappear, once they were properly nourished again. But her father and Marina had been thrown into a pit.

Anna looked away from the mirror, towards the door of Kolya's room. That's where her father had lain. If she went to the door now, and opened it, she might find him still there, watching the door, reproaching her for forgetting about him. He might stretch out a hand and clasp her in a grip of ice. He might say that it's not the dead who close the door on the living, but the living who close the door on the dead.

No, she told herself. No. He wasn't like that. He wanted me and Kolya to live. He's at peace.

She'd tried to talk to Andrei about it once. He listened, but she knew that what she said only disturbed him and made him unhappy.

He hated it when he couldn't help people. She never talked about those times to Kolya, unless he asked questions. It was impossible to know what Kolya remembered, and what he had forgotten. Thank God they had been able to keep him indoors, because there was always Marina to watch over him while Anna went for the rations or to search for firewood. Plenty of women were not so lucky. Kolya hadn't seen the corpses in the streets and courtyards. He hadn't seen the bread queues, and people's faces as they crammed their rations safely into an inner pocket, and then glared about them like hunted animals. He had not seen what Anna had once seen and never forgotten: a little girl, wrapped to the eyes in layers of clothes, standing beside a woman who lay in the snow and did not get up. And while Anna watched, a man came by and scooped up the child, leaving the woman on the ground. Her eyes stared, as dark as raisins in the hollows of her skull. That memory has tormented Anna. She'd assumed then that the child belonged to the man. But had she been right, or had she been too weak, prepared to see only what she wanted to see?

Andrei was right, she should not think about all that. He was usually right. He never reproached her for anything. Sometimes she wished that he would. There were too many things they never talked about.

But perhaps it was as well. If he ever said to her the words she dreaded, she wouldn't be able to forget them.

Of course a man wants a child. It's natural.

He'd never said that, or even hinted that she and Kolya weren't enough for him. But she knew Andrei. He was too good and too loyal ever to let her know what he truly felt about the fact that she had not become pregnant. Once she'd asked him if he thought that perhaps starvation had affected her fertility. He had looked at her sharply and said, 'Of course not, Anna. At the time perhaps, but not permanently.' She'd known from the readiness of his answer how much he had been thinking about it. Thinking, but never telling her.

Anna straightened her shoulders, took a deep breath and looked back at the mirror. The dress was a success. It made her look quite unlike her everyday self. If she could step out of herself — and if Andrei could step out of himself — then there was no telling what might happen. It was time to go now. Andrei was on call and he'd taken his evening clothes with him, to change at the hospital. She was going to meet him at eight o'clock. It was a shame not to leave for the ball together, arm in arm, but it didn't really matter. Kolya was spending the night at Grisha's. She and Andrei had all the time in the world.

Perhaps they can go home soon. The band has begun to play another polka, and Anna moves back behind a pillar. The hall is as crowded as ever. At the side tables the heavy drinkers watch the dancers with unflagging, morose attention. A man gets up slowly, steadies himself and walks with care and in a straight line towards the door that leads to the wreck of the buffet. He can't possibly want to eat anything that's left in there. Perhaps he thinks it's the toilet. The steady hum of pleasure and music has begun to break up.

This polka, and then perhaps a *sudashka,* and then at last another waltz. She was pinning her hopes on that waltz, but now it seems unimportant. The speeches have been made and the toasts drunk. Why on earth do there have to be speeches at a ball? Of course it's interesting that the hospital has received a delegation of thoracic surgeons from Paris, but still. Just as well for those thoracic surgeons that they're back in Paris now, thinks Anna. The ball supper would have been a disappointment to them. The cold salmon was flabby, and the spiced meatballs needed more sauce.

Anna smiles at herself. Since when did I get so fussy? Salmon is salmon. But all the same I wouldn't have prepared it like that. It needed a sharp sauce, not that greasy mayonnaise. She'd have made sorrel sauce. The potato salad tasted as if it had been lying around for days, not hours. The vodka is first-rate, however. She can't remember how many partners have assured her of that.

My God, there's Andrei dancing. Who can the woman be? She's much older than him, with her hair severe in a bun. Her dress has the kind of ugliness that makes your heart clench. It's bright turquoise, and cut so that it turns her breasts into a bolster. And yet she's a handsome woman. In a white coat she would be impressive — and probably is. She'll be a doctor, or a radiographer. She'll have bought that dress without even thinking about it, because it looked more or less suitable. Anna can't help envying her that degree of detachment. She's not even trying to keep up with the steps of the polka. Her feet move to their own rhythm, dignified and off the beat.

They are coming towards her, not even pretending to dance now. Andrei has taken the woman's arm.

'Anna, allow me to introduce you to Riva Grigorievna Brodskaya, a surgical colleague.'

It's her. The one who operated on the Volkov boy. She's not at all as Anna had imagined her.

'Are you enjoying the ball?' asks Anna quickly.

'Yes. Yes, I think so,' says the other woman, as if the question requires a truthful answer.

'They've got a good band this year.'

'Yes, it seems so.'

She looks so out of place here. Anna wonders why she decided to come at all. No doubt her reasons are much the same as everyone else's. She came because otherwise it would look as if she weren't part of the team. She put on that dress out of duty.

'For me, it's a kind of farewell party,' says Riva Grigorievna, looking straight at Anna.

'Oh — are you leaving the hospital, then?'

'I'm leaving Leningrad. I've accepted a post in Yerevan. Hadn't you heard?'

'I haven't seen any of Andrei's colleagues lately. Not for months, really, until tonight,' says Anna, realizing suddenly that none of Andrei's colleagues has dropped in for weeks. And then, as Riva Grigorievna still looks at her, she understands that the person from whom she might — should — have heard this news is Andrei. 'Congratulations,' says Anna.

'Some might say it was a backward step in career terms,' the other woman continues, her eyes never leaving Anna's face, 'but Yerevan has certain advantages. No one is fighting to work there. It's a long way from Leningrad.'

Anna stretches her lips into a smile. 'Yes,' she says, 'it must be.'

'Two thousand five hundred kilometres. A good distance.'

Andrei is looking uneasy.

'You are young,' says Riva Grigorievna, looking only at Anna and smiling faintly. 'You have everything in front of you.'

Anna laughs.

'Why do you laugh?'

'I suppose I'm not in the habit of thinking of myself that way.'

'But nevertheless you are young enough to start again.'

' "To start again?" ' Anna repeats, frowning.

'Yes. I've been trying to persuade your husband that a change of air will do him good.' Suddenly her face changes. She looks past Anna's shoulder. 'Good evening, Boris Ivanovich.'

It's Russov.

'And how are you enjoying our ball, my dear Anna Mikhailovna?' asks Russov, and to Anna's amazement he takes her hand, lifts it to his lips and kisses it. She represses a sharp urge to snatch it away. Riva Grigorievna has already gone. 'But why aren't you dancing, my dear girl?'

'I'm a little tired,' says Anna.

'Beautiful young women don't come to balls to be tired. You'll give me a turn, won't you?'

The band is still playing the polka. Anna glances at Andrei for support but Andrei is staring ahead, his face set. She mustn't alienate this man. Her skin prickles. At that moment the music rises to a crescendo and then plunges to its final chord. The polka is finished. Anna looks at Russov. 'I'm afraid you were too late,' she says.

'They'll begin again in a minute.'

'Yes, but I think the next dance will be a waltz, and I've promised that to Andrei. Another time,' she says cheerfully.

Russov shrugs. 'I must ask you to congratulate me, all the same. I'm off to Moscow, to the Morozovka. Modesty forbids me to say that it's a promotion. But as you know they are expanding there, creating new facilities —'

'You're going to Moscow? When?'

'In the new year.'

Anna sees from Andrei's face that he already knows. So Russov has got himself out of Leningrad too. No Yerevan for him, though — he's picked a plum. A top children's hospital, in the capital.

'My new post will be largely administrative, although of course there will be a clinical aspect.'

'Of course,' says Andrei.

Russov looks a changed man. He glistens with self-satisfaction, and his glance at Andrei holds something of the contempt that a man who has managed things well for himself feels for one who has not. Hard to connect this Russov with the fearful, sweating figure in the courtyard.

The band strikes a chord.

'It's a waltz,' says Anna, though how she can tell after a couple of notes is beyond him. 'Come on, Andrei, let's have this one and then we'll go home.'

He holds out his arms to her, a little stiffly. He's not a good dancer and he knows it. He'd rather not lead off under Russov's smug gaze. Riva Grigorievna is nowhere to be seen. Russov remains at the heart of things, with the promise of the Morozovka ahead of him; she goes.

Anna puts her left hand on Andrei's shoulder. He takes her right hand, and smiles down into her face.

'Don't worry,' she says, 'there aren't so many on the dance floor now. We'll have plenty of space.'

'I know this music, I think.'

'Oh, Andrei, of course you do. You've heard it dozens of times. But I'm surprised they're playing it,' she says, dropping her voice.

'Why?'

'It's Shostakovich. Surely you recognize it?'

He wishes he could explain to Anna that the sounds which are as legible to her as words on paper make no kind of pattern to him. But he must concentrate on the steps or he will be out of time. The waltz is the easiest dance . . . *One*-two-three, *one*-two-three — yes, that's fine, he's really got the hang of it now. Anna is so warm and soft. She moves without him even having to think about leading her. In fact he rather suspects that she is leading him, even though she can't see which way she's going.

'Look out for the pillars, my treasure,' she murmurs.

One-two-three, *one*-two-three — it's not difficult at all; in fact he's almost enjoying it. He looks down at the curves of Anna's lips. She's smiling at something. 'Are you laughing at me?'

'Of course not. I was just thinking how much you've improved, with all the practice we've done.'

'Good. But shall we make this the last dance? Since we've got the place to ourselves tonight, let's make the most of it.'

'Poor Kolya.'

'It's not "poor Kolya". Our lives revolve around that boy.'

'It's always the way, with children in the house,' she answers thoughtlessly, and then he feels her body tense.

'I love you in that dress,' he says quickly.

'The skirt is a bit crushed. Your friend Dontsov grabbed great handfuls of it when I was dancing with him. He must have thought I was planning to run away.'

'He's a nice chap.'

'I know that. All the same, he has sweaty hands.'

'You did your duty. I watched you dancing with all sorts of people.'

' "All sorts" is right. Thank God I didn't have to dance with that snake Russov.'

'He's changed, hasn't he? He used to be all right.'

'He doesn't like you. I'm glad he's going.

He's dangerous.'

'Anna, you mustn't think about any of that now.'

'No, you're right . . . Listen, let's go now, Andryusha, while they're still playing. Shall we do that?'

The streets are light and quiet. It will be another of those cool, cloudy days. Still, summer is short and you have to make the most of it. Anna and Andrei find themselves talking like this, as if someone were snooping on their exchange of banalities. They walk slowly, close together but not quite touching. Anna listens to the sound of their footsteps. Her own are light, in her mother's evening shoes. Andrei's are crisper and heavier. After a while they fall into step, as they always do.

'Did you enjoy it?'

'Yes,' says Anna firmly.

'Every time I looked for you, you were dancing.'

'You know I like dancing. You used to as well.'

'I do, it's just that I don't get any better at it. I keep treading on people's toes.'

'You think you're worse than you are. You've got to keep on trying. You mustn't end up like my father.'

'I promise you I won't do that. Although he was a fine man, I'm not criticizing him,' Andrei adds hastily.

'You know what I mean.'

He knows what she means. A man sunk into himself. Hard to live with; harder to feel that you had the right to enjoy life in his company.

'He liked it out at the dacha, though,' says Anna. 'You know, sitting on the verandah in the evenings, smoking and reading. He was happy there. Happier than he was anywhere else, at least.'

Andrei doesn't like the direction of this conversation. Her face is sad and pensive, and she's far away from him even though they are still talking. He puts his arm around Anna's shoulder and draws her to him.

'You look beautiful, Anna.'

'Oh, Andrei!' she says, almost dismissively. But he won't let her put him off.

'Beautiful,' he repeats, and this time she says nothing, but moves closer into his embrace. 'Just think,' he continues, 'we can stay in bed until eleven if we want. I'll bring you tea.'

'I expect it'll be the other way round. You'll still be snoring and I'll be cooking the porridge,' she replies in a bantering

tone, which jars on him as much as if she'd pulled out of his grasp. But tonight he's not going to let her fend him off.

'Anna!' He stops, and she stops and turns to face him. He reaches out and very gently traces the line of her cheek, and her jaw. He sees her shiver. Good. Holding her eyes, he traces the line where the low neck of her dress meets her breasts. She glances around quickly, fearfully, but doesn't move away. There's no one else in the street.

'Anna,' he says, more softly, and in a moment they're in each other's arms, blotted out against each other, the green against the black, his head bent, her eyes closed. The pale, quiet street vanishes. They cling together, barely moving, as if each of them wants to disappear into the other. He hears her breathing and the quick, deep sound of her heart through the thin dress. How long is it since he's felt like this? A long time. They're so busy, they have so little time. He'd almost forgotten that none of it matters, compared to this.

It takes weeks for a woman to be sure that she's pregnant. Anna has had too many cycles of gathering hope and sudden, crushing disappointment to trust to anything less than cast-iron certainty. A month late, and perhaps she might begin to believe there is a chance. Years ago, in their easier and more hopeful days, Andrei told Anna that there were ways of testing for pregnancy early on, by injecting a woman's urine into a female rabbit and then examining the rabbit's ovaries a few days later.

'Killing the rabbit first, you mean?'

'Well, yes.'

She'd found the idea faintly obscene — it was something to do with the confusion of human and animal — but as it turned out they'd never needed to make use of the knowledge.

It must be past three in the morning. Everything happens slowly, surely, as if it has always been destined to happen in exactly this way. Andrei is on top of Anna, entering her. Suddenly he smiles, unguarded and childlike, so that her whole body seems to melt with love for him. She has never felt so undefended, or so safe.

Later, after he's fallen asleep, she lies awake for hours. She feels as if she has reached the top of a mountain from which she can see the whole world. She is certain that she has conceived.

12

Anna holds the hands of two little girls while several more cluster around her legs. Some of the littlest ones find outdoor play overwhelming, and even on the coldest days the children are outdoors for at least an hour. In summer they spend much of their day in the courtyard or on the verandah. They're very lucky to have so much outdoor space — grass, and asphalt too for rainy days — but today, in a cold, blustery October wind, Anna will be glad enough when it's time to take the children indoors. In a minute she'll get them going with another game of tag, or a race. Little Masha needs to run about; she must be frozen. Not only is she clinging to Anna's hand, but she's also rubbing her face against it. She's a nervous, sensitive child who looks on with dread at the bigger children with their flaring red cheeks and pounding boots as they rush across the yard.

'Mashenka, do you want to run a little race with me? How about you, Tanya? Shall we see who can run fastest over to the silver birch?'

They are so lucky. They have trees for shade, and a concrete pool (empty now) for the children to splash about in during the hottest days of summer. Anna has to hand it to Morozova: she has a genius for extracting 'special funds' for the nursery and is forever on the alert for new initiatives of which they can be at the forefront . . .

'Have you heard?' demands Irina. Irina isn't braceleted with children; she packs her 'clingers' off with a sharp word, and they soon learn not to come to her. Anna suspects that even Irina disapproves of her softness. These children need to be socialized, for goodness' sake, and they won't learn by holding on to Anna's skirts.

But they learn this way too, Anna believes. The shy or fragile children grow more confident if they're allowed to take things slowly. They start off silent, then they're talking to me, then I can get them talking to one another. Soon we can play a little game, and then other children come along to join in and there you are. They're all playing together.

'Just a minute, Irinochka, let me give these

little ones a race and then I'll be with you.'

'You shouldn't be running in your condition.'

Anna feels a warm flush of pleasure, but answers, 'It's fine. Come on, Mashenka, Tanya — and you, Vova, I bet you're good at running. Let's see who can get to the silver birch first. One, two, three, GO.'

She drops her arm, and they're off. Anna jogs with them, keeping the pace. Nervy little Mashenka, to everyone's surprise, covers the ground first. She hangs her head as they all clap her, but Anna catches a glimpse of a smile.

'What were you going to tell me about, then, Irinochka?' she asks when she comes back. *What fresh horrors are in store for us?* But of course she doesn't ask this question aloud, not even of Irina.

Irina frowns. 'It's no joke. Morozova's latest is that we've got to mark the kids' drawings. Just think of what that's going to mean. Every single one's got to be graded and put in a file so we can do a progress assessment every six months. How much time's that going to take?'

'Oh dear.'

' "Oh dear"? Anna, just think about it, it's worth a bit more than "Oh dear".'

'The last statistics lecture I went to, one

of the group was telling us they've started marking the artwork at their place. Some of the parents don't like it apparently. But they've got different parents from ours. Theirs are all teachers and university professors. Ours probably wouldn't complain.' *Because they're cowed by Morozova, she doesn't add, who represents to them the voice of the high-ups themselves. You can laugh at her behind her back, you can grumble all you like, but you know she'll get her way.*

'It's not the parents I'm bothered about, it's us,' declares Irina. 'Every week it gets worse. More boxes to tick, more things to get wrong. You're so lucky, you'll be getting a break from it soon. My God, if I were in your position I'd think I'd died and gone to heaven.'

'No you wouldn't, you'd be bored to death. Look at all the freedom you have.'

'Freedom to work all my life until I'm one of those poor old half-crazy women bargaining over the price of chicken feet? What kind of freedom is that? Sometimes I really think that's what's going to happen to me. I'll work until I'm worn out. Can you imagine still lugging these kids about when you're coming up to sixty? There'll be a hundred times as many forms to fill in by then. I won't meet anyone. I'll never have children of my own.'

How angry and bitter she sounds.

'Irinochka, don't. You're lovely. Someone will snap you up, just wait.'

'Who will? The men who should have married me are dead. The younger men — the ones who weren't in the war — they want the really young girls, not old hags like me. Oh, for heaven's sake, Anna, how many kids do you want hanging off your arms? Tell them to shove off and play!'

'They will in a minute. Vova, can you start the race for us this time? Just say, "One, two, three, GO," and bring your hand down like this. All you others, don't move until Vova says, "GO." I'll watch and see if you're all running your very hardest.'

Irina and Anna watch as Vova holds up his hand proudly, ready to give the signal just as Anna gave it. The little ones jostle themselves into a line.

'One, two, three, GO!' shouts Vova in his thin, clear voice, and the children surge forward. But Masha doesn't make it. She trips and falls forward on to the asphalt as the others pelt away towards the birch tree. Anna hurries forward to pick her up.

'No, you idiot, let me!' shouts Irina. 'You can't go picking up these kids now.'

Masha is all right once she has got her

breath back. Fortunately she is so thickly wrapped in her padded jacket, scarf and woollen helmet that her face has not even touched the ground. She doesn't cry.

'Good girl! Now off you go to the others and see who's won. Thanks, Irinochka, I know I shouldn't be lifting them, but sometimes you can't help it.'

'Yes, you can help it. You've got to put yourself first. Morozova's not going to care if you have a miscarriage in the cause of picking up some snotty kid.'

'I should be all right now,' says Anna. 'It's past four months.'

'All the same, you've got to be careful.'

Irina is so interested in Anna's pregnancy. It's almost as if Anna were having the baby for both of them. Three weeks after she heard Anna was pregnant, she brought in a beautifully wrapped paper parcel. In it was a cobwebby white knitted jacket.

'Did you make that yourself, Irina?'

Irina shook her head, laughing. 'No chance. I bribed my sister. She knits so fast you can't even see the needles.'

'It's beautiful. He can wear it on special occasions.'

'Do you think it's going to be a boy?'

'No, not really. I suppose I only say "he" because I'm used to Kolya.'

'I expect your husband wants a boy,' said Irina, nodding her head and looking wise.

'I don't think he cares, as long as it's healthy. That's the trouble with being a doctor. They see so much disease and suffering that they forget a normal child is really quite common.'

Irina fingered the delicate wool. 'You put it on over the warm layers. It's decorative, really.'

'It's perfect. You could never buy anything like this in the shops.'

The two women embraced. As they separated, Irina asked with apparent casualness, 'What does it feel like, Anna?'

'You mean being pregnant?'

'Of course.'

'I don't feel very pregnant yet. In a way nothing's changed, but at the same time everything's changed. Also, I feel hungry all the time but when I start eating I wonder why I'm putting the food in my mouth.'

'You've got to eat.'

'Well, of course. It's just that everything tastes different.'

Irina sighed. 'Isn't it strange? A few weeks ago you were just like me — except you were married, of course — and now everything's completely different for you. All your future, and everything.'

'Mmm.'

She couldn't tell Irina about the crazy, fearful exultation that sometimes came over her in the dead of night, long after Andrei had fallen asleep. Her waking self told her not to be too confident. She might easily miscarry; these were early days. But her secret self was sure. She would hold her own child in her arms at last. Those were things you couldn't say to anyone else, especially not to Irina.

The wind is growing colder, and swinging round to the north-east. Snow will come soon. The last ragged leaves will be swept off the trees, and the children will squeal with excitement when the first flakes drift past the windows, and then thicken, resolving themselves into a true snowfall, the first of the year. For the children, it's so long since last year's snows melted. They stare with wide, startled eyes at the new world, and then fling themselves out into it.

'The real trouble with Morozova,' grumbles Irina, 'is that she's absolutely determined to get this nursery on to "the cutting edge of early-years excellence". "Cutting edge"! I ask you. She's so sharp she'll cut herself one of these days.'

'You shouldn't say that, Irinochka.'

'Only to you. You're so calm, Anna, I don't

know how you do it.'

Anna feels a stab of shame. She is always cautious, even with Irina, but Irina trusts Anna enough to share indiscretions with her. Anna wishes she could be more open, but it's impossible. Only with Andrei; and even then there are thoughts she keeps to herself. It's the way she was brought up, no doubt.

'I expect there'll be a course on criteria for early-years drawing assessment,' she says, deadpan, to make up.

'And you'll be sent on it. Morozova always sends you. She thinks I'm thick as a brick.'

'She most certainly doesn't! That's ridiculous. You're our resident hygiene expert, aren't you?'

'Yes. Theory and practice of scrubbing hands and bums, that's me.'

'That's all of us. Come on, it's nearly half past, we'd better get them in.'

Andrei has a meeting about sanatoria quotas. It's a subject dear to his heart. Thalassotherapy, in particular, has a proven record of success with certain types of rheumatism. The problem is getting the beds for the children who really need them: those whose joint articulation is so impaired that they are developing compensating abnormalities of gait and flexion.

In theory, the main criterion for the sanatorium beds is need; in practice, there's a hierarchy, which not only excludes many who could benefit from treatment, but also vigorously defends its own interests.

It's a long, bruising meeting. Sometimes he wonders if he's doing more harm than good to his patients by arguing for them.

'I hope you understand, Dr Alekseyev, that we have to apply the most rigorous and impartial selection procedures.'

'Naturally I understand that.'

'We cannot allow the slightest appearance of special pleading. Your patient group is only one of many that have strong claims to the forty-day-treatment allocation at the Red Star sanatorium. You are aware that there is pioneering work under way with children who suffer from recurrent pneumonia. The climate of the Yalta region is considered particularly beneficial to these patients.'

'And who is the clinician in charge of the pneumonia cases?' asks Andrei blandly. He knows the answer, and they know that he knows it.

'Dr E. V. Denisova is in charge of the research project.'

I bet she is. One of the most single-minded

careerists he's ever met. An average doctor, but as an operator her style verges on the brilliant. Between him and Denisova, there's no contest. But all the same, just for the hell of it, he'll fight it out.

'How many beds are available to us?'

Rustling of papers. Sideways glances. 'For the forty-day treatment, you mean?'

'Yes.'

'According to my latest information, we have been offered a package of twenty-eight beds for the period 1st May to 10th June next year.'

'Twenty-eight beds! But that's exceptionally generous, surely. We've never been offered so many at the Red Star before. Couldn't we divide up the beds between our specialities?'

'But you must understand that this is a block allocation. The purpose of the allocation would be most satisfactorily answered by sending a cohort of patients under the care of a particular specialist.'

'I am sure I could find twenty-eight patients, if that's what's required.' He's determined to push this one to the limits. His only weapon is an assumption of naivety, so that they are forced to explain themselves. But he feels weary. Maybe he should give in, and let Denisova have those beds.

More rustling of papers. Impatient, irritated looks. Doesn't Alekseyev have the sense to understand that the deal is already done?

'I believe' — stiffly, with an air of reproof — 'that it is chiefly due to the initiative of Dr E. V. Denisova that this very significant and satisfactory allocation has been made to us. It seems only reasonable, therefore, that her excellent pioneering research work should represent the hospital in the therapeutic setting of the Red Star.'

And Denisova hasn't even had to turn up and alienate people. Those Red Star places have rolled on to her plate like fat, sweet dumplings. No doubt she's worked hard enough for them, though, behind the scenes.

'I fully understand the importance of sanatorium provision in the case of children with recurrent pneumonia,' he says quietly. 'That is not the issue. Equally, I'm sure that Dr Denisova's work is of high quality and deserves support. But all the same, I'm obliged to make the case for my own patients. I think I'm right in saying that twenty-eight beds is an exceptional allocation. Early intervention is vital for my patients. Otherwise, frankly, the benefit that they can derive from rehabilitation decreases sharply. We end up with severely disabled child together, it would have happened by now. He'd never wanted to drag her into the misery of clinical investigations. Nothing was more likely to ruin their happiness. He knew enough; gently, he tried to make sure they did everything that would give them the best possible chance of conception.

But now, suddenly, when he'd given up expecting it, she had conceived. From the day she told him she thought she was pregnant, he'd been struck by how certain she seemed. After so much anxiety — so much grief, if he were honest — he thought she might have been tense and fearful, in case things went wrong. But she seemed quite calm. His own joy was so overwhelming that he became afraid. Something would go wrong. He had spent too many years telling himself that it didn't matter, because he and Anna were happy and they had Kolya. He thought he had convinced himself.

He won't change towards Kolya. The boy won't notice any difference. He vows this to himself, in silence.

A child. His child. He hurries onward, swinging through the main doors of Radiology.

'Is Sofya Vasilievna about?' he asks one of the nurses.

patients. In some cases — not in all, I'm certainly not saying that — early, intensive physical therapy and thalassotherapy have been proven to be beneficial. I'd like to cite the research of Dr I. S. Makarov, published in Moscow last year. I'd be glad to provide copies to this committee. I'm not asking for twenty-eight beds, or even half that number. Even five beds would make an enormous difference to patient outcomes.'

He has much more to say. He would like a great deal more detail about the patients involved in Denisova's research, her treatment outcomes to date, and what other resources she has already managed to secure. But no. The whole thing is tied up already. Either they are discussing this provision disinterestedly and professionally, or they are not. Why bang on a closed door?

He's getting cynical. He never thought that would happen to him. Sometimes he just wants to say: *Enough. Have it your way, and see what comes of it.* But he can't. The system, for all its faults, is a million times better than what was there for these children before. His little Tanyas are entitled to treatment, and on the whole they get it. Things are not perfect, but every system has its committees, its Denisovas, Russovs and Retinskayas.

You have to remain hopeful. You have to believe that what you do makes a difference.

'You are very eloquent on behalf of your patients, young man,' says old Gerasimov, who has been silent until now. He's one of the old school. He must be close to sixty now. In his youth he was a medic with the Red Army, during the Civil War. He's a Party member who has somehow survived everything and remained a decent man. There is a glint of sympathy in his stern face. He won't like Denisova's machinations — or her backers — but he will believe that 'for the greater good' the committee must show a united front.

'I hope I am,' replies Andrei.

'But in this case, I am afraid we must disappoint you.'

Andrei looks around the committee members. They regard him — or avoid his glance — with an air of faint annoyance. Some scribble busily on their memo pads. Others stretch exaggeratedly, as if to emphasize how physically taxing it is to sit in a chair for hours and make decisions. *These committees are certainly burdensome, but one has to do one's duty.* Andrei knows them all, and yet he has a sudden certainty that if he were drowning, not one would reach out a hand. Except old Gerasimov, perhaps.

He nods, gets up from his chair, thanks the committee and makes his exit.

It's good to go straight to Radiology and the consoling presence of real work. He needs to talk to Sofya about a couple of X-rays that have to be redone. If she's got a minute, maybe they can get some tea and have a quick chat about how things are going. She's always asking after Anna these days. Funny how all the women are so interested in Anna's pregnancy, whereas the men, after initial congratulations, say nothing. It's natural enough, he supposes. In fact, now he looks back, plenty of his colleagues must have become fathers without more than a conventional word from Andrei.

But everything changes when it's your own. Once or twice he's even said the words aloud: 'my son' or 'my daughter'. He felt like an imposter, but he supposes that once the baby is born, it will seem quite natural. A child; their child. His child. When she first told him, tears came to his eyes. He knew then how much he'd wanted this without daring to realize how much he wanted it. He had almost given up hope. He and Anna were young and strong and it was years since they'd used any form of contraception. If they were able to have a

'No, she's got a group of students,' replies the nurse, and pushes her trolley away. He hesitates. Probably better to come back later; she might be a while. But as he's hovering outside one of the doors with its warning sign, Lena rushes up to him.

'I need to talk to you. Come on.'

'But, Lena —'

'Quick, this way.' Something in her tone makes him follow her without further questions, out of the department, down one of the long wards that are waiting for refurbishment. Lena stops outside a door, and glances both ways before opening it. 'Hurry up!'

'But, Lena, it's a cupboard.'

'I know it's a cupboard, for heaven's sake!'

They are inside. Lena feels for a switch and he hears it click before a feeble light comes on, showing shelves up to the ceiling, piled with hospital linen. It's a big cupboard and there's space for three or four people to stand upright inside it.

'Isn't this a bit melodramatic, Lena?'

Lena shrugs. 'If you like. But we can't waste time, I've only got ten minutes.' For a bizarre instant he thinks she's offering him sex, but of course that's impossible. Not Lena; not him, either. 'Listen,' she carries on, 'I've heard something about the Volkov boy. He's coming in later today.'

Whoever is in charge of this cupboard seems to like their job, thinks Andrei. The sheets are ranged immaculately, with all the sharp, starched edges matched. He can see the double line of sewing by the seam, where they've been turned sides to middle. Nothing wasted. That's how it should be. *Only people are to be wasted.*

'For a check-up?' he asks, fending off what he already knows.

'No. He's developed further symptoms. They've been to their private doctor, and now he's coming in for a chest X-ray. Persistent cough and shortness of breath.'

'I see.'

'There's a hell of a panic on in Admin. My friend works there.' Lena, so discreet. Even to him she doesn't name the friend. 'Borodin or Ryazanova ought to see the boy,' says Lena, naming the paediatric respiratory consultants. 'It's not your area. It was bad enough the way you got dragged in last time. Besides, it may just be flu. It's that time of the year.'

But from the first moment she mentioned the boy's name, certainty plumbed him like a lead weight. 'Further symptoms'; 'chest X-ray'. Of course he sees, and so does Lena. Osteosarcoma is one of the cancers which is most likely to produce secondaries in the lungs. Four months since the operation; that would be quick, but not impossibly quick. There may even have been some nodules at the time of Gorya's earlier treatment, but they were still too small for the X-rays to pick them up then. Tumours in the lung can grow so fast, especially in a child of that age.

It's a while since he last saw Gorya. The boy's done very well in rehabilitation. Andrei's abiding memory is that of Gorya swinging himself on his crutches down an endlessly long corridor. His face was un-childlike in its grim determination. He was being fitted for a prosthesis, but then there were problems with residual swelling and tenderness in the stump and so Gorya continued on crutches for the time being. What an expert he became, in no time. Children were like that.

'Thanks for letting me know, Lena.'

He sees her hesitate. She's got something else to tell him and she doesn't know quite how to say it.

'What is it, Lena?'

'My friend in Admin said Volkov asked for your file to be sent to him again.'

'I see.'

'You should have got out!'

'It's not so easy. Anyway, it's too late for all that now.'

'Probably it won't come to anything. After all, things are better — they aren't like they used to be. It's not as bad as that.'

' "Life has become better, comrades, life has become more cheerful," ' quotes Andrei savagely. Only to Lena, out of all his colleagues, would he dare to say such a thing. Lena gave him her own hostage to fortune long ago, when she told him that she hadn't seen her father since she was seventeen. *'He was taken away, in '37, and we never saw him again. By some miracle the rest of us weren't touched. Of course, my mother had to denounce him — that was a long-standing agreement between them, for the sake of the children. If she'd been arrested, he'd have done the same.'*

'Pity we can't smoke in a linen cupboard,' says Lena now, 'I could kill for a cigarette.'

'Me too.'

If there are secondaries in the lungs, there's nothing more that can be done for Gorya. They can offer palliative care, that's all: morphine, sedatives, physiotherapy and draining away of the fluid that will collect as the tumours grow.

All that child's pain and fear and mutilation and slow recovery might as well never have happened. Sometimes it makes you doubt what you're doing.

'Don't,' says Lena.

'What?'

'You had no choice. He had to have the amputation.'

'Are you a mind-reader, Lena?'

'No. Just good at reading your face.'

He looks away, confused. The cupboard really is very small. He can smell the clean linen, and also Lena herself. Skin, hair, flesh. A warm human being, close to him, her eyes full of concern.

Fear squeezes his heart again, driving out all other thoughts.

'Well, I can't spend the rest of my day in a cupboard with you, more's the pity,' says Lena, with a smile that fails to deceive either of them.

'Lena — thank you. If I don't see you —'

'Don't talk such rubbish.'

'No, listen. If anything happens, you must go to Anna. Tell her to do what your mother did, for the sake of the baby and Kolya. You know what I mean. I can't talk to Anna about it now, not when she's pregnant. Will you promise me that, Lena?'

For the only time, and with shame, Andrei makes use of what he knows Lena feels for him.

'All right,' says Lena, 'although she probably won't listen. I wouldn't, if it were me.'

After this, everything happens quickly. An hour later, Andrei is intercepted on the way to his ward round.

'You are requested to come immediately to Medical Personnel.'

'But I'm doing a ward round with Professor Maslov.'

'He has been informed.'

Andrei follows the clerk's trim, bouncing figure along the corridors. He doesn't know her. A new girl perhaps, or a transfer from another department. She is very young, but she gives him the message with a look of cold, smug disapproval. For some absurd reason he is hurt by this, as if he expected her to smile.

She turns aside before she reaches the main office of Medical Personnel, and opens a door to her left. The small room is empty. She gestures for him to go forward.

'But there's no one there,' says Andrei.

She looks at him as if he is stupid to have expected there to be anyone in the room.

'Please wait,' she says, and he finds himself grateful for that much politeness, as she closes the door on him. He listens to her heels tapping away down the corridor. Well, at least she hasn't turned the key on him, he thinks, and smiles to himself, a little grimly. She can't be more than twenty. Just a few years older than Kolya. Why let the attitude of a chit like that get to him?

The minutes lengthen. His nerves crisp with irritation as he thinks of Professor Maslov on the ward round without him. He'll have the notes, of course, but not the detailed exchange of views and findings that mark his relationship with Andrei. Maslov is a fine physician, one of the very best. Close to retirement now but unsparing in his efforts to pass on decades of expertise. And what is even more remarkable, given his age and status, he is always open to the latest ideas and research. He treats Andrei more as a colleague than as a junior. Andrei considers himself fortunate to have the chance to work with Maslov, and now, with no warning, he's failing to turn up for the ward round. What the hell is Maslov going to think?

He glances at his watch. Quarter to five. He's been waiting half an hour at least. He should sit down and try to relax. Why doesn't he just walk out of the door? It isn't locked. *'You should have got out,'* Lena had said. Perhaps there is still a chance, if he is prepared to take it.

283

He hears a distant clang. A nurse dropping a bedpan, no doubt. What a catastrophe, magnified by the long, bare corridors. Admin can't protect themselves entirely from the sounds and smells of the hospital, although they keep themselves safely out of sight most of the time. Even here in this little bare room, the hospital breathes around him like a huge organism of which he is a part. He cannot separate himself, not by his own choice. If they force him, that's another matter. But no power on earth will make him say, of his own volition, *'I don't belong here.'*

The door opens. The pert little face of the clerk looks round it. She frowns on seeing Andrei, as if she expected him to disappear or to turn into someone else.

'You are to come with me,' she says.

As he follows her for a second time, Andrei is sure she's taking him to Volkov, and he gets the measure of what Volkov has already done. He has turned the hospital into his own place, running by his own rules. A doctor can miss a ward round and cool his heels in an empty office for half an hour. People can be sent for without explanation and even without reason. There is a larger reason, which is that they must learn that they have now entered Volkov's world.

Well, thinks Andrei, perhaps. But what if I refuse? What if I continue to believe that the man I'm going to see is the father of a sick child, and that he's full of anger and vengeance because he dreads what's coming next? You're the parent, Volkov, and I'm the doctor. Nothing's going to change that.

13

This time, the room to which Andrei is taken contains Volkov. He's seated at the desk, like a man at work in his own office. His chair is larger and slightly higher than the empty chair on the other side of the desk. Volkov gestures to Andrei to sit, without greeting him.

'Good afternoon,' says Andrei, but Volkov plunges in without preamble.

'You know why we're here. The boy is worse.'

'I heard that.'

'He has a cough. He's losing weight. He's tired.'

'And your own doctor has seen him, I believe?'

'Yes. So, what do you think is wrong?'

'It's not possible for me to say that before he's had a full range of tests. If he were my patient I'd arrange a chest X-ray and blood tests straight away, after the physical examination.'

'So he's not your patient, then? I thought we'd agreed that he was. Or is he only your patient when things are going well, is that it?'

The work has become the man, thinks Andrei. Even now Volkov can't stop framing his questions like an interrogator. Keep calm. Don't respond in kind. 'As you know, I'm not an oncologist. I became involved in your son's case because of an initial confusion over the symptoms with which he presented. I remained in close touch with the case at your request.'

' "The case"?'

'Forgive me.' Andrei feels himself flush. He's done exactly the same as Volkov — lost his grip on where they are and what should happen here. A crass, clumsy blunder, worthy of a third-year medical student. He would never have believed he could speak to a parent like that. 'We get used to using certain expressions, and we forget how they sound.'

Volkov's anguish is obvious. He looks worn, and he has aged much more than the few months that have passed since Gorya was first diagnosed. Andrei notices that the nails on his left hand are bitten down and surrounded by raw, bulging flesh. That's new; Andrei remembers noticing how well kept Volkov's hands were, and that his professional life clearly didn't disturb him.

Volkov is far too intelligent not to understand how ill the boy is. Perhaps the private doctor summoned up the courage to warn him about what Gorya's cough and loss of weight might mean. Maybe he even did an X-ray. Volkov wouldn't disclose that yet; it's not his style. He comes in hard with questions, to make sure that the conversation is always on his territory. He finds out your weaknesses.

'You recommended the surgeon, as I remember. What was her name? Brodskaya. Yes, that was it,' Volkov continues, drawling out the syllables mockingly, 'Riva Grigorievna Brodskaya. She performed the biopsy and then the amputation.'

'We discussed the criteria for choosing a surgeon beforehand, if you remember. Dr Brodskaya had the necessary experience, and an excellent reputation.'

'But she doesn't seem to have been very successful in this "case", as you put it. Why do you think that might be, given that she's supposed to be so good?'

'She's a fine surgeon. One of the best.'

'You think so? Let's hope that that her patients in Yerevan think the same. You look surprised, Dr Alekseyev. Did you think we wouldn't know that the bird had flown the nest? So. Let me tell you what really happened. She butchered my boy for nothing.'

'It wasn't like that. There was no alternative to the operation.'

'An operation which has succeeded in spreading the cancer all around his body. His lungs are full of it, do you know that? What kind of surgery was that?'

So the X-rays have been done already. Either here, in haste, or before Volkov brought his boy back to the hospital.

'I haven't seen Gorya's X-rays yet,' says Andrei.

'They show, apparently —' Volkov's hard, aggressive composure falters, but he clears his throat and carries on. 'It seems they show that cancer has spread to the lungs. But you must have suspected that. Apparently, we're now told, it's not uncommon. Met-a-stas-is. Isn't that the word you doctors use?'

'It's a terrible thing,' says Andrei. He would like to remind Volkov that he has always been honest with him. He'd made it clear that osteosarcoma was a highly aggressive cancer. Volkov was told that amputation was the only possible treatment, but never that it was a cure.

It would do no good to say these things now. Out of common humanity, if nothing more, he has to keep quiet. Besides, he feels a corrosive sense of personal failure, as he always does when treatment doesn't work and it becomes clear that medicine has nothing more to offer.

'You remember how he was after the operation? All that,' says Volkov, not raising his voice but striking with his fist on the desk so violently that the pen holder jumps and clatters to the floor, 'all *that* for *nothing*. His mother was right. I should have listened to her, but I trusted you.'

No, thinks Andrei, *you never did, not for a second. You trust no one.* 'Where is Gorya now?' he asks.

'Your Professor Borodin is doing an examination. It's you that Gorya wants to see, though. He never liked Brodskaya. Didn't want her to touch him. Well, she won't be touching anybody for a while. She'll have to shut up her butcher's shop.'

'She is a very good surgeon.'

'When you keep on saying that, it makes me think you're on her side. Maybe you two know each other better than I realized. Were you putting your heads together all the time?'

'Naturally we conferred about Gorya's care.'

'Naturally.' Volkov's forehead is moist. Suddenly his features twist with rage. '*Naturally* birds of a feather stick together!' he shouts. 'Why don't you answer me? What are you made of? Aren't you a man?'

'You're the parent of a sick child, and I'm a doctor. It's not my job to argue with you.'

'You've already failed in your "job",' says Volkov, with a contempt that doesn't quite ring true. Like his anger, it has something in it which is synthetic and theatrical. 'Your job was to find out what was wrong with Gorya and then do everything in your power to restore him to health. Instead of that, you tell me you've got to cut off his leg, you persuade me that's the only possible cure, and like a fool I believe you and allow you to —' he swallows. Genuine emotion fights with the whipped-up anger for a moment, and then anger wins. 'How many other patients have you done this to, eh? How many innocent, trusting workers have brought their children to this hospital, committing them to your so-called expertise and expecting the highest standard of care? The people demand such standards! Nobody is above the people's vigilance! How many mistakes have been covered up? How many incompetents, murderers and saboteurs have been protected?' With each sentence, Volkov slams the desk with his fist. Suddenly he picks up the table lamp, wrenches its cord from the socket, and hurls it against the wall. 'How many?' he shouts. 'How many?'

There is silence, a long, strangely detached silence in which Andrei hears nothing but the race of his own thoughts. He doesn't even glance round at the shattered lamp. These words are not his words. 'Incompetents, murderers and saboteurs.' They're a language he's never needed to speak, although of course he knows it, no one can help knowing it. It seeps across the face of the newspapers like a corruption. Volkov would have learned it all in his young days, when he still had to work at the coalface of interrogation. It's second nature to him now. Outrage and fury are an essential part of the interrogator's repertoire. People who've been 'there' and by some miracle have survived — they don't talk about it. But once or twice, late at night, Andrei's heard a few things. Lies are violent, he knows that. They have their own power.

He's sure that Volkov can't and doesn't believe a word of what he's saying, although the emotion that drives him is real enough.

And yet he has the power to act on whatever he claims to suspect. If he follows his own claims to their logical conclusion, then doctors who believe they are there to do their work will have to admit that really they are butchers, liars and conspirators. He, Andrei, will have to admit it too. Everyone, even the biggest bigwigs in Admin, must understand that this is the delusion of a father who refuses to accept the awful, random fact of his son's cancer. And yet Volkov will make his lie come true, because that is what he does. If he suspects evil, then evil has got to be found. That's what they did to Vasili Parin. He thought he was correctly following his instructions about scientific exchange of research data with the USA. He didn't realize that he was an American spy. Or perhaps Volkov does accept the truth of what's happened to Gorya. He just wants to punish someone for it.

But how has it come about that I'm in this room, with this man? Andrei asks himself, as his clinical eye notes the pallor of Volkov's face, his heavy breathing and the dilation of his pupils. Anna and I were always careful. We believed we'd thought of everything that could happen to us, but we never allowed for this. Is it just chance, or is it fate? If it's fate, then this was coming towards me all my life, even when I was happy and completely unaware that there was any such child in the world as Gorya Volkov. I was here in this hospital, and Volkov was wherever such men have their offices. Anna has always said that the important thing is never to come to their attention. She and Lena thought the same.

Anna, he thinks, *Anna.* But for once he can't see her face in his mind.

'Gorya wants to see you,' says Volkov. His face twitches. 'He didn't want to come back here.'

'It's very hard for him.'

'Last night he couldn't sleep. He said, "Are they going to cut my other leg off?" '

'Of course you told him there was no question of that.'

'He understands.'

Their voices have dropped. There is nothing left but a few bare words to describe the truth. Volkov's look is almost simple, almost intimate. Once again Andrei feels a disturbing closeness to the man.

'He said, "Am I going to die?" — just as if it were any other question. He didn't seem afraid.'

'I've known children ask that. Usually they ask me when their parents aren't around, because they're afraid of upsetting them.'

The faintest shadow of pride crosses Volkov's face. 'I told him he needn't even think about it,' he says.

'I understand.'

'You'll see him, then.'

'Yes.'

Volkov looks away. The thread between them breaks. It seems that the very nature of Volkov's face changes, as if a mask is coming down over it. Very quietly, so that Andrei can't be quite sure that he's heard the words correctly, Volkov murmurs, 'There are saboteurs in every profession, but we always find them out.'

Polina Vasilievna looks so changed. The thick make-up has disappeared. Her hair is no longer jet black and tightly curled, but grey at the roots and twisted into a bun. She smoothes Gorya's hair back from his forehead as she watches his face with anxious, devouring love. As Andrei enters the room she frowns, as if she doesn't quite remember where she last saw him.

'Dr Alekseyev,' he reminds her.

Her face lights up in recognition. Whatever her husband may think about what the doctors have done to Gorya, he hasn't shared those thoughts with his wife. To her, Andrei is simply that young doctor whom her son liked so much. Although of course he's not so very young, not any more.

Gorya's eyes are closed. Perhaps he's asleep, but Andrei decides to say nothing the boy can't safely hear. A cylinder of oxygen stands by the bed, but Gorya isn't wearing a mask.

'He got very tired with those X-rays, and then the doctor had to pull him about all over again.'

'I'm sure it was necessary.'

'They haven't told us what's going on, not properly. He's had this cough. But it's that time of year, isn't it? Everyone gets coughs and colds once winter's on its way.' While she speaks, her eyes are fixed on him, wide with fear, begging him to agree.

'Yes, it's not the best time.'

Gorya's head is raised high on a mound of pillows. His mouth is slightly open and there's bubble of spittle at one corner. Andrei is fairly sure that he's really asleep.

'He gets his breath better when he's propped up,' says his mother. 'It's only with this cough. Normally it's better for them to lie flat. More hygienic,' she adds, as if the word were a talisman.

The boy has lost weight. His jawline is sharp, his skin waxen.

'It's good to make him comfortable,' says Andrei.

'He likes cloudberry juice. That's good for him, isn't it, cloudberry juice? I've got six bottles from last year that our Dunya bottled. He needs the vitamins. Once he's out of hospital I'm going to build him up.'

'Cloudberry juice is good.'

Again, she strokes the hair back from her boy's forehead. His eyes roll under the veined eyelids, but the lids don't even flutter. He's deeply asleep. 'His leg's been bad as well. He even gets pain in his foot. He says, "I know it's not there, Mum, but it hurts me so bad it wakes me up, and then I don't want to go back to sleep."'

'I'm sorry.'

'I should have known. Well, I did know. As soon as they said "cancer", I felt it go through me *here*,' and she touched the place where people think their heart is. 'I ought to have taken him back home with me there and then.'

She is raised up, too, he thinks, above everything but her child and his suffering. She can't blame and she can't hate. Everything petty has fallen away. He's seen it happen before. It doesn't last, though, and besides she has a husband with enough blame and hatred in him for two.

'Stay until he wakes up. He'd be sorry to miss you. He was asking for you.'

'I can't stay too long.'

He must see Professor Maslov before he goes home, and explain his absence from the ward round. Check that all the notes are in order and discuss what's been happening today. Maybe have a quick word with Lena to reassure her? No. Better for Lena if she knows as little as possible.

He sighs, looking at the child asleep in the bed. They have failed. He learned long ago that doctors don't like failure, and he's no different from any of them. The dying do better at home, if there's a bed to put them in. People who are dying need an old granny who's willing to sit by their side, watching for the tiny signals that mean thirst or pain in one who is too weak to talk. Old grannies aren't afraid of death. They meet it on equal terms; they don't believe that it's their job to conquer it. Gorya's mother will cope. If she's allowed to. She surprised him today with the toughness of fibre that lay under all that entitled 'high-up' behaviour. She didn't blame Andrei, but instead reproached herself for going against her instincts. She won't fall to pieces as long as the boy needs her.

'They won't do any more operations on

him, will they?' asks Polina Vasilievna.

'No.'

'I never liked that surgeon. Cold, she was. No proper feeling. Jews. You know, they only care for their own.'

'I must go,' he murmurs. 'Please tell Gorya I came to see him. I'll call in again tomorrow.'

She nods, but already her attention has left him, because Gorya has stirred. He moves his hand, picking at the bedclothes, and then is still again.

'Goodbye,' says Andrei, and quietly leaves the room. He's sweating. The boy is in a bad state. It's all happened so quickly. Already Gorya has that old-man look of a desperately sick child.

The corridor is bright and empty but for the two policemen planted outside Gorya's door. No change there. Andrei walks away down the corridor, half expecting to hear heavy footsteps behind him and feel a hand clamping down on his shoulder. But nothing happens. He turns the corner, beyond their gaze. It's late, much later than he thought. It won't be worth trying to find Professor Maslov now. He must get home quickly, to Anna.

14

They don't often embrace in front of Kolya. He doesn't like it. When he was little he would fight his way in between them. When he was older he would make some little sarcastic comment that was enough to make them self-conscious. It's natural, Anna supposes. After all, they are two, and Kolya is one. Who would like that thrust in their face?

But tonight, when Andrei sits down heavily in his chair and she goes to him and he buries his face against her stomach, Kolya says nothing. With unwonted tact, he steals away, and even closes his door. A few moments later he begins to practise scales. Bless him, she thinks, he wants us to know he can't hear what we say.

'Lie down, my love, you look exhausted.'

'Lie down with me.'

He holds her tight in the circle of his arms, as if he's afraid she'll vanish.

'Things are bad. You and Kolya must get away.'

He speaks very quietly, but every word burns itself on to her brain. Later, she will be able to read back his words as if they are written inside her.

'The Volkov boy is dying. They're already looking for a scapegoat.'

'Not you!'

'Volkov named Brodskaya.'

She feels a shameful surge of relief. 'Brodskaya! But I thought she'd gone off to Yerevan.'

'Of course they know where she is.'

'Andrei, the baby's moving. I wish you could feel him too.'

'You must keep calm. We mustn't let any of this affect the baby.'

'He's fine. I know he is. Tell me what else he said.'

'He claims Brodskaya botched the operation.'

'But that's rubbish.'

'The boy's got nodes in his lungs now. Metastasis, you know.'

She breathes in sharply. She knows enough to understand that the boy will die.

'What we've got to think of now, though, is you and the baby. And Kolya,' he adds quickly, hoping that Anna hasn't imagined for a second that he's forgotten about Kolya.

'It's no good thinking of us all leaving now. It'll just make you look guilty. Besides, they can find you wherever you are.'

He thinks of Brodskaya in Yerevan. *'Birds of a feather,'* Volkov said. Maybe she's already been taken in for questioning. 'But we've got to do something,' he says.

'The only thing is for us both to go to work as usual. You must look as if you've nothing to hide.'

'But you were the one who said before that we should all go to Irkutsk!'

'Yes,' she murmurs, 'it might have worked then, but it's too late now. Anyway, who knows? Probably it would just have brought even more trouble. Kolya's got to go. How can we fix it? Wait. I know. Galya's living out at her dacha all winter this year. Kolya can go to her.'

'He'll never agree to that.'

'He will if I talk to him. The sooner he leaves the better. I'll take a day off work and go down with him. I'll inform the school that he's ill — you'll have to tell me what would be a good illness, something that lasts for a few weeks at least. We can get a medical certificate from someone, can't we?'

'Yes, I should think so.'

'Then that's what we'll do.'

'You should go down and stay with Galya too, Anna.'

'No. I've got to keep on going to work and everything's got to seem normal. Besides, they might not go after Kolya if it's just him who isn't here. Anyway . . .'

'Anyway what?'

'You're an idiot if you think I'm leaving you.'

'You know Lena?'

'Of course I do,' she says with a touch of asperity.

'Her father was arrested in '37. She said her parents had an agreement that if one of them was arrested, the other would denounce them so there'd be someone left for the children.'

'Hmm. That didn't work for most people.'

'It did for them.'

'A miracle.'

'That's what Lena said.'

'Anyway, what's that got to do with us?'

'You know what it's got to do with us, Anna. You've got to think about the baby, and Kolya. If that means you have to —'

'Denounce you, you mean.'

'Yes.'

'You can't seriously think I'm going to do that.'

'I'm asking you to think about it. I would understand. I would know it was for the children and it was nothing to do with us.'

'No, it wouldn't be anything to do with us, because it's never going to happen. You can stop talking about it.'

'But if they arrest you too, Anna —'

'Don't talk like that! No one's been arrested. You've done nothing.' But suddenly, hearing herself, she's shaken by a desire to laugh. *You've done nothing!* Whoever heard of anything more childish and unrealistic? *It wasn't me! It's not fair!*

'Anna, please don't! Don't cry.'

'I'm not crying. If you could see my face you'd know I was laughing. I was just thinking — well, it's stupid, but I was just thinking how much better off we'd be if you were a murderer.'

He releases her, and stares into her face. 'You're not getting hysterical, are you? You have to think of —'

'I know: the baby. I'm not hysterical, I'm only laughing, Andryusha, because it's really very funny, except of course that it's not funny at all. But we survived before, didn't we? We got through.'

'Yes, we got through. Will Galya really be all right about having him?'

'I think so. She's very fond of Kolya, you

know. Also, she's down there, tucked away . . . I shan't tell her any more than I have to, I don't want to drag her into it. I'll just say, you know, there are reasons. She'll understand.' *And when I take Kolya,* she thinks, *I'll take the diaries, too, and bury them. Everything's got to go now. But the less you know about that the better.*

He strokes her hair. 'Listen to that boy. Notes going off like firecrackers.'

'Those Maleviches will be round any minute. My God, how thrilled they'd be, if they only knew what was going on.'

'Their dream come true.'

They listen to the piano. Kolya had finished his scales and is on to the arpeggios. He's playing much too loudly. His technique is really growing strong, Anna thinks. The notes are perfectly even and he doesn't hesitate at all.

'Do you think he could go to a conservatoire?' asks Andrei.

She smiles, hearing in his voice the naive respect of a man who doesn't know much about music and to whom a boy playing well seems extraordinary. 'No. He's not good enough for that. Maybe if he'd started earlier . . . But he didn't have that kind of drive. Or maybe I didn't push him.'

Then it starts: the banging on the wall.

Thud, thud, thud. They'll keep it up now until Kolya stops playing.

'We'll have to tell him to stop.'

'In a minute.'

They're so close, covered by the cascade of notes, Anna in his arms, the baby inside Anna. But his skin prickles. Those Maleviches won't give up. Thud, thud, thud. It feels as if they're inside the room.

'It'll be all right,' he says.

'I know. I'll talk to Kolya tomorrow night.'

'Don't tell him too much.'

'I'll have to explain, or he'll refuse to leave.'

'He'll know we wouldn't ask him to unless it was important.'

Anna laughs. 'Andryusha, he's only sixteen.'

'He's not a child any more.'

That night they lie awake, not talking, not touching, each intensely aware of the other's wakefulness. At about two in the morning she murmurs, 'I'm getting up for a while,' and clambers out of bed. She goes to the window, and pulls the curtain aside. There is a moon, high up in a clear sky. She opens the inner window, and then the outer. A flood of cold air enters the room, and she pulls her dressing-gown around her. She leans forward. Out of the darkness there comes a gull's cry. The bird must be circling high above, his wings sailing through the night. Another gull answers harshly.

'I didn't know gulls flew at night,' Anna murmurs.

The noise of traffic and the background roar of the city has died away almost to silence. Not quite; never quite. There's always the far-off rattle of a train, or footsteps, or a van driving fast down deserted streets until it stops in front of a particular building, and four men jump out —

Anna shivers. *Don't be stupid,* she tells herself. *Listen, there's no traffic. All the apartments are sleeping.*

'Aren't you coming back to bed?'

'In a minute.'

'You'll get cold.'

'It's a beautiful night. Not a breath of wind, and there's such a moon. If I didn't have work tomorrow I'd get up and go for a walk.'

'I suppose we could, if you really wanted to.'

'You'd fall asleep in your clinic. I get so tired, anyway, I daren't be any tireder.'

'It's freezing, Anna. Come back to bed.'

'All right. I'll never sleep now, though.'

But she does, and so does Andrei. The next time he wakes it's about five. He lies still for a while, and then, very softly, he clicks the switch of the dim little bedside light Anna has had since she was a child. Anna is sleeping on her side, facing him, her knees drawn up and her arms crossed. She frowns, as if she has a puzzle to solve in her dreams. He won't go back to sleep now. He'll just lie here, and watch her sleeping. Within her the baby, too, will probably be sleeping.

At six in the morning, the telephone rings. Instantly, as if he's been expecting this all night long, Andrei jumps out of bed, crosses the room, grabs the receiver and lifts it slowly to his ear.

'Alekseyev, Andrei Mikhailovich?'

'Yes.'

'This is a message from Medical Personnel. I am to inform you that, with immediate effect, you are suspended from your duties, pending investigation of serious irregularities —'

'But, but —'

'You are required to hold yourself available for investigatory interview without notice. You are not permitted to enter hospital precincts during the period of investigation.' The line clicks. The caller has rung off, leaving behind a singing, listening silence.

'Andrei, what is it?' Anna is bolt upright in bed, pale and frightened.

'It was a call from the hospital.' He swallows. 'They are suspending me from duty.'

'What?' Anna cries.

'You heard me. Hush, you'll wake Kolya.'

'You mean — just like that? But, Andrei, it's only six o'clock. There can't be anyone in the offices at this time.'

Andrei does not reply.

'Andryusha, sit down, you look awful. I'll make some tea. Oh no, there's Kolya.'

The door opens and Kolya's face peers round it.

'What's the matter? Why were you shouting? Who was that on the phone?'

'It's nothing. Go back to sleep.'

He hesitates, looking from one to the other of them, his face sharpening. 'Is somebody dead?'

'Of course nobody's dead, go back to sleep. I'll wake you at quarter to seven. It was just a call from work for Andrei.'

'You don't look like that when it's just a call from work.'

'He's not a child,' Andrei says. 'He's going to have to know.'

Now Anna looks from one to the other. Andrei is grey with shock. Kolya is frowning, not yet sure whether to challenge them or not. She goes over to Kolya, and puts her arm around his shoulders. He's taller than her now, and she has to reach up. He smells like a man. When he was little and he woke up in the mornings, even his breath would be sweet.

'All right, Kolya, get dressed quickly now, and use the bathroom first. No one else will be in there yet. I need to talk to Andrei. I'll explain everything to you later.'

'Why not now?'

'Kolya, please. I need you to help me.'

'It was a call from the hospital,' says Andrei. 'They are suspending me from my duties. You understand what that means?'

Kolya looks from Andrei to Anna. 'You mean, you can't go into the hospital?'

'That's right. They are holding an investigation.'

'Did one of the patients die, is that why they're suspending you? But it won't have been your fault!' cries Kolya, in a burst of instinctive loyalty that makes Andrei's eyes sting.

'You're right,' says Anna. 'He did nothing wrong. It's — you know — political. I'll tell you in a minute. Go on and use the bathroom now.'

He nods silently, and asks no more questions. Andrei was right, he's not a child any more and shouldn't be treated like one. She turns back to Andrei, and out of the corner of her eye sees Kolya slip past with clumsy, silent tact, on his way out to the bathroom on the landing.

'Andrei, Andryusha, my darling, don't look like that —'

'It's my fault, Anna. I should have listened to Lena and to you.'

'You couldn't have avoided it.'

'But now all this has come down on you. I'll never forgive myself.'

'You've got nothing to blame yourself for. Maybe the suspension will only last for a few days. Volkov just wants to lash out at someone. You must drink some tea. Eat something. I shan't go to work, I'll stay with you.'

'No, you should go. Everything's got to seem normal. You go to work and Kolya must go to school. Tonight we'll arrange everything, and tomorrow you take him down to Galya's.'

'Do you think it's safe to wait a day?'

'Yes. You'd better get ready, Anna, or you'll be late.'

The morning routine shapes itself almost as usual except that Andrei sits unshaven in a chair by the window. Anna washes, dresses, drinks her tea with extra sugar because she cannot face eating, and collects her things.

'Are you sure you'll be all right? I can call in sick.'

'No.'

'I think you should call people to find out what's going on. How about Gerasimov? Or Maslov, he's always given you wonderful references. They might know what's happening.'

'I can't talk to them on the phone, Anna.'

'You mean the phone —'

'There's no point in putting other people at risk.'

'You're always saying that Lena knows everything that goes on.'

'I can't involve her.'

'So everyone else has to be protected, while they set you up as the scapegoat for the whole hospital!'

'It's not like that. Go to work, Anna. You'll be late.'

The door bangs, and she's gone. A quarter of an hour later, Kolya leaves, after lingering awkwardly by the door and blurting out, 'Sure you'll be all right?'

'Of course I'm sure. Try to concentrate in maths for once, Kolya, your last test results were very poor,' snaps Andrei.

Kolya shrugs, mutters something under his breath, and disappears. Heaven knows how much Anna's told him. He heard their whispered, rushed voices coming from Kolya's room. He should have explained it all to Kolya himself, but he just couldn't.

He couldn't face it. The humiliation is too raw. To be suspended, as if he'd pawed a woman patient, or killed someone. The sound of the telephone voice still raps in his ears. He didn't even argue, just bleated, 'But, but —' like a naughty schoolboy. *You are suspended from your duties, pending investigation of serious irregularities —'* Everyone in the hospital will know about it soon. His real friends will be shocked. He has decent colleagues who will be concerned for him as well as for themselves, but there are others who will make haste to separate themselves from him as fast as they can. They'll find the 'correct response to the situation', which usually seems to be pretending that the person who is in trouble has never existed at all.

What will Lena think, or Sofya?

He can't remember an idle morning like this, on his own, without Anna. He should be swinging through the double doors of Rheumatology by now. He should be scanning his clinic lists. There's so much to do that you never have quite enough time to do it. Frustration boils up in him. Who will see to his patients? Everyone will do their best to fill the gaps but no one will gun for that sanatorium bed for Tanya, or make sure that little Lyova gets included in a promising clinical trial.

He must write notes. Surely he can telephone with instructions, if it's a clinical matter? *'You are suspended from your duties, pending investigation of serious irregularities —'*

He gets up and begins to walk about the apartment, clenching his fists. A good long walk, that's what he needs. *'You are required to hold yourself available for investigatory interview without notice.'* If they phone again, and he isn't here, what would that mean?

He'll make tea. Where does Anna keep the things? No, what he would really like is a drink. A shot of that vodka they get out only when there are visitors. *'Not only was Dr Alekseyev under suspension, but he was also noticeably under the influence.'* That certainly wouldn't do. Besides, he doesn't like drinking in the daytime. It blunts your reactions. You can't risk it as a doctor, although of course there are those who do. But they are not suspended from duty, pending investigation.

He should have let Anna stay home with him. They should be together. Or perhaps that is completely wrong. Perhaps the only way to save her is for them to be quite separate. He should go off somewhere, far away. She should say that she threw him out because she was so ashamed of having a husband who had to be investigated. Yes, the example of Pavlik Morozov was the one for Anna to follow. Let her denounce him.

Anna would never do that. Going away would solve nothing; it would only make things worse.

They will all know by now. He stops pacing and slumps back in the chair. It's ten o'clock. He looks at the telephone, but it doesn't ring. Kolya will go to Galya's dacha, Anna will keep on working, and I'll do what? Wait. Just wait. Is it possible that there's going to be day after day like this?

Suddenly the thought comes to him, as clear and bright as if it had been written on the wall for him to read: *I could kill myself, and then it would all be over. Anna and Kolya would be safe.*

A fly buzzes, trapped between the inner and outer windows. How did it get there? Oh yes, when Anna opened the window in the night. It's twelve o'clock, which means that he's been sitting here for two hours.

People don't come to arrest you in the middle of the day. Anna will be eating lunch with the children. It's a very important part of their social education. They learn to eat with their knives and forks, they learn to wash their hands carefully beforehand, to cut up their food and to chew with their mouths closed. They have conversations. Anna says that sometimes these are so funny that she has to jump up and fetch the water jug, so they won't see her laugh. If she laughs, they always want to know why.

He finds that he's smiling. He can almost hear the children's shrill voices and the clatter of the crockery as they pursue a carrot around their plates, and learn to 'cut it up nicely'. Anna has described the scene so often that he feels as if he's been there. *They sound just like a flock of little birds.*

What should he be doing? Perhaps he should write down everything that happened, in order, clearly, so that he can set the record straight. Make a case history of it, as he's been trained. If only he knew what was best. Brodskaya has almost certainly been suspended too, if not worse. If they arrest her and take her in for questioning, who knows what might happen. She might say anything, if they put enough pressure on her. They'll know what they want to get out of her.

He told Gorya he would come in and see him today. God knows what they'll tell the boy now. Nothing, perhaps, because he's already so ill. They may just let him think that Dr Alekseyev forgot about him. Couldn't be bothered.

He's like one of those cartoon characters who run over the side of a cliff and then keep running on empty air.

No, he won't kill himself. He doesn't know how he could have imagined it was even possible. He could never do that to Anna. Protect her! It would destroy her.

He won't make things easy for Volkov. *'Of course, Alekseyev killed himself once he suspected that his criminal conspiracy was about to be unmasked.'* He won't give him that.

Anna is home early, laden with shopping as usual.

'You shouldn't carry so much.'

'I'm pregnant, not ill. Look at this boiling fowl — nearly as plump as a roasting bird, don't you think? Usually they're such scraggy old things. And a good price too.' Her eyes search his face. 'Did you go out?'

'No.'

'You're right, perhaps better not, in case they call again. As soon as I'd gone this morning, I knew I should have stayed. I should have been with you. I'll just unpack the shopping —'

'For heaven's sake sit down and rest for a minute. The shopping can —'

The bell rings. They freeze, then Anna says, her voice carefully steady, 'I expect Kolya's forgotten his key again.'

They both know that when Kolya forgets his key, he bangs on the door, and shouts for Anna. The bell rings again, a long impatient peal.

'I'd better open it.'

'No, I will.'

Andrei goes to the apartment door, and opens it. In the dim light of the landing he sees a single figure. Heat rushes through his body. Only one. It's all right. The shadowy figure resolves itself into a boy of about fourteen, holding a bunch of flowers.

'Dr Alekseyev?'

'Yes.'

'Flowers for you.' The boy thrusts the bunch at him.

'Oh — thank you. Is there a note?'

'No, just the flowers.' The next moment the boy is away, clattering down the stairs. Andrei goes back into the apartment, and closes the door, frowning. He stares at the flowers as if they have nothing to do with him.

'Roses!' says Anna. 'How beautiful. Who's sending us flowers?'

'I don't know. There isn't a note.'

There are four yellow roses, and a mass of dark foliage and fern, tightly and skilfully wrapped, as flowers are wrapped in winter to protect them from the frosts.

'I'll put them in water,' says Anna. 'It's strange though, isn't it? These are expensive flowers. You'd think someone would have put in a note.' She thinks that probably the flowers are from Julia. It's the sort of thing Julia would do. Carefully she unwraps the paper, taking care not to rip it. It's thick, silvery paper, worth saving. She fetches the scissors and snips through the thick band of string that binds the stems.

The tight bunch relaxes. Anna lays it down and shakes it gently to loosen the flowers from the tangle of foliage without breaking any leaves. As she does so, she glimpses something white, deep down between the stems. A thorn catches on her hand as she reaches in to separate the stems. It's a small envelope. So there was a note after all, so well hidden that you couldn't see it until the bunch was taken apart. She turns it over, but there's nothing written on it.

'Look, Andryusha, there's a note.'

'Why don't you open it?'

Anna hesitates. Why would the note be concealed like that? Julia would flourish Anna's name across the envelope, and tuck it in on top of the flowers. Julia has nothing to hide. All of a sudden the roses look too bright and perfect, and the foliage so dark that it appears sinister. The thorn has pricked her skin. Slowly, as she watches, a bead of blood rises to the surface and holds there without spilling.

She'd better open the note.

Anna blots her finger, and unfolds a small sheet of paper, densely covered with handwriting that she doesn't recognize. She looks for the signature, but there is only a letter: L. The note is not addressed.

'It's not for me, it must be for you,' she says, passing it over without allowing herself to read it.

'For me?'

'Take it.'

The boy has been transferred to Moscow, to the Morozovka. V alleges serious professional irregularities in treatment. They say that B has been arrested. Panic here, people being called in. No news of

R or R. Please don't call me. Be very careful. Burn this. Good luck, L.

The words 'Be very careful' are underlined with a thick, black score of the pen. As if Lena feared that he might miss the most important point. Andrei reads through the note twice, and then holds it out to Anna. 'It's from Lena,' he says.

'From Lena!'

Anna reads the note without comment, and refolds it. 'You'd better burn it straight away,' she says. 'She took a risk, with her children.'

Andrei lights a match, holds the note over the ashtray and sets fire to a corner of it. Flame races up the paper, and he drops it, still burning. Soon nothing remains but a frail, curled sheet of ash.

'Wash it down the sink,' says Anna. 'We can keep the flowers, I suppose.'

He rinses the sink and the ashtray until there is no trace of burnt paper.

'It reminds me of those stories they used to tell us in school, about anti-Soviet spies and agitators,' remarks Anna. 'They were always burning notes and writing in invisible ink. And then some brave young Pioneer would unmask them.'

'My God,' says Andrei, not hearing what

she says, 'if it's true that they've arrested Brodskaya —'

' "R or R" — who does she mean? Russov must be one, I suppose?'

'Retinskaya's the other, the radiographer. She transferred to Moscow too, with Russov. There's something going on between them, apparently.'

'If they question Brodskaya, and she says something about you . . .' says Anna in a low voice.

'Brodskaya's not that type.'

'Everyone is that type, if things are bad enough.'

They look at each other in silence. What she's said is true, Andrei knows. Brodskaya hasn't got children, but she's got her old mother. All they would have to do is threaten to arrest the mother as well. But not everyone gives way, even so. Brodskaya is tough. Besides, what the hell is she supposed to confess to, anyway? A conspiracy to cause the cancer to metastasize? What kind of 'professional irregularities' are there supposed to have been?

The worst thing is that he's left in a fog, not knowing. He can't ring any of his colleagues. Lena thinks the phone's not safe. *Please don't call me.* She's probably right.

What if he just went to work tomorrow,

and walked right into Admin and demanded to know what was going on? He's got nothing to hide. He has no reason to skulk at home like a criminal.

'I am to inform you that, with immediate effect, you are suspended from your duties, pending investigation of serious irregularities —'

Suspended; left hanging. They've arrested Brodskaya, but not him, although he was involved with the Volkov boy before Brodskaya was: through him. If it hadn't been for Andrei, she would never have become Gorya's surgeon. He wonders what Brodskaya is thinking now. Why should she protect Andrei? If it weren't for him, she'd still be here in Leningrad, probably working late, calmly busy and on top of things. So many new cases come in each day that there's never quite enough time. You get used to living like that.

'Suspended from your duties, pending investigation.'

'She'll have to shut up her butcher's shop.'

'As soon as Kolya comes home, I'll tell him about going to Galya's,' says Anna. She is very pale but she appears calm. 'The books, Andrei. We must go through them.'

'What?'

'And my father's papers as well, just in

case there's anything there we overlooked.'

'I thought we took everything down to the dacha.'

'There are always a few things that get missed.'

But not by them, thinks Andrei.

'You know more about the books than I do,' he says. 'You get on with that. I'll cut up the chicken and put it in the pot.'

She looks at him, startled. 'But do you know how to?'

'Of course I do, what do you take me for? I've watched you any number of times. Besides, think of all the dissection I did in training. Don't bother with my text books, though, Anna, there's nothing in them.'

'Remember to take out the gizzards. And then cover the meat with water, and add pepper and one of those bunches of herbs I dried last year. It won't be long before we can pick fresh ones again.'

He laughs.

'What are you laughing for? I don't know what they taught you in dissection.'

'Quite enough to deal with an old boiling fowl. I could always begin a second career as a butcher.'

She jumps up, puts her arms around his neck, presses herself against him so close that he can feel the new, awkward swell of her belly. He wraps his own arms around her, hugging her hard. Too hard, he knows from her intake of breath, but he can't bear to let go of her.

By the time Kolya gets home from Lev's, so late that he's almost genuinely sorry, the living room is full of the rich smell of chicken soup. Books and papers cover the floor.

'Whatever are you doing, Anna? You say my room's a mess, but this is like a war zone.'

'Kolya, come and sit down, we need to talk to you . . .'

15

'But you must be careful cycling now, in your condition,' says Galya, handing a glass of tea to Anna. 'Your sense of balance won't be as good. I was delighted when I got your letter about the baby. Your mother would have been so happy.'

'I know.'

'It's always been my dream to stay here all winter. I'm tired of the city,' says Galya.

'But isn't it very lonely?'

'No. There are a few of us old full-time dacha-dwellers, you know. We look after each other. At least, I hope we do! This is my first winter, so I'll find out. There'll be snow soon. My barometer's dropped right down.'

'It won't snow today, surely?'

'I don't think so, but it's on its way. Drink your tea, and then you must get going. Don't worry about Kolya. He'll be fine with me. He's got his school books with him, hasn't he?'

'Yes,' says Anna, smiling slightly as she recalls Kolya's indignant disbelief when she'd told him that even at times like these, his exams still mattered.

'I can help him with science and maths, although I daresay they do everything differently these days. It'll be good to have a young man about the place, to chop the wood and keep the stove going. He seems like a worker.' Kolya's outside, digging over Galya's potato patch so that the frosts can break up the earth. He'd volunteered, to Anna's surprise. 'He'll earn his keep, that boy,' says Galya with a smile.

'I have to tell you, he doesn't do that much at home.'

'He will here,' says Galya with easy certainty. 'You know what they're like.' Galya had only one son, who died in the war. She and her husband divorced long ago. 'I shall enjoy the company.'

'I hope it won't be for too long. As soon as all this is over —'

'You don't need to explain, Anna. Anyway, it's best if you don't. Kolya's the son of one of my dearest friends, that's all I need to know, and he's going to stay here until his health improves. Country air, plenty of exercise . . . it'll do him the world of good.

And naturally you brought him to me, given that I'm a doctor and well qualified to keep a close eye on him.'

'I don't know how to thank you, Galya.'

The older woman bats this away with her hand. 'Look after yourself. I'll make sure Kolya's all right. It might be a bit dull for him, but he can always do some work.' She laughs. 'He'll pass all his exams with top marks.'

'That's not really Kolya. Oh dear, I hope he doesn't miss the piano too much.'

'It wasn't you either, if I remember. You were always drawing when you were meant to be studying.'

'I used to dread my mother reading my reports.'

'My dear child, if your mother could see the way you're living your life, she'd be so proud of you.'

Anna wipes her eyes with the back of her hand. 'Anything makes me cry these days,' she says apologetically.

'It's because you're pregnant. I was the same. Especially anything sad to do with children.'

'I must go. I need to get back before dark.'

On her way out, Anna slips an envelope on to the table. Galya isn't well off, with only her pension, and Kolya eats so much.

Now to say goodbye to him. She straightens her shoulders and lifts her head, ready to smile.

It won't be dark for a while yet. She has just enough time to go to their own dacha, and bury the diaries and sketchbooks she's brought with her. Neither Andrei nor Kolya knows about this. She sent Kolya out to the kiosk to buy some smoked sausage, asked Andrei to take down the rubbish, and then quickly dismantled the secret hiding place, cramming everything into her two saddle-bags. She had nothing to wrap the papers in this time, but she remembered that there was an oilcloth on the table in the dacha. It would be a terrible waste, but it would do.

The dacha is dark and quiet. It looks as if it has taken up its own winter life, which has nothing to do with her. There is no feeling of welcome. All the leaves have fallen and the ground is covered with them, some rotting and some still fresh. There are a few leeks left in the vegetable plot, and she pulls them up. She will dig down here, and then replant them.

Anna fetches her spade. Slowly and carefully, she begins to dig, piling the earth beside the hole. It needs to be deep. The earth is heavy with autumn rain, and the top layer is already frosted. The spade slices down into it, but turning the earth is hard. There's a gust of wind and a few last birch leaves scatter down, bright as coins. Surely the hole is deep enough now. She spreads out the oilcloth and opens her saddlebags. There are her father's diaries. The 'Marina notebook' is on top, and then there are Anna's sketchbooks and all the loose drawings. She'll have to fold the drawings. Later on, if there's ever a right time to recover them, she can get rid of the creases somehow.

Place them all right in the middle of the oilcloth. Fold it over once, and then the other way. Tuck the corners right over, and fold again.

When she has made her parcel, Anna gets out a ball of string and ties the bundle securely, wrapping the string over and over so that it won't come apart. It still doesn't seem enough. The rain will seep in, and then the frost. What else can she do to protect everything?

She gets up, goes inside the dacha and starts searching, but there is so little there. She opens cupboards and peers into drawers. Nothing that's any good.

She'll try the shed where they keep their tools. An axe, a fork, a hoe, a rake, several buckets, rows of plant pots. Labels. And there, thrust into the darkest corner behind the ladder, she sees a pile of old sacks.

Perhaps she could hide the oilcloth parcel under the sacks. It would be dry there. Surely no one will go through the contents of the shed.

Anna bends down and lifts a sack. She gives a cry, and stumbles back, hitting her head on the rake that hangs from the wall. Pin-like squeaks come from a nest in the sacking. Ratlings, naked and squirming. My God, the mother will be somewhere about. A rat with young will fly at your throat. Anna backs towards the light of the shed's doorway. As soon as she's out she slams the door and bolts it. There's no using the sacks, then. She'll have to clear out the nest and the adult rats as soon as possible. She can borrow a dog from the farm. But not now. She knows she ought to kill the ratlings but can't bring herself to do it.

The oilcloth will have to be enough. Anna crouches and reaches down into the hole, gripping the parcel of notebooks, sketch-books and drawings. She doesn't want to throw them down there. She ought to have fetched one of the sacks to kneel on. Never mind, she can brush the dirt off. Anna kneels. The thickening of her body keeps taking her by surprise. She feels clumsy and unlike herself. Never mind. There, the parcel lies flat at the bottom of the hole. She presses it down as if putting it to bed.

Now to cover it. And quick, it's getting late. She keeps glancing behind her, although there's no one there. She can't understand why she feels so frightened. She stands, and picks up her spade. The handle is cold and heavy, and she is very tired. Hurriedly, she shovels the earth back into the hole, stamps it down and spreads the last few spadefuls carefully over the surrounding area so that the site of the hole is concealed. Smooth it all down a bit. Good. And now for the leeks.

One by one, she eases them back into the earth, and then presses down the soil around them. It still looks darker and fresher than the surrounding plot. She stares down at it for a moment, dissatisfied, then goes across to the little grove of young lilac and birch, and gathers up an armful of fallen leaves. Returning, she scatters leaves all over the disturbed soil. There, that looks more natural. If Galya's right, and there's snow in the next day or so, everything will be hidden.

Her father's words are buried, just as he was buried. *If they rot too, there'll be nothing.*

But I can't think of that now. I must get home.

Suddenly she remembers. It was like this the last time she came here alone and frightened. The dacha was deserted. She kept glancing round then too, because the Germans were coming. She knew how close they were but it didn't stop her. She went on heaving onions and potatoes out of the earth, so that she could take them back to the city. What she couldn't take with her she smashed into the soil, so that the Germans would never be nourished by them.

It had been a risk, but it had paid off.

She shakes her head to rid it of the memory. Trying not to look as if she's in a hurry, she puts away the spade — propping it just inside the door of the dacha, because she doesn't want to open that shed again — and buckles her saddlebags back on to her bike. Galya's right, it's much colder. The sky has changed. It is heavy and yellow with a weight of coming snow. Anna pauses, staring intently at the clouds, judging the wind, which has suddenly got up and is chasing the last leaves. It's all right, she'll get home before the snow falls. She wheels her bike down the path, and looks back one last time. A plot of earth, covered in leaves. She has scuffed out all her footprints. The leeks look as if they've been growing there all the time, forgotten, their leaves already dark with frost.

As soon as she reaches the track she gets on her bike and starts to pedal away, much faster than she should, over the bumpy ground. She looks neither to right nor left, but straight ahead. She doesn't look back.

16

You can get used to anything. A new pattern emerges, in which Anna gets up a little later, because there's no Kolya to be chivvied out of bed and off to school. Andrei rises at the same time, and goes through the routine of washing, dressing, drinking tea and eating porridge. He doesn't shave. He hasn't shaved for three days now. Anna detests the stubble but she says nothing. Andrei is working on a letter that sets out his position, explains in detail his handling of Gorya Volkov's case (approved and agreed by Admin at every stage), and demands reinstatement. He refuses to call this letter an appeal. No specific accusation has been made against him. It's a professional matter, that's all. A misunderstanding which will be cleared up once the facts are known.

He's at his desk before she leaves for work, with his pen and a pile of books and papers beside him. She kisses him and he looks up, distracted for a moment.

They've stopped him from being a doctor. With one phone call they have ripped through the fabric of Andrei's life. Her heart clenches with pity and fury. Andrei, who walked to the hospital along freezing, deserted streets all through the siege, to give whatever medical help could be given. He never flinched. He improvised, made do, eked out the pitiful stock of drugs. He believed it was his duty to be there, even when all he could do was unwind a baby's wrappings, and tell the mother to chafe its hands and feet and put it inside her clothes, against her bare skin, so it could share her warmth. And lie down, conserve your energy, drink water, give your milk a chance.

He was there when a father with wild, staring eyes rushed into the clinic. *'It's my little girl. The bakery wall collapsed when we were going for our rations. Her leg's trapped, you've got to come.'* He knew what it was like to kneel in the snow where the child's blood was already congealing as it spilled, and help to lift the mess of shattered brick and mortar off her. She survived, that child.

It was Andrei they were attacking, who'd supervised the boiling of pine needles to make a remedy against scurvy, who'd operated by candlelight on blast injuries, who'd directed infants who had a chance of survival to the feeding stations. They were like one body then, those who were still alive and on their feet. Fourth-year med students, junior doctors, professors, they were equals as they battled through the lines of patients. People came to hospital not so much in hope of a cure, as not to die alone. The corridors were full of the dead. Doctors, nurses, cleaners, physiotherapists, radiographers all struggled to keep the stoves alive. It was no time for hierarchies and protocol.

He'd thought the world would change after all that, just a little. People would remember what they'd suffered and how they'd got through it. In the years of the Terror their human feelings had been suffocated by fear and distrust, but those feelings were still there, alive, like fire sleeping under a crust of earth. People had helped one another during the siege; not all the time, perhaps, but even in the most extreme circumstances they hadn't just survived as animals do. Some, maybe — the cannibals whose eyes had lost all humanity, sunk in the gloss of their flesh. But they were a small number. They were real, but they were not the true story. He'd seen people make sacrifices for one another that he would never forget. A cube of bread or a pannikin with soup in it, taken home from the canteen instead of swallowed. The offer of a share of the wood from a chopped-up bookcase. These things may not sound much now, but in those days they were life instead of death. People wouldn't forget. *Things will be better, Anna,* he said, at the worst times. *When all this is over they're bound to be a little better.*

Things will be better, Anna, they're bound to be . . . She remembers his words and the iron smell of cold and death in their apartment. Did she believe him then? Probably not. She was less optimistic, perhaps.

There hasn't been a second phone call. No letter; no further communication from the hospital. They have dropped Andrei into silence, she thinks, to see if he breaks it and what he says. None of his other colleagues has been in touch. Well, that was what happened. Lena took the risk but you couldn't expect it. Anna remembers what that's like. People didn't come to see her father, except when they were sent to try to persuade him of the error of his ways. Even then they were sweating. Her father was lucky. They stopped him from publishing, they denigrated his writing and called him in for reprimand, but he was never arrested. Looking back, she finds it almost incredible that

338

he could have survived in those times, when so many were destroyed.

Yes, he could be called lucky, but all the same it hollowed him out, like drops of water falling repeatedly on his heart. Shame, isolation, abandonment. She never used those words then. She became impatient with him, and sometimes even angry. Why couldn't he make the best of it? She hadn't understood her father; not really. He turned inward on himself, and although she never said a word she criticized him in her heart.

She'd been a good daughter. She'd gone to work, she'd taken care of Kolya, she'd cleaned the apartment, shopped and prepared the food. She'd grown their vegetables and fruit at the dacha. All these things had been done and she'd found pleasure in them. As far as she can remember she never complained to her father. He had his tea, his books, his papers, his thoughts.

But it wasn't enough. She hadn't wanted to enter his inner world, because she was afraid of it, as a child is afraid of a gloomy forest. She'd left him to wander in it alone.

When she was little she used to believe that the dead could see all the thoughts of the living. She doesn't believe it now. She has to fight not to see the clenched, frozen flesh of her father, as hard as a board.

■ ■ ■ ■

Yesterday Andrei said, 'I've had enough of this. How long do they think I'm going to sit here like an idiot? I'm going in. If there's an investigation going on, I should be part of it. I shall demand to see Ivanov, or Kalinin.'

The room was full of reflected snow light. Full winter had come, quite early. She'd always loved the clarity such light gave to everything. You noticed one leaf hanging from a frozen shrub, or the shape of a child's lips as he threw his snowball and laughed. Stubble sprouted from Andrei's chin. It was darker than the hair on his head.

'Don't,' she said, in her softest voice. 'Don't do that, my darling.'

He shrugged impatiently and flung away from her, towards the window. For a long time he remained standing, looking at the buildings opposite and the floating mass of white roofs that stretched away into the distance. Soon the children would be talking about Father Frost, Anna thought. How quickly the year went round. But all that seemed to be happening in another world, to which she no longer had access.

'You don't need to worry,' he said at last.

'I shan't do anything.'

She looked at his back, and her throat ached. *It won't go on for ever,* she wanted to say. *They'll come to their senses. You're one of their best doctors, everyone knows that.* But she knew it would do no good to say these things aloud. It wouldn't lift his burden; it would just be pretending that the burden was lighter than it was.

She had to go to work. They'd said nothing about Andrei's pay, and she thought it was very likely that he wouldn't be paid from the date of his suspension. They had some savings, which wouldn't last more than a couple of months. Her money was essential. Maybe Morozova was right, and Anna should be fighting for promotion. The main thing was to hold on to her job. It wouldn't be easy if Morozova ever found out that Andrei had been suspended.

She knew all these things and had known them since the moment she woke to see Andrei holding the telephone. Andrei knew them too.

This morning seems a little better. Andrei slept most of the night, and he looks more like himself. She wonders if she should suggest that he shave, then decides against it. She is cooking their porridge when suddenly her head feels strange. A flood of heat comes up in her. The air grows thick with particles. She's about to call for Andrei, but she masters herself, steps back from the stove and draws in a deep breath. Hold it for a moment, release it all the way, and again. She isn't faint, really. She won't sit down or he'll ask what's wrong.

Slowly she stirs the porridge so it won't stick to the pan. Her body has steadied itself. She is fine.

It's because she doesn't want him to look at her too closely that she eats her porridge standing up. He's deep in thought, jotting something in the margins of what he has written. He looks up without seeing the room, then returns to his papers.

'See you later,' she says.

'What?'

'I'm leaving for work.'

He looks up properly this time and smiles at her with that sweetness which she has never seen in another man's smile. 'Of course you are,' he says. 'I wasn't thinking. Are you warm enough? Have you got your shawl on under your coat?'

'I'm fine. The baby keeps me warm. It's like having a little stove inside me.'

'Be careful. Don't slip on the ice.'

'I'll be fine. And you'll be all right?'

'You don't need to worry about me, Anna.

This will all be over soon.'

In spite of the stubble he looks himself again, strong and capable, her Andrei. She smiles with love and relief. 'I'll see you later, then.'

'Of course.'

It's not until the nursery day is over that Irina gets a chance to talk to Anna properly. Anna is anxious to get home, but she's already left on the dot every day this week. She accepts the glass of tea Irina offers, and sits down, arranging her face to look relaxed. She doesn't want anyone — even Irina — guessing there's something wrong.

Irina is fed up: really fed up this time. Her sister has let her down. She's got a steady boyfriend now, which is bad enough given that she's two years younger than Irina. Natasha had suggested that she and Yura and Irina and another boy who's a friend of Yura's go as a foursome to a dance at the Palace of Culture.

'The other boy is supposed to be really nice. He's only twenty-five, but that's not too big an age difference, is it?'

'Three years is nothing,' says Anna.

'But now, would you believe it, he's suggested bringing another girl along as well. She's not his girlfriend, apparently, just someone from work.'

'Well, surely that's all right, then? I mean, if he's still really going to the dance with you and she's just tagging on.'

'That's what he *says,* but you'd have to be a bloody fool to believe it, wouldn't you? He just fancies having two girls for the price of one. And nitwit Natasha goes along with it. She hasn't got the sense she was born with. Besides, she's nicely set up with Yura, so what does she care? I won't go, that's all.'

'You should. You never know what might happen. You could go there with them, and then you might meet someone else. Someone much nicer! No, you really should go, Irinochka. I mean, sitting at home doesn't do any good, does it?'

'True. The only person who comes knocking on my door is our mad old neighbour who's always trying to borrow an egg. *"Just one little eggie, my darlings, and I'll let you have it straight back tomorrow, as sure as I'm standing here."* '

Suddenly Anna remembers the green dress. She promised to let Irina borrow it.

'You could wear that dress I made to your dance.'

'You mean the green one?' asks Irina immediately, and Anna knows she hasn't forgotten the offer for a moment.

'You said you liked it. I'll bring it in tomorrow and you can try it on. We're pretty much the same size — well, we were, anyway.'

Andrei won't want her to lend the dress. She was wearing it that night, at the dance, and then after the dance; the night the baby was conceived. He hates her borrowing or lending clothes. To him, they seem to be part of her, like her skin. She's promised it to Irina, though, and Irina will be careful with it.

'Oh, that'd be lovely,' says Irina, her eyes bright. 'I'll definitely go in that case. Natasha hasn't got anything half as nice, and I bet Miss Gooseberry hasn't either. But are you really sure?'

'Of course I am. Besides, I think that dress is lucky, Irina. It was for me, anyway.'

'Was it? How?'

'I can't really say. It's a bit —' Anna feels herself blush.

'Intimate?' Irina offers, laughing, and Anna laughs too.

'Something like that,' she says.

'Let's hope some of the luck rubs off, then. I could do with a bit of intimate. My God, Anna, you're looking better. You've been miserable as sin for days.'

'Have I?' asks Anna quickly. 'I'm all right. There's nothing wrong.'

Irina stretches, examines her nails and then slides a look at Anna. 'How many years have we been working together?' she asks.

'I'm not sure — five, it must be.'

'Exactly. So I do know a bit about you, and when you come in one day all happy, the way you've been for weeks, because of the baby, and then the next day your face is pinched up and you jump when the door bangs, then I know something's happened. Something bad,' she adds quietly, her eyes intent on Anna's face.

'Irina —'

'Don't worry, I'm not asking questions. I shouldn't think anyone else has noticed. Certainly not our dear leader, the exceptionally brilliant manager of our showcase workplace, because she's one hundred per cent thick about people. Alla's wrapped up in herself, and the others don't know you well enough. The kids notice, though. That little Masha's been hanging off your hand all week, and she was coming on nicely before.'

'You see too much, Irinochka.'

'I always have done. It's very inconvenient. Probably the reason I haven't got a man. Damn it, this nail's cracked. It always happens to me in the cold weather. You haven't got a file, have you?'

Anna rummages in her bag, keeping her head down. 'Here you are,' she says at last.

'Thanks. You look after yourself, Anna. With the baby coming and everything.'

'I'll do my best.'

When Anna gets home from work she is greeted by Andrei, clean-shaven. She presses herself against him, nuzzling his cheeks and drinking in the smell of his skin.

'You're so lovely and smooth.'

'I realized that a beard didn't suit me.'

'Good.'

'Did you have a good day?'

'Not bad. The children are making an igloo. You wouldn't believe the number of skills it teaches them. Spatial awareness, practical mathematics . . . Their mittens get sodden, though, and then they cry. We've got rows of mittens hanging by the stove and they're more or less identical. They're supposed to have their name stitched in but you know how it is. Nobody bothers, no matter how many notices Morozova pins up. I mean, the mothers are all doing overtime and late shifts and God knows what, they haven't the time. And so they were furious at home time about their child getting a pair with a hole in the thumb, and everybody was having rows. And just listen to this. Morozova's latest bright idea is that we should use the experience of making snow bricks to teach the children about the cooperation required for a production line.'

'Well, I suppose it does teach them to cooperate,' he murmurs.

'Of course it does, but why does everything have to happen *for the sake of something else? *Why can't it just happen for its own sake?'

'You'll have to ask Morozova, and I expect she'll have a very good answer.'

'I'm sure she will. She's probably writing it up into a research paper as we speak.'

Beneath their conversation there lies another, shadowy and un-spoken.

Any news?

No, nothing.

Six days now. You'd think at least they'd have sent a letter to confirm the phone call.

They're leaving me to sweat.

There must be something we can do?

I've written another draft of the letter.

Don't send it, Andrei. Please.

All right then, you tell me what I'm supposed to do. Meekly accept that I'm not a doctor any more? Let them take my profession away from me as you take a toy from a child who has

348

misbehaved?

Andrei, please. Please don't get angry with me.

I'm not angry with you. How can you think that?

I'm sorry. I was just tired.

Of course. You've been working all day.

They eat their supper. Lena's roses are on the table, wide open now but scentless. Anna has made vegetable soup with dumplings, and there is sliced sausage on the table. She eats conscientiously, although she isn't hungry. Andrei leaves half his soup. He should go out for a walk at least, she thinks. Surely that wouldn't matter. No wonder he has no appetite, stuck in like this all day long.

'Shall we go out for a while after supper?' she asks. 'Just for a breath of air?'

He looks at her, surprised. 'But you're tired,' he says. 'You've been on your feet all day.'

'I wouldn't mind a little walk. Have you been out today?' She asks the question casually as she gathers up the plates.

'No.'

She goes over the telephone message in her mind, for the thousandth time. She asked Andrei to tell her every single word that was said. He is trained to remember such things, from years of listening to symptoms before he forms a diagnosis.

'This is a message from Medical Personnel. I am to inform you that, with immediate effect, you are suspended from your duties, pending investigation of serious irregularities. You are required to hold yourself available for investigatory interview without notice. You are not permitted to enter hospital precincts during the period of investigation.'

Available without notice. Clearly that meant there would be no appointment made beforehand, and no warning given; but did it also mean that Andrei had to sit beside the telephone day and night? If they went out for just a quarter of an hour, and the telephone rang, then it would ring again, surely?

The caretaker would see them go out. He might be asked about their movements. *They* might say that Andrei had gone out in order to meet someone, or to communicate with someone.

'You're right, I am quite tired after all,' she says slowly. 'Do you know what I'd really like to do?'

'What's that?'

'Just have a quiet evening. Be really lazy. Put my feet up on the sofa and you read to me. Would you mind? You know how I love being read to.'

Andrei smiles. 'Of course I will,' he says. 'What do you fancy? That's right, you lie down. I'll fetch a rug and a pillow.'

She considers what book to choose. 'I'm not sure . . . You know, I think my brain is dissolving with this pregnancy. By the time I get back from work I can barely think.'

Andrei eases a pillow beneath Anna's head. He unfolds the rug and carefully tucks it around her knees and feet.

'How's that?'

'Perfect.'

'I could read you some poetry,' he offers tentatively, and Anna's heart contracts. Andrei is one of those people who doesn't believe that he has the right to read poetry aloud. He remembers her father, a real writer who had Pushkin, Lermontov and Nekrasov by heart, and would recite with every inflection perfect. Even though Anna has never written a word, Andrei believes the inherited gift is hidden in her somewhere.

It's true that he doesn't read aloud particularly well. His voice becomes stilted. His breath comes from his throat, and not his chest. The rhythm of the lines falters. Her father read so well. She remembers the deep, sonorous note in his voice as he recited Lermontov's 'The Dream'. All the same, she is more at ease listening to Andrei's voice than she ever was her father's, once she'd left behind the fairy stories she used to love.

'Do you know, what I really feel like is one of those old stories of Kolya's, from the blue fairy book. "The Mountain King", maybe, or "Little Anastas". You know where it is, on the shelf above his bed. It's the one with gold lettering on the spine.'

'I'll go and have a look.'

She lies back, closes her eyes and listens to his footsteps. Kolya's bed creaks as Andrei puts his weight on it. He'll be kneeling as he scans the shelf. It's the third from the right at the end, she thinks, but she says nothing. In a way it's even nicer when someone you love is just close, in the next room, not actually speaking to you but doing something that will bring him back to you.

It's funny going into Kolya's room these days. The bed is always made. She misses the sound of the piano more than she would have thought possible. You get so used to it. It becomes part of the rhythm of your life.

'Got it,' calls Andrei, and then there's a silence. Idly, Anna wonders what he's doing. She's intensely aware of the rug over her feet, the pillow under her head. The rug prickles a little. They ought to replace it with something newer and softer, but it's good quality. Rugs are expensive. She wonders if there was enough money in the envelope she left on Galya's table. It was all she could afford. She'll send more as soon as she can.

'Here we are,' says Andrei, pulling up a chair to sit by her side.

'What were you doing?'

'Looking at the inscription. I'd forgotten that the book used to be yours.'

'Let me see.'

The inscription is in her mother's handwriting. 'To our dear Anna, from her loving Mama and Father, 7th May 1925.'

'I think it's the only book left that has her writing in it,' says Anna. 'We burned so many books.'

He nods, thinking back to the little stove they had fed with books, in the darkest, coldest days of the winter of '41/2. Anna still has the *burzhuika,* put away 'in case', just as she makes sure there is always a row of jars at the back of her store cupboard, 'for emergencies'. Jam she's made from fruit they grow and berries they gather out at the dacha — wild raspberry, elderberry and blackberry, bilberry, apple jelly. There are pickled cucumbers and dried mushrooms, and always two jars of Sokolov honey. It's all there to be eaten, of course. Anna's not one of those obsessives who fill pillowcases with crusts of black bread. But Andrei has noticed that Anna never opens a jar until she has another ready to replace it.

'Isn't it strange,' says Anna, 'to think of my mother opening that book when it was new, and writing in it.'

'Do you remember getting it?'

'Oh yes. I was about seven. I'd won a small prize for recitation at school. It was only a certificate, but my parents were so pleased that they bought me this book. It was probably the only prize I ever won, but in those days they were still hopeful. My mother was so busy. I was always longing for her to be ill so she could stay at home and I could bring her tea in bed, but of course she never was.'

'Why "of course"?'

'Oh well, she was so strong. Everyone relied on her. I can't remember her taking a day off work until she was pregnant with Kolya.'

He frowns. He's intensely aware of Anna's mother's death, immediately following Kolya's birth. Part of the placenta must have been retained. Maybe the death couldn't have been avoided. She suffered a heart attack after an uncontrolled haemorrhage. Anna's younger, of course, but he's determined that she will have the best obstetrician he can arrange. Andrei will explain the family history. He doesn't want to worry Anna, but a quiet word will do no harm. A doctor who knows he's attending a colleague's wife is bound to take extra care.

A stab of fear goes through him. Who will want to be associated with the birth of his child if he is disgraced? He's hardly surprised that no one except Lena has been in touch with him, but what will Anna do, if she's left alone?

Anna mustn't be frightened.

The book falls open easily, as books do when they've been read dozens of times. 'The Mountain King' is the first story. Andrei clears his throat. He's glad Anna has her eyes closed. He feels self-conscious, reading in front of people. He didn't like it at school. He would never have got a prize for recitation, although he has to admit he got so many prizes in maths, chemistry, biology and physics that his parents took them for granted. If he hadn't won, they'd have wanted to know what was wrong.

' "In the place where night sits on top of

the highest mountain, there dwelt a king who had never been seen with human eyes . . ." '

He reads on. The mountain king is angered because the people who live at the foot of the mountain have forgotten about him and no longer leave fruit and flowers and loaves of fine wheat bread on the lowest slopes. He decides that he will punish them. Very slowly, so slowly that even if you were watching you would never see it, he begins to shrug his giant shoulders. A tiny pebble comes loose from the very top of the mountain. As it skitters down the slope it loosens another pebble, a bigger one, and this pebble loosens another, until the sides of the mountain echo with the rumbling of boulders chasing one another down the steep valleys, smashing into trees, hurtling across rivers, gathering speed until they . . .

' "Until they reached the shepherd's hut where the shepherd was sleeping while his daughter guarded the flock on the mountain pasture . . ." ' recites Anna.

'Who's reading this? "And then the mightiest of all the boulders smashed into the walls of the hut and sent them spinning down the mountainside until there was no piece of wood left that was bigger than a matchstick. But the shepherd, who was sleeping, was thrown high into the air on his mattress of straw." '

Anna shifts restlessly under her rug. 'Don't go on, Andrei. I don't want to hear any more.'

'But Kolya used to love this bit. Anyway, the shepherd isn't killed.'

'I know, and he finds his little daughter alive because she's been playing in a cave instead of looking after the sheep. He clears away the stones from the entrance with his bare hands.'

'So it's a happy ending, what's wrong with that?'

'How about the sheep?'

'What?'

'Do they get crushed to death?'

Andrei skims the pages. 'It doesn't say anything about the sheep.'

'How about the people who lived at the bottom of the mountain, when the boulders came hurtling down on top of them?'

'No, nothing about them either.'

Anna opens her eyes. 'Funny, isn't it, all I used to care about was the shepherd and his daughter. I suppose it was because they were the main characters. Maybe that's the moral: you can't care about everybody.'

'It's just a children's story, Anna.'

'I know. Sorry. Doesn't it seem odd without Kolya playing the piano?'

'Not to the Maleviches.'

'I hope he's getting on all right.'

'I'm sure he is.'

'At least he's old enough to understand why it's all happening.'

'He'll be fine, Anna. I expect he's glad to miss some school.'

'D'you think it would be all right to write to him?'

'Maybe not just yet. Let things settle down a bit first.'

Suddenly, without warning, a terror which she hasn't felt in years seizes on Anna. Her hair is parted by icy fingers. Her skin crawls. Her heart pounds in her throat, suffocating. 'Andrei!'

'What is it? Are you ill?'

'Andrei, I don't feel too good.'

'Lie still. Don't move. Have you got a pain?'

'No, it's not that. Hold me a minute.'

He kneels beside her, awkwardly, and gathers her to him. 'You're not bleeding? No cramps or anything like that?'

'No. It was just a horrible feeling. It's going already.'

She won't tell him any more, not a word. Things are bad enough as it is. It won't help for her to blurt out that she felt as if someone were standing over her with a hammer in his hand, ready to smash it into her temples. And that his face was unemotional as he looked at her carefully, judging the best and most vulnerable spot.

'I'm all right now,' she says. 'Hold me tight. Tighter than that.'

'I don't want to hurt you.'

'You won't hurt me.'

He shifts position, easing her into his arms. 'There, is that better?' He feels her nod. Freeing a hand, he begins to stroke her hair. 'You and the baby, that's all that matters.' He feels *And Kolya* start in her, but she says nothing aloud. 'There, there,' he says, jogging her slightly, rocking her in his arms. 'It's all right. Don't worry, my darling, I'll make sure you're all right.'

17

Andrei lies awake, listening for cars. There are few at this time, because it's almost two in the morning. He hasn't been able to sleep. No wonder, given that he's had no exercise. He thinks of getting up, but it would wake Anna. She is deeply asleep, turned away from him, breathing softly and evenly.

He lies on his back, stretched, rigid. He thinks of the letter. He has written draft after draft, and destroyed each of them. Anna thinks it would be madness to send a letter. He thinks she's probably right, and yet he can't stop planning the paragraphs in his head. In part of his mind he can't get rid of the picture of Volkov reading his letter.

And then what, you fool? He reaches for the telephone and calls you to say that he understands you were only trying to do what was best for his boy?

Anna murmurs in her sleep. She doesn't sound upset, or anxious. Just as if she's talking to someone about something perfectly ordinary.

Anna had insisted that he burn the drafts, just as they'd burned Lena's letter. She said he could commit to memory everything that he wanted to say. It would be safer. He thought she was mistaken, but he went along with it. He didn't want to distress her now.

Another car, going fast down the empty street. He listens, as if the walls of the building are a skin through which he's trying to catch a pulse. It's coming closer. It must have turned into their street. Suddenly, there is a sound of brakes. Not a screech, but brakes being applied firmly. It sounds too big to be just a car.

Andrei slides out of bed and puts on his dressing-gown in the dark. He feels under the bed for the slippers Anna made for him last winter. They haven't drawn the curtains round the bed, with Kolya away.

He hears doors slam. They don't care who they wake. The caretaker will have to open up for them.

He takes a deep breath. His heart is pounding and his thoughts race. The caretaker will open up and then they'll all climb the stairs to the apartment. That's how it happens, everybody knows. The caretaker is witness to the arrest.

Is there anything he should hide? No. They've got rid of everything hat could possibly be compromising. Anna is still asleep. Should he wake her? No. He should get dressed. No, there isn't time. He doesn't want them to find him half naked, struggling into his clothes. Fortunately he went to the toilet only an hour ago.

He listens for sound from the depths of the building. Yes. The caretaker has opened up for them. It's happening, now. Andrei reaches for the switch of the bedside lamp. In its dim light he sees Anna motionless, curled in on herself. He must wake her before they do.

'Anna,' he says, and shakes her gently by the shoulder. 'Anna, my darling.'

She stirs, and mutters a protest.

'Anna!'

He feels her go rigid under his hand. She is awake instantly. Just as instantly, she knows what's happening. She twists round and the pupils of her eyes contract as her face fills with horror.

'I think it's them,' he says.

'Oh my God.'

Yes, the caretaker has let them in. They're

coming up the stairs. Several pairs of boots, heavy, tramping. They don't care who they wake. *They're on the first floor now,* he thinks.

'I can't hear anything,' says Anna.

'Here's your dressing-gown. Cover yourself up.'

Seconds pass. He finds he's staring at the alarm clock. It's just after ten past two.

'What can we do? Andrei, they're coming!'

He leans forward, cups her face in his hand. The footsteps are growing louder and he knows from her face that she can hear them too. They aren't hurrying. They know they don't have to.

'Remember what we agreed,' he says. 'Go straight to the dacha. You must keep out of sight. Tell the nursery you have a threatened miscarriage and you've been told to stay in bed.'

The boots stop. They are still on the stairs, not at the apartment door. For a second Anna's mind floods with hope. They are not coming here. They are after someone else.

'It will only be an investigation,' he tells her. 'Don't be frightened.'

'You must put on your warmest clothes,' she answers.

They hear a shouted order, and the boots come to their door. Anna is already out of bed, and as if by instinct she pulls the covers over and straightens them, so that the men won't see into their bed. She hasn't time to pull the curtains round.

It's not so much knocking as thumping on the door. Probably with the side of a clenched fist, thinks Andrei, as he goes to the entrance.

'Just a moment,' he calls, as if it's any ordinary neighbour in the middle of the night.

'Open up!' shouts a voice, as if they can't hear him unlocking the door. Andrei braces himself, and opens up.

There are four men in uniform. Blue caps. An officer and three soldiers. At the side of the door stand the caretaker and his wife in their nightclothes.

'Alekseyev, Andrei Mikhailovich?'

'Yes.'

'We have here a warrant for your arrest.'

There's a pause, and then the officer says impatiently, 'Stand aside,' and in a moment they are all pushing into the apartment, thrusting Andrei in front of them. One of the soldiers takes Andrei by the arm, in a grip that Andrei hasn't felt since he was a boy in trouble at school. Another snaps on all the lights.

Anna stands at the side of the bed. One hand is at her mouth, the other at her breast. He sees her with terrifying clarity, as if he will never see her again. Under the old flannel dressing-gown her body is rounding out with pregnancy. Her eyes are stretched wide with terror.

'Move away from the bed,' the officer tells her sharply, and Anna moves to one side, stumbling slightly but recovering herself quickly, even before Andrei has started forward and then been pulled back by the soldier closest to him.

The men fan out and begin to pull out drawers, rummaging through the contents and then emptying them on to the floor. They go along the bookshelves, picking out some books for examination and dropping others to the floor. They open Marina's trunk and upend it. Marina's red satin slippers skid across the floor. A soldier picks one up, looks inside it, and then drops it with an expression of disgust. They pull clothes out of the cupboards, and throw shoes on top of them. There goes the green dress. One soldier pulls back the bedclothes and then the bottom sheet and the old blanket that covers the mattress.

Of course the mattress is stained, thinks Anna. Everybody's mattress is stained. But she feels a deep blush rise into her face.

'Turn the mattress over,' says the officer,

and two of the soldiers heave the mattress, sweating.

'Get your shoulders under it.'

The mattress flops over. The men beat it perfunctorily, as if they know they will find nothing inside it, but are bound to go through the motions. Once the mattress has been searched they throw it back on to the base. The youngest soldier, forgetting himself, punches the surface flat as he must once have seen his mother do. The caretaker and his wife watch from the door. How sharp their noses look in their pale faces. Neither of them will meet her eyes. What have they said? Have they denounced us? No, they are just frightened. Perhaps they have to sign the warrant as witnesses.

'Sit in that chair,' the officer orders Andrei, 'and you' — gesturing at Anna — 'sit on the bed, there.'

'I need to go the bathroom,' says Anna.

'It is not permitted for anyone to leave the apartment during the search.'

'My wife is pregnant,' says Andrei.

The officer doesn't reply. He looks down at the papers in his hand, frowns, shrugs, then in a loud, dramatic voice he orders, 'Search the other room!'

They leave the door between the rooms wide open. They throw Kolya's mattress on the floor. Books are tossed from the shelves with hardly a glance. Two of them tip out the chest of Kolya's old toys, which Anna put away years ago 'in case', and the sheets and towels she stores in the cupboard above his bed. Meanwhile the third soldier is in the food cupboard, sweeping packets off the shelves, emptying out flour and rice. He's reaching right into the back of the cupboard. He has got hold of her jars. As he pulls it out, Anna sees it's one of the jars of honey. He rips off the top, breaks the wax seal and stabs the honey with a short knife. She gives a cry of protest but Andrei says, 'Anna.' The soldier glances at them before digging his knife deep into the honey and emptying it into the sink. He returns to the cupboard and takes out all the jars. One by one, he tips them into the sink. The jams, the other jar of honey, and now the pickled cucumbers and mushrooms. He works fast, frowning. Another soldier has picked up a few books from Kolya's floor and is slitting their spines and then shaking out the pages. A piece of paper falls out of one and the youngest soldier picks it up.

'What's that?' asks the officer sharply, striding towards him.

'It's a shopping list,' says the boy naively.

'Bring it here.' The soldier tramps into the

living room, holding the paper. The officer studies it at length, frowning and shooting a glance at Anna and Andrei as if to say, *You can't fool me. Shopping list, indeed!* 'Put it aside for full examination with the other articles,' he raps out at last, and the soldier obeys and puts the paper into a box that they must have brought with them, because Anna doesn't recognize it.

There's a crash from Kolya's room. They are pulling the front off the piano. Keys jangle as the men delve into the body of the instrument. The officer goes to look, leaving the young soldier to guard Anna and Andrei. Anna glances up at his face, taking care not to meet his eyes. He's just a boy, she thinks, not much older than Kolya. His face is round and smooth, but he wants to be a man. He won't have been out on many night-fishing expeditions like this yet. He'll want to prove that he's tough, in front of the others. No use asking him for anything. Her bladder hurts, but she can hold on. If she could go to the bathroom she would have a moment to think.

'I expect you feel tired, getting up in the middle of the night like this,' she says to the caretaker's wife.

The young soldier frowns and says gruffly, 'No talking there.'

The officer comes back, but the cacophony inside the piano continues.

'Please ask your men to be careful,' says Anna. 'I can't afford to have the piano repaired.'

He stares at her. She sits upright and looks him in the eye. She's been afraid for so long and now here they are: only people, after all, like the man who stole her sackful of wood during the siege. He thought of killing her; she saw it in his eyes. But she outfaced him and she survived.

They've destroyed all that food for no reason. How could they do it? They even stabbed through a loaf of bread with a knife. But there are four of them and so they look sideways at one another and they carry on. Behind them they know there are hundreds and thousands more, all in their blue caps, all ready.

'If you have nothing to hide, then you have nothing to fear,' says the officer, and then he shouts to the caretaker and his wife, as if they are a hundred metres away instead of standing against the opposite wall, 'You two can clear off now! Be off with you!'

They scuttle off without a backward look. Their part is played. I suppose they were needed as witnesses to Andrei's arrest, thinks Anna. Does that mean I'm not going to be arrested? No, because if they needed they could easily order the caretaker back upstairs again. In a corner of her mind she sees the caretaker and his wife going up and down, up and down, as person after person is arrested. Each time they would open up the doors, each time they would watch, each time they would scuttle away.

Through the open door Anna sees that the piano stool has been upended. All the music has spilled out on to the floor, but there was nothing else to find. Now a soldier is pulling pictures and photographs off the walls, one by one. He lifts each one high as he scans the back of the frame, and then dumps it down by the skirting board. She hears glass crack.

It seems as if she can't think of anything but what is actually happening in front of her. As if it's the jar of jam she ought to think about, and the mattress.

Andrei looks straight ahead, refusing to watch what they are doing. He is pale and his lips are pressed together. How long will the search go on? They must let him get dressed. She's heard of people being taken away in their nightclothes, or in a thin dance dress like the one she made. Sometimes they search for hours, she knows that. She will have to go to the bathroom. Andrei must take a bundle of things.

I burned the letter, thinks Andrei. Was that good, or bad? They are only taking me. They have no reason to touch Anna. If she does as I tell her and goes to the dacha then she has a chance. She's young enough, she's strong, the baby can be born there as safely as anywhere. Galya's a doctor, after all.

'Officer,' he asks, 'have I your permission to get dressed?'

Anna thinks the man is going to refuse, but after a few moments he says, 'Very well.'

'Your warmest clothes, Andrei,' says Anna quietly. 'Let me help you.'

'Sit there!' barks the officer, as if she might hide a knife in the sleeve of Andrei's jacket. Anna's eyes fill with tears as she watches Andrei bend down under the gaze of the officer and the soldiers, and pick out under-wear, shirt and tie, jacket and trousers from the heaps of their clothes on the floor. He wants to look right for the interview, she can tell. She wants to tell him not to worry about that. The first and only important thing is to be warm. Who knows how long he might have to wear those clothes?

'Wear a jumper over your shirt,' she murmurs, and he looks at her, sees the anguish in her face and picks up a dark blue lambswool jumper she knitted for him down at the dacha the summer before last. She smiles at him. Her fingers know every stitch of that jumper. It fits him so well, and the yarn is triple-ply. Her fingers remember the touch of the wool that will keep him warm. *And two pairs of socks,* she wants to say, *who knows what you will need?* But she must be careful. If she says too much they will put her in the other room and then she won't be able to be with Andrei.

One of the soldiers stands close to Andrei as he dresses. Anna looks away. What do they think he's going to do? Make a run for it? Swallow poison?

Perhaps people do those things. But it won't happen here. She and Andrei are prepared. Everything seems not only unreal but also absolutely familiar, as if she's been waiting for this all her life. All the stories she's heard, all the whispered, shattered phrases, are suddenly alive in the front of her mind, like a set of instructions. People go off, taking nothing with them because they think they won't be away for long.

Andrei is dressed now. The officer asks the soldier who was guarding him to help with the search of Kolya's room.

'Is it permitted to take a bundle of personal belongings?' she asks the officer, quietly.

'That won't be necessary,' he answers.

She seizes on the words. It won't be necessary, because Andrei is only being arrested temporarily, as part of the investigation? Or it won't be necessary, because she will be able to visit him and bring him whatever he needs? The thoughts fly through her mind, full of hope, but her heart doesn't listen. It knows that the officer is saying *That won't be necessary* merely because it is something he's been trained to say. It has no meaning, except to keep her quiet.

The red leather photo album is splayed out on the floor. Some photos have fallen out and the soldiers have walked over them. Anna sees a photograph of herself. It's not very flattering — she's smiling and squinting into the sun — but Andrei has always liked it.

'With your permission,' she says to the officer boldly, 'I should like my husband to take with him that photograph of me,' and she points to the floor.

The officer looks surprised by her boldness, but his gaze follows hers. Something stirs in his face. Maybe he too has a red leather photo album. They are common. At this moment all the soldiers are in Kolya's room. He gives a sharp jerk of the head, which she takes as permission. The next moment she is on the floor, picking up the photograph. She holds it out to Andrei and he tucks it into his jacket pocket. She hopes that he will hide it better than that, as soon as he gets a chance.

The tallest soldier comes to the doorway, holding a box that contains the shopping list, two medical textbooks, a small note-book in which Anna keeps accounts, and her father's English dictionary. He salutes and says, 'Search completed!'

'Are the articles fully itemized?'

'Itemized in full!'

The officer plants his finger on the list, runs it slowly down, checking.

'All correct. You are required to sign the list for the items,' he says to Anna.

She takes the list and reads it quickly. 'It says "Financial documents", but this is only a small book that we use for domestic accounts.'

'Precisely. Financial documents.'

She doesn't know what to do. What if they try to make out Andrei has been receiving money from somewhere? Why should they try to say that Andrei has financial documents, when all he's ever had is his pay from the hospital?

'Sign the list, Anna,' says Andrei.

The English dictionary. *Why did you have*

an English dictionary, given that no one in the household is a student of English? What is the purpose of that?

She mustn't antagonize this man. Andrei will be in his hands. She takes the officer's pen, and signs. She writes her name slowly, clearly. Every second now is a second that Andrei remains with her.

'Time to get going.'

'Where are you taking him?' asks Anna, but this time the man simply gives her a look of contempt, as if her question is final proof of her stupidity. He doesn't reply. He takes out another paper and shows it to Andrei. The warrant for his arrest, all filled out with words in the correct places. The witnesses have already signed it. It's happening now, this minute. Andrei is being taken away.

'Your overcoat!' cries Anna, and for the first time Andrei hears panic in her voice. 'I must get it for you.'

No one stops her this time, so she goes to the entrance hall, takes Andrei's coat off the hook, with his hat, his gloves and his muffler. Her heart is pounding. In less than a minute he will be gone. There must be something she can do. There they are, standing in the centre of the room. Four men in uniform, and Andrei. The rusty band around their caps is the same colour as dried blood. It is happening now, the thing for which her father stayed awake night after night.

She comes towards Andrei, holding his coat.

'Search everything,' orders the officer, and the youngest soldier takes the coat from her, turns it inside out, empties the pockets, feels along the lining. There are a few kopecks and a white handkerchief. The soldier shakes out his hat.

'You can put them on.'

Andrei puts on his muffler, coat, gloves, hat.

Her heart is stifling her. Her bladder hurts. They will be gone. Andrei will be gone.

'Andrei,' she says. Her mouth is numb, as if she's stayed out too long in the cold. He is very pale but his face is calm. She devours his face with her eyes. His lips, his skin. Thank God he shaved. He looks at her and no one else. The soldier behind him gives him a push in the back. Not hard but not gentle either. It says, *You are ours now.*

They are going. There is a soldier on either side of Andrei and one behind. The officer is peering into the box and frowning. Then he jerks his head and the tallest soldier picks it up. They all have guns. Their uniforms are full of detail and her eyes blur. All she sees is how strong they are, because of the uniform, all of them together. It makes them sure of what they are doing. It is their work.

She can feel the baby. She looks at Andrei now, only him.

'The baby is moving,' she says. He nods. Now he is going past her. She reaches out her hand. His hand brushes it, grasps her fingers, then lets go. 'I'll look after everything,' she says.

'You'll have some clearing up to do,' he says, speaking only to her and as if no one else is present. 'I'm sorry I can't help you, my darling.'

'Everything will be all right,' she says, but already he has been swept away.

One of the men takes her by the shoulders and pushes her back, not hard but as if he means it. They're all crammed into the little entrance hall and she is still in the living room, their room. The soldiers' backs hide Andrei from her. She starts forward as they open the door to the landing. Now they are through it and already letting the door swing back. She stops the door, holds it while she jams the wedge under it to stop it closing on her, and moves out on to the landing, after them. Already they are on the stairs. The noise of their boots rings through the stairwell, bouncing around the walls. She sees the tops of their heads, almost at the turn of the stairs. Andrei, in his fur hat.

'Andrei,' she says. She can't speak loudly but she knows he's heard her. The boots are going down. They have passed the turn of the stairs. Suddenly they are all swallowed by the dimness of the stairwell with its weak lights screwed into the walls. She can still hear the boots, going down. She strains her ears to pick out the sound of Andrei's feet, but there is nothing now but the sound of men tramping downstairs, not caring how much noise they make.

She waits, holding her breath and listening. She knows exactly how long it takes to get down all the flights. They are at the bottom now. They will be opening the heavy outer door.

Yes. She hears it. For a second there are still voices and footsteps and then there is a bang, and the door closes. The echo always goes on for half a second, like an overtone. There. It's finished. She listens to the empty stairwell.

Behind her there is the sound of a door being unbolted, unlocked, and very slowly and cautiously opened. She looks round. A line of light appears and fattens around the Maleviches' door. Yes, she thinks, they would be listening. She moves quickly back across the landing to her own door, but not quickly enough. The Malevich door opens more widely and a face peers around it. Old Ma Malevich, her face greasy and her hair in rags. She stares at Anna without expression, drinking in the look on Anna's face. Anna turns away, removes the wedge from her door and goes inside. In a moment, when that bitch is back inside her apartment, she will go to the bathroom. She leans her back against the door, and closes her eyes.

She finds Andrei's alarm clock under the bedding that has been pulled on to the floor. It is twenty-five to five. She looks at the chaos of the two rooms. She will sort it out. She will clean the place until not a trace of them remains. Her jar of face cream has smashed, and cream has spread on the green dress. It's difficult to remove such stains.

She stands still, in the middle of the room, her arms hanging by her sides, her face vacant. Several minutes pass. The clock is still ticking. They haven't broken it.

At last she moves slowly and stiffly to the

edge of the room, stretches out her hand and places it flat on the wall. The wall feels solid, but she knows it is not. It's just a membrane, the thinnest possible covering that shields them from the street outside, or from the eyes of their neighbours.

It has happened. Andrei is with them now. They are driving him through the streets where there's just a little early traffic. People are going to their shifts, wrapped to the eyes against the cold morning. Andrei will hear the trams.

She wonders if they came for Andrei in a car or in a van. If it's one of their vans, people will look away and hunch deeper into their clothes. You feel afraid of those vans, swerving and swooping across the city. She remembers the Black Crows before the war, how thick they were on the city streets. She would think of the people inside, men or women, ripped away from their lives, still warm with the warmth of their beds. But like everyone else, she looked at those vans sideways, and never for too long.

She'll find out where they are taking him. She must think. You have got to think of every single contact, everyone you know who might have a little bit of 'pull'. Even someone you haven't seen for years might be able to do something. You have to fight.

They will find out that it's all a mistake and they will release him.

They might be there by now. The doors clanging, the locks turning one by one. Will they take him to the Kresty? No, not at first. They will have a procedure. She must find out everything. As soon as it's light, she'll begin.

With intolerable sharpness, she sees Andrei being shoved down a flight of stairs into the cellars. She sees a cell which is so small that a man can't sit or lie down but can only stand up. She hears the clang as the door shuts on him.

No. Don't allow yourself to think of anything but what you must do next. And while you are waiting, there is this mess to be cleaned up.

18

She'll go to the hospital first. She'll ask to see Professor Maslov. He's a good man, Andrei has always said so. The hospital must know that Andrei has done nothing wrong. She will force them to support him.

There's Julia as well. She's married to Vesnin. He's a powerful man in the film world and he's bound to have contacts. Anna will go there tonight.

Who else?

Anna stands stock-still, her thoughts flying. But she must go to work. She can't risk losing her wages now that there's no one else to support Kolya. Work first, and then she will telephone Maslov. Perhaps better not to see him at the hospital, anyway, in case her visit makes him feel compromised. People know her there. Better not telephone him either. She'll go to his apartment this evening. It's not too far. Maslov knows her; he's met her any number of times at social events, and she and Andrei have been to the Maslovs' apartment. He won't refuse to talk to her. His wife, though; Anna's not so sure about her. She dresses very elegantly and her manner is gracious, but the one visit she and Maslov made to Anna and Andrei wasn't a success. She was cold and uninterested, and she ate none of the cake.

Cake! Anna digs her nails into her palms. *You fool, why are you thinking of cake?*

Maslov first, and then she will go over to Julia's. Julia is always up until all hours.

She must wash, and dress. There isn't time to clear up all this mess, but she must eat. The baby needs it. Porridge. *They have taken Andrei.*

With slow, trembling fingers she measures out milled oatmeal, heats milk in a pan, adds a tiny pinch of salt and then the grain. She turns down the heat and for a long time she stands by the stove, stirring the porridge with a wooden spoon. It thickens, while small bubbles pock the surface. If Andrei were here she'd add a pat of butter for him, but she prefers her own porridge plain. After a moment's thought, she adds a small amount of butter, and stirs it in. It will be good for the baby. Besides, the baby may share his father's taste for butter.

Will they give Andrei anything to eat? She

mustn't think of that. It's her job to stay calm and purposeful, as long as she's free and can act for them both. She will go to the prison, as soon she's found out where they're holding him. He'll be allowed a parcel, surely? She'll put in cigarettes, and chocolate, and clean linen. You can hand parcels in at the inquiry window, she knows that. You have to queue for a long time and sometimes they slam the window shut just before you get to it, but often you can hand in a parcel. Galya told her that, one autumn when they were sitting in the dusk together, stringing onions. She never asked Galya whom she had waited for, or why, and Galya didn't say. But her words struck deep, and now, when it's needed, the information rises up in Anna's mind. A parcel. You can't put a letter in with it, you must send the letter separately. *I was permitted to send one a month.* Cigarettes, soap, chocolate. Always cigarettes, even if the person doesn't smoke.

Nobody will know anything at work. It'll be a normal day. She'll buy cigarettes on the way home, she'll see Maslov and Julia, and then she'll clear up the flat and clean everything. Andrei would hate to come back and see it looking like this.

A stink of burning porridge startles her. She hadn't realized that she'd stopped stirring. Never mind, the top layer should be all right.

But the taste is tainted all through. She can't swallow the porridge. She holds it in her mouth, gagging, and then spits it out in the sink.

She bends over the sink for a long time, retching, gripping the cold enamel with both hands. Slowly, she raises her head. The tap has a crust of dirt around the bottom. You can't see it from above, only from this angle. She must clean the taps more thoroughly. Anna takes a deep breath, and turns on the cold water. She holds her wrists under the stream of water, then cups her hands and fills her palms. She splashes her face and the back of her neck, then rinses out her mouth before she fills a glass and drinks it off in one draught, sucking up the water like an animal.

As she straightens herself, she catches sight of the clock. She's going to be late for work if she doesn't hurry. She'll have to leave everything as it is.

The corridor is long and Andrei is still dizzy. The stout guard walks on his right, the young, bored one on his left. They pass door after door, all closed. Apart from them, the corridor is empty. The light is reddish and dim. Already Andrei isn't sure if it's day or night.

Suddenly, the stout guard stops dead, opens a door to his right and barks, 'In here!' The other guard gives Andrei a shove in the small of his back, and he stumbles through the doorway. As soon as he is inside, the door slams and the locks turn.

At first he thinks the guards have mistaken a cupboard for a cell. But there is a dim lighbulb in a metal cage, screwed to the ceiling. The floor is bare, and there is no window. He turns back to the door and sees that there is a slit cut into it, with a peephole above.

There is a stench of excrement. It comes from an uncovered bucket on the floor. Someone else has been in this cell, perhaps recently. There is no bench or sleeping platform, because the cell isn't big enough. There is room to stand, and to sit on the floor. If Andrei puts out his elbows, like chicken wings, he can touch both walls.

He decides that the best thing is to sit with his back resting against the cell door, until they come for him again. They will come soon. This can only be a holding cell. He could sit against the opposite wall, and then he could watch the door, but that would mean sitting right next to the bucket. He could move the bucket, of course. Suddenly these thoughts make his head pound once more, and another wave of nausea rises in his throat. He's not going to be sick again, though, not into a bucket filled with someone else's shit.

Andrei sits down. The cold of the stone strikes up through his trousers. He no longer has his overcoat, his scarf, tie or belt. He has been processed.

There was a long time of form-filling and then they took photographs, full-face, left profile, right profile. He tried asking questions but almost immediately realized that not only was it a waste of time, but it was also weakening his position. No one was going to answer, and it made him into a man whose words no one bothered to acknowledge. They removed his watch, his belt, his shoelaces, tie and the contents of his pockets, and entered details of all these personal possessions on a long sheet of paper which he was required to sign. The photograph of Anna was taken too. At last he was led away, to spend the rest of the night in a cell, as he thought then. But it wasn't over yet.

He was taken to another room, smaller and more brilliantly lit. A man in a white coat looked up from a double desk as he was brought in, and said, without meeting Andrei's eyes, 'Strip.'

There were four men in the room. Two were the uniformed guards who had brought him here, one wore a white coat, and the fourth was sitting beside the white-coat in another chair at the long desk, with a pile of forms in front of him. He was very young, and wore wire-rimmed glasses. His skinny neck looked vulnerable inside his stiff collar. His expression was petulant, as if Andrei's arrival had interrupted important work. Beyond the desk was another table, half hidden. Instruments glinted on its surface. Andrei let his shoulders drop, and took a deep, slow breath. There was a small sink, too, set into the far corner of the room, with a frayed towel hanging down.

Andrei took in the details as if they were the symptoms of a patient, while he undressed quickly and methodically, as he did at home. He knew they wanted him to show his shock, or even to protest at what was happening to him. But there was nothing strange to him in the abandonment of human dignity. He'd seen corpses sticking out of snowdrifts, clothes stripped from their limbs. He'd come home and death had been living there too, in their apartment, with his feet under their table like a cousin. Nevertheless, they had survived.

Oddly enough Andrei felt easier once he was naked than when he was undressing in front of the four of them. One of the guards took up a position by the door. He stared ahead, his face blank. He was only a young lad. Andrei knew from his accent that he was a country boy, not a Leningrader. The other guard, who was stout and asthmatic, had more to do.

'Clothes on the chair. Shoes under the chair,' he ordered. As Andrei obeyed, he glanced quickly at the medical instruments on the table by the wall. Stethoscope, otoscope, penlight, swabs, blood-pressure cuff. Speculum.

'Open your mouth. Wider,' said the man in the white coat. Andrei opened his mouth, but still not wide enough for the guard, who suddenly seized Andrei's lower jaw and yanked it down hard. The temporomandibular joint clicked and pain shot through Andrei's ear. The man in the white coat shone his penlight into Andrei's mouth. Andrei smelled the two men's breath and heard the wheeze in the guard's lungs. The guard seemed almost more interested in Andrei's mouth than the doctor was.

'Move your tongue to the left. To the right.'

They thought he had hidden something under his tongue, perhaps. A message, or a poison capsule. But that was ridiculous, like something out of a story for overeager Pioneers. The guard released his grip, but did not step back.

They looked into his ears. They came too close, both of them. The guard's heavy uniform brushed Andrei's naked flesh. It was cold in the room, and the lights were cold too. The other guard shifted his boots. Andrei could not see him but he could hear the creak of the leather.

'Turn around. Legs apart. Bend over. Not like that. Right over. Touch your toes.' Hands took hold of his buttocks, and parted them. He knew what was coming, but even so his body flooded with outrage as the speculum was pushed into his anus, twisted around, opened.

Andrei had performed anal examinations many times. The thing was to reassure the patient. *'Lie on your side. Yes, that's right, like that, with your knees drawn up.'* You had to make sure their entire body was decently covered by the gown, leaving just an opening for the examination. Even children have that fierce instinct for physical privacy. And then you proceeded slowly, gently, all the while telling them what was going on. You were two human beings in this together, trying to find out what was wrong. You had to be sure that the patient was relaxed. Some doctors were more brusque, but usually, Andrei thought, that was because they were not at ease with the procedure.

Thinking these thoughts, he made himself safe. He was back in his own world. If this man were a medical student he'd have had him thrown off the course.

His body throbbed with pain and anger. The white-coat — Andrei wasn't going to call him a doctor — closed the speculum and pulled it out.

'Stand up. Legs together. Turn around.'

God knows what they thought he might have hidden up his backside. But of course that had nothing to do with it.

The examination went on. They took his blood pressure, timed his pulse, sounded his heart and lungs, weighed him, measured his height. The man was a doctor, there was no getting away from it. At the very least, he had medical training. The young clerk was there to record the figures that were droned out to him. Those figures would join the photographs, the arrest forms and the list of the personal possessions that had been taken from him. Surely it must mean something, that they'd bothered to make a list? If they documented his possessions, it must mean that at some point these would be given back to him.

But his heart knew it had no further meaning. Lists and questionnaires signified nothing beyond themselves. If he looked for logic he would go crazy.

He was not ill, but since they already had the outer, public information of name, age, date and place of birth, parental occupation and class status and so on and so forth, they'd moved on to the inner man. They needed to know how his heart beat. If they could have sawn off the top of his skull and peered into the workings of his brain they'd have done so gladly. But then they would have lost him.

The examination dragged on. They didn't tell him when it was over, but the doctor went to the sink, ran the water and began to wash his hands thoroughly. Andrei heard the scrubbing of a nail brush against finger-nails. He was still standing in the middle of the room, naked.

'Shall I get dressed?' he asked, but no one replied. It was as if he hadn't spoken. The doctor continued scrubbing his hands. The clerk wrote a final, careful sentence. The light directly above Andrei's head began to buzz like an angry fly. That bulb is about to go, he thought. He was cold now. He felt shrivelled and his eyes stung with fatigue.

But this is not really cold, he reminded himself. He brought to mind the room where he and Anna and Kolya and Marina had slept night after night, huddled together, dressed in their winter coats, in hats and scarves, under every layer of bedclothes they possessed. And still the frost ate its way to their flesh, easily. Anna had the child in her arms. She was sure that if Kolya slept alone he would be dead of cold and hunger by morning. She was probably right.

Those days, when he walked so slowly to the hospital, leaning on his stick, the wind had time to flay the few centimetres of skin that were exposed. None of them was ever warm, not for a second.

Where was this man then? he wondered. This doctor.

He'd finished washing his hands. He was turning. His face was busy with its own preoccupations. What had just happened was not very important at all. Just another examination of another newly arrested prisoner. He was probably well on his way to fulfilling his norm for the week.

'Your speculum,' said Andrei aloud. 'Don't forget to sterilize it.'

The doctor was not as practised in blankness as the guards. He glanced across at Andrei and his face showed a trace of surprise that Andrei had used the correct name for the instrument.

'Yes, I'm a doctor,' said Andrei. 'What about you?'

The man stopped dead. He wanted to show no reaction but he had not quite learned the art of it yet. He tightened his lips.

'Colleague to colleague,' said Andrei, 'I must tell you that the way in which you performed that rectal examination was a disgrace. It should be done with the patient lying in the left lateral position. You used too much force. You might have caused injury. Didn't they teach you anything in medical school?'

The stout guard stepped forward, to the doctor's side. 'Is he giving you lip?'

The doctor looked at the guard, then at Andrei, and finally at the door, where the second guard was taking an interest at last. He sniffed hard, and jerked his head. The guard took it for assent.

'Give me your revolver a moment, Petya,' he said to the boy by the door.

Andrei saw it happen very slowly. The boy detached his revolver from its holster. The stout guard held out his hand, received the weapon and seemed to weigh it.

I'm going to die. Not in a while but now. He saw snow, piled high. He saw Anna coming down the street, very slowly, a black dot in all that whiteness, towards him. At the same time his mind said, *Why doesn't that guard use his own revolver?*

The guard finished weighing the revolver. His arm whipped back. There was a blur as the revolver butt cracked into the side of Andrei's head.

He fell. He was at the doctor's feet, looking at his shoes. Brown, cracked leather. That was very important. Now he could not see them because they were going into a mist. He was making a noise, a grunting sound. Above him someone was shouting, 'Get up! Get up!'

But it was impossible. He was fighting too hard to stay conscious. If he gave way they could do anything to him. He rolled sideways, shielding the soft underpart of his body. He was sure that now he was down they would kick him. He watched for their boots. There was a rabble of voices, accusations, shouting. 'What the hell have you done? You've killed him!'

And even the guard's voice was frightened. 'He was trying to have a go at you, doctor.' He knew he'd gone too far. 'He was trying to escape, you'll back me up, won't you, Petya?' He had just wanted to do it, smash that revolver into the side of Andrei's head, and he'd tasted the power of the moment so strongly that he'd given in to it. Now he was afraid.

'Give me a bucket, I'm going to be sick,' Andrei groaned. There was a flurry and then the doctor was kneeling beside him, holding out a kidney dish. Far too small. Andrei vomited, over the dish, over the doctor's hands, over the floor.

Let him wash his hands, he thought. *Let him wash his hands now.*

After a while the doctor was feeling Andrei's head. Blood was running down over Andrei's mouth, and he tasted it, hot and salty. It looked like a lot of blood, but for a head wound it wasn't too bad. He didn't think he was concussed. A bad place to be hit, at the temple. The guard had been lucky.

Slowly, Andrei got to his knees, and looked up, shaking his head to clear the blood away from his eyes. He raised his right hand and pushed it across his forehead. It brushed against a hanging flap of skin, and came away bright and sticky. His eyes were fine; no double vision. He could not stand without taking the doctor's arm, and he wasn't going to do that. The guards were conferring, the clerk was putting his papers together with small, scared movements.

'He doesn't look too bad,' said the stout guard.

'You could have killed him,' said the doctor.

They were all afraid. It had happened against orders. There was a time and a place for everything. Now the prisoner was a mess. The blood was still flowing fast. The doctor went to the table, picked up a pad of lint and pressed it to the wound.

Blood and vomit were mixed on the floor.

'Don't move my head,' said Andrei aloud. He was going to be sick again. No, it was passing. Just then everything thickened in front of his eyes. He could no longer see the doctor or the clerk beyond him. A feeling he had never experienced before was growing distinct. It was rising, ready to overwhelm him. *Doom,* he said to himself. He had never spoken that word before, but here it was and he recognized it. He must not let go. He must not fall into it. Whatever happened, he must remain conscious. Andrei took a deep breath, and lowered his head, but even so the blackness behind him swept forward and overcame him.

■ ■ ■ ■

Now he is in the cell. Blood has caked and crusted on his shirt. The pullover is stiff with it. Anna would know how to get it out. The doctor has fastened the pad of lint to his head with sticking plaster. Andrei doesn't remember putting on his clothes.

Suddenly something above his head rattles sharply. It's the cover of the flap on the door. A voice shouts, 'Stand up! It is not permitted to sit!'

Slowly, Andrei gets to his feet. Dizziness returns, but it's not so bad this time. He will lean against the wall.

'Stand up! It is not permitted to lean against the wall!'

Andrei stands in the middle of the cell, facing away from the door. He lowers his head, so he won't feel faint again. There is the bucket, stewing in the corner. Fortunately, he can't smell it any more. There's no plaster on the stone walls. Three quarters of the way up the wall there are two large hooks, set about a metre apart. The floor is also stone. There is a smell of damp and he feels very cold, but that may be shock. Perhaps they are underground. He tries to remember leaving the brightly lit room, and what happened next, but his memory won't give back anything except that last walk down the corridor. Perhaps they came down a flight of steps; perhaps not.

He listens. There is a very faint sound of dripping, far away. Water perhaps. From the corridor outside he hears footsteps, slow and regular. It must be one of the guards, patrolling. There is a pause, a cough and then the footsteps move on. He strains his ears, trying to catch any other trace of human presence. They passed doors all the way down the corridor, on both sides. There must be other newly arrested prisoners behind them.

They can't be going to leave him here for long. Andrei supposes that it's deliberate to keep the prisoner ignorant of what's going on. Some doctors do that. The patient is reduced to a meek cipher, who doesn't know what's about to happen to his body, or why. Andrei has always fought against that approach.

But it works. Of course it works: that's why they do it and have done it for centuries. That dripping sound again. He wonders where it's coming from. For a while he seems to sleep, standing, then he comes back to full awareness. There is wetness on his face. The blood is flowing again, leaking out from under the lint. The wound needs stitching, but that's beside the point. That idiot didn't even know how to bandage it correctly. He should have applied pressure for longer. And of course the patient should lie down.

Andrei looks down at the stone floor. The dripping sound comes again and he realizes that it's his own blood. He watches it pattering down.

The flow isn't dangerous, but it will weaken him eventually. It needs to be stopped. Very slowly, so as not to attract the attention of the guard if he's looking through the peephole, he wriggles his left hand back inside the sleeve of his pullover. Fortunately, Anna knitted the sleeves just a little too long. Now the cuff is free. He raises his hand and presses the cuff hard against the saturated pad of lint. The sleeve brushes his face. It smells of home, and also of blood.

Anna takes a tram directly from work to the Maslov apartment. The tram is packed but she pushes her way through and finds a seat. She closes her eyes and sinks into the darkness. What luxury, to sit down and be carried along in the dark. The tram sways and rattles. A man standing beside her lurches across her and puts his hand down on her shoulder to keep his balance. She looks up, straight into his eyes. He is about sixty, worn and seamed with work.

'Excuse me,' he says.

'That's all right.'

She closes her eyes again. For ten minutes there is nothing she need do except make sure she doesn't fall asleep and go past the stop. Her body yields to the motion of the tram. Inside her the baby swims in its own darkness. She feels it move. The fluttering grows stronger each day. Perhaps soon she'll be able to say that the baby is kicking. People always say 'kicking' — it's obviously the only correct word.

She has thought through exactly what she's going to say to Maslov. It's pointless to ask him to intervene directly on Andrei's behalf. She might as well suggest he sign his own arrest warrant. He hasn't been involved in the Volkov case. But if a man of Maslov's standing were willing to act as a character witness, that might count for something. She won't plead. She knows that only embarrasses people and makes them more determined to refuse. Her father taught her that when she was very young.

'Why don't you make more of an effort to keep in touch with your old friends?' she demanded once, with all the callowness of a girl who had been managing a household and bringing up her baby brother for a full year already. 'All those people who used to come to the house when I was little. Some of them are really famous now. Surely they'd be able to help you get published?'

He'd frowned sternly. 'You understand nothing, Anna. I am like a man who has a dangerous and highly contagious disease. I am lucky to be alive. Naturally they are all terrified of catching it. Please don't speak about such matters any more.'

She remembers the slow, shamed tide of colour that rose in her face as she realized that she had known this all along. She'd just chosen to ignore her own knowledge, because her father's acceptance of his fate was unbearable to her. And so she'd hurt him, even more than he was already hurt. She said nothing more that day, but the following evening, when she brought his tea to where he was sitting in his usual chair, she put it down on his little table with more than usual care. As he reached out to take the glass, she intercepted his hand, and gave it a quick, light pressure. She would have liked to kiss it, but she knew that would only embarrass him.

The tram's brakes screech, and Anna's

eyes fly open. Not her stop, thank God. She gathers her things together, and buttons up her coat under her chin. The man who leaned on her shoulder is gone, but the tram is still packed. Where do they all come from, she wonders, and where do they go? We know nothing of one another's lives.

The Maslovs have a spacious first-floor apartment. There is a lift, but she doesn't take it. The stairs are clean and there is no smell of cabbage. Perhaps, in apartments like these, they never eat it. Their front door is as she remembered it, beautifully painted and with the Maslov name engraved in flowing letters on a brass plate. Such confidence and permanence!

Anna rings the bell. After a few moments it is opened by a young woman in a white blouse and black skirt. Anna recalls that it was this same young woman who took their coats when she and Andrei visited, and who later served them drinks. She must work for the Maslovs full time.

'Good evening,' says Anna. 'Is Professor Maslov at home? I'd like to speak to him.'

The woman frowns slightly. 'Are they expecting you?'

'No, it's just — just an informal visit.'

'What name shall I give?'

'Anna Levina. Professor Maslov knows me

from the hospital.'

'Excuse me a moment.'

Anna waits in the hall. She can hear voices from the living room. Perhaps the Maslovs have guests. That would be awkward; she'd have to leave immediately. But a moment later the young woman comes back, followed by Professor Maslov, who wears an expression of genial readiness mingled with slight annoyance at the interruption. As soon as he sees Anna, his face changes. The young woman nods, and disappears through a door into the back of the apartment.

'But — but you are Alekseyev's wife!'

'Yes.'

'You gave a different name.'

'I kept my own name.'

'I see. I see. I was confused, that's all.' He rubs his hands together. 'So what can I do for you?'

She looks at him in amazement. Surely he must have heard about Andrei's arrest? She is sure the whole hospital will know about it by now. But perhaps Maslov didn't go to work today, for some reason. 'Andrei was arrested this morning,' she says.

Maslov glances behind him at the open door of the living room. 'Please talk more quietly,' he says, almost in a whisper. 'My wife . . .' He knew. He is not surprised.

'Can we go somewhere and talk for half an hour? I need to ask for your advice.'

He looks at her searchingly. 'What do you mean?'

'About what has happened to Andrei, of course,' she says, more sharply than she intended.

Maslov nods. He no longer looks confused. 'My dear young lady,' he says, 'sometimes, you understand, it's safer not to intervene. Better for — the person concerned — if things take their course. Outsiders can do more harm than good.'

She stares at him, too shocked to speak.

'You'll see,' he says in a hurried voice, 'if it's just a misunderstanding, it'll soon be cleared up. These people know what they're about. Andrei will be back at work in no time.'

Anna's hands clench. 'How can you say that?' she whispers fiercely. 'You know that's not what happens. This isn't a misunderstanding. I'm not asking you to get involved in the case. But you know Andrei well, you've worked with him for years, you know how good he is. All I want is for you to say that. They're bound to make inquiries at the hospital.'

Maslov blinks, but says nothing. Suddenly Anna understands that the inquiries have already been made. Probably Maslov has been interviewed today. But he's not going to tell her, because he's already decided on his position.

At this moment the living-room door opens and Maslov's wife peers into the hall. Sonya, that's her name. She doesn't see Anna at first, because Anna is shielded by Maslov's back.

'Who is it, Volodya? For heaven's sake, don't keep guests standing out in the hall.' Her voice is bright and social, if a little ir-ritated. She moves forward, and Maslov steps aside, casting his wife a look of relief as he does so. At this moment Sonya Maslova sees Anna. The hostess frown deepens on her forehead as she tries to place this strange woman who was talking so intently to her husband. Someone from the hospital, come to badger her husband at home during one of his precious evenings. Probably after something. Sonya's smile is wearing thin

'This is Anna Levina,' says Maslov, low and even. 'You remember, my dear, you've met her before. Andrei Alekseyev's wife. We were speaking of him earlier.'

Anna watches Sonya Maslova's face turn to stone. 'What are you thinking of?' she asks, her voice quick, cutting, direct. 'How dare you come here!'

Anna is speechless. Maslov puts out a hand to his wife. 'My dear —'

'You should have sent her packing straight away.' Sonya takes a few hurried steps forward until she is standing right in front of Anna. 'Don't you appreciate that Professor Maslov is engaged in scientific research that is of the utmost importance to the State? There is a serious possibility that his name will be put forward for the Stalin Prize!'

'My dear, please — that was only a rumour.'

She gives him an angry, sparkling glance. 'You never push yourself! You let other people who are far less talented than you snatch all the prizes!'

Anna feels as if she has fallen out of the life she knew, and into an ugly dream. This can't be Maslov, with whom Andrei has worked so long. Andrei's mentor, the man he admires and almost loves. This is some kind of puppet who has taken Maslov's name. A storm of protest seethes in her head. She will shame him. She will force him to change his mind. And yet another part of her, the part that is her father's daughter, understands everything and knows there is no changing it. She licks her lips. 'I'd better go,' she murmurs. All she wants now is to get out of the place as fast as she can, before this woman picks up the phone to denounce her.

Maslov gives Anna a helpless glance. Sonya has forgotten her elegance and stands with her arms akimbo, like a market woman. 'Get out,' she says. 'Get out and don't come back.'

Anna crosses the hall, opens the handsome door, steps out on to the landing. Down the stairs, and across to the ornate street door. People who live in these apartments have really made it.

She is in the street. She must rest for a moment, because she doesn't feel too good. Anna leans against the wall, taking deep breaths of the frosty night air. At that moment the door to the building opens again. A figure comes out, and looks up and down the street. It's Maslov. Anna stands still, unresisting, as he comes up to her. If he were to get out a knife and stab her, it would seem perfectly in keeping with the logic of the day.

'Are you ill?' asks Maslov.

'No. I expect Andrei told you that I'm pregnant.'

'Yes. Yes, he did tell me.'

They are both silent, one remembering

and one imagining that moment when Andrei gave the news he'd been waiting to give for so long.

'You must look after yourself,' says Maslov, 'for Andrei's sake. The baby is very important to him.'

'How dare you say that to me, after —' she jerks her head back towards the building.

Maslov shakes his head. 'You mustn't blame her,' he says. 'She lost her whole family, you know, in the war. I'm all she's got. We have no children.'

'In the siege?'

'Yes, and she had two brothers who were taken prisoner. We never heard what happened to them. She's terrified, you understand —'

'I can't think about that,' says Anna harshly. 'I have to think about Andrei.'

'I have to think about her, can't you understand that?'

'And so you'll go along with it,' says Anna, 'as long as it's happening to someone else. It's not just your skin she's thinking about, it's your *reputation*. She wants you to be a great man, as if we hadn't got enough of those.'

'You should be careful what you say.'

'Why?'

'In your position, I would be very, very cautious.'

'I can see that.'

Maslov peers at her in the gloom. 'Haven't you ever gone along with it?' he asks.

'I can't think about that now,' says Anna again. 'You won't do anything for Andrei. That's all that matters to me. You'd better get back to your wife.'

But still he hesitates. He wants something from her and she has no idea what it is. At last he says in a hurried whisper, 'Don't you understand that it would be better for you if you did the same?'

'What?'

'Tell them you knew nothing about what was going on. Apologize for your lack of vigilance. It's the only way. You're pregnant. Andrei would want you to save yourself. You should think about your child.'

Anna takes a step back from him.

'I'm only trying to help you. You're young, you've got your life ahead of you. Are you in need of money?'

Her lips feel numb, but he's waiting for her to answer. He wants her to denounce Andrei. A 'family denunciation'. *Save yourself. You should think about your child.* A hot sudden flush of rage releases her. 'Professor Maslov, I think you'd better go in now. That man across the road has been watching us for quite a while.'

He freezes, his eyes fixed on her face, and then very slowly he turns his head until he's able to scan the empty street.

'Goodbye,' Anna says, and walks away swiftly towards the tram stop. Her heart thuds with anger and satisfaction. That gave him a fright. Just for a second he felt a touch of what they've had to live with for weeks.

By the time Anna reaches the tram stop she feels cold and wan. Why did she act like that? Andrei would have hated it. He's always hated anything mean or petty. Maslov was no worse than anyone else; it was only that she'd expected more of him. But why should he risk his career and even his freedom for Andrei? That was never part of the deal.

19

It's not too late to call at Julia's, if she hurries. When did she last eat? Soup and sausage with the children at lunchtime. That seems a long time ago. She isn't hungry. She's tired, but she dreads going to sleep without Andrei beside her. As soon as she falls asleep, it will set a seal on everything that has happened today. Time hasn't moved on too far yet. It's still the same day, the one on which Andrei was arrested. She can still say, *'I saw Andrei this morning. This time yesterday, we were at home together.'*

If only Julia's alone. With Vesnin at home it will be more difficult. Anna doesn't know him, and he's not going to welcome this kind of trouble. Much better if she can explain everything to Julia, and Julia will find the right moment to talk to her husband and ask for his help. You can't just throw a thing like this at him without warning. He might not know how far back Anna's friendship with Julia goes.

Probably he won't be at home. Julia said he was out most evenings, and she didn't always go with him. He was meeting colleagues, and besides —

'You get tired of eating out all the time.'

'Do you?'

Another tram, clanging and clanking through the dark night. Anna gets on gratefully, and sits down. The streets are quiet now. A few people plod along, huddled against the sharpness of the wind. They're going home, to their own homes. They'll close their doors and feel safe. They don't know how quickly home can be cracked open, like an egg.

A granny with a huge basket gets on, and heaves herself into the seat next to Anna. Lumps bulge through the cloth that covers the basket. It's a dark blue embroidered cloth, so shabby now that you can hardly see the stitches. It must have been a tablecloth once. Idly, Anna wonders what is in the basket. Potatoes probably . . . or turnips . . . or they might even be lumps of coal.

The old woman glances at Anna. Her face is nutlike, dark and withered, with small bright eyes. She nods as if satisfied, and smoothes the cloth over her basket with her knotted hands.

Suddenly the tram lurches, braking hard. There's a commotion — some idiot running across the tramlines. The old woman clutches at her basket but the force is too strong for her. Anna makes a grab as the basket slips away, falls to the floor upside down, and empties itself.

Apples. Big green cooking apples, greasy-skinned. They tumble away under seats, around feet, beneath the hems of winter coats. The tram fills with the smell of apples.

They'll be bruised, thinks Anna. Once they're bruised they won't keep. Already people are stooping to pick up the fruit. Anna doesn't move, because she's afraid of falling if the tram lurches again. Already it is picking up speed, and apples roll everywhere. A man kneels down to gather them and clambers back up with an armload.

'Thank you, my dears, thank you,' murmurs the old woman, who seems paralysed by the disaster and doesn't try to pick up either the apples or her basket.

'Here you are, granny,' says the man, settling the basket back on her knees and replacing the apples he's rescued. 'Hold on a bit tighter, eh?'

As if the man has been appointed to the job, everyone starts to pass apples along to him, to put back in the basket.

'You know how to handle them,' the old woman approves. 'You put them in gentle, that's the way, so they don't bruise. These are good keepers. They'll keep till March.'

Everyone is handing back apples now, as if they were on a production line. The basket is almost full again. The old woman looks up into her helper's face, and carefully chooses two large, unmarked fruit. 'Take these for your little ones, son,' she says. 'They're cookers, mind.'

The man pushes the apples carefully into his pockets. They only just fit; the cloth bulges. He settles his cap firmly on his head. 'Hold on tight to that basket now,' he says, and then he's gone, swinging his way down the aisle and off the tram.

She'll have come into the city to sell those apples at market tomorrow, thinks Anna. They won't fetch much now that they're bruised. That's why she's turning them over so anxiously. That basket is too full. Another sudden stop and they'll be all over the floor again.

'Why not tie the cover back?' Anna asks gently.

'My fingers aren't good for that,' says the old woman. 'My man, he ties it tight for me at home, and then I've only to get it to my daughter's. It's just the one tree we've got but it's a real Trojan. Every year it bears and bears.'

She's not selling the apples, then, she's brought them into the city for her family, from whatever little plot she has. Anna looks at the twisted, arthritic hands. 'Let me tie it up safe for you.'

The old woman nods. Anna draws the cloth over the basket, makes sure that it is secure under the rim, and then knots the ends tightly. She sits back, the incident dissolves, and they are in their own worlds again. There is still a faint scent of apples.

It's Julia who answers the door. Her face brightens when she sees that it's Anna. 'Thank goodness it's you, I hate answering the door at night, in case it's some bore looking for Georgii. He's out, he's got a meeting — well, a discussion about some project. I thought they were all coming back here but it seems not. But, Anna, you look worn out. You shouldn't be doing so much in your condition. Come in and have some tea.'

Anna takes off her things and sits silently while Julia makes tea with her usual quick, light movements. 'I won't be a moment, the samovar was lit anyway — you know what a demon for tea I am in the evenings —'

The heat of Julia's apartment sinks into Anna. They have money, you can see that, but this is money spent as Anna would spend it herself. Not like the Maslovs' apartment with that stiff girl in her black-and-white uniform. Julia has silk cushions, and a long curved sofa upholstered in the same beautiful deep blue silk. There are paintings everywhere. Anna recognizes a Popova still life — and that portrait of a peasant child looks like a Goncharova. Brilliant trees bend down while the young girl's fingers move so surely that she doesn't even need to look as she milks her goat. Anna draws a deep breath. She and Andrei have slipped into darkness but the other world is still there, guarded by colour and form.

'Your tea, Anna.'

'Oh! Thank you, Julia.'

She looks away from the paintings. Opposite her, at either side of a huge, sleek mirror, there are tall white vases filled with branches of beech leaves. Their leaves gleam bronze, as if they've just been picked, although the trees are leafless now. Julia's gaze follows Anna's.

'They're lovely, aren't they? You have to preserve them by standing them in water and glycerine as soon as you pick them.'

'Really? Is that why the leaves haven't dried up?'

'Yes, and it preserves the colours. It's quite easy, you just stand them in hot water and glycerine for a day. You can do it with all kinds of leaves.'

'They're beautiful.' She stares around the room. Everything has Julia's fingerprints on it, or her husband's. It is intact.

'Drink your tea. Would you like sugar, or jam? Some poppyseed cake? Georgii's mother makes it. We drown in cake here.'

'I'm not hungry, thank you.'

'You need to eat. You're so pale, Anna.'

Anna takes three lumps of sugar. Julia's right, she's got to think of the baby. She drinks the tea thirstily, realizing as soon as the hot liquid touches her lips how much she needs it.

'Let me give you some more. Anna, darling, what's wrong? Do you feel faint?'

'Just a minute —' The heat, the tea and Julia's concern are too much for her. The mask of composure she's worn all day cracks, and melts. Anna leans forward and covers her face with her hands.

'Anna!' Instantly Julia is beside her, kneeling by the chair. 'What's happened? Is it the baby?'

Anna shakes her head.

'Then Kolya? Andrei?'

Anna gathers herself. She must not give way now. She pushes her fingertips hard into her forehead. Get a grip on yourself. Julia can't help if you just sit here crying.

'Here, here's my handkerchief —'

Anna wipes her face, breathes deeply. 'I'm sorry, Julia.' She feels embarrassed and ashamed. She hates to be seen out of control like this. Good, the tears are receding. She swallows them back, blinking, and pushes her hair off her face.

'It's Andrei. They arrested him this morning.'

She feels as well as sees Julia's recoil. 'My God. My God, Anna!'

Anna notes what Julia doesn't say. No cry of 'It must be a mistake!' or 'That's impossible.' She has suspected before that Julia has knowledge of the world into which Andrei has disappeared. Now, she is sure of it.

After the initial shock, Julia speaks calmly. 'Tell me what it's about. If you know, that is.'

'Andrei was involved in the treatment of this boy — the son of someone very influential. I won't tell you his name. The child had cancer and he had all the right treatment, but now the cancer's come back in another place. It does that, you know. Every doctor knows that's the main risk. But now they're saying that the boy wasn't treated correctly.'

'I didn't know Andrei worked with cancer patients. I thought you said —'

'I know. He doesn't usually, it's not his field. It's complicated, Julia. It was a colleague who dragged him into it, and then the boy liked Andrei — well, I won't go into it too much. It's better if you don't know.'

Julia nods. Without taking her eyes off Anna's face she reaches out to the small table behind her, feels for the packet of cigarettes that lies there, takes one out and puts it between her lips. 'Do you want one, Anna?'

Anna shakes her head. Julia's fingers find her lighter, and she lights the cigarette. She draws smoke deep into her lungs, half closing her eyes.

'Andrei's done nothing,' says Anna. 'All he thinks about is his patients —'

'Of course I know that. But it's what they decide to think he's done . . . Where are they holding him? The Shpalerka, I suppose.'

'I don't know yet. I've spent all day at work and then I went to see his professor to see if he could help. I'm going to make a lot more inquiries tomorrow — I'll go to the Shpalerka —'

'Don't.' Julia's voice raps out instantly.

'What do you mean? I've got to —'

'Don't, Anna. Keep away from them. Queue up with a parcel, but believe me, it's not a good idea to go "making inquiries" in a place like that. Your name gets into the system. The next thing you know, you're part of the investigation too.'

'So you're saying I should just do nothing — not even try to help him?'

'Anna!' Julia leans forward, crushes her cigarette out in the ashtray, and seizes hold of Anna's wrists, shaking them gently. 'Anna, listen. Believe me, I know what I'm talking about. Do you want that baby to be born in prison and shoved into a children's home? They give them new names, you know. You can never find them again.'

'But Andrei —'

'All he cares about is you and the baby. And Kolya, of course,' adds Julia quickly.

'I've got to do something. I went to see his professor but that was no good. If I can just find out what the charge is —'

'No, Anna, it doesn't work like that. Drink your tea, for God's sake, you look as if you're going to pass out on me.'

Anna swallows hot, sugary tea. Warmth

spreads through her veins but her head feels icy.

'You've got to disappear,' says Julia.

'Disappear! How can I disappear? My papers have to be in order, I've got my residence permit here, my job — we can't live on air. I've got to support Kolya as well as the baby —'

'For heaven's sake, Anna, don't be so naive!' says Julia in a ferocious whisper. 'What do you think is going to happen to them if you're arrested as well? It's because of them that you've got to stay on the outside. Do you think you'll be getting three meals a day in prison, and a nice nurse coming in to make sure the baby's all right? You'll get bread, and a bowl of soup made with fish that's gone off. If you're lucky and anyone on the outside has got any money to send you, you can buy some sugar from the prison shop. As soon as the baby's born, it'll be taken away. What's Kolya going to live on if you're arrested? Oh no, I forgot, he's already sixteen. That problem will soon be solved. They'll arrest him, too. He's getting a bit old for a Home for Juvenile Delinquents, so it'll be prison for him as well.'

'Julia —'

'No. *Listen.* You've already made one serious mistake. You mustn't go traipsing around asking people to help you. All you're doing is creating witnesses to testify against you. I don't mean me, I'm glad you came here. But that professor you were talking about — I don't suppose he was falling over himself to offer his support, was he?'

'No.'

'Exactly. And if he thinks it will protect his own position he'll tell them all about your visit, and every word you said. He wants to survive. He'll throw you to the wolves.'

To the wolves. Sonya Maslova's expression flashes through Anna's mind. *'Get out and don't come back.'* Julia's right. If it would benefit Maslov, Sonya would certainly denounce Anna. But that doesn't mean that other people won't help — they aren't all the same —

'I know what I'm talking about, Anna,' says Julia, in a tone of weary certainty that silences Anna's protests.

'Julia?' she says at last, tentatively.

'Yes?'

'Tell me . . .'

'There's nothing to tell. It's the same story as everybody else's, only in my case a miracle occurred.' Julia smiles ironically. 'Are you sure you want to hear about my little odyssey? All right then, but I'll keep it brief. It's not so lovely that you'd want to dwell on it.

'My father was arrested in '35, when I was seventeen. My parents had already been divorced for years, as you know, and they were poles apart. My mother had got herself into a very strong position one way and another, and she made sure she stayed in it.' Julia's left eyelid twitches. 'She had no contact with any of us, and she changed her name. No doubt she rewrote her entire autobiography so that my father didn't feature. I suppose it's possible that she denounced him; but I've no proof of that and I don't want to think about it.

'He got five years, which didn't seem too bad, except that he had angina and so I was very worried about that. You know I told you I was with the Kazan Ballet Company? Well, I was, but not for as long as I said. I had a fantastic stroke of luck. I got into Moiseyev's new company — you've heard of it?'

'Yes, I think so —'

'It was a new world. It was wonderful. Exactly the kind of dancing I'd always wanted to do. I'd begun to feel so dead and stuck. I'd never realized dancing could be so — oh, I don't know. Witty. Funny. Full of life. He was exacting, of course he was, but he had something you don't come across very often — just once or twice in a lifetime. He had fire. Georgii has it too — that's why —

'Moiseyev had a vision and he would do anything to fulfil it, and he made you see what it could be like. We worked and worked and worked. I loved it, Anna! I was so happy. I realized that I'd never been happy in my life before, not really. You know what it's like when every part of you, every fibre, is used — not used up — but used *for a purpose* — so that you can go on and on and you're not worn out, you're getting stronger all the time?'

Julia's eyes shine as if they are full of tears. Anna is impatient. Why is Julia going on like this, when Andrei has been arrested? At any other time she'd have been glad to hear Julia's story. But Moiseyev has nothing to do with what's happening now, today, to Andrei.

'It doesn't happen very often,' Julia goes on more quietly, as if she senses Anna's thoughts. 'And it soon came to an end. Late in '37, just when everyone was going crazy about us — the Company, I mean . . .' Julia pauses. The light goes from her face. She coughs, and swallows. 'You remember those times. They started doubling everyone's sentence, or worse. You were afraid all the time. It was like a disease. So many people were being arrested. I can't imagine why I thought that being in the Company would make me any safer.

'They asked me to come in for an interview, because they needed to make "certain inquiries". I remember those exact words. I really thought it was just a formality — or at least, I convinced myself that was what I thought. I didn't take anything along with me, no money, not even a spare pair of knickers. Can you imagine? I hurried along dead on time for my appointment because I had a rehearsal that afternoon and I didn't want to be late for it. That's how much of an idiot I still was, in spite of what had happened to my father. I could at least have given them the trouble of coming to look for me! But no. They only had to pick up the phone and I trotted along, as good as gold. Don't you think, Anna, if they'd had to do all their own dirty work, it might have slowed down the process a bit at least?'

'I don't know, Julia.' Anna looks into Julia's dilated, glittering eyes. 'You had no choice really. We didn't fight. I'd have done the same as you.'

'Would you? I don't know. It still seems to

me that we make it too easy for them. If everyone fought right from the first moment then they'd need a lot more Blue-caps. And a lot more guards in the prisons too. The whole performance might even become un-economic.

'But all that's beside the point. If you don't betray yourself, there's usually some-one ready to step forward and betray you. Anyway, so there I was, with my little pale blue leather bag which had nothing in it but a few sticks of stage make-up, some tights and a couple of pairs of dance shoes. The guards who searched me didn't seem in the least surprised by my collection. I suppose they'd seen everything.' Julia seizes hold of Anna's hand. 'Listen. Are you thirty-four now, or thirty-five?'

'Thirty-four.'

'The same as me. And I was nineteen then. We've nearly lived our whole lives all over again, and it's still going on the same. *But you mustn't be like me.*' Julia drops her gaze. 'Sometimes,' she murmurs, 'it doesn't seem like any time at all. I wake up and I think I'm there.' Her voice quivers, while her grip on Anna tightens.

The moment breaks. Julia reaches for another cigarette and lights it, narrowing her eyes against the smoke before she resumes her story in a calm, matter-of-fact tone. 'As it turned out the charge wasn't connected with my father. It was about a joke someone had made at a party. I could prove I wasn't there, because I'd been sick that day and so I'd only just got through the performance and then gone straight home. But they still got me for "insufficient vigilance". However, and this is where my miracle occurred: I only got a year, can you imagine that? In '37! It was like being handed a bunch of flowers. Maybe the judge was a fan of the Company. Every day I expected to be hauled in front of another court and given an additional sentence. It was happening all the time. They were giving ten years, twenty years, anything that came into their heads by then, and of course the prisons were stuffed full so everybody was being sent off to the camps. But, do you know what, my sentence stayed the same. I came out.'

Anna reaches out and takes Julia's hand, squeezes the soft, slender fingers.

'My father died in '39,' says Julia. 'Heart disease. He was out east, at a place called Elgen. We got the notification.'

'Oh, Julia.'

'You remember him?'

'Yes, of course.'

'I was such a fool. I should have run away, but I stayed in Moscow, like a plum on a tree, waiting for them to pick me. I was like nearly everyone I met in prison. Until the very last moment I couldn't believe it would happen to me. But there were a few who saw clearly, right from the start. They just dropped everything, stepped out of their lives and went as far away as they could, as soon as they caught wind of trouble. They went off to any little place they could find in the back end of beyond. There were so many easy fruit to pick — the authorities only had to reach up a hand — and so the ones who'd vanished weren't always pursued.

'I heard about a university professor who went out to Central Asia, slept under the stars and lived on mare's milk and wild honey — he must have had contacts out there, I suppose. It's difficult, I know, especially for us, because we've all been brought up to fill in all our forms and have the right papers and notify everybody of everything. That's one of the things that drew me to Georgii. He's not like that, he cuts through everything.' Julia leans forward and whispers almost inaudibly, 'I know, you're thinking about that Stalin Prize. But Georgii didn't crawl for it. He made the films he wanted to make, that was all. He likes what it brings, of course, and it means he can keep on doing the work he wants. The one thing I know about Georgii is that he would always put me first, whatever happened, and try to keep me safe.'

Anna's mind whirls.

'So . . . after you were released, did you go back to the Company?'

'No.' Julia stares down at her feet, and in a flash Anna remembers. *I kept getting injuries . . . everything was messed up . . . Dancers' feet are horrible . . .* Something else happened to Julia in that time; something bad. That limp she has . . . They did something to her, in there. Anna's skin crawls.

'Anyway,' says Julia, 'it wouldn't have been good for the Company to have me back.'

Anna takes a deep breath. Even as she begins to speak, she knows it's no good. 'I was going to ask, Julia, if your husband might be able to . . . Well, you know. Put in a word for Andrei somehow. But now I see . . .'

'No,' says Julia quietly, 'I'm sorry. I couldn't ask him, after everything he's done for me. You can imagine, for example, what he had to do to get my papers sorted out so I could live here in Leningrad. That was my second miracle, when I met Georgii.'

Anna understands. Georgii and Julia are in their little boat, and only they know how low it lies in the water. One more passenger might send them all to the bottom.

'It's all right, Julia, I do understand.' Her body feels so heavy, as if she'll never be able to move again. 'But if I go away, Andrei will think I've abandoned him.'

'Drink your tea. You're so pale, Anna, you've got to look after yourself. Andrei won't think anything like that. He'll guess what's happened. In prison, you learn a lot of things very quickly. But until you've been "there" you can't have any idea. There was a woman in the Lubyanka who'd been outside, standing in a queue to deliver a parcel for her husband. Or maybe there were two parcels . . . Yes, that was it! They accepted one parcel but started to make a fuss about the other. All at once, she was pulled out of the queue and taken inside "for interview". That was that. She was arrested too. There was no one left on the outside to bring parcels for her. The worst of it was she had two children. Remember, there's nothing easier than for them to arrest you too. Don't think it can't happen.'

'But I can't let a chance that I might get arrested as well prevent me from trying to do anything for Andrei. I'm not talking about causing trouble, just making inquiries.'

'You really don't know anything! How can I help you when you won't even try to help yourself? Listen. There was a woman in our cell, Anna, who was pregnant. A bit further on than you, about six months I think. That didn't stop them putting her on the conveyor belt.'

'What do you mean?'

'It's a form of interrogation. They kept her awake, standing up, all day and all night for two days — it's something they do, and sometimes it's not two days, it's five or six or even more. When she came back to the cell she vomited all over the floor, and then collapsed. The next night she miscarried. She stuffed her blanket into her mouth because she didn't want anyone to hear. I think she thought there was a chance the baby might be born alive. But it was dead, of course. They took it away. The guard put it in a bucket. They took her away too and I didn't see her again. You haven't been there, Anna. You think it can't happen to you. But I tell you they can do anything. Anything at all.'

A long silence. The air of the room bristles with what Julia has tried to forget. Julia sits, head bowed. At last Anna stirs, leans forward, and strokes Julia's hair. Her hand remembers the feel of it so well. In the old days, playing under the table in the communal apartment, they used to plait and unplait each other's hair. Julia's was always longer and thicker, like the hair of a princess.

'Thank you, Julia. You're a good friend. I'd better go now, before Georgii comes home.'

20

'Prisoner Alekseyev, A. M., has been transferred to the Lubyanka Prison, Moscow.' The official does not look up. He makes a mark on a form, his face blank.

'But —'

'Next!'

The woman behind her in the queue pokes Anna in the small of her back. Anna turns and sees the muffled face, the shadowed eyes. The woman's expression is not impatient, but warning.

Anna stands aside, still clutching her parcel. The queue shuffles forward. Everyone watches the little opening where the official's face is framed, and the shutter above it, which can be opened or closed only from the inside. At any moment, the official might slam down the shutter. It often happens. And then you wait an hour, two hours, hoping against hope that your turn will come. The snow is trampled flat, and has the thick blue glisten of ice. Cold strikes up through your boots as you wait and wait and wait. Sometimes the inquiry window opens again and the official begins to 'deal with' the queue. Sometimes it doesn't. You come back the next day. You come back again the day after, and if you have to you'll keep on coming day after day, with the same parcel. You shift from foot to foot. Sometimes you have to stamp your feet to keep the circulation going, but you try not to draw attention to yourself.

The first time, you can't believe that so many people would wait for so long, and yet the window would fly shut, spitefully, while a long line still snakes across the snow. It seems as if the official has calculated exactly the amount of despair that each person in the queue needs to feel, each day. Soon you get used to it. You know the ropes and you just shrug wearily when someone new tries to question the officials. All questions achieve is to make trouble for everyone else. If an official gets into a bad mood, the window will soon slam down.

That woman standing over there with her parcel in her hands, looking lost, you can tell she's new. She hasn't learned her lesson yet. Those officials are all the same, even though the faces change. None of them has the slightest interest in pleas or tears. They have a job to do, and that's that. What do you want? Special treatment?

Anna stares down at the parcel. In it are two sets of clean underwear, cigarettes, a bar of chocolate, a warm sweater and a pillowcase. She packed them in so carefully. She knew she couldn't risk enclosing a letter, or even a note. Julia had told her what to do.

Transferred! She never imagined that. Oh God, to the Lubyanka. She never thought of them taking him away from Leningrad. Why have they done it? What does it mean?

She stands still, irresolute. The cold sinks into her mind, paralysing it. Should she join the queue again, and beg the official to tell her more? But she's had to wait for over two hours to get to the front, and there are many more people waiting now than there were when she first arrived. She couldn't possibly reach the window again before closing time. Why should they care? It's a job. They have to take their lunch breaks and go home dead on time. Why should they put themselves out for the families of prisoners? Especially prisoners of Andrei's type. Common criminals are one thing. Even if you don't steal or rape or murder yourself, you can understand such crimes, and you know what to do with them. Prisons have been dealing with those types since time began. But these wreckers and spies, saboteurs and socially dangerous elements are a completely different matter. No matter how many you deal with, they keep on coming, like bedbugs.

Anna could come back tomorrow. On the other hand she daren't take another day off work without a certificate. Morozova is rigid about such things. If Anna can't produce one . . .

There mustn't be any inquiries. If Morozova hears even a whisper about Andrei's arrest, she'll soon find a way of getting rid of Anna. Her pioneering model nursery can't be contaminated by association. It'll be obvious that Anna can't have been 'sufficiently vigilant' herself, otherwise she would have denounced her husband. The authorities would support Morozova in sacking Anna, given that she's in charge of impressionable young minds.

If you don't have a job, you're scarcely a person any more.

Andrei won't know that she came here with the parcel. They took him away with nothing, just the things he had when he was arrested. What if he thinks she didn't come because she was afraid? Like a fool, she'd thought he was still close.

She'll go to Moscow. She'll have to arrange it somehow — but how? She'd have to show her passport to buy the railway ticket. Anna clutches her parcel tighter as her thoughts fly one way and then another like a flock of sparrows. She doesn't know anyone who can help them in Moscow. The Lubyanka . . .

No, she tells herself. It's a name, that's all. It's probably no worse there than the Kresty. Except that in Moscow, there's the Kremlin, which is the centre of it all —

Anna stands stock-still, her lips moving. She's making herself conspicuous. One or two people glance at her uneasily. The next thing she'll be down on her knees in the snow, howling like a dog. They've seen it all before, and what happens next, too.

The woman who was behind Anna in the queue turns away from the window. She's empty-handed now; they've allowed her to hand in her parcel. As she passes Anna, she brushes against her, as if accidentally. 'It's not good to stand about,' she murmurs, and then she's gone and Anna's not even sure if she heard the words or imagined them. But they have their effect. Anna comes to herself as the queue shuffles forward a couple of paces. Heavy, huddled figures that look neither to right nor left, but only ahead, or down at the crushed snow beneath their feet. It is so cold. The wind is rising again. That icy wind that sweeps off the Neva and funnels up the streets, twisting and turning, fingering its way into every stone crevice. Later on it will snow, Anna thinks. The marks of the shuffling queue will be wiped out.

She turns away, and begins to walk briskly, head lowered into the wind. She must be careful. If she falls, it might hurt the baby. She walks faster, feeling as if a thousand eyes are watching her back.

She's walked only a couple of blocks when she knows she must stop. Cold sweat covers her body, and she can hardly breathe. She stumbles into an entrance, out of the wind. Anna leans against the stone. Just to be out of that bitter wind feels like a reprieve. It's an entrance like any other, deep-set, with a closed double door. It smells of damp stone. Rubbish has blown into the corner, and no one has swept it away. People hurry past along the street, taking no notice of Anna. They want to get home before the snow thickens into a blizzard.

She's always wanted to get home, too. It didn't matter how many chores there were, or how heavy the bags of shopping she had to lug up the stairs. She could cope, never mind if Kolya was being difficult, or Andrei was late home for the third time that week. Of course she'd grumbled sometimes. Sometimes she greeted Andrei with a dry, cold complaint about the spoiled food. When Kolya pushed her too far she would shout at him, 'You think studying means staring out of the window for an hour with the book in front of you? It won't go in by magic, you know! What's going to become of you if you don't work and pass your exams?'

'So how many exams did *you* pass?' Kolya retorted once, and she replied furiously, 'Not as many as I'd have liked!' and then swallowed the bitter words that were rushing into her mouth. If she hadn't had to care for him, ever since her mother's death, she might have studied art. She used to cherish the idea of being a student, free to do nothing but think, work, develop. Kolya had no idea how fortunate he was.

'I just want to live my life!' shouted Kolya, and she stared at him helplessly, not knowing where to begin to explain to him how wrong he was.

But perhaps it's Kolya who is right. He's taken a close look at the life she and Andrei lead, and decided that he doesn't want any of it, thank you very much. She and Andrei have done everything they were supposed to do. They both believed in work, duty, commitment, self-discipline. Andrei has passed countless exams. Sometimes Anna thinks she's never stopped working. At home as well as at the nursery, there is always one more thing to be done than she can manage.

She tried to keep her father from despair with endless glasses of tea and home-grown vegetables. She made sure that Kolya gave him peace, and protected the time he needed for his writing. She lay awake at night, listening to her father pace sleeplessly from one side of the room to the other, and wondered if she should go to him or leave him alone. All the while she was doing her best to bring up Kolya as she believed she would bring up her own child.

At nursery the work was endless, but she didn't mind that. What was difficult was meeting all the targets set for the children while also giving them a life that was worth living. She almost has to laugh when she looks back on herself, so endlessly busy, cleaning, cooking, preserving, 'getting hold of' whatever she could, running here and there, studying child psychology even though she found most of it incomprehensibly dull, poring over Kolya's school-book Latin. The statistics course; battling with the Maleviches; trying to cope with Morozova; saving seeds from year to year in carefully labelled packets; cleaning out the drains with washing soda . . .

Much good had it all done. It's comic, really, how naive she's been. Always looking on the bright side! Even the siege didn't teach her a lesson. She came out of those terrible years still confident that there was such a thing as normal life to return to, and cherish.

But now she has nothing to go home to. No one would know if she stayed here all night, huddled against this wall.

They've taken Andrei to Moscow. How do prisoners travel? By ordinary train? Do other passengers see them?

No, the authorities won't take that risk. They'll be in sealed cars, so that it looks to the casual eye as though goods are being transported, not human beings. People who are arrested have to drop out of life and disappear without trace. You might know a bit of detail about one or two arrests, if these are people close to you. Suddenly a colleague isn't there. Husbands and wives go about looking dazed and pitiful. Even the authorities can't make a wife fail to notice that her husband hasn't come home, but each tiny circle of awareness is isolated.

Sometimes, though, you are supposed to talk about a notorious arrest, loudly and dramatically, in order to prove that you haven't got the slightest sympathy with the person who's been picked up. Anna is old enough to remember Kirov's murder, in 1934. She was only sixteen but she remembers the loud public declarations as well as the guarded whispers. She even remembers a joke that went the rounds for years: *If all the people who murdered Kirov were laid end to end, the line would stretch from here to the Kremlin.* What is said aloud, of course, is very different. *'Have you heard? Filipov has been arrested.'* And then a careful glance. *'He turned out to be a Trotskyist sympathizer. It just goes to show. I was completely taken in by him!'*

Sometimes they talk about 'ripping away the masks', an expression that makes Anna think of a sinister fancy-dress party. Now they'll use such expressions of Andrei. Of course people who appear to be perfectly ordinary colleagues can suddenly turn out to be spies, saboteurs and wreckers! If you haven't learned that by now, where have you been?

'Haven't you heard? Dr Alekseyev has been

arrested. Thankfully, he didn't succeed in pulling the wool over everyone's eyes.'

Anna leans her cheek against the stone entrance pillar. Its coldness and roughness are comforting. *'I'm stone, aren't I? What else do you expect — sympathy? I'm here to hold the house up, that's all.'*

Inside her, the baby moves. Poor little one, you don't know anything. Just keep on blindly and confidently growing. Don't give up, not for a second, and I promise you that I won't give up either. Wait just a minute. I'll soon feel better and then we'll go home. It's only that your father —

She'll get money to him. There are things she can sell. You are allowed to send money.

Suddenly the face of a former cook's assistant at the nursery comes into Anna's mind. A long, hardened face, utterly devoid of beauty. Skin that looked like bark. She had strong forearms and her muscles bulged as she lifted the heavy soup pots. One day Anna asked if she had children at home. Musya laughed, a short bark of a laugh, slapped down a loaf of bread and began to carve it. 'I know better than that,' she said. 'What's the point? It only makes you soft, see, and then you can't carry on.'

Anna hasn't seen her for years. Not since before the war. She disappeared one day, just didn't come into work, and the space where she had been closed over. Anna remembers another thing. If anyone shivered or complained, Musya would say, 'Cold! You call this cold?'

If Musya were here now she'd say, 'Bad! You call this bad? Look at you, you've got enough to eat and a warm bed to go home to. What's the point of complaining? It only makes you soft, and then you can't carry on.'

If only they don't hurt him. If only he can keep his strength up.

It's Andrei's second day on the conveyor belt. He's standing in a pool of light which is so harsh and dazzling that behind it his interrogator becomes a dark stain on the opposite wall. If Andrei closes his eyes the interrogator shouts and one of the guards slaps Andrei across the face. The wound on his head has opened again and is oozing blood.

There are three interrogators, working in shifts. Dmitriev has just come on duty. He has a soft voice and a sympathetic manner. He tuts whenever a guard hits Andrei, but of course makes no move to prevent it. It's just one of those unfortunate but necessary things which a civilized man has to deplore.

If only he could do something about it!

Dmitriev needs Andrei's help if he's to help him in return. Surely he can understand that? Andrei moves his head sideways. He can't see the pile of papers on Dmitriev's desk, but he knows that they are there and what is in them. The chief document is Andrei's statement. It is all ready, typed out, waiting only for Andrei's signature. There are also witness statements, but Andrei hasn't been allowed to see these. At the start of his first full interrogation, he was given his own statement to read. Dmitriev was on duty then, too. He sat behind his desk and watched Andrei with his arms folded and an expectant look on his face. The lamp wasn't even switched on. Andrei could see the whole room clearly: the desk, the shiny dark brown floor, the oily green paint on the walls, which looked as if it was still wet. There were no windows. He read the document slowly, examining each paragraph. A flush of rage went through him but he kept his eyes moving, and turned the page calmly. *Take your time,* he thought to himself. *No need to rush, given that every second you are reading this is a second when they are not interrogating you.*

They'd made a mistake when he was first

brought in; at least, he's now certain that it was a mistake, from the care they've taken ever since to keep him away from other prisoners. Andrei understands that the plan is for each man to feel utterly alone. When he arrived in Moscow late at night, they'd put him into a van with 'Bread' written on the side, and driven him straight to the Lubyanka. He'd been pretty sure where they were going. This time, he knew what to expect. They processed him, and then pushed him straight into a cell which was full of sleeping bodies.

Full indeed. There wasn't an inch to lie down. A dim greenish light shone from a bulb in a cage of wire on the ceiling. Sleepers were hunched on the two narrow benches let down from the walls, but the rest of the men were on the floor. There must have been eight or ten at least, crammed into a two-man cell. The room stank of sweat, urine and faeces. There was a large uncovered toilet bucket within inches of the sleepers' heads. The air was full of sighs, groans and muttering.

There was no chance of lying down, but it didn't matter. He could stand against the cell door. But suddenly there was a stir from one of the benches, and a figure sat up. 'They just brought you in?' he murmured.

His hair hung long and matted around his face. His eyes were set so deep in their hollows that Andrei could not read them.

'Yes.'

'Did they transfer you from another cell?'

'No. From Leningrad.'

'Right.'

Andrei didn't understand why the man's voice changed on hearing he was from Leningrad rather than another cell in the Lubyanka. Later he would learn that there were certain prisoners — spies — who were constantly moved from cell to cell to pick up whatever information they could.

'Where are your things?'

Andrei indicated his overcoat. 'This is it.'

'Nice and warm, anyway. You'd better lie down over there,' said the man, pointing, but Andrei couldn't see a space.

'It's all right, I'll stand.'

'Don't be a fool, you'll have the guards in again. Lie down there, by the bucket. What's your name?'

Andrei told him, and the man nodded. 'I'm Kostya Rabinovich. Cell foreman. We'll get you sorted out in the morning. What's your profession?'

'I'm a doctor.'

'Doctor, eh? Could be useful. I'm an engineer myself.'

Andrei picked his way carefully across the sleeping bodies. He eased himself down, and the men gave way for him, grumbling and sighing. He lay as still as he could, wedged in by male flesh. He had never slept so close to anyone but Anna since he was a child. The air was fetid but cold, because the small high window was open behind its bars. He didn't mind the cold. The room would be unbearable otherwise, with the smell and the heat of all these bodies. He huddled down. Tomorrow night he would take off his pullover and roll it up for a pillow, but he couldn't do that now, because there wasn't room to move.

An engineer! Perhaps the entire cell was packed with surgeons and architects and marine biologists. Andrei shrugged his head down between his shoulders. The man behind him groaned, heaved his weight over, and then was still again.

Andrei could not sleep. He lay quite still, listening to the sounds around him. In the far corner of the cell, a man sobbed in his sleep. It went on for a while until there was a commotion as another man heaved himself up with a thick curse and pummelled the sleeper's back. 'Give it a rest, can't you?'

From time to time a figure rose and went to the bucket. The splash of urine seemed to go on and on. Andrei's stomach hurt, but it was only nerves. He could wait until morning.

Suddenly, from outside the cells, there was an explosion of voices. A man screamed, on and on. How could he scream like that, without taking breath? The hair crisped on the back of Andrei's neck. At last the scream broke into a howl. There came a clatter and a thud as if something had been thrown on the floor. Guards yelled and cursed. There was the sound of blows raining on flesh. The man yelped like a dog with a choke chain around his neck. At last the noise guttered, and died. Inside the cell there was silence too. Most of the men must have woken up, but no one spoke.

Deliberately, Andrei sought out the tension in his shoulders and arms. He clenched his muscles even tighter, and then let them go. As he did so he named the muscles to himself: anterior deltoid, lateral deltoid, posterior deltoid, rotators, biceps, triceps . . . Over and over again he tensed and then relaxed, taking care not to nudge his neighbours. Little by little, the sounds of the cell flowed back, like peace. A man farted, another muttered in a quick, panicky voice as if he were explaining himself to somebody.

He'd expected solitary confinement. This was better, surely. They were all in the same boat and to some extent it must be organized. Kostya had said he was the foreman. He'd been in here for a while, to judge by the length of his hair.

Suddenly keys grated in the cell door, and it was opened wide. Two guards flung a man through the entrance, and then immediately stepped back and slammed the door shut. The prisoner had fallen forward, on top of the sleeping bodies. Men roused up, swearing, but Kostya was already on his feet. 'Lie down, can't you? Where's that doctor? Over here! Make way for him.'

Andrei got up. This time it was easier to get across the cell. The other men shuffled up so he could kneel by the collapsed prisoner. The pulse was rapid, but weak. He put his head to the prisoner's chest and listened to his heart. 'He's fainted. Call the guards and ask them for ammonia.'

'Call the guards! Can't you bring him round? He's been on the conveyor belt, that's all.'

Before long, the man came round. His legs and feet were horribly swollen. In the dim light his face was distorted, with blackened eyes, cracked lips and a swollen tongue. Andrei wondered if this was the man he had heard screaming.

'He's been on the conveyor belt for five days, no wonder,' said Kostya. All the time they talked in the same almost noiseless murmur.

'What's that?'

'The interrogators work you over in teams. You can't sleep and you have to stand up. Sometimes they move you from room to room so you get disorientated. This is Mitya's third time on the belt, but they've had no luck with him yet. He's tough, this one. They won't be very happy. He just says no to everything. It's hard but it's the way to survive. Start signing things and that's the end of you.'

They gave Mitya water, and he sank into sleep.

'He'll be all right in the morning,' said Kostya, somewhat optimistically in Andrei's view. 'Leave him now, get your sleep.'

But Andrei had barely settled back on the floor when a voice behind him began to murmur: ' "Neither hast thou destroyed me in my transgressions, but in thy compassion raised me up when I lay in despair . . ." '

So they were still jailing believers. Odd, thought Andrei, that you have to be in prison before you know what's really going on. *Raised me up . . .* Can he possibly

452

believe it? The voice of the praying man was like a trickle of water. Surely I'll be able to sleep soon, thought Andrei. *'The interrogators work you over in teams.'* Probably it was best to know these things, or Kostya wouldn't have said them. He seemed a decent man —

All at once there was another racket at the door. Bodies stiffened. Heads poked out of blankets. This time it was his name they were calling.

'Alekseyev, A.M.!'

'I'm over here.'

'Get going, with your things!'

But unlike most of these prisoners, he had no bundle of personal possessions. *'That won't be necessary,'* they'd said when they came to take him away. Maybe that's what they always say. Anna will find a way to get a parcel to him. He thought it might be possible for prisoners to receive money, but he hoped she wouldn't send any. Without his pay, she would have little enough to keep herself and Kolya.

Eyes watched as he was bundled away. The guards seemed angry and agitated, as if this wasn't part of their routine. Something must have gone wrong.

The guards marched him down the corridor and through a door which led to a set of stone stairs. They were back stairs, not like the big staircase he'd climbed earlier.

They went down flight after flight. Lights in wire cages were set into the walls, but there were no windows. Andrei counted the stairs, trying to remember how many he'd climbed before. Surely not as many as this. Now they were at the bottom. The guards opened a heavy door, and there was another corridor, with a low roof and dim lighting. They stopped at a cell door which had three steel panels set across it. One of the guards unlocked the door, and once again he was shoved inside.

The cell was very small, but clean, and filled with the same wan glow as the two-man cell. There was no window. The bed was a wooden bench, let down from the wall but even narrower than the one in the last cell. There was a thin straw mattress, and a pillow, which Andrei examined closely and then put down on the floor. At least the bucket on the floor had a cover.

He lay down on his back. The peephole cover rattled, and an eye examined him, unblinking. His heart began to race, but a few seconds later boots tramped away along the corridor.

He was alone now. It had been comforting to lie down with other men who were in the same boat, torn out of their lives just as Andrei had been. Andrei had spoken only a few words to Kostya, but the exchange seemed even more precious in retrospect than it had done at the time. *'Where's that doctor? Over here! Make way for him, can't you?'*

Those words held the breath of normal life. If a man was sick or in pain, he needed a doctor, and other people would move aside to make sure that the doctor reached him. A doctor was there, not to demean and humiliate, but to heal.

It was good that Kostya was the foreman, willing to organize things and make sure that people behaved as they should. Andrei wondered if the men in the cell had elected him. Again, that was comforting. You need someone to speak up for you.

Andrei realized now what the guards' mistake had been, and why they were so jumpy. He wasn't supposed to have been slung into that shared cell. Someone would probably pay for letting it happen. He was meant to be in solitary, in the bowels of the prison, not knowing what was happening, and above all not knowing that he wasn't alone.

What was Kostya here for, he wondered. And all the rest of them? It made his own arrest seem more ordinary, rather than the extraordinary and terrible blow of fate which it had seemed since that very first telephone call telling him not to come into work. He hadn't been singled out, as he'd thought. Plenty of others must have thought that they were decent, professional men, doing a good job, until that long ring on the doorbell, or the loud knocking that didn't care if it roused the whole building. There were ten men in that cell which was meant only for two. They must be hauling in hundreds.

Footsteps came again. This time the guard tramped past without checking on him.

He would learn every footstep. He would find out who else was on this corridor. He was in solitary but he knew he wasn't alone. There were many others, and even if he couldn't see them he still knew they were there. Andrei closed his eyes. He thought he heard tapping, but it was so faint he was probably imagining it. He strained his ears, but the tapping faded into the beat of his pulse. Sleep rushed up to meet him as the ground rushes up to meet a man who jumps out of an aeroplane.

It's Andrei's third day on the conveyor belt. His legs and feet are so swollen that when the order comes to move, they will not obey him. Two guards take hold of him, one on each side, with their hands under his elbows. They run him out of the interrogation room and down a corridor. His head falls forward and his knees sag to the ground. He knows he must keep on his feet but although he makes a superhuman effort he can no longer do so. The guards drag him into another room, which also contains a desk, a shadowy man and a strong pool of light in which he must stand.

'On your feet! *On your feet, you filthy cock-sucking cunt!*'

They swear at him, and hit him, but he still cannot remain upright. The interrogator gets to his feet, walks around the desk and picks up a heavy jug full of water. He comes over and hurls the water into Andrei's face.

Andrei opens his mouth. A stream of water, mixed with blood, runs down his face. He puts out his dry, cracked tongue and licks the water. A guard punches him in the back.

'Stand up! Stand up!'

They are all melting into one, the guards and the interrogators. Only the jug isn't melting but doubling. Now there are two jugs, and now four, sharp-cut and glittering in the downward dazzle of light.

He is on the floor of his cell. He stretches out his fingers, and they move. They are fat, like sausages. His clothes are wet, with water, with blood and perhaps with urine. There is a bad smell. He has been asleep.

'For goodness' sake,' says a voice mildly, 'surely you realize, an intelligent man like you, that all this is completely unnecessary? You can stop it any time you like. You only have to say the word. All this fuss over something as petty as a signature. It's really not all that important. The trouble is that my colleagues are not as understanding as I am. I've been doing my best to make them see reason, as I'm sure you appreciate, but I'm not going to be able to do so for much longer. Now, let's have a look at this wretched document again. I simply don't see what you've got to object to. Brodskaya's already admitted the whole thing. She couldn't spill the beans fast enough. Russov's corroborated everything. We'll be bringing you face to face with him later on. Pretty upsetting for a decent chap like Russov. But the fact is — and why not admit it? — you were putty in Brodskaya's hands. She thought the whole thing up, didn't she? We're only asking you to admit your own share in it, which isn't that significant, let's face it. Once it's all down on paper, with your signature on it, things will get a lot easier for you.

'We've got most of it already, as you know, since you've read this. But there are just a few details which need tidying up. That Brodskaya! Well, I won't say what I think of her, because it wouldn't be very complimentary. It's not your fault you fell for it. All you have to do is admit your own role, which, let's face it, is only a very minor one, and then we can start to clear up this whole nasty business. And I can go home, and you can get a good night's sleep, and then things will start to look better.'

The words patter around Andrei like rain. He thought he was still lying on the floor of his cell, but it seems that he is here, standing in front of Dmitriev's desk. The guards have placed him much closer to Dmitriev this time. The light glares in his face and hurts his eyes.

Dmitriev takes a cigarette from the packet in front of him, lights it and breathes in the smoke luxuriously. 'I'm sorry, how rude of me — do you smoke?'

Andrei stares ahead. He knows this man now. If he starts talking, Dmitriev will trip him up. At first Andrei tried to give his own account of Gorya Volkov's treatment, but he soon realized that none of his interrogators was interested in that. The facts were an irritation that led to more blows. Kostya was right. Say nothing, and sign nothing. Spit out every word they try to put into your mouth.

Andrei sways. The guard shoves him upright. There is a rushing sound in his ears, but he isn't going to faint. He lost his balance, that was all. A blow to his left ear has affected the inner-ear fluid. It will only be temporary.

'Come along. Have a cigarette. I know you want one. I'll order some food to be sent up. How does chicken salad sound?'

It sounds like a lie, thinks Andrei. *Chicken salad, in winter! He might at least have come up with something more convincing.* Andrei licks his thick, dry lips.

'A glass of wine, perhaps?'

Or perhaps Dmitriev himself has gone completely crazy, after years of this. The period of unconsciousness on his cell floor has done Andrei good. He can join things up in his mind again. He was beginning not to know what was real and what was not.

Dmitriev must have moved the light. It is pointing down, and without the glare Andrei can see Dmitriev's face clearly. He is smiling. He looks clean, mannered, urbane. Perhaps he showers, when he takes a break from interrogation. No matter how wide his smile stretches across his face, his teeth never show.

'All right, all right,' he says to Andrei, with weary, tolerant humour, as if Andrei were a schoolboy in trouble with the authorities. 'You don't want any chicken salad. You don't want a cigarette. Be off with you, then. You've got a visitor coming along later. A very important visitor. You'll want to be at your best for him.'

The guards kick Andrei along the corridor. He knows this is all part of it. Dmitriev must be civilized and smell of cologne and excellent tobacco. The bald one, Bashkirtsev, must scream abuse in a high-pitched voice and end every session with the words, *I'll have you, do you understand? I'll wring your guts until you're shitting blood.'* The third interrogator, Fokin, has to be as tenacious as a rat. He plants his finger on the statement, picks out a different sentence each time, and goes over and over it in a voice that drips through Andrei's head like acid.

'A very important visitor.' Deliberately, Andrei shuts his mind. Here is the cell door. The guards push him through it and the floor comes up to meet him. He is off the

conveyor belt. He falls down and down as the stone floor rocks under him.

Anna has scoured the apartment clean. She has tidied away everything that was tipped out on to the floor. She has folded the linen, rearranged the books, and put drawers and cupboards back in order. She has wiped every surface clean. All the smears and fingermarks are gone. Her feet tap, echoing.

Those men looked so sure of themselves as they emptied the drawers and swept books off the shelves to the floor, as if they were performing to an invisible, approving audience. This is still my home, she thinks. She looks around the room where she and Andrei have lived and worked and slept. She stares through the doorway at Kolya's bed, and the piano. It has been badly out of tune since the men took it apart.

She feels nothing for the apartment or for what it contains. It's finished as far as she's concerned. One day she and Andrei will remake it, but until then she'll eat and sleep here, and go through their possessions to make a list of what can be sold. She needs money to send to Andrei.

By the time Anna gets into bed she is so tired that she falls asleep almost at once, huddled on her own side of the bed.

She dreams that it's summer, and she and Kolya are at the dacha. He's sitting on a low wall, and she's standing beside him so that his face is level with her own. He is barefoot, tanned, dusty. He leans against her and she smells his sun-warmed skin. He chatters about a story he remembers from kindergarten, and she praises him for re-membering it so well. He is slightly offended by her praise.

'After all, Mama, I *am* six,' he says. She looks at his face in surprise, because Kolya never calls her by that name. But as she does so she realizes that this child is fairer than Kolya. There are sun-bleached streaks in his hair, and a scattering of freckles on his nose. His eyes are the colour of Andrei's.

'But, K-K-olya,' she stammers, 'what's happened? Why have you changed like this?'

The boy doesn't answer. Instead he gives her a quick, sweet smile before looking down as if the question embarrasses him. Suddenly she hears Andrei's voice through the trees. It is strong, almost imperative.

'Anna!' he calls. 'Hurry! There's no time to lose. You must go now!'

The child looks up, with Andrei's eyes. Anna stares through the trees but she can't see Andrei anywhere. Again his voice comes, even stronger this time: 'Go now, Anna! Go *now*.'

She wakes, gasping, and switches on the bedside light. It is ten past two. Her nightdress is stuck to her body with sweat. But it wasn't a nightmare, it was just —

She sits bolt upright, listening. Down in the street a car slows. She hears its engine pulse, and then it accelerates again, driving away, turning the corner. She listens until the sound of the car's engine has completely disappeared, then gets up and wraps her dressing-gown around her. She must calm herself. This is bad for the baby. She'll make some camomile tea and then read until she is sleepy again.

'Remember, there's nothing easier than for them to arrest you as well. Don't think it can't happen.'

She feels the baby move in the cage of her pelvis. Not so much a fluttering any more. It's imperative, like Andrei's voice in the dream. *Here I am. You can't forget about me.*

'Anna! Hurry! There's no time to lose. You must go now!'

It's Andrei's voice, coming from wherever he is through the dark of dreams. She won't go back to bed. The dream has woken her for a reason, she knows that now. These hours have been given to her to get things ready. She will collect everything of value: her tablecloths and napkins, the photographs, the little gold chain Andrei gave her to replace her mother's gold necklace, which they sold in the siege. Almost everything went then; books were burned and furniture chopped up for fuel. Her mother's set of porcelain spoons fetched two candles, while her parents' wedding rings and the little gold necklace went for a jar of lard.

It was worth it. You can't eat gold.

It's the same now. Time to get rid of everything in order to survive. If she had time she would even sell Kolya's piano.

Anna fetches her bicycle panniers, and begins to pack them. She mustn't make them too heavy, or she won't be able to carry them downstairs.

She crosses to the window, lifts the blind, and peeps out. The moon is high and sharp. Snow has fallen, but not too heavily. They'll clear the streets, and she'll be able to push her bike even if she can't ride it.

The baby kicks again, warningly.

No, you fool, you won't be able to take the bike. In this weather you'll be exhausted by the time you've gone a couple of kilometres. It's no good loading up those panniers. You'll have to take the train, and then walk at the other end. It's a long walk, but you'll manage it if you pace yourself. It'll be quiet enough on the train on a weekday, but don't make yourself conspicuous by trying to carry a big bundle. Everyone in the building knows Andrei's been arrested. If they see you going off laden down with half your possessions, they might contact the police.

The thought of leaving the bike behind is agonizing. Without it, how will she get around? There's Kolya's bike, of course, which is already at the dacha. They'll just have to manage, sharing it.

She looks around the room, frowning. Kolya's music. He'll never be able to replace it all. She must take the photographs, and her parents' letters, and —

The things she has knitted for the baby fit into a small bag. She must take some linen at least, and as many clothes as she can carry. It's so lucky that Kolya's already got his stuff down at Galya's.

Or no! — she has a better idea. She'll put on layers so she doesn't have to carry too many clothes. She can wear two or three jumpers and a couple of skirts at least. All her skirts are too tight now but she has stitched elastic into the plackets so she should be able to wear them for another month at least. She'll put on a jacket under her coat. If she waits until the last moment to get dressed, she won't get too hot before she goes out into the freezing streets. She'll just have to sweat it out on the train.

Darya Alexandrovna might want to buy these embroidered napkins — or, at any rate, exchange them for food. She loves pretty things. Andrei's photograph of his parents has a silver frame; she'll take that too. And the tea. There must be two hundred grams in the jar.

Anna treads lightly, opening drawers and cupboards without sound. She doesn't want the neighbours to know she's awake. Perhaps it's just as well that the Blue-caps wrecked her food stores. The jars would have been too heavy to carry and it would have been agony to leave them. If only she could say to Julia: *'Come round, help yourself, take anything you want. I know you'll pay me back one day.'* But it's not safe. If Julia were seen in this apartment, the wheels would begin to grind for her, too.

She will leave everything behind, as if she's gone to work as usual. She'd be easy enough to trace if they tried to find her, but perhaps, if she's not here, they'll leave her alone. Surely things have changed a little since Yezhov's time, when processions of wives and brothers and husbands and sisters followed every 'political' to prison.

Here are her lecture notes from the statistics course. She'll leave those behind with pleasure. The cardboard folder with Kolya's drawings and the first little stories he wrote, when he was little. That won't take up much room.

She unties the ribbon and opens the folder. A portrait of herself stares up with manic smile and huge hands spread in welcome. He has even got the number of fingers right. ANNA, he's printed underneath in careful capitals.

She will start drawing again, out at the dacha. There will be no excuse there. She's spent too long filling up every moment of her day so as not to have to look at anything too closely.

Another car slows. Her heart accelerates, then eases as the car drives on.

'*Go now, Anna! Go* now.'

The bag is full. All their money is in her purse. Now she must eat something, and then get dressed in all her layers, because it's past five o'clock.

Everything is ready. Anna wears her brown woollen skirt and cream blouse with her loose blue dress over it, and a long thick jumper of Andrei's on top. Her black jacket, and now her overcoat, boots, a big woollen scarf tied over her head, a shawl across her chest. She picks up her two bags, and weighs them. She can manage them easily. She's only got to walk to the tram stop, and the tram will take her to the station. She can rest on the short train journey, and at the other end it doesn't matter how often she stops on her walk to the dacha. Once she's out of the city she can take her time.

She sits down on the chair by the living-room door. She is really leaving now. Perhaps she will never come back. She'll probably lose her right of residence in Leningrad, anyway.

The room, which has seen so much, regards her calmly. This is the room to which she rushed home from school when she was little, always hoping her mother would be there, even though she knew that nine days out of ten Vera would be at the hospital. Here, in this apartment, she first met Andrei, when he knocked on their door very early one morning to tell her that her father had been wounded. She was afraid of the knock on the door, even then. In this living room she slept with Kolya in her arms and Andrei beside her, blankets and coats heaped over them, while the windows filled with frost and the metronome on the radio ticked and ticked as the hours of the siege slowly passed. This is where she heated the milk to give newborn Kolya his first feed at home, her fingers still shaking from the shock of her mother's death; through the door, in Kolya's room, is where her father died. In this bed, her baby was conceived.

But the room says nothing. For the first time she really understands how old it is. It was here long before she was born or the Levins came to live here, and it will be here long after she's dead. She's part of this apartment's life, but never the whole of it; perhaps, really, not a very large part at all. If the Maleviches moved in tomorrow — and they've always had their eye on all this space — the apartment would make room for them.

Our city is like that, too, thinks Anna. We love it, but it doesn't love us. We're like children who cling to the skirts of a beautiful, preoccupied mother.

I must get going now.

21

It is more than a week since Andrei came off the conveyor belt. He hasn't been called for interrogation again. Each morning he is taken out of his cell, escorted by two guards. This is called 'lavatory drill', and he must empty the stinking bucket, use the lavatory and wash. The guards keep close. Even the lavatory has a peephole in its door. He never sees another prisoner, but on the second morning, as he picked up the wafer of soap on the basin, he saw that there were marks on it. Quickly, cupping it in his hand, he read the letters and then erased them with his thumb. PVN. For a second his mind scrabbled for a meaning, before he realized that they were initials. Another prisoner is trying to communicate his identity.

'Get a move on!'

He had no more time that day. The guard was already chivvying him towards his cell.

'Hands behind your back! Get going!'

The next day was no good either, but on the following morning he managed to pick up the soap, scratch his initials on to it quickly and then lay the soap back so that the marks were hidden. AMA. It wasn't likely that any other prisoner would recognize the initials. In Leningrad there'd have been a faint chance that a prisoner arrested after him might have heard of Andrei's arrest, but not here. Not in the Lubyanka. To scratch his initials was important, all the same. Everything that the guards did was meant to keep you isolated. You saw no other prisoners, and you were always outnumbered by the guards. If he hadn't been put into a shared cell at first, he wouldn't have known those other men existed. The Lubyanka pressed in on him with all its weight. It could obliterate him whenever it chose.

If he dies here, he'll die alone. The last faces he will see will be guards' faces. Outside, he would never have believed that three initials scratched into a piece of soap could be so precious. In here, to know that another prisoner has taken the risk of trying to communicate brings a kind of hope.

For the next hour he was on edge. If the guard found the initials he'd be thrown into the punishment cell, or beaten. After a while, as the prison routine went on its way, he relaxed.

First thing in the morning, when he's woken, he must fold up his bed against the wall, using the iron hooks. His blanket must also be folded, and he must stand beside the folded bed for inspection. It is not permitted to lie on the floor, or to doze during the day. Prisoners must be awake at all times. He is permitted to sit on his stool, as long as his head doesn't droop and his eyes don't close. No sleeping the days away here! Besides, prisoners under interrogation must not be allowed to snatch even five minutes, in case it strengthens them.

Each morning his tin bowl is half filled with kasha, and his mug with a brew of brown hot water, which the guard calls tea. His day's ration of black bread is issued. One day the bread was white. He thought it must be a mistake, but didn't question it.

Each morning, when he is taken out of his cell for lavatory drill, someone comes in and swabs the wooden floor. He never sees this happen, but the floor is always wet and clean when he returns, and the room smells of disinfectant. At midday there is soup; in the evening more soup. It is thin, with a few pieces of potato in it. Sometimes fish scales float on it, and there is a silt of fish bones at the bottom of his bowl. Once he received a whole fish head, which looked back at him with dull, boiled eyes. The soup is always heavily salted.

The guards change frequently, but even so he gets to know some of their faces. Every day they take him to a small yard for exercise, where he is permitted to walk up and down for twenty minutes, with a guard on either side. It seems strange that on the one hand they've spent days interrogating him and beating him, while on the other they inform him of his right to exercise, and that if money is sent to his account 'from outside' it may be spent on certain items from the prison shop. He may buy soap, cigarettes and certain food items. Once a week he has the right to a bath. The system is precise down to the smallest details. Each day, when he's taken out to the lavatory, he is given one piece of paper. This must not be flushed away: it has to be put into the metal bin by the toilet. Presumably they believe that prisoners might secrete the paper and use it to pass messages. He doesn't envy the guard who has the job of checking the used sheets. A guard empties the bin each time a prisoner uses the toilet, presumably, again, so that no prisoner will be able to guess how many companions he has. Or perhaps they think we'll write messages in shit, thinks Andrei. And they're probably right.

The exercise yard is very small, surrounded by high walls. Even there he is always alone. They must arrange the exercise periods very carefully. Clearly the aim of the solitary regime is that prisoners should never meet or even catch a glimpse of one another. On the way back to his cell the guard clicks his tongue loudly each time they come up to a turn in the corridors. It's a warning signal, Andrei supposes. Their tongues must ache by the end of the day.

'Hands behind your back! Get going!'

He asks for a book to read, because he vaguely remembers that in the memoirs of prisoners from Tsarist times they seemed always to be reading poetry and discussing literature. Things have changed, evidently. He is told that he has been deprived of the right to books. He asks if he can write a letter, and is told that he has been deprived of the right to correspondence during the investigation of his case. He often thinks of the slogan that was splashed across walls when he was a boy in the last year of the gymnasium: *'Life has become better, comrades, life has become more cheerful.'*

He decides to go back to medical school,

starting with everything that he can remember from the lectures of the first year. His memory seems to have been strangely sharpened by the Lubyanka. Perhaps it's because he does so little. In normal life his mind is full of things he must do in the next five minutes, the next half-hour, the next day. Now there is nothing he must do except follow the orders that are enforced by blows, and he begins to remember in a quite different way from ever before. He can sit on his stool and concentrate until he sees the exact page he wants in his student notebook. Whenever he likes, he can turn the page. He smells the turpentine polish that they used on the lecture-hall floor. He hears the way a certain professor cleared his throat nervously at the start of a lecture, or the way another spoke too quickly and ran his words together. There was old Akimov, who could spin out 'the riii-ght ayyy-treeee-um' for at least half a minute. They are all before him now.

Andrei has always had a habit of closing his eyes to concentrate, but he soon learns to break it.

'No sleeping! Sit up!'

The cardiovascular system; the nervous and musculoskeletal systems. He will go back to the dissecting rooms. Later he will make his first timid examinations of real live patients. There is enough material for a lifetime of imprisonment, if he paces it right.

As long as he doesn't think of Anna, he can manage. Sometimes, though, she catches him unawares. Usually it's when he's falling asleep, or just after he wakes. He sees her face, soft and open. Usually she is bent over some task: peeling the potatoes, or darning a hole in Kolya's sleeve. She looks up, and smiles at him. He sees the swell of her belly, and that her face is changing too. It is fuller and there are shadows under her eyes. She is plainer, but more beautiful. And then, in his waking dream, her eyes widen with fear. She is looking over his shoulder, at something that looms at her from behind Andrei. She shrinks back, her hands over her breasts.

He forces himself awake. He forces himself to name all the muscles involved in picking up a pen and writing with it. After that, he returns to the yellowed skeleton they studied, bone by bone, until they could name its parts in their sleep. Of course they had a comic name for their skeleton. Of course they didn't really believe that it had ever belonged to a man who got up and ate his breakfast and suffered from a bad cough in winter, just as they did.

On the seventh night there is a search of his cell. A guard shakes him out of sleep, and orders him to stand 'to attention' in the centre of his cell while two other guards begin the search. They examine his bedding and outer clothes minutely, running their fingers down seams as if hunting for lice. They punch the pillow and mattress all over. When this is done they raise the bed and peer underneath it. The bucket is lifted for inspection, the walls and floor examined.

'Everything off!'

Andrei takes off his underwear, which is scrutinized in the same way.

'Legs apart! Bend over!'

But at least this time there is no doctor. They peer into his mouth and his ears. They make him raise his arms above his head and drop them again. They pounce on a fish bone which he has kept back from his soup, with the intention of using it as a needle if he can ever get hold of anything which will make a hole for the thread. They don't even bother to manufacture synthetic anger. All this is to be expected, their faces say. Soon the examination is over and he can dress again. The guards leave, slamming the cell door behind them.

It's night, but what part of the night? He has been lucky this past week. The prison rhythm of meals and washing has allowed him to know how time is passing. But now it might be midnight or four in the morning. You could drive yourself crazy in here, trying to make sense of what goes on. Why suddenly search his cell now? Perhaps it's another part of the routine. *'Random searches must be carried out in the middle of the night, after the guard has made sure that the prisoner is in the deepest phase of sleep.'*

He won't sleep again now. His heart is pounding with rage and frustration. He needs to walk it off, but he can't even pace up and down the cell. Between 'lights-out' and the morning wake-up call prisoners are to be in their beds at all times, covered by a blanket but with their hands in sight rather than tucked in. If a man turns over in his sleep and pillows his face on a hand, a guard is soon there to yell, *'Hands!'*

They call it 'lights-out', but in reality the lights never go out. Sometimes they grow dim, but that always happens in daytime and is probably to do with the electricity supply. At night they burn steadily, like extra eyes guarding the prisoners.

Perhaps they searched him because he was going to be sent for interrogation again. The 'very important visitor' hasn't materialized. Perhaps they just wanted to frighten him.

Now that his cell routine is threatened, it seems precious. Nothing good may happen in it, but nothing too terrible has happened either. Bucket, kasha, soup, walk, bucket, soup, the banging of the door and the eye at the peephole. He's used to it and he can put up with it. Even solitude is not so bad.

At night he goes home, to Irkutsk, plunging through the desire to think of Anna, and out on to the other side, back in his childhood. He must not think of her. The memory of her warm, soft body sleeping at his side leads to terror. What if she's been arrested too? What if they're stripped her naked and exposed the swell of her pregnancy? What if they examine Anna as they've examined him, and interrogate her, and put her on the conveyor belt . . .

He can't imagine how she would survive, pregnant. As long as she is outside, he can cope with everything. He must fill his mind with other things, so that fear doesn't get a foothold.

He closes his eyes. He is out with his mother, gathering blue-berries. The ground is swampy, and both of them wear thick boots. It is late summer, but although the day is warm they wear long-sleeved shirts and trousers because of the mosquitoes. Andrei is lucky, because mosquitoes usually leave him alone. Some people are like that. His mother says it's because he was born here and so the insects recognize him as one of their own. A proper little Siberian. She and his father are not so lucky. The mosquitoes love their city blood.

'Look!' says his mother, pointing upwards. 'The cranes are flying!'

They both peer upwards as three huge white birds sail overhead, slowly beating their black-tipped wings. The wings ripple with each beat. It reminds Andrei of the ripples that he makes with his hands when he plays in the stream. Harsh calls float down behind the white birds.

'We're lucky to see them,' says his mother, shading her eyes. 'They are quite rare now, Andrei.'

Andrei watches the birds as they fly over the taiga, skimming the tops of the birch scrub and the firs.

'They'll be leaving us soon,' says his mother.

'Why?'

'They have to go somewhere warmer for the winter. They can't survive here. They come to us to breed, and then they spend our winter in India.'

'India!' He strains to see the last of the disappearing birds. 'Can they go wherever they want?'

His mother laughs. 'Birds don't need passports, Andryusha. Don't worry, they'll come back to us next year.'

The boggy ground sucks at his left boot. He lifts it carefully, so the boot won't slip off his foot, and steps on to a tussock of moss. His pail is more than half full. They'll keep picking until evening, and then walk home. If he gets tired his mother will carry him on her back for a while. She is strong.

Andrei concentrates. The scent of the taiga is in his nostrils. There is no air like it anywhere in the world. So pure that you feel as if you are drinking rather than breathing it. A smell of resin drifts from a stand of pines. There is the acid sharpness of the bog, and the tang of berries, and his own hot skin and sweat. His mother's smell is so familiar to him that it's simply the climate in which he lives. He is five years old.

The cell door crashes open.

'Name!'

He jerks upright. 'Alekseyev, Andrei Mikhailovich.'

'Get going!'

Along the corridor, hands behind his back, stumbling. Deliberately, he shuts his mind to the thought of where they might be taking him. The guards march him fast and their faces are set in a way which would mean anger anywhere else. His left leg cramps and gives way, but he recovers himself.

'Look where you're going, can't you?'

He will take nothing personally while he is in this place. He knows these guards, and they're not too bad as a rule. He's given a nickname to each of the guards whom he sees regularly. These two are Bighead and Squirrel. Squirrel is the one who always looks sharply cunning, as if he's got a hoard of nuts tucked away somewhere and is on the lookout for anyone who might try to find it. He has an overbite, and pointed teeth. Bighead is a block of a man, with thick, fleshy rolls of stubble swelling over his collar. His features, by contrast, are small, like a child's drawing of a face.

They reach an internal staircase lit by the low-wattage bulbs that seem to be used everywhere in the prison, except in the interrogation rooms. Andrei hears his own labouring breath as they go up flight after flight. He sounds like an old man. But that's nothing. He's not doing too badly. He counts the landings and the locked doors. They are coming up to the third floor, he thinks, or perhaps the fourth. It depends how deep the cellars are, and on what level his cell lies. Without external windows you can't tell.

On the next landing the guards stop at the locked door, fumble for their keys, and open it. They push him through. It seems to be the rule that they must shove and push the prisoner even when he is doing what they want. Another corridor. This time the floor is made of highly polished oak, and the lighting is good. This might be an office block, or the floor of a hotel. Suddenly Andrei is intensely aware of his own physical state. His clothes are filthy. His shoes, without laces, shuffle slipshod along the floor. He has to press his arms close to his sides to prevent his trousers from falling down. He can't smell himself but he is sure that he smells bad.

Down there in the cell, all those things seemed natural. But here, where there's a faint smell of polish and the paint on the walls is clean, they mark him out.

The guards stop. Bighead pulls a sheet of paper from his breast pocket, and unfolds it. For a moment it seems as if the whole process is beginning again: arrest, imprisonment, interrogation. Only this time he'll know what to expect. Both Bighead and

Squirrel look uneasy now. The surroundings have affected them, too.

'Get going!' barks Bighead, as if Andrei were the cause of the delay. They go on, past door after door. *I am in the Lubyanka,* Andrei says to himself. It is like saying, *I am already in the land of the dead.* But he is alive. There are his feet, walking. There are his toes, curled over and gripping hard so that his shoes don't fall off. His head throbs. He'd like to put up a hand to check the wound on his forehead. It isn't healing, although he has cleaned it carefully with water from his tin mug. He must keep his hands clasped behind his back.

Without warning, the guards turn sharply to the right. Andrei's shoe catches on Squirrel's boot. He stumbles, trips over the guard's leg, and sprawls on the parquet.

They yank him up. They don't curse or beat him, as he's sure they would if they were back down in the cells. He is shaken, out of breath. His trousers have slipped and he tries to pull them up, but Bighead orders, 'Hands behind your back! Get going!'

At this moment one of the doors ahead of them opens, and a young woman comes out, holding a stack of files. She walks towards them. She wears a white blouse and a navy skirt. Civilian clothes, not uniform.

She comes level with them. She looks so clean. Perfume comes from her body and the guards move aside to make room for her. Her face is preoccupied. She is pretty, the kind of girl whose face would brighten if she passed Andrei in the hospital corridors.

'Good morning, Dr Alekseyev!'

'How are you? Busy day?'

'Aren't they always!'

This girl glances briefly at the guards, but her look slides off Andrei as if he were a piece of furniture being manhandled from one office to another. He has a terrible impulse to cry out to her and beg her to help him. Surely a girl in a fresh white blouse who washes carefully in the mornings and puts on perfume would look round then, and meet his eyes and recognize him for who he is? A wave of weakness flows over him. He hears the girl's heels clipping away, as calmly as if there were no battered prisoner and no guards. She is used to this.

You fool. Haven't you understood yet that you must expect nothing?

But look on the bright side: she didn't even notice that your trousers were falling down.

Andrei almost smiles. Anna would see why it was funny, even though at the same time she'd fly into a fury with the girl and say,

'I'd like to slap her face!' For once it's safe to think of Anna. The thought of telling her about the girl seems to connect him, just for a moment, to a future where everything that happens now will be safely in the past.

The guards march him onward. Every time they reach a bend in the corridor they click their tongues as usual, so that he won't meet any fellow prisoners. They didn't mind him meeting the girl, because she was part of the process.

And now they stop, with finality, against yet another door. The guards glance at each other. They can't quite hide their nervousness. Clearly they have no key to this door: Bighead raises his hand, hesitates, and then knocks. A woman's voice calls, 'Come in!' as if this were an office like any other.

It's a large outer office. Two women sit at desks, with typewriters and telephones. The windows are high and wide. Light floods in, the first natural light Andrei has seen for days apart from brief exercise periods in the yard, where the walls are so high and there is so much wire mesh that light can scarcely squeak through. His eyes smart. He can see black branches, and behind them buildings. Trees. Trees doing what they always do, moving a little in the wind. Suddenly a crow flies up from a branch, flapping its ragged wings.

One of the women glances up, and then goes back to her work. The other comes forward, frowning, takes the paper that Bighead holds out to her, and says, 'Wait here.' She crosses to another, inner door, knocks, and vanishes inside. Bighead and Squirrel stand at ease, staring rigidly ahead, as if to prove that they are interested in nothing that they see in this office. Andrei shifts his weight.

'Hands behind your back!' raps out Bighead.

'They are already in that position,' says Andrei. The woman at the typewriter glances up at him as if a dog had started to talk. Squirrel sniffs loudly. He doesn't like it in here, thinks Andrei. He's afraid that someone will steal his hoard of nuts.

What is that woman typing? A statement, probably. Some confession dragged out of a prisoner after nights of beating or worse. She types it out and then she goes home, thinking about a tasty supper. The rhythm of it is getting on his nerves. Tap, tap, tap-a-tap-a-tap-a-tap. And yet he doesn't want the typing to stop, or the inner door to open. He's standing on his own feet, in a warm, well-lit room. Outside the window there is the sky. It is a thick winter sky, tinged with yellow. The black branches shiver against it. Even through the double windows, there is a faint sound of traffic. Ordinary life is going on out there. People are scuttling past, heads down. There is a glass on the typist's desk, with a little tea in the bottom, and a sediment of sugar.

He has never seen any of these things so clearly. So many times, when he's had the freedom to stare at the sky for as long as he wants, he's barely glanced at it before turning back to 'something more important'. He has taken a glass of tea from Anna, and continued to work, head down. He has walked under the bare branches of winter trees without so much as a look upwards.

Even the air in here smells clean. He is polluting it, no doubt. The typist will open the ventilation window once he's gone. Or perhaps she's inured to the smell of prisoners. She works on, head down. Her hair is scanty and she has arranged it carefully so that it won't show her scalp. Her skin is pale and although the room is warm she has buttoned her thick cardigan up to her throat.

Underactive thyroid, possibly, thinks Andrei. He can't see her fingernails, because they are hidden by the body of the typewriter, but very likely one or two of them are broken. A few questions would establish whether tests were necessary. *Have you gained weight? Has there been any recent change of mood? Depression, for example.*

The inner door opens. It moves very slowly, as if someone is coming round it with a pile of books or a tray in her arms, and has to push the door with an elbow. His body tenses so that every cell in it seems to tingle, but at the same time it feels as if he is dissolving, as if time will never release him from this moment.

The door. It's still opening. A foot appears; a knee. Fate has seized hold of him and he can do nothing but wait.

22

Of course it is Volkov sitting at the wide oak desk. Who else had he expected? Volkov, heavy and expressionless, giving nothing. The guards salute and stand rigid at either side of Andrei.

'Escort duty, wait in the outer room,' says Volkov. Andrei hears Bighead make a sound which is almost a protest, quickly swallowed as Volkov gives him a glance. The rolls of flesh on the back of Bighead's neck quiver as he turns. He makes for the door as fast as he can, almost stumbling over his own boots. Squirrel's mouth hangs open for a second and then he bundles out on Bighead's heels. The door clicks shut. Volkov and Andrei are alone in the room.

'What a pair of beauties,' remarks Volkov. 'Not, perhaps, the very finest the Lubyanka has to offer. A little re-education is in order. Have they been treating you well?'

Andrei doesn't move and doesn't answer.

'Sit down,' says Volkov.

Andrei crosses to the desk and pulls out the chair that Volkov indicates. It is, of course, lower than his own. You don't have to be in prison long to learn these little tricks. He sits, and Volkov looks him up and down, slowly. In Volkov's face Andrei reads his own physical degradation. Matted hair, scars and bruises, pulpy shadows under the eyes. Stained clothes and flapping shoes.

'Frankly, Andrei Mikhailovich, I would hardly have recognized you,' he says at last.

Andrei gazes back into Volkov's Siberian eyes. Who is this man today? He can't see any trace of Gorya's father. This is the face of a hard, trained top MGB man on his own territory. And yet Volkov has this trick of intimacy. He makes you feel that you owe him something, even if it's only an answer.

Andrei sighs, deeply. He hears the sound of his sigh move out into the room, and he can't call it back. He must get a grip on himself. He must be as strong as Volkov.

'Surely that's the idea?' he says. 'This is the Lubyanka look.'

Volkov raises his eyebrows. 'The idea, as you call it, is to discover what's left after the masks have dropped off,' he says. He looks down at the file on his desk, opens it, and appears to read the top sheet with concentration. Volkov appears entirely at ease. So he should. Wherever there are cells and interrogations, he is at home. They are to him what X-rays and hospital beds are to me, thinks Andrei. Both of us are professionals. I can work in any hospital, and he in any prison.

Volkov looks up again. His eyes meet Andrei's. 'You've been holding out on us,' he says mildly.

Andrei doesn't reply. His body floods with adrenalin, but he holds himself still.

'You should have told us about Brodskaya. It's all going to come out, whether you do or not. Even as we speak, the entire plot is being unmasked. Saboteurs and terrorist elements are being rooted out by the vigilance of the people's security services.'

Volkov speaks rapidly and without expression, as if these words must be said but he himself attaches no particular emotion to them. A feeling of chill begins to invade Andrei's body. His hands hang at his sides, leaden and helpless. If he speaks he'll damn himself, but if he remains silent it will be the same. For the first time, terror seizes him. Part of him, the doctor part, observes. Fear of this order is not an emotion. It is like a virus overwhelming every cell of his body, while his mind struggles to remain clear. He is in the Lubyanka, and it's entirely possible that he'll never come out. Anna will receive an official document. 'Sentenced to ten years' solitary confinement, without the right of correspondence.' Or, in plain terms, taken to the cellars of the Lubyanka and shot in the back of the neck.

'Murderers in white coats,' says Volkov, watching Andrei's face.

'What?' *Keep quiet, you fool. Why did you answer him?*

'Murderers in white coats,' repeats Volkov, slowly and deliberately. 'How does that sound to you?'

Andrei feels his own mind whirr like an engine that can't find a gear to grip.

'You're an intelligent man,' says Volkov. 'You understand what I'm saying. We are only just beginning to realize the scale of it.' He spreads his hands in a gesture of infinite weariness. 'These crimes are attracting attention at the very highest level. You'll appreciate what that means.'

Andrei's head throbs. Is it possible that all this is an hallucination, resulting from his head injury? Volkov is not really here, in this pale, polished room, talking like a madman. If Andrei closes his eyes and opens them, he'll be back in his cell.

'I'll quote you the exact words of Comrade Stalin,' says Volkov. He makes no attempt at the ecstatic reverence that people usually aim for when talking about the Leader in public. He talks like someone who knows Stalin man to man, which no doubt he does. ' "They die so rapidly, first one and then another. We must change our doctors." You understand of whom Comrade Stalin was speaking?'

'No.'

'You don't? Your memory fails you? The names of Zhdanov or Shcherbakov mean nothing to you? Surprising that such men are so easily forgotten.'

'I know their names.'

'Of course you do.'

For Andrei, Shcherbakov is a name out of *Pravda.* Zhdanov, of course, has far greater meaning. He led the defence of Leningrad; and he also led the attack on Leningrad's writers, artists and musicians, once the war was over. Anna talked about it night after night. It brought up memories of how her father was treated in the thirties.

'And you know how they died,' Volkov continues.

But Andrei doesn't remember. Probably he didn't even read the obituaries.

'Heart failure,' Volkov informs him, and

then repeats, *'Heart failure,'* with an emphasis which suggests that the words are well-known euphemisms for something quite different. 'They both died of heart failure. Shcherbakov was a man in his prime. Zhdanov wasn't much more than fifty. Both of them were men who had given and were continuing to give great service to the State.'

There is a silence. What a strange way of talking, thinks Andrei. He sounds as if he's making a speech, but there's no audience. Only me.

'Men whose services we could not do without,' continues Volkov, staring straight ahead with the intensity of one who sees a far and stormy horizon. 'And yet their doctors failed to save them.'

But everyone knows that Zhdanov was an alcoholic. Men like that don't make it much past middle age. If it hadn't been heart failure it could have been a cerebral haemorrhage, or liver disease. Andrei can't remember what they said about Shcherbakov, but it wasn't likely he'd led a healthy life.

'They trusted to their physicians,' says Volkov, and stops again, staring at Andrei as if expecting something from him. But this is absurd. A man like Volkov is far too intelligent to believe a word of all this.

And yet Andrei knows very well that some patients' families do think like that. They refuse to listen to the evidence of disease. Furred-up arteries and bowels eaten away by cancer mean nothing. They continue to believe that if one more thing had been done, their dear ones would have survived. While the patient still lives, they drag him from clinic to clinic, from thermal spring to sanatorium. They cling to hope and won't believe that such treatments are palliative at best. When death finally comes, they turn on the doctors. Accusations fly over injections not given, test results incorrectly interpreted or a failure to visit on that fatal last evening.

Andrei accepts it. It's human nature and usually it does no harm. He's also learned that it's better not to argue. Brandishing the facts of the disease does no good. In the end, except in the rarest of cases, fury spends itself and melts into grief. Besides, it's perfectly true that all doctors make mistakes. It's the nature of the profession. Every day there are so many decisions to be made. You have to feel your way forward, checking symptoms and responses against everything you know, but at the same time you must always keep your instincts alive. You must look, and touch, and smell, and listen. You must accept the need to waste time with the patient.

Sometimes Andrei finds himself working in the dark, at the edge of his own knowledge. Even the accumulated knowledge of the profession doesn't help.

If only he weren't so tired, he could explain all this to Volkov. If Volkov were willing to listen . . .

There is a frill of light around Volkov's head. Andrei blinks, and the light clears. Over the past few days he's had these visual disturbances. He saw double one morning when the guard pushed his kasha through the access door. Just an after-effect of concussion. He's pretty sure there's been no brain injury. If he weren't so tired he'd be able to concentrate better. Volkov is talking again.

'Active steps were taken to do them harm, with the help of hand-picked so-called physicians,' says Volkov, his voice sonorous. 'We are uncovering an international conspiracy of Zionists working as tools of the Americans, who directed these criminal murderers and saboteurs.' Volkov leans back, resting his hands on the padded armrests of his chair, with an air of, *There you are, and now what have you got to say for yourself?*

But Andrei can think of nothing. The real business between Volkov and him has nothing to do with Zionist spies. It's to do with the boy, but Volkov doesn't want to talk about the boy.

'The murderers of Zhdanov and Shcherbakov will be unmasked and will not escape punishment,' announces Volkov, leaning forward again and speaking as coolly as if he were announcing the agenda for a meeting.

Andrei has had this with his other interrogators. They say such things, the most provocative and extreme accusations that they can think up. You answer and you are already on their ground. You have agreed that the impossible can be talked about as if it were the possible. You are already in the quicksand.

Volkov's boy is dying. That's what you have to remember. Everything he says, no matter how preposterous it sounds, is linked to that.

'Your Brodskaya, it seems, had links with these Jewish Nationalist criminals.'

Brodskaya: there's the connection, because Brodskaya is Jewish. She can be fitted into the conspiracy. If she's 'your' Brodskaya, that means Andrei can be fitted in somewhere as well.

'You know that Brodskaya has been arrested.' Volkov is watching him intently now. Perhaps he's waiting for Andrei to lie. Andrei nods.

'Exactly,' goes on Volkov calmly. 'You know that. But perhaps you haven't heard that she's no longer under arrest?'

'You've released her?'

'Her case has been concluded.'

' "Concluded",' repeats Andrei. He has no idea what this means. Perhaps she has been sentenced already. Perhaps they found no evidence of any crime and so the case had to be wrapped up, and she's been sent back to Yerevan.

Volkov leans back. His fingers tap on the armrests. The sound is quiet because the armrests are made of padded leather. 'Regrettably,' he says, 'Brodskaya suffered a heart attack shortly before she was due to appear before a tribunal for sentencing.'

Brodskaya's broad, capable hands. Her strong, solid body, and her tireless appetite for work. Her calm professionalism. *'I am willing to see the family and explain everything to them.'* Were those her exact words? Probably not. His head hurts and he's not sure that he remembers them exactly, but he can still hear her voice. The fact is that she agreed to become involved in the Volkov case, even though it must have been against her better judgement. She did it out of a sense of professional duty. She has been destroyed and Russov is probably still alive, even working.

'She's dead, then?'

Volkov looks at him without replying. Suddenly he swivels his chair, grabs a file from a cabinet behind him, and swivels back to the desk. He slaps the file down on its surface.

'And so now there's no reason for you to hold back. She implicated you in her confession, of course. There are pages and pages of it.' Volkov taps the file and then wrinkles his nose. 'But all the same I wasn't . . . one hundred per cent convinced.'

Volkov's eyes are clear, grey, unflinching. *'She implicated you . . . of course.'* It could be true. If they threatened her mother, for example . . . And yet he is sure that Volkov is lying. He hasn't got what he wanted from Brodskaya. Perhaps she got away; escaped him. Prisoners do sometimes succeed in committing suicide, even though they are forced to sleep with their hands outside their blankets in case they strangle themselves secretly, or gouge their wrists with their nails. Brodskaya might have been killed herself. Or perhaps Volkov is lying in a different way and Brodskaya is still alive. She might be here in the Lubyanka, still holding out. Volkov might have said to her, 'I have Alekseyev's confession here. Of course, he implicated you. There's no reason for you to hold back now.'

He wants to believe that she's still alive, but knows that she is probably dead. For some reason they've held back with him. A few nights on the conveyor belt and a beating-up are nothing. They haven't tortured him. The guards have let him know that he's got off lightly so far. They drop hints about what goes on in the dungeons.

'They'll put you in the meat-grinder down there.'

'You know what a standing cell is? You'll be lucky if you don't find out.'

Don't think of what might have gone on before she died. She is dead now, and out of it. But if it hadn't been for him, Brodskaya would never have become involved. He asked her to do the biopsy and she agreed. And then the amputation.

'It'll be Dr Brodskaya who does the operation, Gorya. She's very good. You've seen her, she's the one who did your biopsy. You remember: she has her hair in a bun, and glasses.'

'I don't like her. Dad says she's a Jew.'

'She was a good surgeon,' says Andrei now.

Volkov's face twists. He leans forward, lifts the file high, smashes it down on the desk. 'Don't think that I will protect you!' he cries.

There is sweat on Volkov's forehead. He wants them all dead, because his son is dying. Andrei understands him.

'It was Brodskaya who recommended amputation,' says Volkov. 'You were persuaded by her.'

He's offering Andrei a chance. Or perhaps pretending to offer him that chance, so that Andrei will betray himself by grabbing at it.

'It was the only possible course of treatment,' says Andrei. 'Any surgeon would have taken the same decision.'

' "Treatment"? You call such butchery "treatment"? My son is dying because of it.'

At the edges of Andrei's vision, black is thickening. Directly ahead of him there is still light. He can still see Volkov's face and hear his voice. He draws a deep, slow breath. He is not going to faint. He should put his head down but Volkov would take that as an admission of defeat.

'I heard that. I am very sorry.'

'Sorry? Why would you be sorry unless you were guilty?'

'I meant it in a different sense,' says Andrei.

Volkov's voice echoes. 'I trusted you. I picked you out.'

'We did what we could. Sometimes that isn't enough.'

'I trusted you. I should have killed him myself before I let you butchers near him with your saws and your knives. I should have taken him home with me.' There is a long silence, and then Volkov says quietly, 'He was perfect.' The fat toes that Volkov tickled when Gorya was a baby. The rosy little legs kicking after his bath. Volkov comes in, dismissing the nurse, takes the baby and jumps him on his knee. How strong he is! The baby laughs at his father. Perfect.

Andrei can barely move his lips, they are so cold and stiff. Blackness advances towards the centre of his vision, but there is still a hole through which he can see Volkov. The blackness is not pure black. It has a texture. He sees Volkov move through it. Now he has gone out of Andrei's field of vision.

Volkov's voice comes from somewhere towards the window. 'They've sedated him. He'll die more quickly that way but he won't suffer as much. That's the choice I made.'

Andrei bows his head. The blackness is

underneath him now as well, rushing upwards. Terror of death sweeps over him.
'Excuse me,' he says aloud, 'I can't —'

He can still hear Volkov. Quick footsteps
across the wooden floor. A hand is under
his chin, pulling his head back. Now Andrei
can see nothing. Volkov's hand is warm
against his icy skin.

'You've taken something,' says Volkov.
Andrei hears a door open and Volkov's
voice, further away now, calling loudly.
'Bring a doctor! Immediately!' and then a
rush of feet, and a door banging.

He was away somewhere but now he is
back. He can see light again. He coughs as
ammonia hits his throat. Someone is taking
his pulse. A sharp voice, not Volkov's, says,
'Have you taken poison?'

'Where,' says Andrei, fighting the thick-
ness of his tongue in his mouth, 'would I
get poison?'

The doctor lifts Andrei's eyelids to peer at
his pupils. Quickly and thoroughly he
checks Andrei over as a vet checks a horse.

'He'll do,' he says. 'Just a temporary loss
of consciousness.'

He does not mention the head injury. It's
not his job. He has only to confirm that the
prisoner is fit for interrogation to proceed.

Rags of darkness swirl through Andrei's head. *When you die, this is what it will be like. Remember this.*

It's releasing him. He's not going to die. It was just an ordinary syncope and now he's been dragged back to consciousness.

'There are no signs that any toxic substance has been ingested,' says the doctor, presumably to Volkov.

At the edge of Andrei's vision darkness continues to fray like rotten cloth. He glimpses a more solid shadow, which slowly resolves itself into Volkov.

'He's all right, then,' says Volkov. 'Fine, you can go.'

Quickly the doctor gathers his instruments, looking neither at Andrei nor Volkov, and makes for the door. Andrei licks his lips. No good asking for help from him. He's not a doctor but a machine. They must turn them out from a production line these days.

'Drink this,' says Volkov, producing a glass of water. 'We haven't finished yet.'

Andrei sips the water slowly. Drops roll over his tongue and into his throat. As soon as he tastes the water he realizes how thirsty he is. He could lie down by the edge of a stream and lap from it like a beast.

'We are treating you well,' Volkov observes.

Andrei looks up. The trouble with Volkov

is that Andrei keeps forgetting who he really is. Volkov has a way of coming close to you. Andrei was on the point of returning the small ironic smile on Volkov's lips.

'Could I have more water?' he asks.

'I said that we are treating you well, not that we are spoiling you.' But nevertheless Volkov crosses to his desk, where someone has put down a jug of water. He fills the glass, and returns it to Andrei.

'Yes, you are alive,' Volkov murmurs, with a slight emphasis on 'you'. 'As alive as life itself, as they say. But soon my boy will not be.' He says it like a parent, with disbelief. The fact is there but the father still can't grasp that his son can really die before him. 'Tell me. When she did the operation, she had the power. Those instruments were in her hands. You were not in the operating theatre; I've checked exactly who was present. Those cancerous cells travelled from the tumour in the leg to Gorya's lungs. Either she let it happen or she made it happen. I'm not blaming you. She pulled the wool over your eyes, too.'

He turns to Andrei as he says this. It's a naked look, man to man. *We are both on the same side. You were tricked too. Deceived, just like me. Why not admit it?* Either Volkov really believes what he's saying — for the moment at least — or he has the power of convincing himself when he needs to. Or possibly it's his training. There's something in Volkov, despite everything, which makes Andrei aware that he must fight down the desire to please him.

'*He'll be so angry with me. The running track cost so much money.*'

'*You don't know how angry he gets.*'

In a sense Volkov is right. The amputation did no good. It turned out to be exactly what Volkov feared it would be: a pointless mutilation. Andrei feels a flush of pain, almost shame. *We did the best we could, in the circumstances,* he tells himself, as he's already told himself many times. *We can't predict whether there will be metastasis or not. We have to proceed on the assumption that a child's life can be saved. And what if we didn't intervene — what would our patients' families say then?*

Andrei gathers himself. Volkov has said too much, and revealed too much of himself. Andrei will have to disappear, like Brodskaya. He's been fighting that knowledge but his body knows that death is coming. That's why he passed out. It was weakness but it doesn't matter. He will go on.

He is in an empty, frozen street. Snow

whirls, sinking and falling. Vast banks of snow lie on either side of him, like pillows. If he lay down the snow would take him in. But he mustn't do that. He has to get to the hospital, where there are patients waiting. There are few medicines left but there are still things he can do and say which will be of use. He walks like an old man, bent and shuffling. He leans heavily on the cherry-wood stick which belongs to Anna's father. On either side the dead lean on the snow-drifts, watching him. Now Brodskaya is there too. She is already covered by thickly falling flakes but he can still see her eyes. They watch him to make sure he keeps on walking.

'That's not how metastasis takes place. Surely it's better to believe that what was done was done in good faith?' says Andrei to Volkov. 'Brodskaya made the only decision she could possibly have made. It was correct to carry out the surgery, following the biopsy.'

Volkov frowns. ' "Correct"?' he asks.

'Yes, professionally correct. What if we had decided to do nothing, for fear of what might happen to us if the surgery didn't cure him and the disease metastasized? Or what if we had pretended we could do nothing for him, and referred Gorya elsewhere?'

'You . . . amaze . . . me,' says Volkov, slowly and softly. 'Where do you think you are?'

Andrei doesn't answer.

'You must think you have nothing to lose. Let me assure you that you have a great deal to lose. You don't understand me yet.'

'I understand that Brodskaya is dead.'

'But you are alive.'

There is a long pause. Andrei realizes that the room isn't really silent. He can hear the muffled clatter of typewriter keys from the next room. He can hear a faint rumble in Volkov's guts. He wonders what time it is. Time to eat, perhaps. Perhaps he'll never leave this room. No doubt people have been killed before, during interrogation. Suddenly, Volkov could attack him. No one would stop him. No doubt there are protocols but Volkov is powerful enough to get round them, as well as to control what is written in the report of Andrei's interrogation. Maybe they'll say he died of a heart attack, like Brodskaya. It could happen now or it could happen later. Before he dies he will allow himself to think of Anna. By then it can do no harm. As long as she remains alive, and the baby remains alive within her, he can sink into that darkness. He will have to go through the terror first, but then it will be over.

He wonders if Gorya feels the same, sedated as he is. He is an intelligent child. He will know that something new is happening to him, and perhaps he will also know that it is called death. His face will change. His parents will see that Gorya has turned away from them. Not because he doesn't love them, but because he has to. Sometimes the mother will cry out and try to drag him back. It may even work for a while, but then the tide will be too strong for her and she will have to release him.

He'd like to be with Gorya. He would know how to look after him. He has learned not to retreat from dying patients, although he understands why that happens. You are frustrated, and you feel a sense of failure, and so you leave the final stages to the nurses. But there's a lot you can do, very small things, to make those stages pass as well as they can. He hopes that Gorya has got someone good with him.

'I am treating you well,' says Volkov. 'Do you understand that? I remember that you're an Irkutsk boy —'

There is a knock at the door. A woman's voice says, 'Excuse me, Comrade Volkov, there is an urgent phone call for you. Would you prefer to take it in your office or outside?'

'Outside,' says Volkov. 'Clear the office. And I need two guards in here for this prisoner.'

The guards stand, one on either side of Andrei's chair. They would have liked to remove the chair but Volkov said over his shoulder, 'He's to remain seated.'

Volkov has been gone for a long time. An hour at least, perhaps two. There is no clock in the room. Andrei retreats, deep inside himself. He will not think of anything except the peace of this moment. The guards are not shoving or beating him. The room is warm. Outside the wind has got up, and the light is fading. Snow falls, not thickly enough to obscure the pattern of the branches. He is in Moscow, in the Lubyanka. The city is going on with its life out there. The typewriter is still clacking. The glass of water is on the desk in front of him, a third full. He considers asking if he can drink it, but decides against it. He doesn't want to stir up the animosity of the guards. He's never seen this pair before and they are in a different league from Bighead and Squirrel.

But the typist doesn't seem afraid of them.

At one point her typing stops, and she opens the door and comes right into the room. She says in a voice which has an edge of flirtation in it: 'Would either of you boys like tea?'

Yes, they say, nodding their heads, they would certainly like tea. Plenty of sugar, please.

After a while the typist returns with two steaming glasses of tea.

'Very nice,' says one of the guards. 'I appreciate that.'

She stands there, just within Andrei's field of vision, simpering. Incredible, but she seems to find the guard attractive. Andrei can smell the tea. Real tea. The guard takes a gulp.

'I don't know how you can drink it as hot as that,' says the typist.

'Always have.'

'Iron mouth, he's got,' says the other guard approvingly.

'My dad was the same,' says the typist. 'A real man.'

She goes out. The guards look at each other.

'Nice tea,' says Iron Mouth, with meaning.

'If you can get it,' rejoins the other.

They must know that there isn't a microphone in the room, thinks Andrei. Presumably Volkov has the power to make sure of that.

He's beyond tired now. Beyond tension, or even fear. Every minute feels so full that he could live his whole life inside it.

I am alive, he thinks. *Everything is complete.*

It is dark and late when Volkov comes back. Andrei has been taken out to pee once, but he has had nothing more to eat or drink. He has just sat there, without moving, barely thinking. It might be midnight, or it might only be mid-evening. The typing in the outer office stopped for a while, then restarted. Probably they work shifts, just as the guards and interrogators do. As Volkov enters the room, the guards snap to attention, their eyes fixed on a point in the distance. Andrei also looks up.

Volkov is exhausted. The bones of his skull seem to push against his skin. He is wearing a dress uniform with military decorations, as if he's been to the ballet. He dismisses the guards and they clump away into the outer office. Someone is still typing. Do they never stop? Yes, the clicketty-tap stops and he hears a murmur of voices. But he mustn't think of outside. He must concentrate on

Volkov, who drops the file he's holding on to the desk, and sits down heavily. Volkov spreads out his hands on the desk top and gazes down at them as if he has never seen them before.

'You're an Irkutsk boy,' he says, as if there's been no interruption. 'Don't worry, you'll soon be seeing your homeland again.'

Instantly, as if their minds are linked, Andrei understands him. Volkov is telling him that he will not be shot or beaten to death. He will not disappear somewhere in the Lubyanka dungeons. He'll be tried, sentenced, and sent to a camp. Everything is already decided, at least in Volkov's mind, and that means it will happen. It's within his power.

Andrei's mind floods with an extraordinary blend of joy and rage. He will not die. Now he knows it, he also knows how afraid he was. And how angry, that Volkov can do this to him.

There was never any possibility of release. You knew that, Andrei tells himself. You are not a child. Arrest and interrogation have to be followed by guilt and sentencing. If he's lucky it will be five years. Surely ten is the most it can be.

'Saboteurs,' murmurs Volkov, still looking at the back of his hands as if they contain an answer. 'Traitors, criminals, spies . . . Can you imagine the scum I have to deal with?' His fists clench. He heaves himself up and his chair crashes backwards to the floor. He leans forward over the desk, breathing heavily. 'Why do they do it, eh? Can you tell me that? Why do these cunts think that they can get away with it?'

Andrei holds himself still. Who is this 'they'? Volkov is glaring at him.

'You don't know, do you?' demands Volkov. 'You don't fucking know anything. There you sit, in your own little world. You're in the Lubyanka, my friend! Things are hotting up! Doesn't that mean anything to you? Listen. I understand you now. You made a mistake, that's all. You kept bad company. *Insufficient vigilance.* But my son liked you and that means something to me. Levina — that's a Jewish name, but she's not Jewish, is she, your wife? Don't worry, we know all about her. She's in the clear. They're Jews, the lot of them. Things are coming to the boil, my friend. Soon they'll all be in the pot together. Listen. My son liked you. That means something to me.' Volkov is sweating heavily. A fume of vodka comes off him. 'At the highest level, concerns are being expressed about your profession,' says Volkov, suddenly pedantic and enunciating each syllable. 'The very highest level. Do you understand me?'

'I'm not sure.'

'I think you are. I think you know what the highest level is. Or if you don't you're more of a fool than you look. Do you know where I've been tonight? Would you like to have a guess?'

'With Gorya, perhaps?' *And then you drank, to wipe it out.*

Volkov bares his teeth. 'No. Not that. My son is dying but I haven't been to see him. I had a more pressing appointment.' He is very drunk. 'Don't you want to ask me what that was?' Volkov's shoulders are bunched with tension. His eyes are bloodshot.

'If you want to say,' says Andrei.

'My son is dying but I wasn't with him. My wife is there. I'll tell you where I was, my fine friend. *I was dancing.*'

The emphasis that Volkov puts on these words is so ferocious that the air between them seems to quiver. He spits out 'dancing' as if it's an obscenity. Does he mean he was out with a woman? That would be natural perhaps. You see death and you want to bury yourself in living flesh.

Slowly, Volkov picks up the fallen chair, and resettles himself in it. 'You're a Siberian boy, like me,' he says. 'You'll know the dance: Krasny Yar.'

'Oh,' says Andrei. A folk dance. Not with a woman then. Krasny Yar: beautiful ravine; red ravine. He knows the dance and Volkov will know it better, being a boy from Krasnoyarsk.

' "Oh",' echoes Volkov mockingly. 'Oh, oh, oh, oh. And have you no further questions, Dr Alekseyev? All the symptoms appear perfectly normal to you? With your medical eye you will already have noticed that I've been drinking. You're right. I've been drinking and dancing, and now I'm talking to you, and then my driver will take me to the Morozovka to see my child, by which time I shall be entirely sober.'

An urgent phone call, and then he spends the evening folk dancing? Andrei shakes his head. He can't understand any of this.

'You may well shake your head,' says Volkov, as if to himself. 'What kind of man dances when his son is dying? But when certain tunes play we all have to skip about.' He makes a dismissive gesture. 'That's by the way. Let's get down to business. There's nothing you won't like. Sit down and read it.'

He flips open the file and pushes it over to Andrei, who takes it and begins to read. Yes, it's a statement. Someone has typed it out beautifully; perhaps the woman who gave tea to the guards.

It begins with a lengthy biography and outline of his current professional work. The tone is sober and accurate. Everything is entered into in detail: his parents' settlement in Siberia, his own education. It is noted that he was not a member of the Pioneers. There are his exam results, the move to Leningrad and his entry into medical school. Service with the People's Volunteers at the outbreak of war. His war service in the besieged city. The tone so far is neutral and even respectful. His marriage to Anna; her family circumstances, class background and occupation. A note that her family is not of Jewish origin. Full details of her mother's professional career; no mention of Mikhail's writing. Strange. Andrei glances back, to check if he's missed anything. No, there's nothing. A brief mention of Mikhail's service with the People's Volunteers and his death from wounds during the siege, and that's it.

Extraordinary. Andrei would have thought they'd go to town on Mikhail's fall from favour during the thirties.

He reads on. This is like a novel, there is so much detail. It is like a description of the life of another man, but perhaps that's always the case when you read about yourself. His further studies, his specialism, even some detail of particular cases.

Andrei turns the page. Here is the record of his arrest. And now pages of his interrogation record. He reads it carefully but there seems to be nothing there which was not actually said during the interrogations. There's no mention of Brodskaya. But then there is a question which he knows was never put to him:

Do you accept, Dr Alekseyev, that you have shown insufficient vigilance?

A. M. Alekseyev: I accept that I have shown insufficient vigilance.

He looks up. 'This question was never put to me.'

'Which question?'

Andrei indicates the place in the text. 'This one.'

'Ah. Turn the page.'

Andrei turns the page. The next one is blank. He turns again. The next sheet is also blank. He riffles through the rest of the file, but there is no more writing in it.

'Sign it,' says Volkov. 'I am giving you a chance.'

'But it's not accurate.'

'It's accurate enough for the purpose. Sign it.'

Andrei rereads the last part of the statement. No one is named. There is no accusation of any crime. 'Insufficient vigilance' will get him five years, perhaps, ten at the most. Kostya Rabinovich said, *'Start signing things and that's the end of you.'* But isn't there just a chance that Volkov really is giving him a chance? Brodskaya isn't named. No one is named. No one else is being dragged into this.

'Full name,' says Volkov.

Andrei picks up the pen. This is his life; he can't deny it. He has not been sufficiently vigilant. He has not protected any of them: Anna, the baby, Kolya, himself. If this investigation continues they will spread the net wider. The best thing for all of them is for the case to be concluded as soon as possible. He's not fool enough to think that anyone gets out of the Lubyanka with a slap on the back and an apology: *We made a mistake, we pulled you in for nothing.* Can he trust Volkov? Of course not. But has he any alternative?

Volkov is watching him. Impossible to know what to make of his expression. Andrei pulls the statement towards him, and writes his name immediately under the last line of typing.

'Good,' says Volkov. 'Now listen carefully.

You may not be seeing me again. Do you understand what I'm saying?'

Andrei looks at the sweat on Volkov's forehead, the slight tremor of his hands. He sees the dilation of Volkov's eyes. This man has had some shock, perhaps physical, perhaps mental. He is not the same man as he was before he received that telephone call. He's been drinking, of course. But dancing is something else — Andrei can't make sense of it. From the way Volkov spoke you would think he had been forced to dance. But who can force a top MGB man like Volkov to do anything he doesn't want to do —

Oh.

Volkov is still waiting. He's quick. He sees the change in Andrei's face. 'I see that we understand each other. Listen. Sometimes a man receives a — let's call it a hint. An intimation. In my line of work you become quick at picking up such things. I received such an intimation tonight. Some men would ignore it; they would convince themselves that their position was secure and they had nothing to fear. But I am not such a fool. I know what it means. I've danced my dance. I can tell you that, my friend, because you're not in a position to betray me. As for your case, I've done what I can.'

522

And am I supposed to thank you? You were the one who got me arrested. You made the case against me. It was you who brought me here, to the Lubyanka.

But in spite of himself, Andrei can't help feeling something — not warmth, not sympathy, but a kind of recognition perhaps. He knows Volkov. Volkov has made sure of that. He has a strange way of coming close. If he's right and he's finished, then his downfall is going to be a hundred times greater than anything Andrei has experienced.

He destroyed Brodskaya, Andrei tells himself, pulling back from his own thoughts. Well, she will have vengeance. But she wouldn't have wanted that. It was her life she wanted, and her profession. Volkov took it all and didn't even think it was worth taking.

'You must go to Gorya now,' he says, not wanting to say, *While you still can.*

'Yes,' says Volkov. He sighs deeply. It's as if the alcohol in his veins swirls up one last time, freeing his tongue. 'Gorya is better off out of this shit.'

Gorya will be fast asleep by now. From time to time a nurse will check his breathing and all his vital signs. Andrei wonders if the mother is still there, sitting by the bedside. Perhaps she's dropped off to sleep. If Volkov falls, she'll be in danger. Will they take her, too? Surely not before the boy dies. But even as Andrei says those words to himself, he knows that he doesn't believe them. Anything at all can happen to anyone at all, and Volkov never forgets it.

'I'll go in a minute,' says Volkov, but he doesn't move. Outside the window it's still snowing. Moscow is filling up with snow. Even in the dark there's a faint glow from its whiteness.

23

A shaded lamp burns in Gorya Volkov's room. He is propped high on his pillows, so that he is almost sitting upright. Beside the bed there is an oxygen cylinder. A mask covers Gorya's mouth and nostrils. Tumours have swallowed most of the space inside his lungs. Each day they take away more of his breath. They have moved so fast from invasion to conquest that they have already surrounded his heart. This morning the doctors drew more fluid from his pleural cavity, to ease his breathing.

The child is full of morphine. If it depresses the automatic functions of his body, that doesn't matter now. His face looks peaceful, as far as it's possible to judge through the mask. On the other side of the bed from the oxygen cylinder, his mother sits upright on her chair, although her head droops. Her sleep is very light; she would wake at the slightest sound from her son.

Just ten minutes, she tells the nurses, is enough to keep her going for hours.

She isn't wearing any make-up. Once again she looks like the peasant woman whom Volkov married all those years ago.

The door handle turns very slowly. Someone pushes the door and it opens without a creak. Volkov steps into the room, wearing a civilian overcoat and a fur hat. He stands by the door for a few moments, surveying first his son and then his wife. Perhaps he's waiting for the cold which he's carried in from the winter night to dissolve into the warmth of the room. He wouldn't want the boy to feel that chill.

Now he moves to the foot of the bed. The oxygen cylinder hisses. Volkov stands there for a long time, looking down at the boy. His face shows no particular expression. At last he leans forward to touch his son's foot through the covers. His hand stays there, on the thin cotton coverlet, for more than a minute. The boy doesn't stir. His mother's head slips down a little further, towards her chest. Volkov straightens himself again, goes noiselessly to the door, opens it and leaves without looking back.

Once he's outside, he squares his shoulders and frowns at the empty corridor. For some reason there is no one guarding his son's room tonight. His hand goes to the right-hand pocket of his overcoat and pats it lightly, as if for reassurance.

Outside the hospital, his car is waiting. Volkov looks as if he's about to get in, but then appears to change his mind. The driver has already sprung from his seat to open the passenger door. Volkov says something to him. The driver looks surprised, even a little alarmed. He seems as if he might be about to argue with Volkov, but he thinks better of it, gets back into the driving seat and puts the car into gear. Slowly, he rolls away down the street. His winter tyres cut a sharp pattern in the snow, but within a minute the swirling flakes have blurred it.

Volkov watches the car until it is out of sight, and then glances rapidly all around him. He appears to see nothing that disturbs him. He hesitates a moment longer before seeming to come to a decision. He sets off, walking north at a brisk, confident pace. Soon his hat and shoulders are covered with snow, but he keeps going. It's not until there's the rumble of a militia truck behind him that his pace falters. However, he does not look round, and the truck goes by, churning up old and new snow. Volkov slows to walking pace, and then stops. It is now about two in the morning and he is conspicuous in the empty street. He seems to realize this, because suddenly he speeds up, moving more erratically now, and plunges into the entrance of a narrow alleyway on the left. The snow is even thicker here. He keeps close to the shelter of the wall, but stumbles on something that is hidden by the snow. A piece of rubble perhaps. He saves himself from the fall with surprising agility, takes a couple more steps and then stops and leans against the wall.

The noise of his breathing is loud, and in spite of the cold he has sweat on his forehead. He pulls off his fur hat, shakes it, and drops it into the snow. He pats his overcoat again. There's the sound of an engine on the main road. Perhaps it's the truck again. Volkov looks to his right. Yes, it is the militia truck, but it passes in the opposite direction this time, slowly and steadily, as if on patrol. There is a possibility, of course, that it might be a different truck.

Volkov appears to consider for a while, and then he takes off his leather gloves, puts them together carefully and drops them into the snow close to his hat. It is very cold; his breath smokes. He reaches into his pocket, takes out his Makarov service pistol and pushes the safety lever to the 'fire' position.

He opens his mouth and puts the muzzle inside. He seems to know which is the correct angle, because he makes a small adjustment with his other hand. His hands are shaking, but not enough to interfere with what he's doing. His breath comes hard. He seems to taste the metal of the gun and a mask of anguish and disgust comes over his face, as if he has tasted poison. For a few seconds he remains still, apart from the shaking of his hands, and then he leans forward, as if about to vomit, and pulls the trigger.

24

Kolya misses Leningrad, but he doesn't talk about it. Anna doesn't know what Galya said to him in the weeks before she joined them, but he seems different. Older, perhaps. More guarded. He is going to look like his father: it's quite clear now. When he thinks she isn't looking he gives her a quick, watchful glance, as if checking that she is safe.

Anna arrived at Galya's exhausted by her walk from the local station. Galya made her lie down, and drink tea that was heavy with sugar. Anna drank the tea and then lay flat, staring up at the ceiling. She was neither happy nor unhappy. There was only the mattress underneath her, and the narrow white room. She could let herself sink into it. There was nothing she could do and nothing that she needed to do. She heard Galya's footsteps, and a murmur of voices.

The dacha was small and it echoed like a wooden box.

She had taken off the layers of clothes she'd worn for the journey. The baby turned inside her, kicking, insistent. *I am here. Don't forget me. I won't allow you to forget me.* She put her hands on her belly and watched the wall, thinking of nothing.

After a while Kolya put his head around the door. He'd been out fetching wood. She searched his face, looking for her Kolya, her boy, but he wasn't there. This was the face Kolya would have from now on, she thought. It was defined, with strong eyebrows. Not yet a man's face, but you could see the man he would be.

'Are you all right? Galya said you weren't feeling too good.'

'I'm fine, Kolya. Just tired.'

'You'll have to rest more,' he said seriously. He came over and sat down carefully on the narrow bed. This slip room had belonged to Galya's son, long ago. It had been a junk room for years; Anna remembered towers of books and broken chairs.

'Do you like it?' he asked.

'The room? Yes, it's lovely. It seems so much bigger.'

'I cleared it all out. Most of the stuff was junk but there were some good pieces of wood. I'm using them to repair the hen-run.'

'Are you?'

'Don't look so surprised. I do know how to use a hammer and nails. There are a lot of jobs that need doing around here.'

'Well, Galya's not so young any more.'

'She's ancient!'

'We're all ancient to you. Do you two get on all right?'

'Of course we do. I like Galya, she leaves you alone. She doesn't talk all the time. She can't manage those hens any more, though. They keep getting out of the run and laying away. The vegetable plot's too big for her as well. She's only been growing stuff on about a quarter of it. I'm going to dig it all over as soon as the ground's clear.'

'I'll help you, once the baby —'

'Galya says you've got to rest. I white-washed the walls, did you notice?'

'Of course I did. It's so nice the way the light comes through on to it. I could lie here and watch it all day.'

He looked anxious. Has she really changed that much?

'Of course I won't, Kolya! When have I ever lain in bed all day? I'm going to do the cooking. We can't expect Galya to cook for the three of us.'

'She's hopeless, anyway. She makes the same soup all the time.'

'She's never been interested in cooking.'

He sat there, watching Anna as if she might disappear. He didn't ask any questions about Andrei. Perhaps Galya had told him not to, or perhaps he understood the whole situation.

'Anna,' he said at last, 'what if they come here looking for — for us?'

'They won't.'

'They might.'

'The morning I left, I gave the caretaker the impression that I might go out east, to be near Andrei's people when the baby's born.'

'But his parents are dead.'

'Yes, they are — but no one in our building knows that, do they?'

'Do you think he believed you?'

'I think so. I'd never have thought I could lie like that — do you want to know what I said?'

'What?'

'It was so early when I left that I didn't think he'd be around, but he was sweeping snow out of the entrance. He was in a bad temper about it as usual. He stopped sweeping and stared at me. I was sure he'd noticed the bags I was carrying and all the clothes I was wearing. I nearly panicked and then I thought of what I could say. It just came to me. I pointed to the snow and said, "This is nothing to what they get where I'm going." I could see his mind working. He said, "Where might that be?" and so I made out I hadn't meant to let it slip. I said, "Oh, it's nothing, I was only talking about where my husband's family live, out east." And he nodded, you know how he does, very slowly. As if he knows something which he can use against you, and he's filing it away.'

'That was good,' Kolya approved. 'But won't he know that you'd never say anything to him if you were really going to do it?'

'No,' said Anna, 'I don't think he will. He wants us out of the place, anyway, so he was happy. If a man like that is ever happy. And then he said, "No offence, but if you're ever thinking of leaving us, what about that piano? I've always had a fancy to learn the piano." '

'That's unbelievable!'

'It's what he said. "Would you be thinking of parting with it?" So I said, "Maybe. I'll think about it and let you know." I thought that would keep him sweet for a while.'

'It was a risk, even so,' said Kolya soberly. 'What if he informs on you?'

'Then our apartment would be sealed, and

he'd have no chance of getting the piano. I bet he has his eye on our furniture as well. I don't think he'll inform yet, and if he does, he'll tell them we've gone to Siberia.'

Kolya laughed with pleasure, like a child, and then the anxious look came back. 'But won't they take all our stuff if they think we've gone?'

'Not yet. The rent is paid and the apartment is all locked up. They'll wait for a while before they take the risk. But, Kolya, I'm going to have to talk to you properly about the piano —'

'It's all right, Anna, I know all about it. You don't need to say anything.' Kolya spoke rapidly. His face was set, like a man's face and not a child's.

Yes, Kolya understands the situation all right. It's a relief not to have to explain everything. It's even more of a relief that he doesn't complain, or say he misses his friends, or that he is never going to pass his exams at this rate. He seems to have accepted that they are in limbo, and in return he has taken the freedoms of a man. He'll come and go when he wants, because he's not a schoolboy any more. He will grow vegetables. He'll fish, and trap rabbits. He will take over hammer and chisel, axe and saw. What he thinks of his future is a mystery. He never even says that he misses the piano.

One day, a few weeks after her arrival, she picks up a sheet of paper from the floor by Kolya's couch. There is music written on it.

'Is this yours, Kolya?' she asks, but he whips it out of sight as if she's tried to read his diary.

She doesn't ask again, and is surprised when he says, out of the blue one evening when she's resting on the couch, 'I've been writing a march. It's almost finished.'

'What?'

'A march,' he repeats patiently. 'You know, Anna, music for people to march to.'

'Oh! You mean you composed it? Without the piano?'

'It's not as hard as you'd think.'

'It would be for me.' She thinks, but doesn't say, that surely they've had enough of marching.

'It's dedicated to Andrei,' says Kolya, who has rarely mentioned Andrei's name since his arrest.

'To Andrei?'

'Yes. It's called "Prisoners' March".'

'Oh, Kolya.'

'Obviously I haven't written down the title, or the dedication. I'm not an idiot,' he says quickly, as if defending himself.

'Could you sing it to me — or hum it, or whatever?'

'It wouldn't work. I could show you a bit on the piano. But it's not one of those nice lyrical pieces you like.'

'I'll get you another piano, Kolya.'

'I know.' He says this as if humouring her own emotion rather than comforting himself.

'Maybe we'll be able to send you to a conservatoire one day.'

'You must be joking. I don't play anywhere near well enough.'

'But if you compose —'

'It's all crap, anyway. What they want in those places is crap. Even if you do what you're supposed to and make nice musicky-music which says all the right things, you still get stuffed. Someone doesn't like the sound of it and there you are: banged up for twenty years. I won't be hanging around waiting for someone to pat me on the back and say, "All right, young man, we're going to allow you to be a composer! For now!" ' He stares at her as if willing her to dare contradict him, his underlip pushed out. In his eyes she sees — or thinks she sees — a spark of the child he once was, longing for her reassurance.

No. She is deceiving herself. He wants her to tell him the truth.

'I suppose you're right,' she says at last.

A muscle twitches in his cheek. In a different, quieter voice he asks, 'But how are we going to know what's happened to Andrei?'

She's glad she is lying down. The bare thought of what might happen to Andrei makes her feel as if every particle of strength is draining from her body. She won't think of it. Even when they were starving she had refused to believe it, and they had lived.

They have Julia to thank for the sale of the piano. She has a friend — someone in the film business, with money — who wanted a decent piano for his daughter to learn on. Julia quickly said that she knew of one, and arranged for Kolya's piano to be taken away and repaired first. The apartment hasn't been sealed. Julia didn't go there herself — too risky — but Anna sent the keys to her and Julia passed them on to another friend who had an interest in second-hand furniture. He was to supervise the removal of the piano and at the same time look at the apartment's contents to see what could be sold.

He reported back to Julia. Was it just a bit

of surplus furniture that her friend wanted to sell, or was it everything? If she wanted, he could clear the whole apartment.

'What do you think?' Julia asks Anna, when they meet at the local railway station. She hadn't really wanted Julia to come, but Julia thought a brief meeting at the station would be safe. She wouldn't risk coming to Galya's.

Anna hesitates.

'What do you think, Anna?'

The rent for the apartment is paid until the end of next month. She won't be able to pay after that. The nursery has been informed that she won't be returning to work: 'High blood pressure causing serious complications of pregnancy,' it says on her medical certificate. The doctor was a friend of Andrei. He asked nothing; didn't even ask where Andrei was, but the certificate was prepared, ready to sign.

All the furniture, the books, their clothes. (*Thank God,* she thinks again, *that I made Kolya take so much with him when he first went down to Galya's.*) Their china and their linen; the kitchen equipment. But the apartment has got to be emptied, and it's impossible to bring the stuff down here. For one thing she hasn't the money; but more importantly, it might draw attention to them. It could lay a trail to bring the arresting officers to Galya's door. Safer to lose everything than risk that. And better to sell now than to hang on in hope. Everyone in the building knows about Andrei's arrest. The caretaker or the Maleviches might seize their chance, break in, and help themselves. She's heard of apartments being stripped bare after an arrest if there's no family to stay and protect the place.

She will never go back. That life is over. But she has a room to sleep in, and Kolya has a couch in the living room. There's food on the table. When the snow melts Kolya can begin to cultivate Galya's vegetable plot, and their own. Once the baby is born she will work there too. They can grow enough to have food for barter as well as for their own use. Next winter is a long way away, and by then the baby will be six months old.

She should have registered for maternity care. The baby's birth will have to be registered too. The baby will need its paperwork, like everybody else. Don't think of that now. Galya will be able to deliver the child. Anna never liked the idea of giving birth in hospital anyway. It brings back too many memories of her mother: the smell of blood and disinfectant, her mother's colourless face, and the baby Anna fetched from the hospital nursery, and brought home.

Andrei is alive. She would know if he were not alive. He'll come back and they will have a life together. She can't imagine now what that life will be like, but she doesn't need to. She must think of today, only today, or she will freeze with fear. If she thinks of the future it must only be in terms of spring coming, and the baby being born.

'Get him to sell everything,' Anna says to Julia. 'I need the money to send to Andrei, and we've got to manage until I can get work again.'

'Or until Kolya can,' says Julia.

'Kolya?'

'Yes. He's not a child any more, Anna. He can always go to university later on.'

'I doubt if they'd let him in, the way things are,' says Anna. 'What's he going to put on the forms? And if there's anything you want to take, Julia, just say. I know you've got lots of stuff, but —'

'I'll take what I can,' says Julia. 'I'll keep it for you.'

'But not if it can be sold.'

'No, not if it can be sold. And I'll get the money to you. I'll have to think how to do it, because it's not a good idea for me to come out here again. I'll write to Galya once everything's sorted out.'

'Julia, you are — well, I don't know what to say. Thank you.'

'There's my train — I'll have to rush. I'll be in touch, Anna!'

But she isn't in touch. No letter comes. Anna lies awake, fearing that Julia too might have been arrested. In mid-January, Galya goes to the city to visit an old colleague. Just an overnight stay; they arranged it months ago and Galya's been looking forward to it, even though she finds the city too much for her these days.

Anna is sitting at the window, staring idly into the falling snow, when Galya returns. She's walking slowly, head down, shuffling in her heavy boots. She looks like an old woman, thinks Anna. She has never thought of Galya as old before. Galya comes in, stamps her boots on the mat and brushes the snow off the shoulders of her coat before hanging it up. She sits down heavily in her chair.

'It's the end for my profession,' she says. 'They're calling us murderers now.'

'What do you mean?'

'It's in *Pravda*. We are fiends and killers who disgrace the banner of science, apparently.'

'Who are?'

'Doctors. Us.' She sighs heavily and begins to unlace her boots. 'Read it. The paper is in my bag. I don't want to talk about it.'

Anna seizes the paper.

Today TASS news agency reported the arrest of a group of saboteur-doctors. This terrorist group, uncovered some time ago by organs of State Security, had as their goal the shortening of the lives of leaders of the Soviet Union by means of medical sabotage . . .

She reads on, heart pounding. Victims are named: Zhdanov . . . Shcherbakov . . . My God, are they saying that Andrei killed Zhdanov? But it's impossible. It's crazy. No one can believe a word of it. 'Recruited by the Americans . . . International Jewish-bourgeois nationalist organizations . . . poisonous filth . . .' The words pour on but she can make no sense of them.

'But Andrei was arrested weeks ago,' she says aloud. 'Long before all this.' It can't have anything to do with Andrei. These are eminent doctors who have treated Party leaders, generals and admirals. That's why they are supposed to have been part of a plot: because they had access to such senior figures. You couldn't possibly say that a paediatrician whose clinics are crammed with Leningrad children is part of an American conspiracy.

Of course you couldn't. Sense and logic defy it. But even while she is reassuring herself, Anna knows that sense and logic have nothing to do with it. *Pravda* isn't simply reporting these cases, but signalling the start of another campaign against yet another profession. In the thirties scientists and engineers got it — and before long everybody was getting it. After the war it was writers and artists and musicians. The only thing that doesn't change is the language. Anna reads on. 'War-mongers and their agents . . . spies . . . traitors who plot to destroy our Motherland . . .' She can hear her father's voice in her head, saying with bitter irony, *'Yes, this is all just as it should be, just as normal.'*

How happy Volkov will be now. He'll be able to build a case against Andrei with no trouble at all. He's just the kind of high-up Party man these doctors were supposed to have tried to murder. But a child — how could anyone think that a doctor would deliberately kill a child with cancer? Even the most perverted imagination would be hard put to it.

'Galya, did you talk to anybody, what else are they saying?'

Galya eases off her boots, first one and then the other. 'Andrei's not a Jew, be thankful for that. They're talking about deportations. Special settlements for Jews. They've arrested hundreds of doctors, apparently, far more than it says in the paper, and nearly all of them are Jewish.'

'But those are just rumours, surely, Galya —'

'Rumours? Everything's a rumour in this country, until it happens to you. When you've lived as long as I have, you won't dismiss rumours.'

Galya sounds as if she were angry with her, Anna. Perhaps she regrets taking them in now. Even Galya might be afraid.

'We could go back to our own dacha,' Anna says.

Galya's hand, which has been massaging her calf, freezes. 'What are you talking about?'

'It might be safer for you if we left, now that all this is happening.'

'Safer! What kind of a person do you think I am?'

Galya's eyes flash. Suddenly she's the Galya of Anna's childhood. She is Vera's friend, who can be suddenly and terribly

545

stern if she finds you doing anything which would upset your mother.

'Safer! I'd be safer if I were dead. That's the only kind of safety there is for us now. At least I'm old, and out of the profession. I don't have to see my colleagues terrorized. Can you imagine what Vera would have said? When I think how we studied, how we worked, how we thought nothing of going whole nights without sleep — and now they say that we want to murder our patients. You'll stay right here, Anna. You have the baby to think about. If I can do nothing else, I can help you deliver that child. As for Kolya, he's rebuilding my house for me, so I'm certainly not going to risk losing him. We'll put that rubbish in the stove,' she says, reaching for the newspaper. 'I should never have brought it home. But you'd have been bound to hear it on the radio, anyway.'

'I have to read it, because of Andrei,' says Anna, drawing back and keeping hold of *Pravda*.

'It's not Andrei they're after,' says Galya quickly. 'All the names they give are senior doctors. Some of them have world reputations, and they're almost all Jews. This isn't to do with Andrei.'

Anna sits with her head bowed. Let Galya think she's reassured me. She knows, and I know, that this has everything to do with Andrei. Probably this is why Julia hasn't been in touch. Her husband must have excellent contacts, and he might have got wind of what was happening before it was made public. He might have warned Julia that she must keep right away from Anna now.

What will they do to Andrei? The paper talks about treason. Zhdanov, Shcherbakov. . . . Tomorrow there could be another name: Gorya Volkov. Her stomach hurts. She splays the newspaper out on the table and leans forward as if she's studying it, to hide the pain from Galya. It's nothing to do with the baby. Just indigestion.

'You should go and lie down,' says Galya.

'No,' said Anna, 'I'm fine.' She stares at the sheet of dirty newsprint without focusing. 'I'm going out in a minute.'

'What? In this?'

Anna raises her head and looks out of the window. It's still snowing. 'I'll wait a bit.'

It's when she looks down again that the name draws her gaze like a magnet. The newsprint swims, then sharpens. S. I. Volkov, it says. The heading to a tiny paragraph, close to the bottom of the page:

The death is announced from heart

failure of S. I. Volkov, formerly Commissar of State Security.

She scans above and below the item, but there's nothing more. *Volkov is dead.* She puts her fists on the table to support herself. *Volkov is dead.*

'Anna! Are you ill?'

'I've just seen something in the paper. Volkov is dead. You know, the man whose son Andrei —'

'Give it to me. Now, where are my reading glasses — wait a minute —'

'There, Galya.' Anna points to the announcement.

Galya takes it in. ' "*Formerly* Commissar of State Security . . ." Now what does that mean, I wonder? Do you know, Anna, I'd say that the wolf had fallen from favour.'

'Surely he can't have.' Her heart leaps. If Galya's right, then that changes everything.

'You remember when Yezhov fell? It can happen, even to them. All the signs are there, look. No list of titles and honours. No fulsome testimonials to his war service. They've only given him a couple of lines. And I've never liked the look of "heart failure". "Shot in a cellar", more likely. And good riddance. Let *him* taste the bullets.'

Anna looks at Galya in amazement. She's

never heard Galya speak like this. 'Do you think it can really be true?' she asks. 'Volkov's really dead?'

'Would they put it in *Pravda* otherwise? Either he's dead, or someone intends him to be dead very soon.'

'I'm glad,' says Anna. 'I hope he suffered.' Volkov is dead. He is dead, and Andrei is alive. 'I'm going out now,' she says.

She crosses her shawl over her chest and ties it at her back before putting on her overcoat. Kolya has gone over to see Mitya Sokolov, and no doubt he'll stay to supper with them if he's asked. Darya Sokolova welcomes him these days: Kolya is a piece of the past. She likes to have him about the place.

'You remember, Anna, how your Kolya and my Mitya used to play all day long down by that stream, when they were little? And before that it was you and our Vasya.' She sighed. 'It's hard, isn't it, when you don't have a grave to visit?'

'Yes.' Vasya lies somewhere at the bottom of Lake Ladoga. He was driving a lorry with food supplies for Leningrad; the ice broke, and the lorry plunged through the crevasse. Or at least that's what she thinks happened.

Vasya was as passionate about dam-building as she was. Often they quarrelled, because they each had their own ideas about what would 'really make the dam hold'. But when the lakes they made began to swell and brim like real lakes you could swim in, they would grab hold of each other and hop about with glee. Do bones dissolve, after more than ten years?

'It'll be nice to see another little one playing down there,' Darya said. 'Only you'll have to hurry up and fill the cradle again, because it's no fun playing on your own.'

Darya seemed to have made a decision not to ask any questions about Andrei. She behaved as if he were any absent husband, off working somewhere. That was the way things were. You had to take what you could get, and a family couldn't always be together.

Anna smiled. She felt grateful to Darya for the simple normality of the phrase. *Fill the cradle* . . . Of course she would.

'Are you thinking of buying any honey this year? I've got a few jars left.'

'That depends on the price.'

Darya named one so outrageous that Anna just smiled and shook her head. Simple normality was one thing; but Darya hadn't changed all that much.

■ ■ ■ ■

Anna buttons up her overcoat and ties her scarf over her head. She doesn't want to see Darya today. She wants to be on her own. Her boots are by the door. Balancing carefully against the weight of the baby, she wriggles her feet into them.

'I'll be back soon.'

'Don't go far.'

The snow is easing. A sharp lemony light shines between the young lilacs, but the snow is blue in its folds and hollows. Everything is effaced. The whole world seems to have been put to bed. Anna follows the path that Kolya cleared just this morning. It's covered again, but not too deeply. She'll go a little way into the woods.

The fresh, powdery snow squeaks under her boots. It's very still, very quiet. But of course not so quiet, once you start to listen. There is the whine of a chainsaw, a long way off but distinct. A lump of snow slithers off a branch and drops close to Anna's feet.

She reaches a little clearing. This is where she used to climb trees when she was little. She remembers it as full of leaf shadows, and secretive, but today light pours down from the pale sky to the glistening snow. She looks up. A ragged crow flaps across the sky.

Black crows. She shudders. But Volkov is dead. Maybe he's already buried. He can do nothing more. If Galya's right, and he's fallen from power, then perhaps the case against Andrei will collapse.

Of course that can't really happen. She's not such a fool as to think they'll simply let him out. But a lighter sentence, perhaps. If Volkov's no longer there, driving the case on, then the prosecutors might lose interest.

It's cold. She ought not to stay here, but she can't bear to go back to the dacha and talk to Galya like her normal self.

She would like to howl like a wolf, with fury and frustration. Volkov has reached into their lives and torn them apart, and for nothing. He was already falling himself, but he dragged them down with him. Now he's dead, and he's got out of it. Why should he escape? If she could find his grave she would spit on it. He doesn't deserve to sleep. He should be dragged out of his coffin and hung in the wind, for the crows to eat him.

Anna shivers again, and crosses her arms over her breast. She would never have believed she could feel like this. As if a new self has grown up, inside the shell of the old

Anna. Perhaps she'll become one of those old women, the widows with their bitter, exhausted faces, who believe in nothing and trust no one.

The baby thuds, deep inside her. In less than two months he will be born. She thinks it will be a boy, but probably that's only because Kolya is a boy. The baby is strong. Sometimes when he kicks now, she sees a little foot push out under her ribs. She ought to go to a maternity clinic, but she doesn't want to go anywhere near officials. Galya says things are going well. Anna is in excellent health and there's every indication that the birth will be normal.

'I'm not going near a hospital,' Anna says to her.

'But your mother —'

Galya is thinking of the post-partum haemorrhage that killed Vera, after Kolya's birth. Anna thinks of it too, but says, 'It didn't help her, being in hospital, did it?'

After a pause, Galya shakes her head.

'We'll manage,' says Anna to the baby now. 'Don't worry, I'm going to make sure you're all right.'

The baby kicks again. He's so strong, so imperative. He doesn't know anything about Volkov. None of it matters to him. He just wants to be born. To push his way out of

Anna, just as the buds will push their way out of these trees. It's almost frightening, how powerful that force is, thinks Anna. As if Andrei and I don't matter, as long as he gets born. We've served our purpose, in making him. But perhaps that's as it should be.

She feels calmer now. She'll be able to go back, and talk normally. She'll ask Kolya what's happening at the Sokolovs', and whether Darya has had second thoughts about the outrageous price she's asking for her honey.

'I'm here, Andrei,' she murmurs, surprising herself. 'Don't be afraid.'

The wind sifts, but nothing answers. Anna straightens her back. She looks up at the sky, and clenches her fists. The baby kicks even harder, as if he senses her fury — or as if he shares it. 'We're going to be all right, you bastards!' she calls into the empty sky, as she called once before, long ago. 'Just wait and see! We're going to live!'

Galya meets her at the door. 'I've been looking out for you.'

'You shouldn't stand here, it's much too cold.'

'Look.' Galya holds up a package. For a wild moment, Anna thinks it might be something from Andrei. But no, the package has been delivered by hand.

'You just missed him. He didn't give his name. A tall chap. He said this came from a friend of yours in Leningrad.'

Sure enough, there are fresh footprints in the snow, not Anna's.

'He said he couldn't stay,' says Galya. 'He was so muffled up that I didn't really see his face.'

'Oh.' Anna turns the package over in her hands.

'Close the door. That child of yours may be a Spartan, but my bones are growing old. Come to the stove.'

Anna sits by the flank of the stove. There is string around the parcel, and she unties it carefully and rolls it up. She takes off one layer of paper, and then another. Inside, there is a thick envelope. Nothing is written on it. Her heart beats fast as she opens the flap.

There it is. A pile of banknotes, used and shabby, held together with a rubber band.

'Julia must have sent it,' she says. 'It's the money from the furniture.'

She riffles through the notes, counting them. Halfway through, she looks at Galya with disbelieving eyes. 'It's far too much. Our stuff can never have fetched all this.'

'You sold the piano, didn't you?'

'Yes, but it was just an ordinary piano. It had a good tone but it wasn't especially valuable.'

'I suppose that depends on what the buyer was prepared to pay. And you sold all your household stuff as well, remember.'

'But it can't have been worth all this. This will keep us going for months if we're careful, and I can send plenty to Andrei. It's Julia who's done this.'

'Good for her.'

'She shouldn't have. It's too much. No one can afford to give away all this.'

'Not in our world, that's true. But didn't you say her husband was a Stalin Prizewinner?'

'Yes.'

'There you are, then. Why shouldn't you have it?'

'I don't know. It doesn't seem right.'

'Of course it's "right",' says Galya with such finality that Anna says no more.

Besides, it means that she can give Galya money, and buy food and things for the baby. Only an idiot would refuse. Julia hasn't put in a note. She wouldn't have wanted there to be anything with her name on it.

'I expect that the man who brought it was

her husband,' says Galya. 'I only hope he knows how to keep his mouth shut.'

'Of course he will.'

'There's no "of course" about it, and you know it. But he'll be careful. It would come out that his wife is your friend.'

'That's why I worry about us staying here with you.'

'I know you do. I can see you worrying away, Anna, you have a very transparent face.'

Have I? I think you might be surprised, even so, if you could see into my mind . . .

'But you don't need to worry about me. I have nothing to lose.' And Galya smiles calmly, as if this were the most obvious and incontrovertible fact in the world.

25

The train creaks to a halt. Andrei stirs, and shifts his swollen legs. If he turns his head a little to the right he can see through a chink in the wooden slatting. He can taste the air.

Outside there is a platform, bathed in bluish light. There's a low wooden shed, not much more than a shack. Someone is walking up the platform in heavy boots. Andrei can hear their tread but he can't see the figure. There is a sudden ringing clang. His heart jumps, then settles. They are only testing the wheels. He's sure that's all it is.

All around him, men stir. Old Vasya groans. He's probably not that old, but with his yellow skull-like head and huge eye sockets, he looks a hundred. He has dysentery; probably amoebic dysentery, Andrei thinks. The pail in the corner of the truck brims and reeks.

There is never enough water for Vasya to drink. His tongue is cracked and swollen.

'What's going on?' murmurs Kostya.

'Don't know. Just a halt, I think. We're at a station.'

'What can you see?'

'The platform. A shed. Some birch trees.'

It had seemed like a miracle when he had met Kostya again, in the 'bread-van' that took him to the railway station. Kostya had got twenty-five years.

'You only got ten! You lucky sod. I thought they'd stopped handing out tens. The rest of us are all halves and quarters.'

A 'half' was fifty years, and a 'quarter' twenty-five. Why sentence a man to fifty years when there was no chance he could survive that long? For the same reason, Andrei supposed, that they did everything else.

When the prisoners were offloaded at the railway station — in a special area screened from the public — he saw how pale Kostya was. The dead-white look you get from being locked away from the light for months. All the men were blinking in the winter sun as the guards lined them up and crammed them into the trucks. Vitamin deficiencies, as well as lack of exposure to light, Andrei thought. What a rabble they look. If he saw himself coming along the street, he'd probably cross over to the other side.

'Stick close,' said Kostya. 'We'll get ourselves sorted. It's good to have a doctor on board.'

Once they were in their truck — a cattle truck lined with wooden plank beds all the way up to the ceiling — Kostya began to organize them. There was no argument about electing him as their foreman. They needed someone who could speak up, who knew their rights and yet wouldn't antagonize the guards. It was bitterly cold in the truck.

'We'll have to get this stove lit,' said Kostya, but there was no sign of the guards. Andrei spread out his blanket and rolled himself up. He would get some sleep. He didn't feel the cold as much as some of them; his Siberian upbringing must have seen to that. He had his padded jacket, too. He had done a deal with one of the guards after he was sentenced and knew that his winter overcoat wasn't likely to be much good for 'corrective labour'. It was a good overcoat. Anna had saved up her wages for months, and surprised him with it. But the padded jacket was thicker, and very little worn. As long as he could hold on to his things he would be all right. He needed padded trousers but God knows where they could be obtained. Maybe the camps issued some kind of work uniform.

The clanging sound runs up and down the train.

'Maybe this is it. Maybe we're there,' says one of the men uneasily. Old Vasya moans loudly.

'I wish he'd shut the fuck up. He'll have the guards in,' someone hisses angrily.

Old Vasya has scurvy as well as dysentery. There are petechial haemorrhages all over his body. Several of the men have bleeding gums, but Vasya is by far the worst, probably because he's not absorbing what nutrients there are in the soup. It is even more salty than the Lubyanka swill.

'Do they think we're animals?' the men mutter in disgust as their bowls are filled.

Probably, Andrei thinks. If you treat a man like an animal, then you have to believe that he is one. He's learned that the guards hate it if you look directly into their eyes. It can lead to a beating.

There is supposed to be absolute silence when the train is at a halt. The logic must be that if civilians heard human noises coming out of a cattle truck, they might get uneasy. But it's so cold that Vasya can't help groaning.

'Can't someone shut that bugger up?'

The moon shines on outside. Andrei puts his face as close as he can to the chink in the slats, and snuffs up the air. There is a smell that tantalizes him. It is so near, so familiar. He breathes more deeply, and suddenly the smell hits a part of his brain that almost remembers it.

A charking sound comes from Vasya, then stops. After about half a minute, it begins again, louder and more agonized.

'Oh, for fuck's sake!'

'He's dying,' says Andrei. 'Let me get near him.'

There's nothing he can do. Old Vasya is lying on his back, with his nose jutting towards the roof of the van. His mouth has fallen open like a cave. It stinks of decay, as if he has already begun to rot from within. Andrei takes his wrist. A pulse flutters, and then jumps. Vasya's trousers are sodden with liquid faeces. He's been like that for a while, because a couple of days ago he lost the strength to go to the bucket. The charking noise begins again, rising in pitch, then dying back.

Andrei takes his hand. There's nothing he can do. The hand is limp, and already cold. The sound will go on for a little while longer, and then it will stop.

■ ■ ■ ■

In the morning, when the guards have heaved Old Vasya's body out of the van, Kostya persuades them to bring water with disinfectant in it so they can wash down the floor.

'We've a doctor in here and he says there's a risk of infection. We could all be going down with it.'

The word 'infection' works. Andrei watches the guards jump to it. They are terrified of lice, too. 'You'll all be fumigated once you get where you're going,' one of them announces, as if this is a reward. *I must remember this,* Andrei thinks. They are afraid of typhoid epidemics, because disease doesn't know which is the prisoner and which is the guard.

'Who's the doctor, then?' asks the old guard they call Starik, the one in charge of their van.

'I am,' says Andrei.

The guard's eyes find him in the gloom, and assess him. 'Name?' he asks.

'Alekseyev, Andrei Mikhailovich.'

'Right.'

The guard's eyes rove over the rest of the men. You have to watch yourself these days.

These aren't like the prisoners you got back in the thirties. Most of these men are war veterans and they know how to handle themselves. You have to act accordingly.

'Right,' he says again. 'Full disinfection will be ordered at the next halt. Any noise, you'll find yourselves in the punishment cell.'

For of course, even on a train travelling the breadth of Russia and on to Siberia, there has to be a punishment cell.

At that moment Andrei remembers the smell that filled his nostrils the night before, when he pressed them to the gap where icy air poured in. It seemed all the sharper in contrast to the fetid air of the cattle car. His brain comes alive, remembering, recognizing. It was the smell of the taiga. It was the cold, wild air of home.

26

'Make sure she latches on properly. That's right. Don't let her chew the nipple.'

Anna strokes the baby's head. It is hot and fragile, like an egg when the chick is ready to be hatched. The baby looks up at her and sucks frantically, as if she doesn't believe she will ever taste milk again.

They call her 'the baby' still, for she has no name even though she's eight days old. She was born in late February, a little earlier than Galya or Anna had expected. Already, it seems as if she's been with them for ever.

'Do you think "Natasha"?' she asks Galya, who is rinsing out nappies at the sink.

'I don't like it, personally. There was a spiteful little girl at school who used to pull my hair — she was called Natasha.'

'It's difficult, isn't it? So many names have associations.'

'You could always call her Vera,' says Galya. She doesn't turn round, but Anna sees from Galya's sudden stillness that this is important.

'I don't think I could do that,' she says gently. 'I'd be thinking of my mother every time I said her name.'

'Wouldn't you want to do that?'

'Of course. But I want to think of her and the baby separately.'

Galya nods, and plunges her hands back into the sink.

'When Kolya comes back, I'll ask him if he's had any more thoughts,' says Anna.

Kolya got up at first light and went over to their own dacha, to clean out and repair the guttering there, as he has done at Galya's. He needs to get out of the house. It's a bit too much for him, the smell of milk and blood and baby faeces, with nappies in buckets and baby clothes hung up to dry all around the stove. He'd rather be out, alone.

Everything has changed since the baby's birth. Kolya is part of a different generation. He is an uncle now; not Anna's child, but a brother who is almost an adult.

'Don't you worry, Anna,' he said this morning, as she lay there floating, exhausted, with the baby in the crook of her arm, 'I'll look after you while Andrei's away.'

He's bored, she knows that. He needs to go off, tramping through the snow. He needs to mend things and make things and relieve his restlessness with action. He's not a country boy but he's shaping himself that way, as if he thinks Leningrad has turned its back on him.

She's not going to start thinking about Kolya's future, because she always comes to the point where her mind hits rock and stalls: *What kind of future have we given him?* This is their life now. He has to chop wood, feed the stove, repair the ravages of winter, plan the spring planting, do odd jobs in exchange for eggs or honey. She wants to tell him that it won't be for ever. He will get his own life back. He'll be able to study, and one day they'll have a piano again. But she says nothing. He's not a child, to be comforted with promises. He doesn't want her to make him feel better. He pulls on his boots and goes off on his own.

Anna strokes the baby's head. She's sucking well now. Last night she woke for feeds every two hours while Anna slipped in and out of sleep, feeling the baby's lips pull and smack. She is small and needs to put on weight. When she was born it seemed impossible this could be the big, vigorous baby who had kicked so hard in the womb. She was a little, curled-up creature with a slick of dark hair and long, spidery fingers. When she opened her eyes they were pieces of a darker sky than ever shone over Leningrad. She cried if she was left alone; she wanted to be held tight, as if she were still inside Anna. When you gave her a finger she gripped as if she would never let it go. Even the soles of her feet curled when Anna touched them, and her toes tried to grip too.

Anna cannot believe she ever thought the baby was a boy. As soon as she was born that idea dissolved as if it had never existed. She was herself and nothing else. Anna watched her for hours, learning how expressions flitted over her face and how she drew up her knees and screamed with pain if she fed too quickly.

'Poor little mouse,' Kolya said once, touching her cheek with the back of his finger.

'She's tough,' said Galya. 'She'll be fine.'

There's no snow on the twigs outside her window. Already, Anna sees signs of the coming spring, still locked inside winter. The sun grows stronger every day. By noon yesterday the temperature was up to two degrees, and there was a steady tick-tick-tick as water dripped from the icicles on the sunny side of the verandah.

She loves the way the seasons follow one another. No one can take that away. Newspaper faces and radio voices can rant as much as they like, but they can't make a single bud open, or a bird build its nest.

Yesterday Kolya was on a ladder outside the window, making repairs. A piece of loose guttering had to be fixed before the thaw began in earnest, or the weight of water might pull it off the roof. She lay and watched him, as Galya passed up tools and told him what to do. And he turned round, looked down over his shoulder at her, and smiled, not with the resentment of a teenager but with the reassurance of a man. She couldn't hear his words through the double glass but she saw his lips move, and knew that he was saying, 'It's all right, I know how to do this. You go indoors and keep warm.'

He was afraid when Anna went into labour. It was evening, and Galya sent him off to the Sokolovs'. He came to see Anna before he left, peering around the door nervously, as if he expected to see her bathed in blood. She smiled with more confidence than she felt and said, 'It's all right, Kolya. When you come back in the morning I expect the baby will be here.'

When he came back in the morning, the

baby was there, sleeping by the bed in the old cradle Galya had dug out from somewhere. Anna was asleep. Kolya sat by the bed in the little bentwood chair that just fitted between bed and wall, and waited for her to wake up. When she did, at first she didn't remember anything, and then a creaking cry made it all true again.

'Do you want to pick her up?'

'I won't know how to,' said Kolya.

'Pick her up carefully and put your hand behind her neck to support it.'

'She's so wobbly!'

'Yes, I know.'

He sat beside her, holding the baby, who had subsided back into sleep. 'Are they usually as small as this?'

'She's not that small. Galya says she's almost three kilos.'

'She's just a mouse. Was I like this?'

'You were bigger,' said Anna, remembering how Kolya had been put into her arms while her mother lay dead in the hospital bed. They hadn't even had time to take Vera to the morgue.

'I'm an uncle now,' said Kolya, prodding the baby's foot doubtfully.

'So you are,' said Anna in surprise. She had almost been thinking of the baby as Kolya's little sister.

'Are you all right, Anna?' he asked, embarrassed, not looking up. 'Is there anything that you want?' She recognized that these were a brother's questions, not a child's.

The radio is broken. Anna is glad of it, but Galya misses it terribly.

'I can't manage without my radio. I'll have to get it repaired. I asked Darya if she knew anybody who might be able to fix it, but she doesn't.'

Much better the silence, Anna considers, than what's been on the radio lately. More and more doctors are being arrested. Confessions are pouring out of them. They are spies, traitors, murderers in white coats, collaborators with American agents. The radio voices thicken with synthetic outrage.

'You have to know what's going on,' says Galya.

No, thinks Anna, *you don't.* You can decide not to allow such poison into your ears. It doesn't help Andrei if I listen. I have to think of him, not of these madmen. I have to try to reach him. If he's thinking of me at the same moment that I'm thinking of him, then perhaps our thoughts can touch. 'Galya,' she says aloud, 'do you think that Andrei has received that money yet?'

'I should think so by now,' says Galya.

'But we haven't had a word from him. Not one.'

'Sometimes prisoners are deprived of the right to correspondence.'

'Can they receive parcels, if that's the case, do you think? Do they still get their letters?'

'I'm not sure.'

They've gone over all this so many times. Each time the conclusions — or lack of them — are the same, but even first thing in the morning Anna can't leave these questions alone.

Suddenly the baby pulls off the nipple and begins to scream. Anna rocks her, and tries to coax her back, but the baby turns her face from side to side, frantically. Deep crimson floods her skin, darkening to purple. Her hands bat the air. 'Oh, Galya, what's wrong with her?'

Galya leaves the sink and comes over to where Anna's lying on the couch with the baby. Her firm, experienced hands feel the baby's forehead.

'She's all right. She just got into a lather. They can feel your tension, you know. We shouldn't have talked about Andrei while she was feeding. Give her a minute and then try again.'

The screams rise, ricochetting around the

room. Sweat starts under Anna's arms. She is a bad mother, on top of everything else. She can't even feed her own baby properly. Tears sting her eyes. *Stupid, idiotic — I forbid you to cry —*

'Give her to me a moment.' Galya picks up the baby and walks away with her, humming. After a while the screams begin to lose conviction. The baby still shudders and hiccups, but she is calming down. 'There, that's better. Now, in a minute, you're going to settle down and have your feed. Poor little one, she doesn't find life easy. Some of them do and some of them don't.' Galya rocks the baby, swaying from hip to hip. She looks like a mother. Her brisk professional expertise is still there, but cloaked by tenderness. 'Here we are, you have her back. It'll be fine now.'

And it is fine. The baby shivers all over as she latches on and shuts her eyes, sucking vigorously. After a minute she opens one eye and gazes up at Anna reproachfully, before losing herself in the milk again.

'She's happy enough now.'

'Yes,' murmurs Anna, 'perfectly happy.' Her heart contracts with pity as she watches the baby suck blindly, her fingers palpating the air. Now she is happy.

'I'll look after you, my darling,' she whispers. 'Don't be frightened. I won't ever leave you.'

The baby feeds until she falls asleep. Slowly, her mouth comes away from Anna's nipple, still connected by a glistening string of saliva and milk. In her sleep, her lips move. She is utterly relaxed.

There's a bang on the door. One blow, and then another. A rain of blows, rattling the door in its frame. Anna jumps violently. The baby startles and flings out her arms and legs with a piercing cry.

'Oh my God!' says Galya.

The knocking goes on, but this time a voice comes too, shouting, 'Anna! Galya!'

'It's Darya,' breathes Anna.

'Darya!'

'Yes, it's only her.'

The women look at each other, their eyes still dilated with fear. But it's all right, Anna tells herself. Only Darya, in a state about something — that's nothing unusual. The knocking goes on. You'd never think one woman could make so much noise.

'There might have been an accident down there.' But Galya still hesitates.

'You'd better open the door,' says Anna, shielding the baby's head with her hand.

No sooner is the door open than Darya bursts in across the threshold. She looks as if she's rushed out of her house, throwing only a shawl over a jumble of clothes. Her head is bare. She's panting and her eyes are wild.

'Sit down, for goodness' sake,' says Galya. 'No, don't try to talk. Get your breath back.'

Darya must have run all the way, and she's far from young. Her face is pale and sweaty, with a patch of crimson in each cheek. She collapses into a chair, her hands on her knees, heaving for breath. Galya gives her a glass of water. 'Sip it slowly.'

But Darya pushes the water aside. 'Did you — hear it?'

'What?'

'The news.'

'No. Our radio's broken, you know that.'

'No one's been and told you?'

'Told us what?'

'They said last night — he was critical — in a critical condition they said.'

'Who?'

'And then today — early this morning — well, you know how I am, I don't sleep so I'm up no matter how early — they said —' She pauses as if not daring to say it, as if the words themselves may burn her mouth. 'They said — "This is Moscow speaking" . . .'

'Yes — Yes — ?'

It's obvious Darya hasn't paused for dramatic effect. She simply can't get the words out.

' "D-dear" . . .' she stammers, ' "Dear c-comrades — and f-friends" —'

Galya bends down over her. As if Darya Sokolova were an hysterical girl she takes hold of her sholders and shakes them firmly. 'Now, tell us sensibly,' she says.

'Stalin is dead,' bleats Darya. Her eyes look like a doll's eyes, rolling.

'What do you mean? Are you sure?' demands Galya severely. 'Because, you know, it's a very serious matter to make up something like this.'

'I'm not making it up! It was on the radio! "This is Moscow speaking." ' Darya is beginning to regain some self-possession. She dashes her sleeve over her face, as if wiping away tears. 'I can't believe it. It's too — too —' she pauses. 'Too terrible. I didn't know what to do with myself. I just sat there frozen, hours it was. And then I thought of you, not having your radio, and I thought, I've got to tell them, it's not right they don't know . . . And I just up and ran, fast as I could. What are we going to do without him?'

What, indeed, thinks Anna, letting her hair fall forward over her face so that it is completely concealed. Her heart beats so fast she's afraid she'll be sick. Let Darya think she's overcome. The baby has stopped crying, as if the news has shocked her into silence. Her mouth is open, and a small, pearly milk blister shows on her upper lip.

'You're right,' says Galya. Her voice trembles a little, then steadies itself. 'No one can take in such news all at once. Excuse me, I must go and lie down. And Anna will need to rest; such a shock is very bad for her, you know. Anna, dear, are you feeling faint?'

Galya's worn, intelligent face is as pale as curd, but she's already mastered herself. She won't betray them.

'A little,' mutters Anna.

'You'll have to forgive us, Darya. Anna must go back to bed. Such terrible news; no wonder she feels ill.'

'I was just the same when *I* first heard it,' says Darya with an edge of competitiveness in her voice.

'I'm sure you were.' Galya is steering Darya to the door. 'Now, walk home slowly. Take deep breaths. Remember, you've had a shock; we all have.'

' "The breathing became more difficult and the pulse," ' continues Darya, as if she's memorized the entire radio broadcast.

' "Boundlessly dear to the Party," that's what they said.'

'Are you sure?' asks Anna sharply. 'Are you really sure that's what you heard? They announced that he was dead?' For if it's a trick, some gigantic, monstrous plot to make people betray themselves —

'As sure as I'm still breathing,' says Darya, and then gives an incongruous smile, as if the fact that she is still breathing while Stalin is not has suddenly struck her with all its force.

'Go home, my dear,' says Galya, like the doctor she will always be. 'Go home and rest.'

Galya stands and watches Darya hurry away, huddling her shawl around her. Slowly, she closes the door and turns to Anna.

'Come to the stove,' says Anna. 'You shouldn't have stood in the cold like that. You're shivering.'

Galya pulls back her shoulders and settles her glasses on her nose. This is how she must have looked, when she was working, after she'd dealt with some emergency on the ward.

'Well, there we are, then,' she says.

'You think it's true?'

'It has to be, if it was on the radio. They

wouldn't dare say it otherwise.'

'It didn't seem as if he would ever die.'

'None of us is immortal,' says Galya. The words ring strangely in Anna's ears. Someone else said that, a long time ago. She pulls back a corner of the baby's shawl, and gazes at her face. The baby's eyelids are almost closed.

'What do you think it will mean?' asks Anna.

'Who knows?'

'Can it really be true, though?'

'He's capable of dying, I suppose, like everyone else,' says Galya drily.

'Everything will change. It's got to.'

Galya sighs. 'Maybe. There are plenty to step into his shoes.'

'I hope he suffered,' says Anna, smoothing the baby's cheek with one finger. 'I hope he was alone and suffered for hours, and no one came to help him.'

'That's not very likely. He'd have had phalanxes of doctors.'

'I hope that just before he died, he saw the ghosts of all the people he'd murdered, and knew that they were waiting for him.'

'Good heavens, child! Don't be so superstitious. Death is death, and there's an end of it.'

'Do you really believe that, Galya?'

'Of course I do. Why else would we work so hard to make the world a better place? I remember when we were students, your mother and me. You would get old women coming in with terrible prolapses that had never been repaired, and ulcers all over their legs. They could barely walk. They believed in the next world, and no wonder, when this one had given them nothing. But we believed in making this world a better place. Of course things went wrong — mistakes were made —' She sighs deeply, convulsively.

'I know.' Anna is not really listening; she has heard all this a thousand times. It was the theme tune of her childhood: these women, Galya and her mother and all the others, with their handsome, dedicated faces, their hair pulled back, their glasses and their professional expertise. Galya hasn't really taken in the news yet; she's living in the past.

Anna's mind is full of Andrei. Does he know? Have the prisoners been told that Stalin is dead? No, probably not. There might be a riot. But they will find out.

'Look at her, fast asleep,' says Galya. 'That's all we can ask for, a better world for these little ones. We have to keep on working and hoping. You can't go backwards.'

'No.' *But Stalin is dead. He is stiff and cold. His hands can't move. He can't write as much as a single word. He can't give another order. He and Volkov —*

'You'll have to find a name for her. We can't keep on calling her "the baby".'

Anna looks down at her daughter, who has fallen asleep. *They are dead, and the baby is here. Andrei's baby, and hers.* 'It's so hard to decide without Andrei. It seems wrong.'

'She can't be nameless,' says Galya briskly. 'Didn't you two ever discuss names?'

'No.' But at that moment, gazing down at the baby, Anna knows what her name has to be. 'I shall call her Nadezhda,' she says.

'That's good. Yes, I like it. Little Nadya.'

'My God, Galya, you know something? I'm beginning to believe it. He's dead. It doesn't sink in all at once, does it? He's dead, and we're alive. But do you know, it frightens me to say it out loud.'

Galya looks at Anna with the child cradled in her arms. 'You're alive twice over,' she says.

Anna's eyes glow, and her cheeks are bright. She smiles at Galya as a woman might smile on the battlefield after she has stripped and mutilated the corpse of her enemy. 'Let the earth fill his mouth,' she says.

Involuntarily, Galya glances round. No one is there. The broken radio is silent. She thinks of sitting here with Vera, years ago, when Anna and her own little Yura were babies playing on the floor. Anna's too young yet to know that the past is just as real as the present, even though you have to pretend that it isn't, and carry on towards the future. Vera would sit there, in the wooden rocking chair that Galya kept in her bedroom for years afterwards. Anna sits in it now, to feed the baby. Mikhail would be out, walking, smoking, composing lines in his head. He would come back when the supper was ready. That was before Marina, and all the trouble she caused between them. Dear Vera. What strength she had, and what dignity.

Thank goodness Anna didn't notice Galya's stupid, tactless slip when she said, 'None of us is immortal.' Imagine her being so crass as to apply Vera's words to Stalin! She was getting old and losing her touch. Those were Vera's exact words, when she was pregnant and they were all teasing her for getting caught out when she was forty. There she stood in her cotton maternity smock, smiling. Galya can see her now. They teased her, and Vera said, *'Well, none of us is immortal.'* And then they laughed even more, and Vera said, *'No, I don't mean that, do I? What's the right word?'*

'Infallible?'

'Yes, that's it.'

Immortal! No, you weren't that. My dear friend — my dearest friend — there's never been anyone else to touch you, thinks Galya now, remembering how she stooped to kiss Vera in her coffin. How cold she was then, and how hard. They were both women who were used to death, being doctors, but Galya has never been able to forget that kiss on Vera's iron brow. And the little baby, Kolya it was then, in Anna's arms . . .

She sighs. They are all here, even though Anna doesn't see them. Vera, Mikhail, baby Kolya, Anna herself tumbling on the floor like a puppy, with Yura.

Yura is laughing. Today Galya can see his face plainly, just as it was. That doesn't always happen, so this is a good day.

Anna doesn't see or hear any of them. She's too young. She's got her life to live yet. And now there's this new little one, Nadezhda, Vera's grandchild.

None of us is immortal. But look, my darling. Look at that baby.

■ ■ ■ ■

'Galya, would you pass me my sketchbook?'

The sketchbook is on the corner of the kitchen table. Anna leaves it there most of the time, and picks it up when she has a moment. She draws only the smallest things. An onion top, or a crumpled dishcloth. She draws birch twigs that Galya has brought inside so that they will open their leaves in the warmth of the stove. She draws bits of bark, and the marks on the wall.

Yesterday, when she was changing the baby, Anna reached out for the sketchbook. Without thinking, and in a few seconds, she drew the baby's foot.

Anna opens the sketchbook. It is beginning to fill up. These are not good drawings, because she is rusty. She's allowed herself to lose the discipline that says, *Draw every day, no matter how you feel.* She's hung back, hovering over the quality of her work until she does none at all.

You need only draw the smallest things. Not the whole world; don't try for that. Anna picks up her pencil and draws the line of Nadezhda's cheek.

She will draw every day. There will be a record.

There are no miracles, but for a second she believes that one day Andrei will see his child.

27

In March 1953, following the death of Stalin, an amnesty of Gulag prisoners was initiated by Lavrentii Beria. More than 1,200,000 prisoners serving sentences of five years or less were released. However, few political prisoners were released under this amnesty, since most of them had been sentenced to terms well above five years. In addition, the amnesty excluded those convicted of 'counter-revolutionary crimes'.

Over the next few years, case reviews and rehabilitations of political prisoners swelled from a trickle to a flood, although this never became, as Nikita Khrushchev later said he had feared, 'a flood which would drown us all'. Anastas Mikoyan, a member of the Politburo for more than thirty years, observed that it would be impossible to declare at once that all the former 'enemies of the people' were innocent, because that would make it clear that 'the country was not being run by a legal government, but by a group of gangsters'.

In April 1953, *Pravda* announced that an investigatory committee set up by Beria had found that 'illegal methods' had been used by the MGB to extract confessions from the doctors accused of taking part in the 'Doctors' Plot'. These doctors were exonerated, and, if still alive, released. The guilty MGB officials were arrested. *Pravda*'s editorial on this policy reversal promised that the Soviet Government would respect the constitutional rights of Soviet citizens.

During the years following the death of Stalin, thousands upon thousands of prisoners began to make their way back from Siberia across the vast expanses of the Soviet Union. Among them was Andrei.

SELECT BIBLIOGRAPHY

The following books and articles were especially valuable to me during the writing of this book. *The Betrayal* also draws on research undertaken for *The Siege* (for more detail, please see the Select Bibliography for that novel). I am deeply grateful to all these sources.

BOOKS

The Cure: A Story of Cancer and Politics from the Annals of the Cold War by Nikolai Krementsov, University of Chicago Press, 2002

Cold Peace: Stalin and the Soviet Ruling Circle, 1945–1953 by Yoram Gorlizki and Oleg Khlevniuk, Oxford University Press, 2004

Stalin and His Hangmen: An Authoritative Portrait of a Tyrant and Those Who Served Him by Donald Rayfield, Penguin, 2004

Stalinism: New Directions (Rewriting

Histories), ed. Sheila Fitzpatrick, Routledge, 2000

Everyday Stalinism: Ordinary Life in Extraordinary Times by Sheila Fitzpatrick, Oxford University Press, 2000

Tear Off the Masks: Identity and Imposture in Twentieth-Century Russia by Sheila Fitzpatrick, Princeton University Press, 2005

Revolution on my Mind: Writing a Diary under Stalin by Jochen Hellbeck, Harvard University Press, 2006

Stalin: The Court of the Red Tsar by Simon Sebag Montefiore, Weidenfeld & Nicolson, 2003

The Unknown Stalin by Zhores A. Medvedev and Roy A. Medvedev, trans. Ellen Dahrendorf, I. B. Tauris & Co. Ltd, 2003

Stalin's Wars: From World War to Cold War, 1939–1953 by Geoffrey Roberts, Yale University Press, 2007

Stalin's Last Crime: The Doctors' Plot by Jonathan Brent and Vladimir Naumov, John Murray, 2003

The Lesser Terror: Soviet State Security 1939–1953 by Michael Parrish, Greenwood Publishing Group, 1996

Bolshevik Wives: A Study of Soviet Elite Society by James Peter Young, PhD thesis, Department of Government and International Relations, Sydney University, 2008

Till My Tale is Told: Women's Memoirs of the Gulag, ed. Simeon Vilensky, Virago, 1999

Into the Whirlwind by Evgenia S. Ginzburg, trans. Paul Stevenson and Manya Harari, Penguin, 1968

Within the Whirlwind by Evgenia S. Ginzburg, trans. Paul Stevenson and Manya Harari, Harvill Press, 1989

Remembering the Darkness: Women in Soviet Prisons by Veronica Shapovalov, Rowman & Littlefield Publishers, Inc., 2001

Gulag: A History of the Soviet Camps by Anne Applebaum, Allen Lane, 2003

Night of Stone: Death and Memory in Russia by Catherine Merridale, Granta, 2000

The Whisperers: Private Life in Soviet Russia by Orlando Figes, Allen Lane, 2007

Kolyma Tales, by Varlam Shalamov, trans. John Glad, Penguin Classics, 1994

Red Miracle: The Story of Soviet Medicine by Edward Podolsky, Books for Libraries Press, 1972

Daily Life in the Soviet Union by Katherine Bliss Eaton, Greenwood Press, 2004

Children's World: Growing Up in Russia 1890–1991 by Catriona Kelly, Yale University Press, 2007

Writing the Siege of Leningrad by Cynthia Simmons and Nina Perlina, University of Pittsburgh Press, 2002

The Legacy of the Siege of Leningrad, 1941–1995: Myths, Memories and Monuments by Lisa A. Kirschenbaum, Cambridge University Press, 2006

Nursing the Surgical Patient, ed. Rosemary Pudner, Elsevier Health Sciences, 2005

ARTICLES

'Building the Blockade: New Truths in Survival Narratives from Leningrad' by Jennifer Dickinson, University of Michigan, in *Anthropology of East Europe Review,* Vol. 13, No. 2, Autumn 1995

'Lifting the Siege: Women's Voices on Leningrad, 1941–1944' by Cynthia Simmons, Canadian Slavonic Papers, 1998

Pravda, 13 January 1953

'Above-knee Amputation' by Paul Sugarbaker, Jacob Bickels and Martin Malawer in *Musculoskeletal Cancer Surgery: Treatment of Sarcomas and Allied Diseases,* ed. Martin M. Malawer and Paul H. Sugarbaker, Kluwer Academic Publishers, 2001

'Survival Data for 648 Patients with Osteosarcoma Treated at One Institution' by Henry J. Munkin, MD; Francis J. Hornicok, MD, PhD; Andrew E. Rosenberg, MD; David C. Harmon, MD; and Mark C. Gebhardt, MD, in *Clinical Orthopaedics and Related Research,* No. 429

'How to Wrap an Above-the-knee Amputation Stump' by Denise D. Hayes in *Nursing,* January 2003

'Secondary Lung Tumors' by Rebecca Bascom, MD, MPH, Professor of Medicine, Pennsylvania State College of Medicine, Division of Pulmonary, Allergy and Critical Care Medicine, Milton S. Hershey Medical Center

I am grateful to Memorial (International Historical-Enlightenment, Human Rights and Humanitarian Society Memorial) and to The Shalamov Society.

I owe a lifelong debt to the works of Anna Akhmatova, Isaak Babel, Olga Berggolts, Alexander Blok, Mikhail Bulgakov, Nikolai Gumilev, Nadezhda Mandelstam, Osip Mandelstam, Vladimir Mayakovsky, Boris Pasternak, Alexander Solzhenitsyn, Marina Tsvetayeva, Alexander Tvardovsky, Yevgeny Zamyatin, Mikhail Zoshchenko and many more than I can name here.

No contemporary bibliography is complete without reference to the wealth of material now available on the internet. To give just a few examples, I was able to listen to a recording of Radio Moscow's announcement of Stalin's death; view declassified Top Secret CIA papers from 1953 that relate to the death of Stalin and to the Doctors' Plot; and consult research into the health and fertility of women who survived starvation during the Siege of Leningrad. Such access would have seemed incredible in the late 1990s, when I was writing *The Siege.*

■ ■ ■ ■

A BLACK CAT READING GROUP GUIDE BY LINDSAY TATE: THE BETRAYAL
HELEN DUNMORE

■ ■ ■ ■

ABOUT THIS GUIDE

We hope that these discussion questions will enhance your reading group's exploration of Helen Dunmore's *The Betrayal*. They are meant to stimulate discussion, offer new viewpoints and enrich your enjoyment of the book.

More reading group guides and additional information, including summaries, author tours and author sites for other fine Black Cat titles may be found on our Web site, www.groveatlantic.com.

QUESTIONS FOR DISCUSSION

1. Set in post–World War II Russia, *The Betrayal* chronicles life in Leningrad ten years after the infamous siege. Begin your discussion of this novel by considering how the city itself affects and shapes the characters' lives on both a physical and a spiritual level. Consider Anna's quote: "Our city is like that. . . . We love it, but it doesn't love us. We're like children who cling to the skirts of a beautiful, preoccupied mother" (p. 470).

2. Dunmore writes with compassion, celebrating the simple things in the life of a society that has known true horrors. What does Andrei mean when he wants "to live out an ordinary, valuable life" (p. 30)? In the context of the time and place of the novel, what does this mean? Why is it so important to be ordinary?

3. The redemptive nature of love lies at the heart of the narrative, buoying Andrei and Anna forward as they struggle to survive the daily grind. Find other instances throughout the novel where love — be it parental, familial, or romantic — bravely pushes forth shoots of hope and compassion among the grim circumstances of life.

4. In speaking of compassion, how far would you agree that it propels Andrei into danger, into the hands of Volkov?

5. "He recognizes it already as one of those moments that has the power to change everything" (p. 14). Looking back at Andrei's conversation with Russov in the hospital courtyard, discuss how closely his dire imaginings turn into reality. Despite his very concrete misgivings, why then does Andrei take on the case of Volkov's son? Does he really believe that everything will be fine?

6. Especially effective is the mood of quiet paranoia surging through the novel, reaching its crescendo in Andrei's arrest. Examine how Dunmore captures this in the thoughts and actions of her characters.

7. Find examples throughout the novel of the ways that Stalin's rule and emphasis on society and "collectivism" has entered the human psyche. One of Dunmore's strengths throughout the novel is to rise above stereotypes in depicting these people. Discuss the role of the neighbors; the Maleviches, and the principal at Anna's nursery school, Larissa Nicolayevna Morozova. Do you feel any kind of sympathy for them? How have Anna and Andrei become like them?

8. Volkov's very name — from "volk" in Russian — brings fear into the lives of those around him. In his dealings with Andrei at the hospital, does he ever show only his paternal anguish or is it impossible for him to separate himself from his position in state security? Are you ever able to sympathize with him as a desperate father? What about Gorya's mother?

9. Discuss the constant specter of the siege of Leningrad, the memories of the dead. Anna, especially, is reminded of the past on a daily basis. How does it affect her in the ways she lives her life on a practical level and on an emotional one? Would she ever want these memories to leave her if

she could make them do so? Do you consider these memories as a negative or positive in her life? Why do you think we learn so little about Andrei's past? Did it bother you to only know about Anna's memories?

10. Anna's memories about the siege inevitably relate back to her father and her questions about her relationship with him. Even ten years after his death she is still defending herself against him, still trying to please him. Why is this? What does it mean to her when she buries her father's writings? How does Andrei's arrest lead her to a better understanding of her father, and ultimately a closer relationship with their uneasy shared past?

11. Anna believes that it's not a question of remembering or of forgetting. "The past is alive. It claims what is its own" (p. 148). Discuss what is meant by this statement.

12. Talk about the place of optimism in the novel. How far would you agree that the author sees it as a necessary part of the human condition, as a means of survival? Consider the instinctive hope during the siege that things would be better in Lenin-

grad afterward. How do people deal with the harsh reality of post-siege Leningrad? Are some of the characters more optimistic than others? Anna, Andrei? How does it affect them? Discuss how optimism is responsible for their downfall but also perhaps, ultimately, their salvation.

13. Anna's younger brother, Kolya, lives with her and Andrei as a "son." Discuss this situation and the impact it has on all three. What about the strained undertones of Anna and Andrei's desire to have their own child? Would you say there is a great difference between their two generations in the way they view life, Russian society, the future?

14. What does the dacha represent for Anna and her family? Why do they all seem to become different people there? Talk about Kolya's transformation when he moves there to live with Galya. How likely is it?

15. How far do you agree with Anna's words as she buries her father's writing, "We didn't choose any of this" (p. 224)? How realistic is it to think that they could have avoided the whole situation?

16. Anna's childhood friend, Julia, plays an interesting role in the novel, one that is not clearly revealed until the end. Her life seems to be one of ease with a husband whose work is approved by Stalin himself. Yet, what is it that sets her apart from being a Malevich or a Morozova? What are your feelings about her when you first meet her? Do you trust her? Why does she tell Anna that she is so lucky (p. 127)?

17. Discuss the relevance of the story of the mountain king that Andrei reads to Anna just before his arrest. Anna takes the story to mean, "You can't care about everybody." How prescient are her thoughts in light of what happens after the arrest?

18. The scene of Andrei's arrest vividly brings the terrifying outside world into Anna and Andrei's most intimate, private life, ripping apart everything they have carefully cobbled together. Discuss the ways in which tiny domestic details speak of intrusion and violence, of the cruel indifference of the police state. Talk about Anna and Andrei's reaction, and the volumes it speaks about who they are.

19. Find instances throughout the novel of

kindness, of humanity slipped into the dreary fabric of everyday conformity. How far would you agree that it is possible to divide the characters of the novel into two groups: those who will risk a part of themselves for others and those who won't?

20. What were the most striking images for you in the prison scenes? Was it the physical violence perpetrated against fellow humans or the inhumane living conditions? Why was it so important for the guards to keep Andrei in solitary confinement? Discuss the psychology behind such a method. Consider also the contrast in the lives of the prisoners and those of the women in the administrative offices. What does Andrei find hardest about prison life?

21. Talk about the scene at Lubyanka when a prisoner collapses into Andrei's shared cell and Kostya, the foreman, shouts out, "Where's that doctor? Over here! Make way for him" (p. 451). Why are these words so important to Andrei at that moment? Think about them too in the context of the whole novel.

22. When Andrei meets Volkov again at the

Lubyanka prison he meets two very different Volkovs — one before the phone call that will change Volkov's life and one after. Discuss the complex nature of Volkov's character, and his relationship with Andrei. Do you think that he really does care about Andrei? Talk about Andrei's understanding of the situation: "Andrei can't help feeling something — not warmth, not sympathy, but a kind of recognition perhaps" (p. 523). What are your feelings toward Volkov at this moment? When he takes his own life?

23. On leaving her home to head out to the dacha to join Kolya, Anna reflects on everything the apartment has meant to her over the years: as her home that she shares with Andrei and Kolya; her childhood home, the one she lived in during the siege, the one where her father died. What does it mean to her when she realizes that "she's part of this apartment's life, but never the whole of it" (p. 470)? Is she saddened or liberated by this thought?

24. When Volkov says about his dying son, "Gorya is better off out of this shit," it's hard not to disagree. Yet Anna and Andrei's baby becomes, in many ways, a

reminder of the simple joys of being human and a symbol of a better future. Talk about the ways in which Anna's unborn child takes control of Anna's actions, honing her instinct for survival. Do you think her story, her actions, would have been very different if she hadn't been pregnant?

25. Talk about the ending of the novel. Did you find it satisfactory to know that Andrei would make it home to his family or would you have preferred to see the reunion with his loved ones — and his new baby? Why do you think Dunmore ended the novel in this way, moving from the individual story to the story of a nation?

26. In retrospect would you consider *The Betrayal,* with all its Orwellian undertones, to be a bleak novel or is there a convincing message of hope? Is it really possible for the characters to believe in a brighter future? Consider parallels with the fairy tale about the mountain king.

Suggestions for Further Reading:
The Siege by Helen Dunmore; *Into the Whirlwind* by Eugenia Semenova Ginzburg; *1984* by George Orwell; *City of Thieves* by David

Benioff; *The Master and Margarita* by Mikhail Bulgakov; *The Bronze Horseman* by Paullina Simons; *The Madonnas of Leningrad* by Debra Dean; *The Stalin Epigram: A Novel* by Robert Littell

The employees of Thorndike Press hope you have enjoyed this Large Print book. All our Thorndike, Wheeler, and Kennebec Large Print titles are designed for easy reading, and all our books are made to last. Other Thorndike Press Large Print books are available at your library, through selected bookstores, or directly from us.

For information about titles, please call:
(800) 223-1244

or visit our Web site at:
http://gale.cengage.com/thorndike

To share your comments, please write:
Publisher
Thorndike Press
10 Water St., Suite 310
Waterville, ME 04901